RAGE OF THE SERBS

RAGE OF THE SERBS

Marjorie Radulović

The Book Guild Ltd
Sussex, England

This book is a work of fiction. The characters and situations in this story are imaginary. No resemblance is intended between these characters and any real persons, either living or dead.

The Book Guild Ltd
25 High Street,
Lewes, Sussex

First published 1998

Set in Baskerville
Typesetting by Keyboard Services, Luton,
Bedfordshire

Printed in Great Britain by
Antony Rowe Ltd,
Chippenham, Wiltshire

A catalogue record for this book is
available from the British Library

ISBN 1 85776 372 0

ACKNOWLEDGEMENTS

This book could not have been written without the love, support and encouragement of my husband, Sava Radulović, whose ability to transmit something of his profound knowledge of Serbian history and his love for pre-war Belgrade has supplied whatever ambience the writer has captured. He also spent considerable time in research and translation of the substantial volume of material available in the French, Serbian and German languages and in relating to me his own personal experiences during the war, all of which made a significant contribution to background material. His help has, quite simply, been incalculable.

For details concerning activities of the guerrilla fighters of General Draža Mihailović I am especially grateful for Branko Lazitch's *The Tragedy of General Mihailovitch*. With regard to Croat *Ustaši* atrocities I have taken care to rely only on reports or affidavits by prominent Croat citizens themselves or eyewitness reports from Croat allies as investigated and reported by German and Italian writers and scholars. In the latter case I am greatly indebted to Dr Lazo M. Kostich's *Holocaust in the Independent State of Croatia*, which is a compilation and translation of these reports.

M.R.

A NOTE ON PRONUNCIATION

ć	as in church – Ristić becomes Ristich
č	similar to ć but with slightly more stress – Čiča becomes Chicha
c, š	ts as in cats; š as in shrill – Šlivovica becomes Shlivovitsa
j	as y – Jelena becomes Yelena

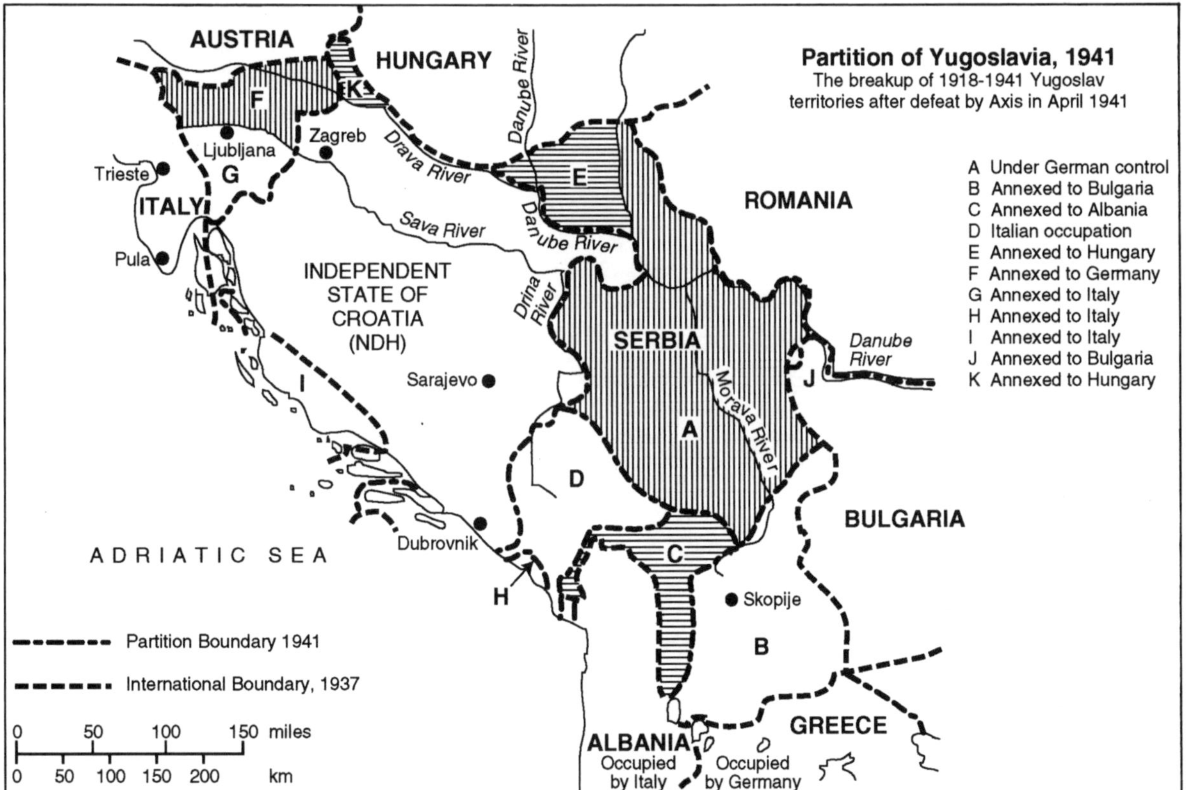
Partition of Yugoslavia, 1941
The breakup of 1918-1941 Yugoslav territories after defeat by Axis in April 1941
A Under German control
B Annexed to Bulgaria
C Annexed to Albania
D Italian occupation
E Annexed to Hungary
F Annexed to Germany
G Annexed to Italy
H Annexed to Italy
I Annexed to Italy
J Annexed to Bulgaria
K Annexed to Hungary
AUSTRIA
HUNGARY
ROMANIA
BULGARIA
GREECE
ALBANIA
Occupied by Italy
Occupied by Germany
ITALY
SERBIA
INDEPENDENT STATE OF CROATIA (NDH)
ADRIATIC SEA
Trieste
Pula
Ljubljana
Zagreb
Sarajevo
Dubrovnik
Skopije
Drava River
Sava River
Danube River
Drina River
Morava River
Partition Boundary 1941
International Boundary, 1937
0 50 100 150 miles
0 50 100 150 200 km

PART ONE

Early this morning the Yugoslav nation found its soul.

Winston Churchill
27 March, 1941

The German nation will now settle its account with that Serbian clique of criminals in Belgrade which believes that it can once again place the Balkans at the disposal of a British attempt on European peace.

Adolf Hitler
6 April, 1941

1

As usual, Belgrade was full of life. Strolling along the *korso*, pausing now and then to chat with friends he encountered walking along by themselves or sitting in small groups on one of the numerous hotel or café terraces overlooking Knez Mihajlo Street and the Terazije, all of them busily engaged in the favourite Yugoslav pastimes of talking, drinking, eating, arguing and laughing, David asked himself why on earth he had ever left his beloved native city. Not that he had really had any choice! As a lieutenant in the army reserve, he had returned home that morning from military exercises in Negotin, a small provincial town over three hundred kilometres east of Belgrade, just one of the many young men called upon to take part in the temporary mobilization of the Yugoslav army during that uneasy summer of 1939.

The talk, he noted, was still all about the paranoic German guttersnipe, Hitler, his Nazi war machine, and the shameful appeasement of the democracies in Munich, all of which had contributed to Belgrade's decision to hold the half-hearted army exercises that had just taken place on the Bulgarian and Rumanian frontiers. It had all, David told himself, been quite unnecessary. But of course, his country, with its turbulent history, had, almost as a gut reaction, braced itself at the first sign of fascist aggression in Europe. With its chilling remembrance of things past, Yugoslavia could not help assuming an undercurrent, a subconscious awareness, of the ever-present danger of war. So perhaps it was only natural that its capital city should seem uneasy, restless, like an old warhorse pawing the ground at an imagined smell of blood in the air, even though on this beautiful summer afternoon it was clear that life was too good, too fair, and full of promise to be replaced overnight by the terror and destructiveness of war. No, no. That sombre forecast was merely a nightmare propagated by the pessimists. War, quite simply, was unthinkable.

David was about to cross the square leading to the Balkan Hotel on Brankova Street when he felt someone timidly take hold of his arm. Turning, he found himself looking into the gentle, limpid brown eyes of his friend, Jack Cohen.

'Jack!' He reached out and shook the other man's hand with genuine warmth. 'I'm so happy to see you. Aunt Draga told me you called at the apartment last week. Sorry I wasn't home.'

'Yes, yes. Your aunt told me you were in Negotin. When did you arrive back?'

'Yesterday. Had quite a nice trip along the Danube. Via Kladovo, you know?'

Jack nodded. 'Kladovo? Yes, of course.'

'Look, Jack, I'm on my way now to meet Stevan and Bogdan. Why don't you come with me? Join us for a drink.'

Jack blushed. 'Oh, no. I mean ... I don't drink, you know, and ...'

'Well, you can have a coffee then. Come along.' In the friendly manner of the Serbs, always touching, hugging, embracing, David placed an arm around Jack's shoulders and began to draw him across the street, chuckling as the other man shook his head, drew away.

'Look, Jack, I know you don't like Bogdan. But he's not a bad fellow at heart. Truly. I will see there are no tricks played on you today.' He was referring to the time he had persuaded Jack to join them, when Bogdan had slipped half a tumbler of vodka into the glass of lemonade Cohen had ordered. Poor Jack had been sick for a week.

'No, no. It's not that ... I'm on my way to my father's office. But I do want to talk to you, David. I really need to talk to you.' The soft eyes blinked rapidly behind the thick glasses. 'If you have any free time?'

'Of course I do.' With an ironic grimace David gestured towards his uniform. 'I'm stuck in this for another couple of days. Then I return to the bank. But for the moment my time is more or less my own.' He looked around, then pointed towards his favourite outdoor café. 'How about meeting me at the Russian Tzar tomorrow morning? Say around ten? We can have coffee ... talk ...'

'Yes, yes. That would be fine.' Jack's eyes were shining, and he broke into his rare, charming smile. 'Thank you, David. Until tomorrow then.' He lifted his hand in a half salute, backed away a little, then turned and hurried off down the street. David watched him go with an affectionate smile, then, glancing at his watch, gave a start and began walking briskly towards the Balkan hotel.

He spotted Stevan and Bogdan the moment he entered the hotel lounge. They were sitting at a small table in a corner of the room. In front of them was a bottle of *Šljivovica*, the potent plum brandy most Yugoslavs loved, and a huge plate of hors d'hœuvre. Stevan was the first to catch sight of him and was on his feet when David reached the table, holding out his hand with a delighted smile.

'Welcome home, David. How good it is to see you.'

David shook his hand, then playfully cuffed Bogdan, who remained seated, although with a huge grin creasing his narrow, rather sly face. 'Hey, you. On your feet when you greet a king's officer.'

Bogdan sniggered. 'King's officer indeed! Little boys playing games. That's what *I* call it.'

Laughing, David sank into the chair Stevan held out for him. 'Well, for once, Bogdan, I think you may be right. As a matter of fact I was just thinking on my way here, what on earth was I doing wasting my time with the army while here in Belgrade everyone is having a wonderful time? Mind you, there is nothing like being away from home for a while to make you appreciate it.'

Bogdan leaned forward eagerly, the hound-dog eyes glittering. 'But girls! Did you meet any interesting girls in Negotin?'

'In Negotin? You must be kidding. Even if I had, there would have been no time to do anything about it. As a matter of fact, the only interesting people I met were a couple of German tourists. They turned out to be journalists. But that was on my way home.'

'Germans?' Stevan looked up. 'Great! You were able to practise your German then?'

David nodded. 'Which is always useful.'

'How did you come to meet them?'

'Well ... it was rather strange, really.' He leaned forward to pick up the bottle of brandy, poured himself a small glass, and settled back to tell the story.

On the ship bringing them back to Belgrade, David and two fellow officers had found themselves surrounded by tourists taking advantage of the beautiful summer weather to cruise along the Danube. The three young men had flirted for a while with a group of young Slovene girls, then strolled around the deck and taken a position against the rails to better admire the forbidding Golubac Fortress that loomed up in the distance with its seven tall towers overlooking the entrance to the Iron Gate Gorge. As usual when faced with evidence of his country's turbulent past, David had become lost in reverie, marvelling to himself at the fortress' state of preservation, considering the endless battles that had taken place around its solid walls over the centuries. He had been quite startled when a deep voice had addressed him in German.

'Können Sie mir, bitte, sagen, wie heisst diese Festung?'

He had turned around quickly, and found himself looking into the level grey eyes of a man who seemed to be a tourist. In fact, there were two of them. The man who had addressed him, tall, with the thoughtful sensitive face of an intellectual and his companion, also tall, but more heavily built with round, rather blank looking blue eyes.

'The name of the fortress?' He hesitated, then replied in German. 'Sie heisst Golubac.'

'Golubac?'

He nodded, then added quickly as the men thanked him and began to turn away, 'Wie wissen Sie dass ich Deutsch spreche?'

The German who had first addressed him turned back, shrugged, smiled. 'Wir haben schon bemerkt dass in Jugoslawien vielé Leute Deutsch sprechen und . . . Sie sehen wie ein Deutscher aus . . .'

It was David's turn to smile. Certainly, he himself, with his blond hair and clear blue eyes, probably did not fit the stock image of the dark-haired, dark-eyed Yugoslav, but on the other hand, he thought, he had noticed from films and pictures of the Nazis that many of them seemed to be swarthy, brown-eyed and stocky. A far cry, more often than not, from their Aryan ideal. In any event he returned the German's smile, nodded, and turned back to his friends who were standing to one side, listening uncomprehendingly to the exchange.

'What was that all about?' Vladimir Petrović asked.

'I wish I could speak a foreign language,' his twin brother, Janko, added.

'All you have to do is study, Janko.' David turned to Vladimir. 'They asked me the name of the fortress.'

'That's all?'

'Well, I asked them how they knew I understood German. They said that I looked like a German, but that in any event they had found that quite a surprising number of Yugoslavs speak their language.'

'But of course they are surprised!' A wide grin split Vladimir's broad, good-natured face. His expression suddenly assumed an exaggerated look of dimwitted naïvety. 'Who would expect us primitive Slavs to speak a foreign language?'

David joined in with Janko's laughter. They had almost reached the fortress and he decided that he would just have time to go below and get a drink and still be back in time to admire at closer quarters the historic building that had been guarding the entrance to the gorge since the fourteenth century. 'Save my space here at the rail, eh? Shall I bring you both a beer?'

They both nodded 'And some cigarettes too, David, please,' Vladimir added before turning back to watch the two Germans who had also taken up a position next to the rails a few yards away.

Unexpectedly, there was quite a crowd gathered around the bar and David hesitated, undecided whether to join the queue and perhaps miss a close-up view of Golubac. Still, he had often taken the trip down the Danube that led to the fortress, so he decided to wait. By the time he returned to the upper deck the ship was well past Golubac, but what caught his attention was the sight of two burly looking men in civilian clothes handing identification papers back to Janko and Vladimir.

Frowning, David hurried over to his friends, just as the two men were turning away. 'What was that all about?'

Janko shrugged. 'The police. They asked us what you were talking about to those tourists. They asked for our identification.'

'And you gave it to them?'

'Why not?'

David's eyes flashed. 'Because the civil police have no right to question uniformed army officers about *anything*,' he snapped. 'That's why not.' He glared angrily towards the two men who were standing close enough to hear. They returned his glance with cold imperturbability. 'Let them ask for *my* identification papers,' he challenged loudly and provocatively. But there was no reaction. To add to his irritation, one of the men yawned.

'Oh, what does it matter, David?' Neither Vladimir nor Janko seemed the least bit perturbed. But then, he had thought with a mixture of affection and contempt, it took an awful lot to perturb either of the twins, both of whom looked upon life in the army reserve or out of it as one big joke.

He wanted, however, to make some gesture to further show his displeasure, and found an opportunity as the two Germans again walked past with a friendly nod.

'Gentlemen!' They paused a little disconcertedly at the loudness of his voice, spoken in his own language. He held out his hand, continued in German. 'David Ristić! At your service. I take it you are on vacation? How are you enjoying our country?'

'Wunderbar! Wunderbar!' They shook his proffered hand and smilingly went on to tell him that they were, in fact, journalists, and thus enjoying something of a 'working' vacation. 'You see,' said the blue-eyed man, who introduced himself as Werner Dietrich, 'if you are a writer, then you are always working.' He explained that they would be staying in Belgrade for a couple of days before returning to rejoin their wives, who had opted to stay at a hotel on the Dalmatian coast rather than continue on with their husbands to Belgrade.

The name of the second journalist was Heinz Wiesinger. David introduced them both to the Petrović brothers then, on sudden impulse, after again glancing towards the two detectives, said loudly in Serbian. 'I would like to invite you to dine with me while you are in Belgrade. Should you have the time, of course.' Quickly he translated his invitation into German.

'Why, that is kind of you.' The Germans exchanged pleased if somewhat puzzled looks as he wrote the name and address of the Madera Hotel on the back of his card. 'Tomorrow evening, then? Say around eight. The hotel has an excellent restaurant. I think you will enjoy it.'

The time and place agreed upon, David then went out of his way, much to the amusement of the twins and to the apparent disinterest of the watching detectives, to give the Germans a running description of further historical sights along the Danube, including a short history lesson about Smederevo, the most important port before they reached Belgrade, and about the last mediaeval Serbian ruler, Despot Djuradj Branković, who had built a fortress there in 1430.

By the time they had passed Pancevo and reached the junction of the Danube and Sava rivers facing the huge Kalemegdan fortress, the game had palled a little. He might almost have regretted his impulsive invitation if it had not been for the profession of the two tourists.

'You see,' he now told Stevan and Bogdan, 'it might be an interesting experience. They should be able to throw some light on what is really going on in Germany.'

'What papers do they work for? Did they say?'

'No. Nor did I ask, as a matter of fact, Stevan. They did say they were both from Hamburg, though.' He looked at them both expectantly. 'Well?'

'Well what?' Bogdan was busy refilling his glass with *Šljivovica*. He held the bottle up inquiringly at Stevan, who shook his head. David's glass was hardly touched.

'What do you mean? "Well what!"' David glanced towards Stevan, who seemed to be off in some reverie of his own. 'Don't you want to come with me?'

'What for?'

'Come on, Bogdan! What do you mean "what for"? To learn something. That is what for! Besides, how often do we get a chance to practise our German for a whole evening? Stevan? What do you say?'

'What? Oh ... yes ... well, you are right, David. I wish I could go with you. But tonight ... the truth is I have to go to a party.'

'And *I* have a date.' Bogdan looked at them both with a wide grin.

'You do?' David and Stevan stared at him. Bogdan seemed to spend half of his life trying to get a date. With his unprepossessing looks and sly manner he had, however, little success, despite his occasional and surprising flashes of dignity and the efforts of his two friends to help him meet and mix with girls of their acquaintance.

Now he smirked, finished off his brandy, and endeavoured to look mysterious.

'Is it someone we know?'

'I doubt it.' He reached out, took a piece of the delicious

local cheese *kačkavalj*, and began to nibble at it fastidiously with an air of infuriating smugness.

After a moment David stopped frowning. He shrugged, grinned, glanced across at Stevan, who winked back at him. The only way to get any information out of Bogdan when he was in this kind of mood was to pretend complete indifference, as they both knew. And as a matter of fact, except for being glad that at last Bogdan had found *someone*, David for one was not all that interested. He was simply glad that his friend had found a girl willing to go out with him. *I hope to God she is kind*, he thought. Then forgot about the subject.

'Where's the party?' he asked Stevan.

'At the Miletićs'. Funny ... I thought Olga was going to send you an invitation. Have you looked at your mail yet?'

David shook his head. 'No, though come to think of it there were some letters on my bureau ... you know how it is at home ... so much excitement just because I arrived back ... I just never got around to opening them.'

'I think you'll find one of them is from Olga. Are you sure you can't come?'

'No, no. Of course not. I can't let those two fellows down. But you might explain to Olga what happened. Tell her...' His voice trailed off as he became aware of a sudden movement from Bogdan, who was rising to his feet.

'Well, I'll be off. You two will be wanting to talk about your social plans.'

Oh God, David thought. *We've done it again!* Olga had never liked Bogdan. It was a sore point with him that she had never invited him to the Miletić home.

'But wait, Bogdan. Don't be in such a hurry.' He glanced across to Stevan for help, but only received a slight shrug in return. Bogdan stood looking at him sullenly, shifting his weight from one foot to another. 'Listen. Aunt Draga was asking about you. She wants you to come to dinner one evening. How about Friday? Both the girls will be home. They'll be going out later, but I'm sure...'

Bogdan glared at him suspiciously for a moment, then his face softened. He had a soft spot for David's aunt, who had always treated him with warmth and kindness. 'Well,' he muttered, 'you tell her I'd like to come. But I can't. I'm taking my girl to see *The Merry Widow.*

'*The Merry Widow*? Where is it on?'

'At the State National. A revival.'

'Really?' David thought for a moment. 'Listen. Could you get me a couple of tickets? That's Aunt Draga's favourite operetta. It would be a great treat for her.'

'Well...' Bogdan was becoming more relaxed. 'Yes. I could pick up a couple more tickets.' He hesitated. 'How about your sisters?'

David shook his head. 'No, no. We were just planning on having dinner together. Andjela and Zora are going to a dance afterwards. But listen. Why don't you bring your girl along? You can both have dinner with us, then we can go on to the theatre together. Unless,' he added quickly, 'you would prefer to be alone?'

'No, no. That sounds fine. I'd like you to meet her.'

'That's settled then. Shall we see you around six? Or if that is too early...'

'Six is fine. I'll bring the tickets with me. My treat, too, David. For your Aunt Draga. All right?'

'She will appreciate that very much, Bogdan,' David replied gravely.

Bogdan had been making a point of not even so much as glancing in Stevan's direction, until the latter suddenly reached out and slapped his hand down hard in the centre of the table, making brandy slop over and the plates of meat and cheese jump. 'Friendship!' he yelled so loudly that for a moment a hush descended over the room. Heads turned briefly, then the hum of conversation began anew. Three noisy young men were nothing to get too excited about at the Balkan Hotel.

'Friendship!' David had instantly followed Stevan's lead, slamming his hand down hard over the latter's. It was a ritual left over from high-school days when the three of them had formed what they swore would be everlasting friendship. A ritual that Bogdan, out of the three of them, always found it impossible to resist. A broad grin spread from ear to ear. He slammed his hand down hard on top of David's with a force that made the latter wince.

'Friendship! Friendship!' he cried, moved as always by the concept of brotherhood with these two young men he admired so much, had striven so hard to emulate. To hide his emotion he picked up David's glass, still half full of *Šljivovica,* drained it, wiped his hand across his mouth and stalked awkwardly out of the room.

'Whew!' David shook his head. 'He's still so touchy. I always forget.' He sighed, nodded assent as Stevan picked up the brandy and refilled his glass, then frowned. 'I'm sorry, Stevan, I'm forgetting my manners. About Friday – you, too, are of course welcome. Aunt Draga would be delighted. Could you . . . ?'

Stevan shook his head. 'I would love to come, but I have something else. You know, family,' he added vaguely. 'But I wish you could come along to Olga's tonight. I'd like to see what you think of her now. She's changed a lot. I'm sure you would hardly know her.'

David put an elbow on the table, rested his chin in his hand and studied his friend thoughtfully. 'Mmmmm . . .' he said. During their high-school years Stevan had always had what David considered to be something of a fixation about Olga Miletić, something he, David, had always found difficult to understand. 'Well,' he said now, 'I suppose I'll get around to meeting her again sooner or later. Let's see . . . it must be at least three years now. But you . . . I suppose having been in London both at the same time . . . you must have kept pretty much in touch with her?'

'In a way. But the only way I could get to see her there was to attend some pretty boring political meetings. She was friendly with some English leftists. And, of course, I could always be relied upon to say the wrong thing. Still, now we are both back in Belgrade . . .' He leaned across the table, suddenly extremely serious. 'Look here, David. I'm relying on you, you know. You must convince her that I am to be taken seriously. She has always admired you. If you show her you consider me to be a mature man I'm sure she will listen to you. She will take notice.'

David shook his head, half flattered, half irritated. He had, as a matter of fact, never cared over much for Olga Miletić. Certainly, from what he remembered, she was attractive enough. But self-opinionated. A little too overbearing for her own good. Never known for his tactfulness, he was about to say as much when, perhaps fortunately, Stevan changed the subject.

'Those detectives you mentioned. When you were returning to Belgrade, I mean. What do you suppose it was all about? Because they heard German being spoken? Since when has that been illegal?' He paused, then went on thoughtfully. 'Do they really expect trouble here from those bloody fascists?'

'God only knows. But I hope not. What chance would *we* have against Germany alone, let alone Germany and Italy . . . and you can bet if they struck at us, Bulgaria would join the vultures. We are simply not prepared, you understand? You should have been with us during army manoeuvres. No modern arms, no organization. The only thing we had plenty of was chaos. Army chaos, not army manoeuvres, is what they should have been called.' He picked up a small piece of bread, began to knead it thoughtfully. 'So far as the detectives were concerned, I suppose it was because they heard me speak German to those two. I think there is no doubt that some kind of Fifth Column exists here in Belgrade, and you know it is years since I can remember there having been so many German tourists here. What annoyed me – what irritated me – was that they should dare suspect army officers of disloyalty, indiscretion, whatever. I was furious, I can tell you.' He laughed ruefully. 'And because I lost my temper, here I am now stuck with two fat German tourists! I would have much preferred to have gone with you to Olga's party.'

Stevan chuckled. 'That temper of yours, it's going to get

you into trouble for the rest of your life, you know?'

'Probably! Still, what I said before still holds true. I will be able to practise my German and, who knows, I might get some useful piece of information from them. They might let something slip.' He beckoned the waiter. 'Let's pay the bill and get out of here. I could do with some fresh air.'

Outside the sun was still shining. They stood there, blinking a little in its bright light before, by tacit agreement, slowly making their way to Kalemegdan Park. Although it had been some time since they had met and both had been full of things they wished to tell each other, both young men fell silent, busy with their own thoughts.

Oddly enough, considering the beauty of the day, the park was almost deserted. But it was, after all, late afternoon. The watchful *babas* would have already taken the children home and the housewives were all hurrying back to begin to prepare supper. There were still a few old men drowsing in the sun, however, and they passed a couple of young men who, like themselves, seemed free of work for one reason or another and were taking the opportunity to enjoy the weather and the beauty of the park, and at the same time exchange views about women, sports, the gathering war clouds in Europe and national politics.

Stevan had been thinking about Olga. He threw a friendly arm around David's shoulder. 'Tell me. Do you have a permanent girl yet? I mean, anything serious?'

'No, thank God. Who wants to get serious at our age? No, no. I want to play the field for a few more years. And if you will take my advice, Stevan . . .'

He stopped walking, looked at his friend inquiringly. Stevan burst out laughing. Removing his arm from around his friend's shoulder he grinned broadly. 'I was just thinking. Do you realize? If we walked like this in, say, a London park, the English would think we were homosexuals!'

It took a moment for what he said to sink in. David's wide blue eyes stared back at him uncomprehendingly, then he slowly shook his head. 'Are you serious?' he asked. 'Is it true?'

'Yes, yes.' Stevan was still chuckling. 'It's true.'

'My God,' David said as they resumed walking along the pathway, breathing in the scent of the lilac bushes, pausing occasionally to admire the cool little ponds, 'are the English so degenerate then?'

Stevan shrugged. 'Well, they are a strange people. So cold in a way. Also, they act a lot, I think.'

'Act?'

'Well, for instance. You and I are both good at languages. Right? And neither one of us is shy about telling anyone that.'

'Why should we be?'

'Exactly. But in England it would not be what they like to call "good form". I told some people there I had a wonderful talent for languages and they thought I was simply boasting.'

'Boasting? Because you told the truth?'

'I told you, they are a strange people. Olga seemed to like them, though.'

They had reached the impressive naked statue *The Warrior*, which stood on guard at the prow of the old fortress, and now they paused to lean against the rail and gaze down at the Sava River as it began to lose itself in the Danube.

'You mentioned something about her knowing some English leftists?'

Stevan nodded, chuckled. 'That's another reason I think they act a lot. They are not like our mad communists. Picture if you can, David, these upper-class people, living very well indeed, and they gather together and serve tea and cucumber sandwiches and talk about the wonderful social experiment going on in Russia. I found them ludicrous.' He grimaced. 'But Olga found them impressive. So there you have it.'

'Members of the British upper class? You are saying some of them admire the Bolsheviks? Hard to understand.'

'Well, that's just it. If the Bolsheviks took over England, these people would be amongst the first to go. Even if they survived, which I doubt, well, from what I hear is going on in Russia, that would certainly be the end of their cucumber sandwiches and tea, to say the very least.'

David laughed. 'I would say so.' He gave a last look at the swiftly flowing river before joining his companion, who had begun retracing their steps. 'But damn it, Stevan. If the English have become so degenerate who is going to stop Hitler eventually? Maybe the French, do you think?'

'Maybe.'

'Yet in this very park we have a statue honouring the French who died with our fathers during the last war. Wasn't that enough? Is there some great unwritten law that says Europe must run mad every generation or so and spill its own blood?'

'Seems like. But let us hope we can stay out of it this time. We had to fight the Turks for five hundred years for God's sake. We still need time to straighten out our own problems. A war now would be disastrous for us.' Stevan squinted up at the sky, as though searching for rain. 'You know, David, sometimes I think my father is right. He thinks we should have kept Stoyadinović as prime minister.'

'That bandit? That wolf?'

'Well, you know what they say. If you live amongst the wolves, you have to howl with them! Anyway, according to my father, Stoyadinović had as much time for those maniacs Hitler and Mussolini as you or I. A friend of the family was with him when he made his last trip to Italy, you know. Stoyadinović, I mean. He told us that as the prime minister stood saluting before a parade Mussolini put on for him, he turned around to his party and muttered: "One must trick the tricksters!"'

'Is it true? Yet what about all of those young fascists he packed his meetings with? Yelling *Vodja! Vodja!* Leader indeed! And all wearing green shirts! No, no. I have the greatest respect for your father, as you know. But Stoyadinović. No! That is more than I can swallow. Prince Paul was right to get rid of him.'

Stevan nodded agreement. 'Yes. You are right.' He chuckled. 'But you know how it is with my father. When he talks, I keep silent and listen!'

They spent the rest of the afternoon wandering around Kalemegdan Park which, built as it was around the famous fortress that had played such a historic role in protecting Belgrade from hordes of invaders for centuries, presented Serbs not only with the calm peace of its flowers, trees and beautiful little bridges, but with a perpetual monument to their proud and turbulent past.

As their ancestors had done for hundreds of years, the two young men became lost in discussion of local Belgrade gossip, of memories from their school days, of plans for their own future. A certain amount of boasting was mandatory upon them both, but as they talked and laughed and occasionally shouted, it was inevitable that their talk would again and again return to the eternal Serbian preoccupation with politics, both internal and external.

While it was a good thing, they both agreed, that Stoyadinović, with his penchant for flirting with the fascists, was gone, just how much could Paul, the Prince Regent, be trusted? Rumour had it that he was liked by Hitler, which was hardly a recommendation, although on the other hand, if it kept Yugoslavia out of a war with that bandit, it could be a plus, too. What a pity the last war had taken the lives of so many of Serbia's finest sons, men whose experience and wisdom was desperately needed in these chaotic times. Who was there left with the maturity and wisdom to guide Yugoslavia, a country that desperately needed time to sort out its own internal divisions before becoming embroiled in the rest of Europe's latest madness? And, if war did come, how much could the country rely on its tumultuous provinces to unite under the Belgrade government?

'Montenegro would be with us,' David said, 'for all of their complaints about Belgrade being the cause of their poverty. You would think the government had created their barren land instead of God!'

'Slovenia?' They both sighed.

'But Dalmatia! Better the Serbs than the Italians she would think. She was robbed long enough by Venice to know on which side her bread is buttered.'

'And Macedonia, too, despite her grumblings. Better we Serbs than the murderous Bulgars. That is one thing they have learned.'

And so on, through all of the provinces that for one reason or another had grumbled continuously about their central government in Belgrade since the historical manifesto of 1917 had been issued by the Serbian government that was to unite all South Slavs under the protection of the glorious Karageorgević dynasty and that would ensure that all those who had for centuries been robbed and ravished by the Turks, the Italians, the Austro-Hungarian empire and by marauding bands of barbarians of all kinds dating back to the time before the Illyrians, would at last stand as one democratic country, united against all forms of totalitarian tyranny.

Until they came to Croatia.

It was true, they agreed sadly. Most provinces could be relied upon to unite with Serbia in the face of Nazi aggression, except for Croatia.

'When will they realize they are our brothers?' David asked.

'Never!' Stevan replied loudly. 'They will never realize it. Because they are *not* our brothers.'

'Yet they are Slavs.'

'Slavs, but not Serbs. They cannot forgive us because they know that not one Serb bowed his head under the Ottoman yoke, while the whole of Croatia knelt in surrender to the Austrians, who thanked them for their docility, by the way, by plundering and murdering them. They not only bowed their heads, you know, but they fought like wolves for the Habsburgs. For their oppressors! Imagine that! Can you imagine that?'

'Yes. And look at the way they keep shouting about so-called Serbian hegemony! They know as well as we do that in the 1915 Secret Treaty of London the Allies offered us all of Bosnia-Hercegovina, not to mention a good part of the Dalmatian coast. And did we grab this territory? No! What we wanted was simply a state that would protect all Slavs.

Mind you, it's only the power-mad politicians and so-called intellectuals in Zagreb, you know. The people themselves – Serbs and Croats – live together peacefully enough in the towns and villages.'

'You are right. That is what my uncle says. And yet, will they fall in love with Hitler, he asks? Will they fight for Hitler the way they fought for the Habsburgs? And listen to me, Stevan,' he cried with an urgency that belied the fact that he had said the same thing to his friend a thousand times. 'Listen to me. Do you think they will ever forgive us for Kaimakchalan? Can they forgive the fact that our brave Serbian army conquered an impregnable mountain during the great war and drove every single one of our enemies out of our country?'

'What you say is all true. And then there is their religion. How could they give up our ancient and beautiful religion for perfidious Rome?' He shook his head in wonder. 'They gave up our religion. They rejected our culture which, of course, is the richest culture in the world. How could they do these things?'

They both stopped in their tracks, gazed at each other in amazement. It was incomprehensible that anyone would give up either the glorious richness of the Orthodox church or the brilliant Byzantine culture that had been the Serbian heritage from the tenth century Nemanyan Dynasty, for the barbaric and shallow civilization of the West. Incomprehensible, their expressions said as they gazed at each other. Incomprehensible!

'Yet what can we do?' David draped a consoling arm across his friend's shoulder as they began slowly to walk again.

'There is nothing we can do. Unless we South Slavs join together we will never have peace. Not while the Italians and the Hungarians and the Austrians and the Albanians and the Bulgarians crouch on our borders ready to pounce the moment we show the slightest weakness. Not to mention the Germans! Serbian hegemony? What they should worry about, I say, is German hegemony!'

Stevan's voice was raised to such a pitch that a couple of old men passing by looked up and shook their heads. Such noisy youth, their expressions proclaimed, then immediately changed into sly complicity. They, too, had done much shouting in their day.

A slight breeze had sprung up and the sun had disappeared behind a cloud when David glanced at his watch. 'Look, Stevan, if we hurry we might just have time to join the *korso*.' He was referring to the evening procession of Belgraders who took a pre-dinner stroll in order to be seen, to exchange a word or two of gossip.

'Is it really that late? My God! Yes, of course. Let us go.' They hurried out of the park, still talking excitedly.

The *korso* was in full swing when they arrived at the centre of Knez Mihajlo Street. They strolled along, stopping occasionally to greet and talk with mutual friends, until they reached the Russian Tzar Hotel, where they found Bogdan loudly holding court with a group of young men who belonged to the Belgrade rowing club. David and Stevan joined them and were instantly caught up in a rowdy discussion about the merits and perceived weaknesses of their new coach.

Time flew. When David again consulted his watch, he gave a start. He would hardly have time to go home and freshen up before keeping his appointment with the two Germans. Before leaving, however, he placed a hand each on Bogdan and Stevan's shoulders, 'Listen, you fellows. We three have to get together more often. It seems to me we have been losing touch over the past few years.'

'Yes. You are right. But you know how busy I have been,' Bogdan said importantly.

'Well, so have I. And Stevan has been travelling. But still . . .'

'I agree with you, David. We must not drift too far apart. Let's get together again soon. Look, I take it upon myself to arrange something.' Stevan's face creased into its ever ready and engaging smile. 'That's a promise. You leave it in my hands.'

'Good. Well, then...' He nodded goodbye to the other young men and left the gathering, well pleased.

* * *

Belgrade's balmy summer evening was a perfect setting for the Madera's huge outdoor terrace at the back of the hotel. David arrived exactly on time and stood at the entrance for a moment taking pleasure, as always, in the beautifully arranged plants and flowers, and looking around at the elegant women with their well-dressed escorts, to see if there was anyone present whom he knew. The jazz orchestra was playing and a trio of singers crooned softly into the microphone as spotlights illuminated the already crowded dance floor in the centre of the terrace.

He gave his name to the rather self-important *maître d'* who had bustled up, and received a bow in reply. Ah yes, Lieutenant Ristić. Of course. Your guests have already arrived. He led the way to an excellent table in the centre of the dining area with a good view of both the dancers and the orchestra. The two men already sitting there rose to their feet, held out their hands. 'Good to see you, lieutenant. We must congratulate you on your choice of a dining place. An exceptionally nice atmosphere.'

David returned their smiles with genuine pleasure. He loved showing off his beloved city to visitors. 'Sit down. Please sit down. What have you been doing with yourselves in Belgrade?'

Heinz Wiesinger smiled, shrugged. 'Very little, to be quite honest. Just wandering around.'

'Soaking up the atmosphere. Just soaking up the atmosphere you might say.' Werner Dietrich's round blue eyes were darting around the terrace, lingering now and then on one or two of the more attractive women.

David nodded. 'Except for Kalemegdan Park, I suppose there is little to see here, really. But atmosphere? Yes, indeed. We have plenty of that.'

Wiesinger lifted a bottle of wine from the centre of the

table, held it aloft. 'Won't you join us? We arrived here quite early. Decided to enjoy a glass of wine with the–' he paused, his eyes following those of his friend's as they rested on the face of a vividly handsome woman two tables away '–scenery!'

David joined in with their laughter, and settled back with his wine to study more closely his two dinner companions.

Werner Dietrich was in appearance more closely Germanic than his companion. In addition to the blue eyes, which on closer scrutiny proved not so artless as David had originally perceived, his thinning fair hair, pink and white skin and heavily-jowelled face seemed the perfect prototype for the much loved Aryan of his Führer. Heinz Wiesinger, on the other hand, with his dark hair, high forehead and pale, penetrating grey eyes, did not so easily fit into any nationalistic mould.

'Your health.' Wiesinger had lifted his glass with an air of amusement at David's scrutiny. The latter responded with a slight smile of embarrassment, was glad when Werner Dietrich leaned forward to speak.

'Do you mind if we call you David?' He gave the correct Serbian pronunciation of *Dah-vid.*

'Please. Of course.'

'Well, David,' Heinz Wiesinger drained his glass, refilled that of his companion and poured the remainder of the wine into David's half-emptied glass. 'We have spent the day strolling around your Belgrade. Tell us what you think we found most fascinating?'

David shrugged, shook his head. 'Well, I suppose it is a city like any other. To tell you the truth, Belgrade has been invaded so many times, torn down and then rebuilt over and over again, that it is something of a hodge-podge. Nothing too interesting, as I said before, except perhaps for Kalemegdan.' His blue eyes lit up. 'And yet, what *I* think it has that *must* be unique, is that its very air reeks of history. Almost as far back as history began men have lived and fought and died here. And for the most noble cause. For their freedom. To protect what rightfully was theirs.'

Werner Dietrich nodded, leaned forward and gave him a keen look that confirmed David's realization that he had underestimated the intelligence hidden behind the bland expression. 'Of course you are right. The thing that struck us both was the vivacity of your people. They are full of life!' He settled back in his chair, nodding his head thoughtfully. 'That is where it comes from. A people who have had to defend their land and their lives so fiercely and for so long must surely come to love that life, to treasure and appreciate that life, more than most. Yes?'

'On the other hand, the thing that really fascinated us about Belgrade was...' Heinz Wiesinger began to chuckle, shook his head.

'Yes?'

'Well, to be quite honest, it was your butcher shops.'

'Our butcher shops?' David laughed, having immediately grasped what Wiesinger was saying. 'Ah, yes. I have heard that there is a food shortage in Germany. It is true, then?'

'Well, as you can see...' Dietrich patted his corpulent stomach and gave a conspiratorial wink, 'we are not exactly starving, despite our chancellor's predilection for guns before steaks. But, yes. It is quite some time since we have seen anything quite like the butcher shops of Belgrade.' He sighed, with a slightly wistful air. 'All of those succulent piglets, the whole lambs, the veal, the beef steaks, the geese and–'

'For God's sake, Werner,' his friend raised his hands in protest. 'You are making me hungry.'

'Well, here is the waiter,' David smiled, 'perhaps just in time?'

Following his suggestion they joined him in ordering steaks with Serbian salad. When the huge platters arrived he was amused when they asked whether it was possible to order steaks like this every day at the Madera.

'Of course. Any time. Any restaurant. As many as your stomach can hold. Night or day. You must understand, there is no shortage of food in our country. In fact we have too much of it. We cannot find enough markets.'

'Lucky Yugoslavia!' Werner Dietrich grimaced with mock envy. He then lifted the glass of Bajloni beer David had ordered to accompany the steaks. 'Priyatno!'

Startled, David lifted his glass and responded warmly. 'Priyatno!' and then added the German equivalent for the benefit of an obviously uncomprehending Wiesinger. 'Guten Appetit!'

In the manner of healthy men they tackled their succulent main course in silence. It wasn't until he was halfway through the huge steak that David lifted his head and glanced towards Dietrich. 'You know something of our language, then?' He smiled. 'Or is "priyatno" perhaps the extent of your ambition?'

'Well, not quite.' He lifted his beer glass and drained it rather noisily. 'You see, a couple of years ago I was stationed in Zagreb as foreign correspondent for my paper. So I know something of your language.' He held up one hand as David started to reply. 'But, please, I beg of you. It does not come easily, and as your German is excellent...'

David nodded, then gave full attention to finishing his dinner. Following the steak the waiter appeared bearing several platters of Yugoslav cheeses and pastries. They completed their meal, ordered coffee and sank back into their chairs with contented sighs.

'A cigar?' David shook his head and watched as Dietrich accepted one from his friend, then tilted his chair around slightly to get a better view of the dance floor. Wiesinger inhaled deeply. 'You know, David, you seem to lead a really good life here in Belgrade.'

'Yes, we do. I hope it stays that way.'

They both accepted the pointed remark in silence, seemingly absorbed in the spectacle of dancing couples. The night was still and warm, a full moon added its glow to the man-made lights and the heavy, sweet smell of blossoms lent the evening a pleasant somnolent quality.

'You were referring, I take it, to the activities of our

Führer?' Without taking his eyes from the dancers, Wiesinger reached out to the ashtray in the centre of the table, tapped his cigar.

'What's that?' The two men had remained silent for so long that David had almost forgotten his previous remark. He had been thinking, in fact, about the job at the State Mortgage Bank he would be returning to on Monday.

'Oh! Well, yes. You must admit, gentlemen,' he added quickly, 'that your Führer, as you call him, has a great many people worried.'

'They needn't be.' Wiesinger turned in his chair and regarded David steadily. 'At least, shall we say, none of Germany's friends have cause to worry.'

'Yes, yes. That's true. And, after all, thanks to your ex-prime minister ... what was his name again?' Dietrich's artless blue eyes were blinking rapidly behind the thick cigar smoke.

'Stoyadinović?'

'Stoya ... yes, that's the name. I do believe he is still quite highly thought of in our government circles. And I must say your prince regent has now also made it clear that Germany and Yugoslavia should remain firm friends.'

'Perhaps.' David leaned forward a little, looked at them both thoughtfully. 'It certainly makes sense. As we have mentioned tonight, Yugoslavia has an abundance of agricultural goods – you probably know your country is one of our principal food buyers – and in exchange we buy your industrial products. Why jeopardize such mutually beneficial trade agreements? Yes, yes. Our two countries must remain friends. It is just ...'

'Don't tell me!' Heinz Wiesinger was shaking his head in disgust. 'You have been hearing some of these filthy rumours about our treatment of the Jews.'

'Rumours?' David frowned. 'Yet from every reliable source possible, we hear about confiscation of Jewish property in your country. Destruction of their businesses. Are you telling me it is not true that the walls of Berlin and Hamburg are plastered with ugly caricatures of the Jewish people? Or that the so-called "crystal night" did not take place last November?'

'No, no. We are not saying that.' Dietrich had become agitated, his plump cheeks trembling as he shook his head vehemently. 'But what can we do? We admit to having a certain, well, let us say radical element in our society. Why, you have them yourselves. Here in Yugoslavia we have heard about disturbances, public demonstrations. Why, only a few days ago while we were still on the Dalmatian coast, we read about student arrests here in Belgrade.'

David laughed. 'Oh, our students! Look, only last year I completed my degree in economics at the University of Belgrade. Certainly, we do have a group of Marxist students. They even tried to get *me* involved. But, you know, who can take them seriously? Certainly not the workers to whom they are supposed to appeal so much, on whose behalf they make so much noise, I assure you. They hardly have one worker supporting them. No, no. They are no more than a bunch of romantic dreamers who find it far more exciting to run around the streets of Belgrade irritating the police than to study. It is so much easier for them to learn a few Marxist slogans than to study, say, Ricardo's theory of qualitative rent! And, of course, to counter them, we unfortunately have our extremist right. In fact, they are the ones who worry me more than the communists. The communists here are considered a joke!'

'Ah, yes. The communists!' It was Wiesinger who now seemed agitated. 'It truly is incredible. But consider. In Germany we make a few Jews feel uncomfortable and the whole of democratic society is up in arms. Yet in the Soviet Union they managed to exterminate – *exterminate,* I tell you – God only knows how many of their own people. Millions have died. Absolute genocide! And what did we hear from our wonderful democratic intellectuals and writers then? Nothing! If that is the word for a deafening silence! And would you believe it? Many of them still rant on about the so-called new society. It works, they say. *It works!* Liars! And even these infamous trials of theirs will eventually be swallowed by these great intellectuals. I truly believe they would rather see the whole world in flames rather than admit they were wrong. And then they have the absolute gall to complain about Adolf Hitler! Incredible! I tell you it is all simply beyond reasonable comprehension.'

'Yes, yes. In that respect Heinz is right.' Dietrich had been listening to his friend carefully. Now he turned to David. 'And, you know, you mentioned something about Berlin walls being covered with unpleasant graffiti about Jews. Well, I would like you to know that I have seen similar graffiti in just about every country I have ever had cause to visit. In the United States, for instance, where so much of the propaganda about our treatment of the Jewish element seems to be coming from, I have seen graffiti about Jews, and about their own Negroes. I have seen that in New York. Yes, I assure you. In every overseas city I have visited.'

'But not in Belgrade. Never in Belgrade!' David spoke so vehemently, so earnestly, that Dietrich broke off what had fast seemed to be becoming a tirade, stared at him for a moment, then burst into laughter.

'You are right, my friend. I have not seen such things in Belgrade.' The blue eyes turned shrewd, began to twinkle. 'But I'll tell you where I *have* seen similar things, and that is on the walls of Zagreb, saying very unpleasant things indeed. Not only about the Jews, but about you Serbs. Yes?'

David scowled. He was about to snap a sharp rejoinder, but then thought better of it. He laughed wryly instead. 'You have me there, Werner,' he admitted, adding rather sadly, 'I'm afraid our Croatian brothers can out-hate anyone.'

'Yes, yes,' Dietrich continued. 'Hate! A terrible word. But I felt it there, you know. They absolutely hate you Serbs. And yet, to me, a German, a stranger, during my entire stay there I found nothing but kindness. Extraordinary!'

'Well, you see . . .'

'No, no.' Dietrich held up a plump, pink hand. 'If you will allow me just one more observation. That hatred – and I use the word in all of its implications – does not seem to be returned by you Serbs. That puzzles me.'

David nodded slowly. 'But your observation is very astute. You must be an observant man indeed.'

It was Wiesinger who replied, rather drily. 'We journalists tend to be, eh, Werner?'

'If you ask me why they hate us, the reasons are rather complicated. I think the main reason, oddly enough, is that we freed them from Austro-Hungarian domination. You know, of course, that they fought alongside the Austrians in the Great War. Yet we demanded no reprisals. Not at all like the Allies who demanded so much from Germany, for instance. In fact we offered them freedom within a South Slav state. No one tried to deprive them of their Catholic religion. They were allowed their own representation in our parliament. But then, of course, there is the fact that throughout the five-hundred years of Turkish occupation, we Serbs did not bow our heads. Except for a few who embraced Islam when a gun was pressed against their heads, we refused the Turkish religion and the Turkish culture, whereas the Croats, they not only embraced the Roman Catholic church in order to please the Habsburgs, they like to pretend that because of that they are more civilized than the Serbs. What a people!' He paused, shrugged. 'Yet how can we hate them? They are Slavs, after all, whatever else they pretend. But you cannot imagine the difficulties they have caused our country.'

'And yet,' Dietrich said carefully, 'what *they* say is that your Serbian police have sometimes acted towards them with great brutality.'

David looked glum. 'Some of our police. Yes, I'm afraid so. A Turkish legacy, you see. Just as the Croat police inherited *their* brutality from the Habsburgs. And just as the Croat terrorists learned *their* legacy of torture and mutilation from Italy. Not to mention their capacity for endless intrigue.'

‘And, of course,’ Dietrich added thoughtfully, ‘they did murder your King Alexander.’

‘Once they no longer feared reprisals for their part in the Great War,’ David said bitterly.

Dietrich nodded. ‘And it was your “great allies” the British and the French who blocked condemnation by the League of Nations of Italy for its role in that barbaric act.’

‘I know. I know,’ David despaired. He became suddenly aware of the waiter hovering expectantly by their table, reached out to take the bill, then glanced at his two companions. ‘Do you have any other commitments this evening? Perhaps we could move to the bar. Have some more wine. Talk. It is less noisy there.’

‘A good idea.’ Dietrich glanced towards Wiesinger, who nodded his head in agreement. ‘Yes. I’d like to continue this conversation. Very interesting.’

A few moments later the three of them were sitting around a table in a dark corner of the bar, sharing another bottle of wine.

‘I was interested in what you were saying about your young communists, David.’ Wiesinger settled back heavily in the comfortable leather chair. ‘You don’t think they are a danger to your country, then?’

‘Of course not. Perhaps I’m doing them an injustice, but I can’t help feeling that there is an element of “fashion” in many of our so-called leftist professors, students, artists, and so on. An element of fashion to this so-called new ideology which, after all, as I am sure you know, is hardly that new. It’s been tried before, and never worked before. It certainly won’t work in Yugoslavia for the simple reason that we have so few workers here. We are an agricultural country. Three-quarters of our people are peasants, most of whom own their own land. And they are too aware of what happened to their class in the Soviet Union to want to embrace Marxism, I can assure you of that.’

Dietrich was nodding his head in agreement. ‘And I wonder if your people are aware just how fortunate they are to have escaped this industrial age of ours? I don't pretend to know – does anyone of us know? – just what we have been put on this speck of dust in the universe we call Earth for, but I'm damned if I can believe it is that so many of us can spend the greater part of our lives in some soulless factory or office.'

Wiesinger laughed. 'Don't listen to him, David. My friend Werner is something of a dreamer. Thank God his dreams have not led him to communism. But, talking about our industrial age, how much longer will it last? Fifty years? A hundred? And then what? My guess is that "then what" will be that the world will need all of the food it can get, and agricultural countries like yours will really come to the fore.'

'I had not thought of that,' David said excitedly. 'Yet, you know, you may perhaps be right.'

'The trick is,' Dietrich's eyes seemed strangely concentrated inward, 'the trick is to keep modern industry out. Of course it does have many advantages, but these simply do not outweigh the disadvantages. Especially for a country like this. Especially for Yugoslavia. I am a foreigner, but I would truly hate to see this country change.'

Wiesinger gave another short laugh and winked at David. 'Ah, I can see that my friend Werner is about to expound upon one of his favourite propositions!'

'No, no.' Werner shook his head and took a gulp of wine, his pink face becoming more flushed than ever. 'It is just . . . you see, I told you, David. I spent a year or so in your country. Of course I happened to be living in Zagreb, but to be quite honest I did not have that much to do. Had quite a bit of time on my hands, so I spent a good deal of it exploring as much of Yugoslavia as possible, learning something of the language.'

'And when he returned to Hamburg, he spent a good deal of this spare time he had so much of telling me about the wonders of Yugoslavia!' His friend slapped him heartily on the shoulder and laughed.

'But wasn't I right, Heinz? You and I, most of our

countrymen I suppose, had and still have such an inaccurate view of this country. "Ah yes", we tend to say, "the primitive Balkans!" And yet, let me tell you, I found such a wealth of history here, of tradition. It is an extraordinary culture. Why, just on a short trip, you can stumble over a Butmir jar or the helmet of a Roman horseman, almost casually. And the monasteries! Such treasures. I have seen extraordinary, *extraordinary*, frescoes. Beautiful, I mean truly beautiful mosaics. Byzantine murals, such a mixture, Turkish mosques. . . ' His plump cheeks were shaking with excitement, the words came tumbling out, almost falling over one another. 'The country must surely be an archaeologist's paradise! And the people! As in Greece, you can find the shepherd still tending his sheep, his clothes in the style of his ancestors going back for hundreds of years. He looks so poor, and you begin to exclaim at his poverty. And then he lifts his pipe to his lips and begins to play this strange, haunting melody handed down to him by his fathers since time immemorial. Then you become aware, you *know*, that he is closer, far closer, to the essence of life than you and I and our miles of asphalt shall ever be. So you discover that far from being poor he is, in fact, a thousand times richer than you.

'Or you stumble across a so-called poverty-stricken peasant sitting under a tree playing the *gusle*, and there it is again, in his music, in the stories he sings, the distilled history and even the origins of mankind. And you find, again, this man is far richer than you. I tell you, you envy him! And the women! The women in the mountains. Beautiful to look at? No! *Heroic*. That is the word to describe the strength in some of those women's faces. And the costumes they *still* wear. Richly embroidered patterns that have been handed down to them since times so far back in history that one must simply lose track. Did you know that in Bosnia you will find what surely must be the last remaining primeval forest in the whole of Europe? Swarming! Swarming, I tell you, with packs of wolves and bears and eagles and vultures. Did I tell you, Heinz? So help me! I even met an American hunter in Sarajevo who claimed to have seen the mythical white wolf! And where else in Europe, I ask you, where else can you sit down *anywhere*, and, if you have the simplest grasp of the language, talk to a peasant whose basic wisdom, let alone his shrewd knowledge of politics – God alone knows where they get it – leaves you yourself, a so-called intellectual, completely without words, completely at a loss.'

He paused, simply out of breath. He reached into his breast pocket, withdrew a large white handkerchief and began to mop his by now damp and perspiring brow.

David had been listening with intense pleasure and interest.

'But it is all true, Heinz, you know.' David turned to Wiesinger eagerly. 'And particularly about our peasants. Did you know that, in fact, your own Werner Sombart, Germany's most famous sociologist, surely? Did you know he once said that the Serbian peasant is the most intelligent peasant in Europe?'

'Sombart? That is true? Well, Werner, you cannot say that your views are not shared by good company.' He smiled at David pleasantly. 'You can see what an eloquent propagandist for your country my friend is. Still, I must agree with him. During *my* short visit, I have been most impressed. And he left out the Adriatic coast, by the way, which is so beautiful that neither of our wives would budge a step further. So you cannot say we do not appreciate the beauty of your country or the history of your people.'

Dietrich had, during this short exchange, spied a folded newspaper discarded at a nearby table. He tilted his chair back, reached out and picked it up, began fanning his flushed cheeks. 'Well, I just hope you can keep it all together in one piece, David.' He shook his head doubtfully. 'Although, I am sorry to say, every time I think of the way the Croatians speak about you Serbs...'

'For myself,' David said earnestly, 'I will be quite honest. Personally, I would prefer to see them given independence – let them be reabsorbed by Austria if you will. At least we would know then exactly where we stand. Slavs or not, our brothers or not, if they really prefer an alien civilization to their own, then let them have it!'

Dietrich nodded. 'I am not sure that I would agree with you except, for all their kindness to me, I did find their hatred for Belgrade and for all Serbs for that matter irrational, to say the least. What is it? The church? I suspect that Rome keeps stoking the fire, but I really don't know enough.'

'But yes, you are right,' David broke in excitedly. 'It is the church and, of course, the events of the last war. You know, perhaps, that although Croatia had been seeking autonomy from the Austrian empire for many years, they nevertheless fought on your side. They never quite forgave us Serbs for fighting so bravely during that war and...'

'Ah, yes,' Wiesinger broke in with a smile, '"Brave little Serbia". I have read about that.'

David nodded proudly. 'We freed them from the domination of the Austrian empire and made no effort to interfere with their religion, for which their church is hardly grateful, I might add.'

'But wasn't there also something about one of their leaders being assassinated in Belgrade?'

'Assassinated? Hardly the right word. What happened was that the Croatian delegation in *Skupshtina* – our parliament – stood up and accused a Montenegrin deputy named Punisha Rachić, of corruption. To compound the insult, when Rachić made a speech calling for unity throughout our nation in the name of all of the Serbian blood spilt in order to give freedom and unity to all South Slavs, the Croatian delegation simply sneered at him and asked contemptuously ... they asked ... "How much did that blood you spilled at Kaimakchalan cost? We will pay you cash for it."' He paused for breath, checked to see that he still had their interest, and went on.

'Now let me tell you about our Montenegrins, gentlemen. They are the bravest of men but, frankly, their heads are as hard and as stubborn as their province, which consists mainly of rock and stone. In addition to this, from the moment they enter their mother's womb they are convinced that they are heroes of epic proportion. Personally, I would prefer to try to move the most stubborn mule than to try to persuade a Montenegrin that black is black or white is white should he think otherwise. In his mind, you see, he is not only a hero, but also is never wrong about *anything*. So to insult such a man, to question his honour, is something you do at your own risk, but then to add cynicism and sarcasm to compound the injury, well ... although, of course, he was a madman. He did a terrible thing.'

'So it was this man ... Rachić ... you said? He killed the Croatian leader?'

David nodded. 'A Croatian called Radić. He was then minister of education. His nephew, Paul, was also killed outright by Rachić. Others were also killed or wounded. This madman simply pulled out his revolver and ran amok, you understand? Of course some unscrupulous politicians in Croatia have spread the story that our king, that King Alexander, was behind it. Nonsense! That story is nonsense!'

Dietrich nodded. 'Interesting ... very interesting ...'

David nodded, sank back in his chair, picked up his glass of wine, sipped it. 'But I'm sorry, gentlemen. I really did not intend to take up all our time giving history lessons. As a matter of fact, what I wanted–'

'No, no,' Dietrich protested. 'This is the kind of thing I could listen to all night.'

'And *I* must admit that never before have I realized just how little I know about your country. Or the whole of the Balkans for that matter.' Wiesinger shook his head ruefully.

'Well, I'm glad you find some interest in what I've been saying.' David was looking at them both carefully. 'But, you know, what I really wanted to talk about tonight, was your country.'

'Germany?' Wiesinger raised a hand to his mouth, covered a yawn, then stretched, smiled. 'I'm afraid we will need at least another night for that.'

'Well, I know it's late.' David glanced towards the bar

clock. 'My God! It's well after midnight. And I suppose you are both tired?'

Werner Dietrich nodded. He had settled back heavily into his chair. The blue eyes that had moments before been alight with interest, were suddenly glazed. 'I must admit–' he began.

'If I could just ask you one thing?' They both returned his look rather wearily. It was as though the tiredness that had been creeping up on them both imperceptibly had suddenly descended in an all-enveloping blanket.

'You see, I have a friend. I will be meeting him for coffee tomorrow. I am sure he is going to ask me what he and his family should do. In what direction Europe is headed. You see, he is a Jew, and–'

Wiesinger sat upright in his chair. 'What he and his family should do? Why should they do anything?' The grey eyes were cold, the voice hostile, brittle. In the silence that followed, Werner Dietrich moved uneasily. 'Tell your friend,' Wiesinger continued icily, 'that in Germany, whatever American and British propaganda says to the contrary, all Jews are protected by the same laws as the rest of us. And if *that* doesn't answer his question . . .' He stood up abruptly. 'Are you ready, Werner? I think it really is time.'

The three of them silently made their way outside and stood at the entrance to the hotel looking at each other uneasily. After a moment Wiesinger relaxed and held out his hand. 'An extremely interesting evening. Thank you very much for your hospitality.'

'Yes, yes . . .' the big man beside him nodded his large fair head in agreement. 'I must say, look, Heinz, there is a cab, I'll just grab it . . .' He loped off down the street, waving both arms. Wiesinger laughed, turned to David. 'How speedily he moves when he wants to, for such a big fellow, eh?' He paused, then: 'Can we offer you a lift, David?'

'Thank you. But I think I'll walk for a while. It's such a beautiful evening.'

'You are right. But I must say, you have more energy than I at the moment.' He reached into his pocket and pulled out a card, held it out. 'Thank you again for an extremely pleasant evening. If you are ever in Hamburg, please do look me up.'

David accepted the card, nodded. 'Of course. I hope to visit Germany one day. If I find myself in Hamburg I shall certainly call you.'

'Here we are, Heinz. I've got a taxi!' A few yards away Werner Dietrich was opening the back door of one of Belgrade's few taxi-cabs and beckoning to his friend. As Wiesinger, with a farewell nod to David, moved towards the cab, Dietrich returned with outstretched hand.

'A wonderful evening. Thank you very much.' David accepted the large, soft hand, shook it warmly. 'My pleasure, Werner. I hope you will look me up should you return to Belgrade.'

'Of course. Of course.' The large head nodded. He gave a gesture of farewell and moved away in the direction of the taxi, then suddenly returned and took hold of David's arm urgently. 'Tell your friend,' he muttered rapidly, 'to get out of Europe. Tell him to get out of Europe anywhere and any way he can!'

And then he was gone, leaving David to stare after the taxi as it pulled away from the kerb and roared noisily down King Alexander Boulevard.

He felt as though a cold hand was very slowly squeezing his heart.

2

'You mean you are going out again? But, son, you are never home. You are away for two months and when you do return we never get a chance to see you.' Aunt Draga's fine dark eyes reflected her disappointment. Turning away from him she abruptly began to bang pots around on the stove.

'But come on, Auntie. You know I have only a couple more days and then it's back to the bank for me. Besides, I promised I would be home for dinner this evening, and I intend to keep my promise.'

'What a great sacrifice! After two months, just one night for the family! And you know the girls are going out after dinner.'

'But so are you and I, Auntie.' David moved over to her, placed both hands about her ample waist and began to whirl her around the kitchen as he sang snatches of *The Merry Widow* waltz.

'What *are* you talking about? Stop that!' Trying to keep a stern countenance and at the same time quite unable to hide her pleasure, she grabbed hold of a wooden spoon as he danced her past the large, well-scrubbed kitchen table and gave him a resounding smack on his knuckles.

'Ouch! What an ungrateful woman.' He deposited her down on a straight-backed wooden chair near the stove and wagged a stern finger at her. 'Here I go to all the trouble of arranging to take you to see *The Merry Widow*, and all the thanks I get is a whack!'

His aunt shot straight up in her chair. 'You mean it? *The*

Merry Widow? But that is my favourite operetta. All those handsome officers singing. They remind me . . .'

'I know. I know. They remind you of Uncle Svetozar and how handsome he looked in the uniform of the Serbian cavalry.'

Aunt Draga smiled, sighed, and wiped a surreptitious tear from the corner of her eye. Her husband had been killed on the Salonika front during the Great War, and mention of his name was one of the few things that could soften the fierce façade she rather enjoyed presenting to her family.

'There. Aren't you ashamed now to go around hitting your only nephew with a wooden spoon?' He picked up a jar of *slatko* and began to unscrew the top, dodging out of her way as she gave an exasperated gasp and tried to take it from him.

'No, no. That's for tomorrow, give it here.'

Too late! He had already pried open the top, scooped out a spoonful of the sweet plum preserve and swallowed it. He undid her apron strings, ducked as she aimed a blow, kissed her on the cheek and made a hasty exit with her exasperated protests ringing through the apartment. It wasn't until he had reached the hallway that he remembered about Bogdan and his girl. He moved swiftly back to the kitchen, poked his head around the door and said: 'By the way, Bogdan will be coming for dinner tonight, too. And he'll be bringing a friend.'

He darted through the living room into the hallway again and through the front door, ignoring the peremptory cries coming from his aunt, asking him to explain about Bogdan, and *which* friend!?

Outside the apartment building he ran lightly down the street, and swung aboard a passing tram that would take him down King Alexander Boulevard to the Terazije. Once seated, he rubbed his still stinging knuckles and gave a rueful smile. What a fiery-tempered dragon his aunt could be. She had come to live with her sister's family during the Great War and had remained with them after her husband was killed. She had become a permanent fixture in their lives. Just as well, too. She had certainly put a stop to any signs of unruliness in David and had acted as counter to his gentle mother's tendency to spoil her children. When their beloved mother had died, Draga had been a tower of strength, not only for the children, but for her brother-in-law, David senior, as well. It was Aunt Draga, too, who had gathered up the pieces once more when the children's father had died of a heart attack, peacefully in his sleep a few short years later.

David alighted from the tram and made his way through the Terazije where he stood looking around the crowded square before crossing over to the Russian Tzar. Jack was already sitting at a small table underneath one of the brightly-coloured umbrellas. He sprang to his feet as he caught sight of David and held out his hand. 'I'm so pleased you could come. So pleased. I've ordered coffee, pastries, is that all right?'

'That's fine, Jack. Just fine.'

'Well. And how were the military manoeuvres? You look so fit! What a wonderful tan.'

David laughed. 'I'll tell you something, Jack. I would have much preferred to have acquired it here in Belgrade at the rowing club, I can assure you of that.' He accepted the sugar Jack was offering, stirred it into his coffee and began to relate a few amusing incidents that had taken place during his short stint with the army reserve in Negotin.

Jack, as usual, was a fine audience, listening intently to every word, nodding and laughing and pressing him to take more coffee, more pastries. When the inevitable pause came at the end of David's anecdotes, however, he sighed heavily, fidgeted with his expensive silk tie, coughed, and nervously rubbed a fine linen handkerchief between his hands until it was a moist, wrinkled ball.

'Something's wrong. What is it, Jack?' David knew what was coming; he also knew it was required that he ask.

'Wrong?' The soft eyes blinked anxiously behind the protective glasses. 'Oh, no. Nothing. Nothing.' He hesitated, then rushed on. 'I was wondering, though. I mean, my father was wondering. He was asking me – he asked me a few day's ago – if I'd seen anything of you. Of course, I told him no, that you were away on army manoeuvres and...' He gave a deprecating gesture, attempted a smile. 'You know how our old people are. He could not understand why they had called up the reserve, why they were holding manoeuvres now. "What is it?" he keeps asking. "Are they expecting war, then? Now that they have got rid of the fascist Stoyadinović, does it mean they expect war?"' The flow of words stopped, Jack sighed, looked down at the wrinkled handkerchief in his hands. Began worrying it again.

'Why would we expect war? Do you think we are mad?' David's vehemence surprised himself. Jack stared at him even more anxiously. David tried to put Werner Dietrich's parting words to him the previous evening out of his mind. The man had simply been drinking too much, that was all. On the other hand...

'Look, Jack,' he went on in a milder tone, 'of course you, your father, all of your family must be worried. All these stories coming out of Germany. Enough to make the whole of Europe worried and nervous. But, now that he has Austria and Czechoslovakia, surely that is as far as the English and French will let him go? As for this madness with the Jews ... it seems to me that small sections of the human race seem to need to go mad once in a while. We are dealing, it seems, with a mad minority, that is all.'

'Not such a minority,' Jack said, shaking his head nervously. 'I was at the movies the other evening. They were showing some news. And the crowds *he* draws. The *enthusiasm*. The whole of Germany seemed to be there.'

'The whole of the rabble, you mean,' David snapped. He sighed. 'As a matter of fact, Jack, I was talking to two Germans last night. Quite intelligent men. Journalists. They seemed very civilized to me. If the majority of Germans are like those two, then...'

'But what did they say? Did they mention the Jewish situation in their country?' Jack sat up straight and stared at him anxiously.

David picked up a pastry and began to chew it glumly. 'Look, Jack. The whole point is, you are nervous, your family is nervous. I don't blame any one of you. But, well, it is a well-known fact. Your father is a wealthy man, right? He can, after all, choose the place in which he wishes to live. I mean, until things blow over, you and your family could–'

'But that's all we talk about. Day and night! Should we sell up and get out of Europe? But to go where? We have made inquiries, you see, at the American embassy, at the British embassy, the Canadians, even. But...' To David's horror, his friend's eyes were suddenly moist, and the full mouth began to tremble. 'Everyone is so terribly sorry! But it seems no one *wants* us. There is nowhere we can go. Nowhere we can turn.'

David stared back at him, fighting down a feeling of revulsion. Of fury against all of the dirty, unseen forces that were filling his gentle, kindly friend with this unreasoning and helpless fear. And here in democratic Yugoslavia of all places! He suddenly slapped his fist down hard on the table. 'Damn them!' he cried. 'You are a free citizen of Yugoslavia! Why *should* you sell everything? Why *should* you get out? Damn them. Damn them!'

There was a slight stirring of interest in the tables around them. Heads turned, shoulders shrugged. But the citizens of Belgrade were on the whole too absorbed in their own affairs to take much heed of the passions of a young and temperamental army officer. Jack, however, was, momentarily at least, startled out of his own fears. 'You are right! Why should we go? My father and his father before him worked hard for everything we have. Why should we leave our beautiful home? Our investments? Our friends? Why should we leave our country?'

They stared at each other. David's burst of fury died as quickly as it had flared. Jack's moment of bravado faded.

'The point is, I suppose, this Hitler. I think he must be a maniac, Jack. Look, you are right about selling out. Why should you? But what you *could* do, is you could leave Europe on an extended holiday. Why don't you?' The solution seemed so obvious that David sat up excitedly. 'Don't you see? Your whole family. You could go as tourists, to visit England, the United States, but only for a year or so. You could just keep moving on an extended tour. Surely these countries would give you visas for short stays?' The idea took hold, gained momentum. 'You could take as much money out of the country as allowed, and jewellery! You could take some jewellery with you. And just travel, *and wait and see*. Surely to God someone will have calmed that maniac down within a year or so. Or at the very worst, things will become clearer. Either the British will get into a war or they will not. And if a war did start and Yugoslavia became involved, then you would be granted automatic permanent immigration status in any democratic country you happened to be visiting. Then, when we have got rid of the filthy fascists, why you need only to return home, reclaim your property, and carry on with your life as usual.'

Jack was sitting up straight, his eyes bright with hope. 'But you are right, David. Of course that is the solution. Why have we been talking about *losing* everything? About leaving Europe *forever*? After all, you know, for years now my father has been talking about taking a vacation in the United States. He has a cousin in New York, you see.'

'Well there you are! You have nothing to lose. And a vacation to gain.' The feeling of relief made David's eyes sparkle. He laughed exultantly. 'Of course! You see, my friend, how simple things become if one only thinks them through.'

'Yes, yes.' Jack was almost trembling with excitement. 'I will tell my father. I will tell my family at once.' He rose to his feet and held out his hand. David also rose from the table, shook Jack's hand warmly, and slapped his shoulder. 'All right then, my friend. You will let me know what you decide?'

'Yes, yes. Of course.' About to hurry off, Jack changed his mind and turned back. 'But look, David, are you busy? Why don't you come to my father's office with me? Right now. You are so much more persuasive than I. You will know how to talk to him.' He gave a self-deprecating half-smile. 'He never takes too much notice of me, you see. But I know he likes you. And he would respect your opinion.'

David shook his head. 'I'm sorry, Jack. I have to pay a courtesy call to the bank, check in with my boss. I don't have to start work until Monday, but I promised I would let him know when I arrived home. But don't worry about your father. Just tell him about our discussion and send him my regards. He is a wise man. He will quickly realize our idea is the only answer.'

Jack nodded, but still looked a little dubious. 'I hope so, David. I hope you are right.' He straightened his tie, smoothed his hair, again gave that self-deprecating little smile, then hurried off down the street.

David watched him disappear across the Terazije with a slight frown. He then smoothed his own fair hair back, straightened his jacket and slowly made his way to the end of the square, past the Albany, Belgrade's one and only skyscraper, and along Vasina Street until he reached the imposing façade of the State Mortgage Bank.

He enjoyed his work at the bank, although he did not intend to stay there much longer; had other ambitions, despite the fact that he had reached a comfortable Grade 6 level in the mortgage loan department which carried with it an excellent salary. The head of the department was Eugene Krstić, a small, slightly-built man with an impressively curled white moustache, darting dark eyes and a powerful, authoritative voice. Well into his late sixties, he determinedly resisted the idea of retirement. The bank without him, he firmly believed, would soon cease to exist!

Krstić caught sight of David the moment he entered the building and began to cross the beige and black marble floor to greet him. 'But here is our soldier! Welcome home, David. How are you? How are things with you? And with our heroic army?' There was no chance to reply. Lowering his voice in a conspiratorial fashion, Krstić frowned importantly. 'When are you returning to work?' David tried to match the serious look on the old man's face.

'I'll be back on Monday, sir.' He always enjoyed, was amused by the air of self-importance that radiated from Krstić.

The white moustache twitched importantly. 'Monday? Wonderful. We have all been very busy since you left.' He frowned sternly from beneath the thick mop of white hair. 'We need you, David. We will be glad to have your extra pair of hands.'

'And I'll be glad to be back, Mr Krstić. I can tell you, sir, I much prefer the bank to the army.'

The old man nodded, jovial now. 'Just give yourself a few days. You will feel as though you were never away from us.' He offered his hand abruptly in a gesture of dismissal and David shook it with a feeling of relief and freedom. Freedom, he told himself as he made his exit, was preferable to either the bank *or* the army.

As though to echo his thoughts a voice hailed him from behind. 'Hello there, David. Still in the army, are you? How nice it must be to be free from the bank routine.'

It was Ernst Halder, bank colleague and fellow soccer player. David turned, smiled, shook hands. 'I'm not so sure I'd call a stint with the army freedom, Ernst. But perhaps now, at least until Monday, anyway. How are you? How have you been keeping?'

'Fit as ever. Yes. I must say I have been keeping fit. Tell me, will you be playing with us tomorrow?'

'I'll just be a spectator. I need a week or so to get back into things.'

'Of course. Well, I'll look forward to seeing you at the club again.' Halder, a tall, solidly built *Volksdeutscher*, born in Yugoslavia of German parents, grinned and ran his hands through his shock of chestnut-coloured hair. 'Have you been practising your German?'

'Not much chance of that in the army! But, as a matter of fact, last night...' David told him about the two German journalists. 'A pity it was all at such short notice, Ernst. I could have invited you along.'

'I would have enjoyed that. But better luck next time.' He

held up a large brown envelope. 'I'd better be off. Have to drop this off at the foreign exchange. If I don't see you at soccer you'll be back at the bank, Monday did you say?'

David nodded. 'I'll certainly be seeing you then.' He watched Halder walk briskly into the bank building before beginning to slowly make his own way back towards the Terazije. If there was one thing he especially enjoyed at the bank, he mused, it was the number of different ethnic groups he worked with. *Volksdeutschers* like Halder, Jews, Croats, Slovenes, Serbs, all with their different cultures, backgrounds, points of view. Ernst Halder was not a favourite of his, although in all honesty there was no good reason for the faint feeling of unease the brown-eyed *Volksdeutscher* always aroused in him. He was a cooperative colleague, and an excellent soccer player, a strong full back with great skill in defending the goal, which certainly made him a welcome addition to the club to which they both belonged. In addition to this, Ernst knew of David's interest in languages and was always ready to assist him with German vocabulary. In fact, now he came to think of it, Halder had gone out of his way more than once to be pleasant and helpful to him. And yet . . .

'Hey! Young soldier! Would you like a trip around the square? Won't cost you much. A few dinars. And you can enjoy this beautiful sunshine.'

Taken out of his reverie, David looked up and realized that a spry old fellow sitting behind two grey geldings was addressing him. The *fiacres* of Belgrade were slowly disappearing with the onrush of motorized transportation and he couldn't resist the offer. 'All right. Why not? Let's take a run down Knez Mihajlo.' He swung himself up into the open carriage, removed his cap, sank back against the cloth-covered seat, and gave himself up to the enjoyment of a truly beautiful day.

*   *   *

Half an hour later he stood shaking hands with another elderly man, Blagoje Nešić, the father of David's favourite girlfriend, Vera, who welcomed him into their home with a warm smile. 'Vera,' he called, 'Vera. He's here. Come and say hello to David.'

Mrs Nešić bustled in from the kitchen. 'How nice to see you again, David. Do come into the living room. Vera will be down in a minute.'

'Thank you for inviting me to lunch.' He took her proffered hand, bent down and kissed her on the cheek. He always enjoyed visiting this family. Blagoje Nešić was an old friend of his Uncle Mikhail. Both were of the 'old guard' who had fought together during the Balkan wars, against the Turks in 1912, and the Bulgars in 1913. In 1915 they had both received medals for heroism shown during the battles of Cer and Rudnik, when the Serbian army had routed the Austrians and Hungarians. Again, in 1918, they had together survived the fierce fighting along the Salonika front against the Austrians, Germans, Bulgars and Croats.

Major Nešić never tired of describing to David the magnificent sight his uncle had made as he led an infantry column of troops through the streets of Skoplje on their way to liberate not only Serbia, but also Croatia and Slovenia. Knowing his uncle as he did, it did not take too much imagination to visualize that proud, six-foot-five-inch bulk astride a huge chestnut stallion, brown eyes undoubtedly afire with determination, his smooth, tanned face handsome and alert above the olive-green uniform of the Serbian army.

'The order of the supreme command,' old Blagoje would relate in his deep, booming voice, 'was to pursue the enemy. Day and night! Imagine. The troops exhausted, the horses, I can tell you, had had enough. We *had* to stop and rest. Occasionally we *had* to stop and rest, orders or no orders from our commanders, far behind the main front line themselves needless to say. But still, we kept going. We kept going north and then west, fighting every inch of the way. On and on we went until we had liberated the whole land, even the blasted Croats, who were being invaded by some of their own sons under the flag of the enemy!' At this point he would inevitably pause to brood, to mutter a few choice Serbian expletives before going on. 'But I must tell you, David. The bravest man I have ever seen – and I have seen many brave men, I can tell you – was your Uncle Mikhail. A magnificent leader. Tireless. Never discouraged. Heroic! His men would have followed him anywhere! And you notice I say *followed*. Because he was *always* ahead of them. Never at the rear. Not for him the rear! Never!' At this point he would shake his head, give a heavy sigh, and peer at David from the fading black eyes to ensure his story was still getting the attention it deserved.

Today, however, the old man had other things on his mind. 'Here, my boy. Let us have a glass of wine together and you can tell me how things were in Negotin.'

'If you will excuse me, David. Something in the kitchen . . .' Having seen him settled in a large, comfortable armchair, Mrs Nešić left him alone with her husband, who opened a box of cigars and offered him one.

'Thank you, sir. I don't smoke.'

Blagoje carefully selected one for himself, lit it, and took a deep, luxurious draw. 'Wise boy. Terrible for the health!' He began to cough, and spluttered a little. 'Terrible! Still. Once one acquires these vices . . .'

David laughed. 'Well, so long as one enjoys them, sir.'

'True. True. Why give up something one enjoys so much?' He leaned comfortably back in his chair. 'But tell me, my boy. How did things go during army manoeuvres? I hope to God the military is shaping up. From the look of things we might need it before too long.'

'Well, let us hope it is not too soon, sir. I'm afraid I can't report to you that we are the most prepared army in the world. No one seemed to know what the devil we were doing, or why we were doing it. I for one felt I was wasting my time. And I really missed Belgrade. I can't tell you how glad I am to be back.'

The old man gave a disgusted grunt. 'Is it true? What is the matter with us then? Doesn't anyone realize there is a maniac loose in Europe? Is there anyone who truly doubts that maniac's intentions? I tell you, unless the army pulls itself together, unless our government finds a way to end all of these internal, and infernal if I might say, divisions in our country, we will find ourselves gobbled up yet again by one of those empire-building bandits who can never seem to keep their hands off the Balkans. I tell you this country *must* have unity. But sometimes I despair. Sometimes I really despair.' He rose and began pacing up and down the large room in some agitation.

'Unity.' David was nodding his head in agreement. 'You know, sir, it is not just by accident that our national flag carries four S's: *Samo Sloga Srbina Spasava*. Only unity saves Serbs! And that is the central word now for our whole country. I couldn't agree with you more. We need a united front to show to the world, particularly to Germany and Italy. A united front and a united army. But...' He shrugged and sipped his wine with an air of fatalism.

'It's the whole story of our history.' Blagoje sank down again into his chair and disconsolately stubbed out the remains of his cigar in a large silver ashtray. 'Divide and rule! Those damned Austrians and Hungarians and Turks with their damned divide and rule! It kept their empires intact for hundreds of years and nobody knows that better than we Serbs. And yet still we–'

'Still we what, Papa?' David looked up and sprang to his feet with a smile at the sound of Vera Nešić's fresh young voice.

'Vera!' He moved over to her ... placed his hands on her shoulders, kissed her on the cheek and then stepped back to really look at her. 'How wonderful you look. Fresh and sweet like an apple.'

'Listen to that, will you?' Blagoje also stood up, beaming fondly at his daughter. 'Nothing but a shameless compliment. And in front of your own father, at that.'

David joined in with Vera's laughter and watched as she crossed the room to hug and kiss her father lightly on the cheek. The fact that she had studied ballet for several years was evident in the graceful swing of her walk, the straight shoulders, the proudly held head. Not a pretty girl, she nevertheless had grace and charm and did indeed look both fresh and sweet.

'Now, Papa, behave. We girls need all the compliments we can get, don't we Mother?' Mrs Nešić had just re-entered the room carrying a large platter of savouries. 'Compliments? What compliments? It's a long time since your father has paid *me* a compliment, I must say.'

Watching the three of them laughing and teasing each other with warm affection, David once again became aware of just how fond he was of the Nešić family. He had known Vera since childhood and there had always been a warm bond between their families. Not for the first time it crossed his mind that this was the girl he would probably one day marry. In fact he had been on the verge of suggesting it to her on his last night in Belgrade before leaving to join his army unit. He had taken her out to dinner and afterwards they had gone dancing. Yet something had held him back. Not yet, he had thought. It is too early for marriage. It is not yet the time.

Later, as they sat around the dining table, and after Mrs Nešić had wagged a finger at her husband and demanded that there be 'no politics' at the luncheon table, Vera began telling David the latest Belgrade gossip. He only half listened as her mother joined in with bits of information about the comings and goings of mutual friends, at the same time pressing upon him his favourite cuts of cold meat and various salads, rich in beans and saukraut, with large slabs of her beautiful home-made bread. With the dinner he knew he would be facing that evening at home he tried to eat as sparingly as possible, accepting only a morsel of each dish, but had trouble getting away with it under the family's watchful eyes.

He was in the midst of laughingly protesting as Vera placed a large slice of cake on his dessert plate when something her mother was saying caught his attention.

'Did you say Alex Miletić? Is he really back in Belgrade?'

'That's right.'

'But I thought he wasn't expected back until the end of the year. Didn't he have a contract to stay in South America until then?'

'Well, Vera heard that the project he was working on was completed earlier than expected, that's all.'

'Strange that Stevan didn't mention it. I had lunch with him only yesterday.'

'Perhaps he assumed you knew.'

'I suppose so. What a pity. Olga invited me to a party at their home last night. I couldn't make it, but if I'd known Alex was home . . .' He shook his head. 'Well, I couldn't have made it anyway.'

'You have seen Olga, then?'

Inexplicably, David felt irritated by the inquiring look Vera was giving him. *Heavens, Vera, we're not engaged yet!* Outwardly, though, he just gave a slight smile. 'I haven't *seen* her. But I called her this morning to apologize. She had sent me an invitation to her party and I received it too late to answer. So I called her and . . . she didn't say a word, though. Not a word about Alex being back.'

Vera sipped her coffee and gave him an enigmatic smile. He was on the verge of telling her that, in fact, he had promised Olga he would call at her house with Stevan on Sunday afternoon after rowing at the club. 'My parents won't be here,' she had said, 'but I have a surprise for you, David.' He assumed now that the surprise must be Alex, began to say as much, then changed his mind. It might be more diplomatic, he realized, to say nothing more to Vera about Olga Miletić. He turned instead to her father and began to talk about a coming soccer match between the Belgrade and Yugoslavia sports clubs. Blagoje listened to him, stern-faced but attentive, until David simply ran out of words. There was a brief silence at the table. Mrs Nešić sighed. Vera stirred restlessly. The major regarded him solemnly, then secretly gave him a huge, mischievous wink.

David burst out laughing. It will be worth marrying Vera, he decided as she looked at her father coldly, if only to acquire the old man as a father-in-law.

* * *

Later that afternoon he returned home to find that all was uproar. His aunt and his two sisters were busy in the kitchen, preparing the soup and bread rolls and the chicken *paprikaš* for dinner that evening. The girls were discussing what they would wear to the dance.

'What's wrong with that blue dress you have that I like?' he asked Andjela.

'Oh, David. I've had that *forever*,' she wailed.

'Well,' Zora decided, 'I think I'll settle for the red taffeta.'

'That red dress? I don't like it. It makes you look fat.' He ducked as his sister pretended to throw an onion at him. 'Just kidding, Zora. Just kidding.'

'Now girls. Leave your brother alone.' Aunt Draga had forgotten her morning brush with him, and was flushed and excited at the thought of the evening that lay ahead. They began to discuss hairstyles.

Women's talk! Time to leave. He poured himself a cup of coffee from the tall black pot on the stove and announced that he was going to his room to read for a while. 'But you didn't say what time Bogdan will be here.' His aunt brushed a strand of black hair back from her forehead. 'And who is his friend? Someone we know?'

'I doubt it. I told him to come at six, but he rushed off without telling me her name.'

'*Her* name?' His sisters stared at him, open-mouthed. Andjela shook her head slowly. 'I don't believe it. Don't tell me that at last Bogdan has found a girl for himself.'

'Andjela, that's not very nice.' Aunt Draga frowned. 'Bogdan is a nice boy. He just needs someone who will understand him, that's all.'

'Well thank heavens,' Zora said. 'Now perhaps he will stop pestering *us* for dates.'

David was already on his way to his bedroom.

'David?' His aunt had followed him out of the kitchen.

'What is it, Aunt Draga?'

'You *will* wear your uniform tonight, won't you? I mean your dress uniform.'

'What for? I've been dying to get into a decent suit all week.'

'But you look so handsome in uniform. I will be so proud of you.'

He laughed. He was pleased, flattered. 'If it means something to you, Aunt, of course I will.'

'And you didn't say, but I suppose Bogdan and his friend will be coming with us?'

'Yes, or course. In fact it's really Bogdan who is picking up the tickets. And he insisted that they be his treat, by the way.'

'You see? I don't know why the girls don't like him. He is such a nice boy, really.'

'Bogdan? Well, anyway, he's certainly fond of you, Auntie.'

'And David, I'll be wearing my black silk. Is that all right? Do you remember it?'

A surge of affection for her swept through him. He leaned over and kissed one of her smooth, flushed cheeks. 'Of course I do. You will look wonderful, as always. It will be the same as that ball you went to, when the king patted your cheek. You will be the handsomest lady there.'

David and his sisters had been brought up on the tale of his aunt and the ball and the famous pat on the cheek accompanied by the 'charming ... charming...' comment of King Peter I, that fascinating Serbian ruler who had not only translated John Stuart Mill's essay on liberty into the Serbian language, but had practised its principles, introducing a constitutional monarchy and ensuring that Serbia benefited from the essential fruits of liberty: a multi-party system, free press and autonomous universities that the people still enjoyed. Their father had often told the story and their mother had retold it, and always Aunt Draga would smile and say nothing. But she loved to be reminded, loved to remember. She could not now quite hide a pleased smile.

'Oh,' she laughed, 'that old tale.' She bustled off, shaking her head and pretending indifference to the glories of her past.

David watched her retreating figure with a smile and then went into his room, sat down at his desk, rested his forehead on the palm of his hands and lost himself in the open copy of Spinoza that lay in front of him.

* * *

There was no way in the world that Bogdan could hide his pride. And David, as always, found himself having difficulty hiding his surprise. Completely spontaneous by nature, his tendency to express the first thought that came to his mind frequently got him into hot water.

This time he managed to restrain himself, however, at least until his aunt asked him to bring the chilled wine from the kitchen icebox.

'Let me help you, David.' Bogdan was on his feet in an instant, and followed him into the kitchen.

'I don't need too much help carrying a jug of wine, Bogdan.' He was amused, well aware of why his friend was dying to get him alone.

'Well?' Bogdan didn't even notice the mild irony. 'What do you think?'

'I think she's a lovely girl,' David said honestly, then couldn't help blurting out, 'but she's Jewish.'

'There is something wrong with that?' Bogdan's face turned a furious brick red. David removed the jug from the icebox and shook his head in exasperation.

'Of course not! Don't be a fool, Bogdan. But for heaven's sake, she's not a girl you just take around. She's the kind of girl you marry. And what makes you think her parents would let an Orthodox Serb get serious about her?'

'David? Is there something wrong? What's taking you so long?' His aunt's voice beckoned somewhat imperiously from the dining room.

'Coming, Aunt!' He placed the jug on a tray. 'Let's talk

about it later.' They returned to the dining room, Bogdan looking sulky.

His face lit up immediately, though, when Rachel Aaron looked over at him and smiled. He began to show off, talking loudly about the car his stepfather had loaned him for the evening. The odd thing about this girl Bogdan had finally found, David mused, was the initial impression of plainness that so quickly changed the moment she opened her mouth to speak, or to smile. Then the colourless hair, too large a nose and dark eyes that were not quite large enough were suddenly infused with a radiance and warmth that startled and confused. It was as though an inner light had been turned on that brightened even her skin and hair. A moment later the smile would fade, she would stop speaking, and there it was again, an immediate transformation – this time into a plain, rather nondescript girl.

At the moment she was talking and laughing with Aunt Draga, who was telling her about some childhood escapade in which both Bogdan and David had been involved. Rachel had clearly made a wonderful impression on his aunt, and when she began to speak with great intelligence to Zora about her medical studies, and then to Andjela about music, it was clear that she had won the hearts of the whole family.

David himself was delighted with her. She was exactly what Bogdan needed and when she casually mentioned that her brother was married to a Croatian girl, the slight worry he had felt about complications with religion vanished.

Shortly after they had finished their coffee, friends arrived to take his sisters dancing, and then Bogdan proudly ushered the rest of the party into the shiny black Ford his stepfather had loaned him.

The National State Theatre was, as usual, crowded.

'Tomorrow is the last night for *The Merry Widow*,' Rachel said as they settled into their seats, 'and then it's back to the symphony and some opera. Are you like your sister, David? Do you enjoy music?'

He nodded. 'Very much. Andjela is the only true musician in the family, though.'

The lights dimmed, the orchestra leader appeared, received an enthusiastic ovation, and led his musicians into the overture.

Afterwards, David never could quite pinpoint the moment he noticed her. He was sitting back enjoying the dazzling costumes and lilting music when suddenly his attention was frozen on a girl in a yellow organza who presumably had been singing and dancing with the rest of the chorus for several minutes. She was small and slender with light-golden hair. He supposed her eyes were blue, but from his seat in the centre stalls he could not be sure. That the oval face and laughing mouth were quite the loveliest he had ever seen was something about which he had no doubts at all.

The curtain fell. The lights went on. It was first intermission. People began to rustle and stir around him, but he could only sit there, quite still, as though stunned. Finally, however, he turned to Bogdan and asked abruptly, 'But who is she?'

'What?'

'Who is she?' His friend stared back at him uncomprehendingly and David felt the impatience that was never far from the surface flare up. 'I said–'

'Who is *who*?' His question had finally penetrated, but Bogdan obviously had no idea what he was talking about.

David took a deep breath and then sighed. No one, he decided, could be quite as obtuse as Bogdan. 'The girl in the yellow dress, of course.' He opened his programme and ran his eyes down the list of names under the simple heading *Chorus*.

'Oh!' Bogdan's slender and surprisingly graceful finger jabbed at a name. Then he pronounced it. 'Irina Mirskaia. She's new,' he added unnecessarily. David was no longer listening, but was busy repeating the name to himself. *Irina Mirskaia*. Several minutes passed, during which Bogdan was joined by Rachel and Aunt Draga in staring at David, who seemed to have turned into a pillar of salt. Finally Bogdan sniggered and took hold of Aunt Draga's arm. 'I think he's fallen in love,' he announced, pointing to the open programme on her lap. 'One of the chorus girls. Irina Mirskaia.'

Aunt Draga leaned over, looked at David searchingly, and then turned to Rachel who was laughing softly. 'Which one was she?'

'I think she's the one wearing the yellow dress.'

'Ah, yes, of course. Lovely. Lovely. Like a little golden butterfly. David? *David.*'

But David was lost. He sat through the remainder of the operetta in a trance. He did not afterwards remember going out to the foyer during the second intermission and returning with chocolates and drinks for Rachel and his aunt. The curtain rose again. He saw nothing until Irina Mirskaia waltzed gaily onto the stage with the rest of the chorus.

'He is mesmerized,' Aunt Draga announced with some wonder. He did come-to, however, after the show. The curtain had come down for the last time. The curtain calls were over and the four of them had moved slowly up the aisle until they reached the foyer, where Aunt Draga ran into a friend and began to exchange rapturous comments about the production they had just seen. David stood there for several minutes, automatically making all the correct responses, then grasped Bogdan's arm.

'Take care of Aunt Draga for a moment,' he said. 'I'll be back.'

* * *

Backstage it was more crowded than he had expected. The cast had already begun to trickle out and it seemed that most of the people waiting were friends or relatives intent on escorting the girls home. David looked around, and wondered with a sinking heart whether she had already left. But what if she hadn't? What if one of the young men clustered around the stage door was waiting for her? He frowned and glared at the best looking of them, just in case, but almost in the same instant four laughing girls exited from the theatre and his imagined rival held out his arm to a plumpish brunette.

Minutes passed. 'The lead singers came out to a burst of applause and a flutter of excitement, followed by a trickle of male dancers.

A *fiacre* with two very large black horses pulled up in front of the stage door exit. He gave it a quick glance, looked back again towards the stage door and there she was, just coming out of the theatre. Alone. She was wearing a green dress of some kind of silken material with a matching shawl draped around her shoulders. She glanced towards David and he saw that her eyes were not blue but light brown with golden flecks and he realized again that he had never in his life seen anyone as beautiful.

He removed his officer's cap, tucked it under one arm, and stepped forward briskly. 'Miss Mirskaia?'

She gave him a startled look. Her eyes moved past him to the waiting carriage, then back again to him. She hesitated. 'Yes?'

'Miss Mirskaia, my name is David Ristić. I wonder if you would allow me the honour . . .'

'No she wouldn't!'

Startled, he turned to find himself confronted by the energetic figure of an angry middle-aged woman with suspiciously bright apricot-coloured hair and prominent eyes of the same golden-brown hue as Irina's. She waved a frilled parasol furiously in his direction. 'My daughter does not speak to stage-door Johnnies, young man. Get away with you! How dare you address her like this! Away with you now!' She grasped Irina firmly by the arm and propelled her into the *fiacre*. He caught the glimpse of a smile as Irina peeped at him with amused eyes, and then the assault on his dignity hit home.

'Madame! Just one moment, Madame!' He roared it out in his best parade-ground manner and was gratified to see the stout figure pulled up short in its intention of following her daughter into the carriage. She turned, gave him a startled look.

He replaced his cap on his head, removed a card from his breast pocket, and handed it to her with a slight bow. 'Lieutenant David Ristić at your service. I am *not* a stage-door Johnnie, Madame! I assure you, I come from a very good family, and I request your permission to call upon you and your daughter.'

There was a sudden hiccup of laughter from the *fiacre*'s driver, a slightly-built man with a swarthy face and a mop of black hair. David glared at him fiercely. The laughter stopped abruptly.

'Well, I must say...' Madame Mirskaia glanced at the card, peered at David. He stood stiffly at attention, too indignant at his intentions having been so crassly misunderstood to be aware of just how impressive he looked in the gold-braided summer uniform of an officer of the Yugoslav army, his blond hair brushed smoothly back to reveal a broad forehead, his candid blue eyes, at that moment blazing with indignation. Irina's mother took it all in. The straight nose, firm chin with its deep cleft, the light summer tan.

'Irina?' She poked her head inside the carriage. A few whispered words were exchanged, and then she was tucking his card away somewhere within the confines of her impressive bosom.

'Very well, young man.' She stared at him sternly. 'You may call upon me *and* my daughter. You may take tea with us next Wednesday afternoon. You will find us home at 15 Miloša Velikog Street. First floor apartment. Three o'clock sharp!' She vanished into the carriage, the driver gave David a wink, flicked his reins, and the *fiacre* bore them quickly away.

He returned to the now almost empty theatre foyer to find his aunt, Rachel and Bogdan looking around for him.

'But David, where *have* you been?'

'I hope you weren't looking for Irina Mirskaia.' Bogdan gave a hoot of laughter. 'You should see her mother! Guards her like a she-wolf her one and only cub.'

David smiled. 'Is that so?' he asked innocently, and gaily

grasped his aunt's arm. 'Sorry to keep you waiting, Auntie. Look, to make up for it I am going to take you all to the *Skadarlija* for supper!'

Laughing and talking he swept them all off to Belgrade's colourful version of the Montparnasse, found an outdoor café with gaily striped umbrellas, and they finished the evening shouting with laughter, talking, greeting friends and singing snatches of music from *The Merry Widow* over their wine until the small hours of morning.

3

Olga had promised David a surprise, so diplomatically he gave no sign that he had learned Alex had returned from abroad. The things he found truly unexpected were Olga herself, and the fact that when the maid showed him into the large drawing room, who should be sitting there but Bogdan Bošković.

Good old Stevan. When he wanted to put himself out he could be extremely thoughtful.

David had known the Miletić family for years, and like most young Belgraders had always admired Alex, who was some five years older than himself. Alex Miletić was a giant of a man, a wonderful athlete with a mild, modest but friendly nature that invariably attracted all kinds of people to him. But Olga had been something else. Even before high school, although Stevan had always adored her, David had found her too bossy and not that attractive. Now, however, he was confronted with a tall, strikingly beautiful young woman who seemed to have little connection with the plump teenager who had forever been tossing her black braids about with a petulant air, or ordering her peers around in an overbearing way.

After exchanging the usual Serbian bear hug with Alex, he had turned to Olga, taken her hand, and kissed her on the cheek. 'Alex hasn't changed a bit. But I would hardly know you, Olga.'

'Do you think I've improved? I hope so,' she laughed.

'Well, you've still got the shiniest black hair I've ever seen.

But you've grown taller, amongst other things.' He stood back and studied her. The pigtails had vanished, her hair was now shoulder length, with thick bangs that softened the too high forehead. The truly striking thing about her, he decided, was her colouring. Large, intelligent black eyes, creamy white skin and full red lips. She wore no make-up and certainly needed none. And then there was her figure. She was taller, slimmer and everything had certainly softened out in the right places. No wonder Stevan was more smitten than ever.

'You look lovely,' was his final decision. She laughed again, obviously pleased, gave a mock curtsy.

He inquired about the health of Judge Miletić and his wife, and learned that they were spending a week or so at Sokobanja, Serbia's most fashionable spa. Courteously he passed on a message from his family for when they returned. Then Stevan arrived. The five young people settled down to talk.

Bogdan was on his best behaviour, carefully accepting the tiny cup of Turkish coffee, nibbling politely at a rich morsel of pastry. He was obviously impressed by the narrow, high-ceilinged room with its rich furnishings. The oriental carpet that sucked thirstily at his feet; the low, deep divans with their lavishly embroidered cushions that matched heavy green and gold drapes; the large circular brass table with its ornate pattern, the bowl of red and cream roses placed upon it; the massive marble fireplace above which loomed a magnificent mural of Olga and Alex as small children. Dressed in Serbian national costumes and holding hands, they seemed to be stepping directly into the room. He could not help mentioning that one day he wanted to have a home with a room just like this. 'The building looks so plain from the outside, and is so spectacular when you enter.'

'Exactly,' Olga said, 'like a mausoleum.'

'No, no ... I didn't mean ...'

She laughed. 'Of course you didn't, Bogdan, but it's true. If you truly had to live here you would soon get tired of it.'

She turned to David. 'I was saying to Bogdan just before you arrived, David. I'm so sorry I lost touch with him after high school. Stevan told me,' she turned again to Bogdan, 'that your father had died ... and your mother remarried?'

Bogdan smirked. 'She did very well for herself. My step-father owns several restaurants. I manage one for him. You know The Three Violins? Caters for the theatrical trade. You must come and have a meal there. On me, of course.'

'Thank you.' The faintest smile crossed her face and for a moment David fancied he caught a glimpse of the old, rather unpleasant Olga. The expression was gone in an instant however, and she continued to talk to Bogdan with such warmth that he decided he was imagining things. Old prejudices die hard, he thought ruefully.

She was telling Bogdan how glad she was that Stevan had suggested she call him, invite him for coffee. 'It's been such a long time. So much has happened to all of us since high school.'

'Well,' Bogdan said importantly, 'I know I'm doing very well for myself. I feel I'm off to a good start. But you and Alex are the lucky ones, Olga. Finishing school in France and a visit to London for you. And Alex ... how was South America, by the way?'

'Yes, Alex. How did you enjoy your travels? Tell us something about your life since you left Belgrade.' David leaned forward eagerly and for the next hour they listened to the big man describe some of the adventures he had experienced since leaving Belgrade, while occasionally Olga or Stevan broke in to comment on the time they had found themselves in London together.

'One day I'm going to travel, too,' Bogdan announced. Again he glanced around the room they were sitting in. 'I'm going to live in a place like this. How lucky you both are to have been brought up in such a home.'

Alex laughed. 'But what Olga told you is true. You would soon get tired of it. It can be very stifling living in such a big place. There are only the four of us, you know. It's very unjust really.' He leaned forward in his chair. 'In a way you are the one who is fortunate, Bogdan. Stevan mentioned your father was a worker, a baker. What a privilege to be brought up close to the masses. It's the only way, really, to learn what life is all about.'

'My God, Alex,' David blurted out. 'Stevan said something about Olga having been bitten by this socialist bug. Don't tell me you have been too?'

Alex smiled good-naturedly. 'That's one way of putting it, I suppose. Yes, it's true. One thing my travels taught me, and Olga too, I was delighted to learn, is that there is a tremendous amount of social injustice in the world. It is the Russians who have found the answer to it. We should be proud, you know, to think that we too are Slavs.'

'You don't approve, David?' Olga had been watching him. She removed a cigarette from the ebony box on the coffee table and leaned forward to accept a light from the eager Bogdan.

'David probably feels the way I do,' Stevan broke in. 'It's not a matter of disapproving ... we simply disagree.'

'But I'd love to discuss it with you both,' Alex said, and turned to Bogdan. 'And with you too, of course, Bogdan. Your input should be invaluable.' He hesitated a moment. 'Do you know what I'm trying to work out? How did you three become such good friends? Olga told me the three of you were inseparable at school.'

'Languages!' Bogdan answered promptly. He nodded towards David. 'He was always first in the class, Stevan second and–'

'And *I* used to be third until you displaced me.' Olga shook a finger at him. 'I used to be furious with you.'

'If it's any consolation, it was never easy. I used to have to work at a bakery in the evenings, you know. My father was always threatening to withdraw me from school, but he died before–'

'You see? That's what I mean about injustice!' Alex shook his head sadly.

Before leaving, the three young men made arrangements to meet with Alex to discuss the 'socialist business' further.

Olga pouted prettily because she had a previous engagement and would not be able to 'make *my* contribution'. 'Another time, Olga,' they assured her. 'We will talk to you about it another time.'

'It's all a lot of nonsense,' Bogdan told David and Stevan as they shared a taxi into town. He could tell Alex a thing or two about socialists, he added. He knew more about *that* subject than anyone would think!

'Good, good,' his companions agreed. 'You can help us put Alex straight about the matter, then.'

They parted ways shortly afterwards, each in his own way looking forward to the coming discussion with Alex Miletić with the profound enthusiasm Serbs brought to their favourite form of entertainment: good food and drink combined with a lively political discussion.

* * *

'Yes, yes. Here he comes. He is here.' Anna Mirskaia turned away from the window with a slight frown. 'You know, I don't know what came over me. Inviting him to tea! We don't know him at all. What was it he said his name was?'

'David Ristić.' Her daughter moved gracefully over to the window and joined her in peeping out from behind the curtains. 'He's not wearing his uniform, Mamoushka. Do you think perhaps he is just in the army reserve? Still, he is very good-looking. Don't you think he is good-looking?'

'Good-looking indeed,' her mother grumbled. 'As though that means anything when we don't even know him.'

'But he said he was from a good family.'

'Is there a man alive who *wouldn't* say he was from a good family? If it suited his purpose, that is.'

Irina laughed, slipped an arm around her mother's waist and kissed her on the cheek. 'He *must* be from a good family. Otherwise, how could he have stood up to my fierce little Mamoushka the way he did?'

'Shall I answer the door? Shall I let him in?' Marya Mirskaia, the other woman in the room, looked up from her embroidery. She was a tiny woman with a sallow face and rather hard black eyes that softened as they rested on Irina's' flushed face.

'What else can we do?' Moments after she had been startled into issuing her invitation to the young Serbian army officer, Anna Mirskaia had begun to entertain doubts. Especially when she recollected the authoritarian tone of voice he had used to address her. Somewhat of an expert in the use of authoritative tone herself when thwarted, she was torn between admiration and irritation as she contemplated the young man standing outside their apartment building. Almost as though he read her mind through the solid brick walls the apartment rang again with several more short, impatient buzzes.

'Very well, Marya. Let him in. Such impatience! Can he not wait for three seconds?' Her instructions were unnecessary. Her sister-in-law had already neatly folded her embroidery, risen from her stiff-backed chair and was on her way to the hallway. A few moments later she reappeared at the doorway of the sitting room with David Ristić standing behind her.

'Ah yes. There you are. Come in. Come in.' Madame Mirskaia adjusted her face into a cold smile and moved forward to greet him. 'Mr . . . Mr . . . ?'

'Ristić. David Ristić.' But he was looking beyond her at Irina.

'Of course. I see you've met my sister-in-law, Mr Ristić.' He tore his eyes away from her daughter, turned to Marya Mirskaia, and gave a slight bow.

She returned his smile. 'Why don't you all sit down? I'll bring the tea, Anna.'

A short time later the four of them were sitting around a hissing brass samovar, sipping tea from dainty porcelain cups. To David's silent amusement, Madame Mirskaia had in short time extracted a great deal of information from him concerning his family, his financial prospects, and the fact that he was not a regular, but a reserve officer in the Yugoslav army.

'We thought you were in the regular army,' she explained, 'because your uniform fitted you so nicely. Forgive me for saying so, but you reserve officers usually dress very sloppily indeed, in my opinion.' She sipped her tea appreciatively.

Irina frowned, shook her head. 'Oh, Mama, that's just not very nice. Not a nice thing to say.' She turned to David. 'My grandfather was a general. I'm afraid my mother judges *all* officers by *his* standards.'

David smiled and leaned forward to accept the cup Marya Mirskaia had refilled for him. 'As a matter of fact I agree with you, Madame. Most of our reserve officers could look a great deal smarter. But, you see, it's a matter of money. We have to provide our own uniforms, and many of us can't afford to spend too much money on a tailor. For myself, I have a cousin who is an officer in the regular army. I managed to get my uniform through the same channels, through the officers' supply cooperative, as he does. I suppose it makes a difference.'

'Oh, it does. Indeed it does.' Anna Mirskaia nodded her head vigorously. 'But perhaps Irina is right. I tend to judge by my father's standards. But those were such beautiful days, you see. When I was young, I mean. And Irina's grandfather, my father, he was such a handsome man. I was always so proud of him. And yet, after all, what is the use of judging things by times past? What is the use of judging things by the standards of our beautiful country, lost now to us forever?' Unexpectedly, a solitary tear began to trickle down one of her heavily-rouged cheeks.

'Madame!' David leaned forward with genuine concern.

'Oh . . .' She waved a plump hand towards him as though to ward off sympathy, and dabbed at her eyes. 'It's all right . . . all right . . . I just . . .'

'But you miss your country. Of course you do.' David's voice was warm, concerned. 'No one can blame you for that, Madame. Nothing can be worse than losing your country forever, as you say.'

'Yes, yes. Of course, of course.' She took a deep breath,

lightly grasped Irina's hand which had reached out to touch her cheek, kissed it, and then seemed to pull herself together. 'You must not misunderstand me, Mr Ristić. We are *very* grateful to have found a home in Yugoslavia. Very grateful indeed. So many things here remind us of home. The language ... so similar ... the church ... the food ... the people ...'

'You see, Mr Ristić, when we left Russia—' Marya Mirskaia joined the conversation, but was interrupted by David.

'Look, won't you all call me "David"?' He turned to Madame Mirskaia. 'And if you don't mind, Madame,' he went on firmly, 'I would like to call your daughter Irina.'

'Of course you can call me Irina.' She smiled at him, her lips turning up at the corners in a delicious way that made his heart give a sudden lurch.

'Well ...' Madame Mirskaia frowned, smoothed the skirt of her brown silk frock.

'When we left Russia,' Marya Mirskaia picked up the conversation again, 'we settled first of all in Paris. We were hoping my brother would join us, would find us there, but ...'

'But Paris was not Moscow,' Anna interrupted. 'A beautiful city. Many of our friends were already there. But it was not the same, you understand? Just not the same. And as for the French,' she shrugged.

He was surprised. 'You did not care for the French?'

'Oh, I suppose they were kind enough. But, how shall I put it? They do not have the soul, you know? They seemed to me to be so ... so *trivial*, somehow.'

Marya Mirskaia laughed. 'My sister-in-law means that they do not have the Slavic soul, David. That's why we feel so at home here. You Serbs are like Russians. You share the Russian soul.'

'But how can you both be so unkind about the French?' Irina gave an exasperated smile. 'I loved them. They were always so gay.'

'And we Russians are *not* gay, Irina?'

'Of course we are, Mamoushka. But there is always that

undercurrent of sadness. Always the sadness is there.' She turned to David. 'You understand?'

David's mind was on something else. 'But if you lived in Paris . . .' His blue eyes lit up. 'Mais vous parlez français!'

And thus he discovered that she not only spoke French, she spoke an *enchanting* French.

Anna and Marya Mirskaia sat watching them as they began to talk together excitedly in French. They were both so young, so eager, looked so beautiful together that even Anna Mirskaia's watchful face softened. After a little while she joined in the conversation with a warmth and gaiety that David found as charming as it was unexpected. For the first time he caught a glimpse of the enchanting Irina in her mother.

Later in the afternoon they gathered around the piano, which Marya Mirskaia played quite beautifully, while her niece sang Russian and Serbian folk-songs in a light, pretty soprano. And later still, David extracted permission to again visit the Mirskaia's on their return from a short vacation they were about to take in the country, an annual event that had been put off until Irina completed her engagement with the light opera company at the State National Theatre.

At home that evening he was very quiet, very thoughtful. As the evening wore on his Aunt Draga began to watch him with a slight frown. David's work at the bank began at 7.30 a.m., but he was finished for the day by 1.30 p.m. Although he rarely returned home immediately, often joining friends for lunch, or going directly to his sports club for an afternoon of soccer or to take his small canoe out on the river, when he did arrive home he was usually full of talk and laughter about the events of the day. At the very least he could be relied upon to tease his sisters! His time for peace and quiet came when he retired to his own room, firmly closed the door and sat down at his desk to study or to read one of the great philosophers he loved so much.

This quietness, dreaminess almost, even at the dinner table where he seemed to have lost his appetite and only toyed with his food, was something new.

'Listen to your aunt, David,' she told him sternly just before he retired to his bedroom. 'When you finish work tomorrow I want you to drop by and see Dr Popović.'

'Dr Popović?' The blue eyes stared at her uncomprehendingly. 'Do you want me to pick something up for you?'

'For me? Of course not. I am as strong as an ox!'

'I know you are.' He kissed her on the cheek. 'Just see that you stay that way, Auntie.'

She waved him aside, in no mood to be trifled with. 'Of course there's nothing wrong with *me*. But you? Maybe that malaria you had as a child is coming back?' She gave a worried frown. 'You have been so quiet all evening. Hardly touched your food. Now, please don't argue with me, David. I know you are coming down with something.'

She was so offended when he began to laugh – began and could not stop – that she did not begin to thaw until the following evening when he diplomatically arrived home with a large box of her favourite sweet, *alva*.

* * *

The four young men first of all ate heartily from large white dishes of *ćebabčići* and bowls of Serbian salad, washed down with huge draughts of beer. Then they pushed their chairs back against the whitewashed walls of the small restaurant and watched a party of male students link arms around each other's waists and dance the *kolo*, clapping their hands in time with the music supplied by an itinerant violinist. As the steps of the dancers became faster, more intricate, the students' faces became flushed, their smiles dissolving into looks of intense, primeval concentration, their laughter turning into high, bird-like cries.

Suddenly Alex looked around, shook his head. 'But we will never talk seriously here. Where can we go so that we can talk?'

Bogdan suggested that they go to one of his stepfather's restaurants where they could have a private dining room, but after discussion it was finally decided they would all go home with David. His aunt and his sisters were spending a few days with some relatives in the village of Umka. 'We will be quite alone,' he said. 'No chance of being disturbed.'

So for the rest of the night they had sat around the spotless kitchen table in the Ristić apartment, nursing glasses of wine, arguing about politics and occasionally eating from the huge platter of meats, cheeses and bread David provided.

Standing in the shower and vigorously scrubbing himself shortly after his friends had finally left only a couple of hours before he was due to arrive at work, David mentally reviewed the sometimes rowdy discussion.

Alex had told them he was determined to join the Communist Party as soon as he 'felt worthy' of becoming a member. He seemed profoundly committed to 'world revolution'. Still, David thought, smiling to himself, how could anyone really take any of the communists seriously? Certainly, as he had explained to the big man, he himself had at one stage shown an interest in their ideology which was interesting in theory if something of a disaster in practice. Why, he had even attended one of their meetings. It had been held in a building on Vasina Street and he had gone along on the invitation of a bank colleague, a young woman called Vera Kojić. He had had to leave in disgust, though, when all they did was shout slogans, play loud Russian music and absolutely refuse to discuss economics with him simply because he had not finished reading *Das Kapital*.

Bogdan, too, it seemed, had had a mild flirtation with the communists. Except to mutter something about them all being 'mad' or 'criminal', however, he had remained strangely quiet at the beginning of their discussion.

Stevan had wanted to know what was wrong with their own democratic system. He had pointed out to Alex that Yugoslavia's new democratic state had not been born until December 1918. The Russian Revolution had taken place in 1917. Yet in comparison had the Serbs really done so badly? Why only the other day, he had said, a French newspaper had reported that the Yugoslav medical insurance scheme was the most advanced, the most generous, in the whole of Europe. And most of the students who roamed the streets agitating for communism or breaking up classes at the university with their rowdiness were doing so on grants from the government.

'Yes, yes,' Bogdan had suddenly broken in excitedly. 'And remember how our government took responsibility for all of the debts held by our peasants in 1934? Imagine! The entire debt load of all of our peasantry. Where else in the world has something like that been done? As for poverty. Well, the depression is worldwide after all. And at least all of our people have food, and are housed, even if primitively. The depression is worldwide. Yugoslavia did not invent it.'

The big man had stuck stubbornly to his convictions, however. Even after David had reminded him that Yugoslavia did not *have* a proletariat. More than three-quarters of the country's people were peasants. What percentage of workers do we have, he had asked? Seven, eight per cent? Did Alex want them to go through the same comic performance the Russian communists had gone through at the beginning of the century? Their people, too, were predominantly peasants and the communists had made themselves ridiculous before the whole world because they had so few workers that they had to introduce capitalism into their country in order to produce workers who could be exploited and thus incited to revolution. What nonsense!

So on and on they had argued until something, perhaps too much wine, had got into Bogdan. Alex had sought his support with the contention that as the son of 'one of our brave workers' he should understand and sympathize with what the communists were trying to achieve.

Stepping out from the shower and rubbing himself with a huge towel David could still hear Bogdan yelling over and over that his father had been no 'brave worker' but a vicious old devil who had brutalized both his wife and his son. 'Look! Look! Look!' he had shouted as the other three stared at him, disconcerted by the sudden outburst. Impetuously he had risen to his feet and ripped off his shirt in a violent movement that tore at the seams. 'Look at this!' Stevan and David, who had seen the faded scars on his back, heard the story before, exchanged a quick glance as Alex shook his head in puzzlement. 'My father ... *my own father* ... did this. And worse! Do you hear? And my mother. Oh, yes. My mother could tell you some stories. My mother could show you some scars, I can tell you that.' Tears of self pity and rage had flooded his eyes, only to be impatiently brushed away. 'The working class is no different from any other class!' he had screamed. 'Some of them are fine fellows and some of them are bastards! As for the communists,' he had added sullenly, 'I know them too. I know them only too well. A handful of idealists, yes, but many more who turn to the Party to try to find outlets for their own inner mess. The others? Thugs, murderers, malcontents. I know them, you see. Oh, yes. I know them well.'

And that outburst had certainly put an end to the party. A disconcerted Alex had muttered something about what social forces had made Bošković's father so brutal, but David, after a searching look at Bogdan's furious face, had called for a break for coffee and then steered the conversation towards Stevan's eternal problem of what to do with his life.

Stevan had sighed, then, and told them that he had only gone to law school in order to avoid having to work in the family shipping company, but since dropping out of university he was under intense pressure from his father to join the business. What he really wanted to do was simply become a poet, roam the countryside with a *gusle* ...

'Come on, now, Stevan,' Bogdan had scoffed, recovering momentarily from his peeve. 'We all know perfectly well that you would never give up that luxurious apartment of yours. Not for all of the poetry and all of the *gusle* in the world.'

Stevan had flushed angrily, but as both Alex and David began to laugh, he had given a rueful smile. The party had broken up on that note. David had seen them to the front door, and had stood there yawning slightly as they clattered noisily down the steps. Now, leaving the apartment himself on his way to work, he encountered the blue-eyed, rosy-cheeked Frau Gertrude Schmidt, wife of the apartment building superintendent. 'Hope we didn't disturb you last night, Frau Schmidt.' He stepped adroitly around her as she vigorously mopped the front steps. 'I had a few friends in. We were a bit noisy, I'm afraid.'

'Ja, ja. What can you do? You are young people. You must make a little noise now and then. But, no. I didn't hear a thing. And you know my Otto. It would take an earthquake to waken *him*.'

'Good.' He returned her warm smile and hurried off down the street, pausing at the corner to look back and acknowledge the plump arm that was waving a friendly goodbye.

4

Stevan was waiting for him outside the bank and, as arranged, they hurried together to the rowing club, changed in the locker room, then took one of the club's double sculls out onto the river Sava. They were to join Bogdan at The Three Violins for a late luncheon after the noon to three rush hours.

David had left work in high spirits. Irina Mirskaia had returned to Belgrade with her mother and her aunt and the previous evening he had escorted her to dinner and later to the Balalaika, a popular night club haunt of Russian émigrés and young Yugoslavs. He was bursting to tell Stevan all about it and searched in his mind for words that would describe how wonderful the Russian girl was. To his disappointment, however, Stevan had not seemed to be in any kind of mood to invite confidences. In response to David's warm greeting he merely nodded in an absent-minded way, his usual pleasant smile nowhere in sight.

Now they were rowing silently along the Sava. Stevan was still locked into his own seemingly gloomy thoughts and although normally David would have tried to jolt him out of this rare, moody silence, today he was content to let his own thoughts dwell on the enchanting Irina.

He had taken her first of all to a Bohemian restaurant on the *Skadarlija*, where they had dined at a small, candle-lit table, sipped a light wine and talked endlessly about books and music before discovering that they shared a passion for the philosophy of Spinoza. As if this wasn't enough, they then found that they also shared the esoteric experience of having visited some hidden monasteries in the remote mountain country of the Morava Valley, where unusually beautiful works of art and frescoes could be found.

The coincidence seemed to them both to be extraordinary and they gazed at each other in wonder. Irina began to describe one tiny, whitewashed church she had visited. 'There was this painting of Christ,' she said softly, 'not well done. Quite crudely done really, yet created with such deep feeling, such *passion* ... I stood in front of it for such a long time. I was deeply moved. Aunt Marya had simply to drag me away.'

David studied her thoughtfully. 'Yet I would not have thought you to be such a serious person.'

'Serious? Oh, only sometimes. It is the Russian way.' With the quick change of mood he found so fascinating she began to laugh. 'What I *truly* like is to sing, to dance, to laugh. Life is so short. We must enjoy it to the full. You agree?'

He watched the extraordinary way in which the gold-flecked eyes lit up and said yes, yes, I agree. Then he took her to the Balalaika where they hummed along with the music, then danced the rest of the evening away.

On the way home he asked her about the doorman at the nightclub. 'People say he is an exiled Russian prince. Is it true, Irina?'

She laughed. 'Oh, David. They are *all* exiled Russian princes. Or most of them, anyway. At least, that's what they say.'

'Then you must be a Russian princess?' He joined in with her laughter, took hold of her hand.

She left her small hand in his, but with that quick change of mood, was no longer laughing. 'No, no,' she said quite seriously. 'My father came from the landed gentry. His parents owned a huge estate outside Moscow. How Aunt Marya misses it! She always talks about it. And my mother's family belonged to what I suppose you might call the lesser aristocracy, although her father was supposed to be the tzar's favourite general.' She gave a deep sigh. 'Always the past. I get so tired of it! I am so tired of hearing about the past, David!'

The afternoon sun burned down hot on the young men's shoulders and glistened on the rippling water as they skimmed along the river, every breath taken filled with soft, warm air and the pungent smell of freshly mown grass rising from the river-bank.

David's mind, an instant ago filled with thoughts of Irina, became empty; there was only the silence, broken by the splash of oars, the harsh breathing that went with the effort of leaning forward, pulling back. A sudden flow of adrenalin filled his blood with excitement followed by a kind of rage and foreboding that sprang from the terror and beauty, joy and tragedy that had gone into the making of his unique country and his unique people; very faintly he could hear the sound of his forefather's laughter and the babble of their tongues, their shrieks of savage defiance as they battled against every barbaric invader that had dared ravage their land.

'David. David?' The voice seemed to come from a long way off. Then he was back in the present and coolly alert. Stevan was saying something. 'Do you think we should turn back? Bogdan will be waiting for us.'

'Sorry, Stevan. I was day-dreaming. Yes, yes. By all means. Let us turn back.'

An hour later they were sitting down with Bogdan at The Three Violins. The busy lunch period was over and except for two elderly men who were arguing gently over a bottle of brandy, the three friends had the dining room to themselves.

Bogdan, always in an expansive mood when acting as host, plied them with food and wine. 'Drink up, drink up,' he cried excitedly, then shook his head in resignation when David refused the expensive cigar he offered. 'No, no, Bogdan. You know I don't smoke. An occasional cigarette perhaps. That's all.'

'But you will take one, Stevan? Good. Good. You know the trouble with David? He doesn't appreciate the good things of life.'

'On the contrary. It's precisely because I *do* appreciate them that I don't intend to ruin my lungs, fellow. But thank you for the meal, Bogdan. It was a wonderful lunch.'

Bogdan nodded. 'Old Toša is the best chef in town.' He winked. 'All I have to do is keep *him* from discovering that.'

David chuckled. 'Exploiting the workers, eh? Good thing for you Alex isn't here today. What do you say, Stevan?'

Stevan did not appear to see the joke. He shrugged, puffed gloomily at his cigar.

'Ah yes. Alex!' Bogdan too became gloomy. 'I don't suppose he'll want to see *me* again. I suppose I made a fool of myself the other night?' His muddy yellow eyes shifted searchingly from one face to the other.

'Why do you say that? You said what was in your heart. You can never go wrong when you express something that is honestly in your heart.' David nodded his thanks to the waiter who had silently appeared to refill their cups with coffee.

'A man I have always admired! I suppose because I was never good at sports myself. My God, David, he must have won every trophy Belgrade has to offer for swimming.'

'And skiing. I don't know if you have ever seen him ski, Bogdan. You would not credit that such a big man could be so graceful. And calm. Nothing shakes him. Nothing!'

'Skiing? No, I haven't seen him ski. I did see him take part in field athletics once. He ran the one hundred meters and . . . you were there, too, Stevan. Do you remember that day? Stevan?'

'What is the matter with you today, Stevo?' David had decided his friend's uncharacteristic silence and moodiness had gone far enough. 'Bogdan was talking to you, and you haven't been listening to a word either of us has been saying.'

'What? But I have. Bogdan was asking whether he'd made a fool of himself the other night and you said–'

'Be honest, now,' Bogdan interrupted. 'Alex won't want to meet *me* again. Not after what I said about my father and workers and so on. Although it's true, mind you. All of it was true.'

'Nonsense. Of course he'll want to see you again. So will Olga. Which is more than I can say for myself.' He reached out for the bottle of wine, refilled his glass and swallowed it in one gulp. 'Women!' He shrugged and wiped his glossy black moustache, of which he was so proud, and shrugged. 'Who cares anyway?' he cried loudly.

'Ah! So that's it. Olga!' David nodded wisely and privately gave thanks that he had not told Stevan about his own happiness with Irina.

'Olga?' Bogdan perked up. 'She will want to see *me* again? But I thought she only invited me for coffee because . . .' His face reddened as he came under both his friends' scrutiny. 'Of course she only invited me because *you* asked her to, Stevan,' he finished lamely.

'Nonsense! At least, all right, I *did* ask her. She told you that herself. But once she remembered you and recalled that you came from a working-class family, she–' He banged his fist down hard on the dining room table, causing the plates to rattle and the waiter who was changing the linen for the evening trade to pause in his duties and stare over at them curiously.

'This stupid bloody obsession they both suddenly have with socialism,' he shouted. 'God knows, I've been patient enough. But as I told Olga, it's all right to pass the time away in a London drawing-room talking about the oppressed proletariat. I am convinced, you know, it is a way of fighting boredom over there, that's all. But now we are back in Belgrade. Now we are home. It just doesn't make sense.' To his friends' consternation his face suddenly crumpled. My God, David thought, he's going to cry.

He did not, however. He simply took a deep breath and stared into the empty wine glass he was still holding. 'Anyway,' he said finally in a voice so low they both had to lean closer to hear, 'she doesn't want to see me any more.'

'What?' David could hardly believe his ears. 'My God! But, apart from anything else, what does a woman know about politics anyway? I must say, Stevan, I thought Olga had more sense than that.'

'You mean they really *wanted* to meet me?' Bogdan was lost in his own concerns.

Stevan gave a harsh laugh. 'Well, I *did* point out that now you are the manager of a restaurant you must be considered a member of the bourgeoisie. I was joking, of course. But you will be pleased to know, Bogdan, that both Alex and Olga are mesmerized by your immaculate working-class background! All of your faults, all of your *many* faults,' he teased, reverting for a moment to his old gay manner, 'can be traced directly to the fact that your parents were victims of the bloated capitalists!'

'Is it really so?' Bogdan stared at him happily, seemingly oblivious to the irony evident in his friend's voice.

Stevan then went on to tell them about his fight with Olga over her determination to become involved in left-wing politics. It had been precipitated by the fact that he had been offered and had accepted a position as political journalist for one of Belgrade's daily papers, *Politika*.

'What are you saying?' David interrupted. 'But this is wonderful. You have been searching for a career since you dropped out of university. Congratulations! Why didn't you tell us earlier? We could have drunk a toast.'

His friend shrugged. 'That's what I expected Olga to say, or something like that. I thought she would be delighted, and at first she seemed to be, but . . .'

'But what?' Bogdan refilled their wine glasses. 'It is never too late to toast a friend when he has made such a momentous decision.' David smiled at him with affection. Whatever Bogdan's faults, he thought, he can surely rise to the occasion. They both lifted their glasses, clinked them. 'To Stevan! May he have a wonderful career at *Politika*!'

'Thank you. Thank you both.' He beamed at them, and seemed to temporarily regain his good spirits.

'Yes. Well. Now what's this little problem with Olga all about?' Bogdan folded his arms and sat back with the air of a sage.

Stevan's gloom returned. He sighed. 'You see she had submitted an article herself to *Politika*, you know? It had been returned that very morning. So, of course, I asked to read it.'

'Ah,' David nodded wisely. 'And it was bad?'

'Not so much bad as naïve. I mean it was so full of left-wing naïvety that before I could stop to think I had said no wonder they returned it and, well, one thing led to another. And now she absolutely refuses to see me again.'

'Would it do any good if *I* spoke to her?' Bogdan radiated self-importance.

'Why? What could *you* say?'

'Well ... to begin with, I could tell her that she would be extremely wise if she refrained from becoming involved with any leftist or communist people in Belgrade.'

'But any one of us could tell her that.' David covered his glass, shaking his head as Bogdan made to refill it.

'Yes. But perhaps I know a few things you and Stevan do not.' Bogdan gave what they liked to call his 'smile of mystery'.

'The same things you told Alex the other night?' Stevan looked amused.

'There was plenty I *didn't* tell Alex, as a matter of fact.' They both listened with growing interest as he went on to tell them of the time he had carried on what he called his mild flirtation with the Communist Party in Belgrade. In common with Alex and Olga, the Party, it seemed, had been having some difficulty in finding workers to whom it could relate. Bogdan had been talked into going along to one of their meetings by a communist sympathizer who had known his father. After that he had gone to their meetings for some time. Firstly, he admitted, because everyone had made such a fuss of him due to his 'worker's' background. Secondly, he said, with a sly look, because he had heard all that talk about the Party favouring sexual freedom. Communists, he had understood, considered chastity to be just an old-fashioned bourgeois prejudice.

David and Stevan exchanged looks and grinned. 'Details! Bošković. Details!' Stevan banged his glass down noisily on the table. Bogdan grinned sheepishly, looked around furtively before going on to tell them that so far as 'free sex' was concerned, he had arrived too late on the communist scene.

'Too late? Never too late, Bošković,' Stevan cried a little drunkenly.

'No, no.' Bogdan again glanced around the empty dining room, then, noting that even the waiter had vanished into the kitchen, spoke up more confidently.

'You see, what happened is, things were progressing more or less according to plan, it seems, and the communist ladies were being *most* accommodating, and then two of their leaders were jailed and while they were in prison *their* "wives" took advantage of their absence to . . . shall we say . . . offer comfort to some of the other comrades, and the result of that was . . .' Bogdan burst out laughing. 'I tell you, fellows, it caused the quickest change in Marxist ideology you ever did see! Overnight the Party became all for monogamy and virtue!'

'Ah, ha,' David chuckled. 'A new communist morality, eh?'

'Now that,' Stevan grinned, 'is what I would call a contradiction in terms, David.'

'Anyway, I'm not complaining *too* much,' Bogdan went on quite seriously. 'I must say, the women in the Party, you know, not exactly beauties, eh?'

'Beggars can't be choosers, Bošković!'

'No, no, Stevan. Seriously. I don't think I missed anything much.'

'Well, beauties, or not,' David interposed, 'I suppose their sudden reversion to morality ended, what was it you called it? Your "mild flirtation" with the Party?'

'Well . . .' Bogdan's worried, furtive air returned, 'not so much that.' He glanced yet once more around the dining room to ascertain that it was still empty except for themselves. He seemed strangely nervous. His voice dropped to a harsh whisper. 'Not that so much, you know,' he repeated. 'You see, I had made friends with another fellow. Like me, he wasn't a member of the Party, though in fact he helped them much more than I was ever prepared to do. But, well, he liked the girls, you see.'

'Not like *you*, Bogdan.' David gave him a wink.

'He just couldn't stay away from the women. And although the Party warned him several times that he now had to toe the new line, so to speak, it simply wasn't in his nature, you understand?'

'Well?' Stevan prodded him gently when he paused and seemed reluctant to go on.

'Well ... a group of them went on a picnic ... by train. Took this friend of mine with them.' He seemed to have trouble swallowing.

'What's the matter?' David became impatient. 'What happened? Are you going to tell us or not?'

'On the way back from the picnic, he was killed, you see.'

'Killed?'

'He fell from the train.'

'An accident then?'

Bogdan looked up as the lone waiter re-entered the dining room. 'Marko! A bottle of *Šljivovica*, eh?'

He held the bottle up when it arrived, opened it as both David and Stevan shook their heads, and poured himself a substantial draught.

'An accident! That's what they *said*. There were others, though, who said...' He swallowed the brandy in one gulp and wiped his mouth. There was something in the tone of his voice that made them both stare at him intently. Some vague memory began to stir in the back of David's mind.

'My God!' he suddenly exploded. 'Paternoster!'

Bogdan let out a deep breath, and very slowly nodded.

'You mean...?' David stared at him.

'What are you talking about?' Stevan looked at them both in turn.

'Paternoster,' David repeated slowly. 'I remember the name, of course, an unusual name, not Serbian, eh? You were in London at the time, Stevan. But I knew a few students, a few leftist students. They were convinced it was no accident. Changed a few of their political views at the time, I can tell you.' He nodded slowly. 'Paternoster,' he repeated. 'Yes, yes. I remember now. You are saying those rumours were true, Bogdan?'

Bogdan again wiped his mouth and gave a barely perceptible nod. 'Let's just say that I made myself scarce for quite some time after that. Lots of people did, I can tell you! And now, well, I do keep in touch. I was scared not to. Not so much scared,' he contradicted himself hastily, regaining a little bravado. 'But anyway I think they still regard me as a ... as some kind of sympathizer. But, you know, I have as little to do with them as possible.' He nodded wisely at Stevan. 'I know enough to be able to tell Olga to keep away from them, you understand?'

'But you can't tell her *that*.' Stevan was horrified.

'No, of course not. But, look, what is today? Wednesday, eh?'

'That's right. Wednesday the twenty-third of August, fellow.'

'Listen then, I've been thinking. David has met Rachel, but I want you to meet her too, Stevan.'

'Rachel? Ah, yes. That girl you said you were taking out. You met her, David?'

'Of course. We all went to see *The Merry Widow* together at the beginning of the month. You couldn't join us, remember?'

'Oh, yes. Yes, that's right.' He winked at David. 'What did you think of her? Did she pass inspection?'

'She's a lovely girl.'

'Pretty?'

'Well,' David as always was irresistibly frank, 'not until she smiles. But when she smiles ...'

'Yes, yes,' Bogdan broke in anxiously. 'She has a beautiful smile.'

'It is like an electric light,' David went on. 'When it is switched on it lights up everything around it.'

Stevan nodded judiciously. 'Wonderful. Wonderful. You have a girl like an electric light-bulb then, Bogdan?'

David leaned forward and slapped him on the shoulder as the three of them burst into roars of laughter; laughter caused not so much by the nonsensical remark as by the sense of camaraderie they had never lost from their high-school days.

'That's not,' Bogdan shouted, wiping tears from his eyes, 'that's not funny!'

'Then why, why are you laughing?' David rested his forehead on his hands and tried to stop his own gales of laughter.

Eventually the hilarity died down. It was arranged that Bogdan would give Olga a call and invite her to dinner the following week. 'We'll make it Thursday,' he said. 'I can keep a private room available for us here. Thursdays are rarely busy. Are you free too, David? You can bring a girl along to make up the party. I could even ask Alex, too, and his fiancée, then Olga would be sure to come!'

Stevan shrugged. 'I suppose it's worth a try, Bogdan. Thank you for thinking of it. But I don't think it will work.'

'Why not? It will bring you both together again. Also, you see, what I thought I might do when you are both here is suggest we all go to one of those student meetings they hold at the university. You know about them, David. They call them cultural evenings. I can find out when the communists will be speaking there and we can all go along.'

'They allow the communists to speak there, then?'

'It's worth listening to,' David said. 'They go to the university, shout their slogans, complain about their lack of political freedom and don't even seem to notice the contradiction in the fact that they are allowed the use of university facilities to attack the government.'

Bogdan nodded agreement. 'Olga's an intelligent girl, Stevan. They will irritate the devil out of her. You should just hear them shout! And they contradict themselves every five minutes. Then, after the meeting, we can all go and have some coffee together and I can tell her a few things. Not the Paternoster thing, of course. But there's plenty more, believe me. Yes, yes. It will work. You will see.'

'Well, perhaps you are right. I don't suppose it can make things worse than they are now, in any event.'

'If that's settled, then I think I'd better go.' David glanced at his watch.

'Just let me have a glass of water and I'll be with you.' Stevan held out his glass to Bogdan, who filled it. They both again thanked him for his hospitality, and a short time later they left the restaurant, parting at the corner of Vasina and Bitoljska Streets.

It was not until he was running up the front steps of his apartment house that David realized he had not found a moment to mention Irina Mirskaia to either of his friends. So much the better! His face broke into a wide grin as he pictured the impact it would make when he walked into The Three Violins with Irina on his arm. When was it to be? Next Thursday. A week from today. And today's date? He had to think for a moment. The 23rd. That's what Stevan had said. The 23rd of August, he thought gaily, 1939.

* * *

At 7 a.m. the next morning he turned on his radio and discovered that a non-aggression pact had been signed at the Kremlin by Germany and the Soviet Union.

He decided to walk the several blocks between his home and the bank, trying to grasp the full implications of what he knew to be a shattering historical event. Once at work he nodded a good morning to his colleagues and went straight to his office. As usual all of the bank employees were applying themselves diligently to the work at hand, but there was no escaping the sense of excitement in the air.

It wasn't until he joined his friends in the canteen for a coffee break that the matter on everyone's mind could be discussed.

'What does it mean, David?' his friend Ivo Hajduk asked.

'War, probably. And the end of Poland.'

'It also means that we now have the interesting spectacle of two scorpions in a bottle,' chuckled Bora Borović of the foreign exchange department. 'And if they don't manage to sting each other to death, so much the worse for the rest of us.'

David nodded. 'The more you think about it; two totalitarian powers with institutionalized violence within both systems. God help us all!'

'What will Britain do? And France?'

'One thing is certain. It is too late for either of them to do anything intelligent. I suppose they will honour their commitments to Poland. But what a time for them to have to act! Militarily they are pygmies compared to Germany. I don't know what they *can* do, except to declare war.'

'What will *we* do? What will Yugoslavia do?'

'Stay out of it if we know what's good for us!' Borović finished his coffee. 'Anyway, war or no war, I've got work to do. See you later.' He got up from the table, walked briskly away, then paused at a table where a group of left-wing employees sat silent and morose. 'Well, well,' he said loudly, slapping one of them on the shoulder. 'Aren't we all silent today, comrades? Nothing to say today?' He gave a snort of contempt and marched out of the canteen.

Glancing over at the group, David caught Vera Kojić's eye. She looked so miserable that he made a point of pausing at their table on his way out.

'I'm sorry, Vera,' he said, 'it must be quite a blow.' She acknowledged his comment with a slight nod, then clasped her hands together and stared down at them. Everyone else at the table ignored him, so he shrugged and rejoined Ivo Hajduk who was standing aside, waiting for him.

'Serves them all right,' Ivo said with a satisfaction David found himself unable to share. Things, he thought sadly, are too serious for petty gloating. He was glad when the work day was over.

Arriving home a little before two, he found his aunt surrounded by all of the morning papers. He read them while she prepared a light luncheon. There was confirmation of the report given earlier by radio. Signature of the treaty, he read, had been sealed by warm and friendly discussions. A gala reception had followed at the Kremlin, attended by Stalin, his foreign minister, Molotov, and Ribbentrop, Reichminister for foreign affairs. Toasts had been exchanged, so all of the papers reported, quoting one offered by Stalin to the Führer: 'I know how much the German nation loves its Führer. I should therefore like to drink to his health and to a favourable development of relations between Germany and the Soviet Union.'

Aunt Draga sighed, shook her head, and repeated the same question Ivo Hajduk had asked him earlier. 'What does it mean, son?'

Once again he found he really had no reply.

*   *   *

The dinner party at The Three Violins went ahead as planned. Proudly Bogdan Bošković introduced his Rachel to Olga and Alex Miletić, and to the latter's fiancée, the lovely Jelena Marković. Just as proudly David introduced Irina to the group and by the time Stevan arrived the party was in full swing. A subdued Olga greeted him kindly. It soon became apparent that she and her brother were both saddened and disillusioned by the German-Soviet pact. As time wore on, however, the lively Serbian temperament came to the fore and soon the party of eight was laughing, arguing, eating and drinking with joyous Slavic abandon.

Just before they all left the restaurant, in the early hours of the morning, Bogdan glanced towards Stevan and mentioned that he had heard that the Yugoslav communists were to address a meeting at the student cafeteria on Saturday. His not very subtle expression as he gazed over at Stevan, his shrug of the shoulders, indicated that it was obvious, in any event, that the pact had already done the job of turning Olga off communism. Stevan silently agreed. Still, it was an opportunity to see her again, to consolidate the gains of the evening.

'Let me take you, Olga. It might be interesting to hear what they have to say.'

'*You* want to hear what they have to say?' She studied his face for a moment, then laughed. 'Well, why not? All right, Stevan. It could be an amusing evening.'

No one else was the slightest bit interested in going. They laughed about it for a few minutes, then the party broke up. Stevan returned to his apartment and retired immediately. When he wakened and switched on the radio it was to learn that while they had been laughing and dining the previous evening the German army, without formal declaration of war, had bludgeoned its way into Poland.

* * *

By the time they arrived at the students' cafeteria at Belgrade University, the meeting was well under way, but to their surprise there were quite a few seats still available.

'It's because the main speaker has just left,' a lanky and rather grubby young student told them. 'Milovan Djilas! You've missed the main speaker.'

'Djilas! A bit of a fanatic,' Stevan whispered to Olga. 'I listened to him speaking at one of their rallies a few weeks ago. A shouter. Full of contradictions. I don't think we've missed much.'

The present speaker, however, seemed a different kettle of fish altogether. Tall and dark, a solid-looking middle-aged man who from his appearance might have been a prosperous merchant or a bank manager. Quietly, forcefully, he put forward the communist point of view as had apparently just been expounded by Djilas. Quite simply put, it was that Stalin had been forced to sign the pact with Germany because the Western powers were plotting to pit Hitler against the Soviet Union, after which they would move in to defeat whichever side emerged as victor. There should be no doubt in anyone's mind, therefore, that Stalin, as always, was right! One of the first conditions of being a communist, he reminded the audience, was that one must have absolute confidence in the Soviet union and the decisions of its government. In dealing with all non-communist states it did not make one whit of difference to the Soviet Union if they were capitalists, fascists, nazis or a military autocracy. There was, after all, no fundamental difference between Hitler's Germany and the Western democracies. So it naturally followed that if the situation required, at certain moments in history, Soviet cooperation with any one of them, then that was the course that must be followed. Stalin, he said firmly, was perfectly justified, therefore, in signing the pact with Hitler.

'Eh, comrade!' Stevan found himself being nudged in the ribs by the unkempt student. 'I wouldn't want to play a round of poker with *him*, eh?' He gave a loud hoot of laughter at his own wit. Stevan's attention, however, was still firmly on the speaker, who was now tossing off, in a mild and even slightly ironic way, the obligatory Marxist slogans, which were followed by a prediction: Germany's attack on Poland, far from being a disaster, was an event that would prove to be an excellent opportunity for the Soviet Union to spread socialism while the warring sides fought!

That seemed to be it.

'But, of course, Stevan, he's perfectly right, you know. What he says makes sense.' He turned to Olga, who was sitting next to him. She was perfectly still, but the dark eyes were shining and she exuded an air of suppressed excitement.

'Well, I must say, he's rather impressive.' He helped her up. 'Would you like to talk to him?'

'Stevan! Olga!' A hand landed heavily on his back. He turned to find a friend he had gone to law school with, the gangling, swarthy Dragan Dukić, beaming at him. 'This is the last place I would have expected to see you two.' He grinned happily at Olga.

'How are you, Dragan?' she smiled politely. 'As a matter

of fact it's the last place I would have expected to see *you*.'

Dragan shrugged. 'You know how it is. Have to keep up with things.' Like Olga and Stevan, Dragan came from a well-known and well-respected Belgrade family. So far as they both knew, he had always held conservative views, in common with his wealthy parents.

'Look,' he added, 'are you leaving? Let's have some coffee together.' Then, as they both glanced towards the speaker, who was now surrounded by students: 'If you want to speak to Djerdja you won't get near him now for an hour or so.'

So they accompanied him to a small coffee house close to the university and settled into a corner with thick mugs of coffee.

'My God, those communists!' Dragan took a gulp from his steaming mug. 'They can talk their way out of anything.'

'Well, that one was quite impressive,' said Stevan. 'What did you say his name was?'

'Djerdja. Nikola Djerdja. Yes, well, he is one of the saner comrades, I must admit.'

'But you haven't told us, Dragan, what on earth were *you* doing there tonight?' Olga wagged a finger at him. 'I bet your father doesn't know where you spend your Saturday evenings.'

He grinned, not without some embarrassment. 'He'd skin me alive. Still . . .' he shrugged.

'But you're not really mixed up with these people?'

'Well, Stevan, I'm not a communist, of course. If that's what you mean. I occasionally help them out. You know the kind of thing. Distributing leaflets. If my parents are out of town I let them hold meetings at the house. You know. That kind of thing.'

'Communist meetings? At the house of Dragan Dukić, Senior?' Stevan nearly choked. 'My God. He'd more than skin you alive, Dragan. He'd . . .'

'He'd sell you to the Turks!' Olga had thrown back her head, and was laughing out loud. 'Do you realize what you are doing, Dragan? If the police ever–'

'The police? Olga, if the police were searching the whole of Belgrade, my father's house is the *last* one they'd approach.' Dragan was grinning with a mixture of embarrassment and pride. He gave her a sly look. 'Of course, Judge Miletić's home would be the second last place they'd approach!'

'But why?' Stevan was genuinely puzzled. 'Why do you do it? Do you believe those things Djerdja was saying?'

'Oh, not really. Sometimes! Well, at least I know *he* believes them.' He floundered, recovered. 'You see, it's not as big a risk as you imagine. I know the police used to hound them. But lately ... there aren't that many of them, I suppose, so they are leaving them alone. Why, even that meeting tonight, they can always talk at the university and no one stops them. Everyone knows about it.'

'But I still don't understand *why*.' It suddenly seemed important to Stevan to know what in the devil Dragan Dukić was doing hanging around communists. What was their attraction, for God's sake? First Alex and Olga and now ...

'I'm not sure, really,' Dragan replied. Then his face broke into another wide grin. 'Yes, I am,' he contradicted himself. 'I know what makes me do it.'

'What, then?'

'Boredom!' He lifted his mug and finished his coffee slowly as they both stared at him. 'It really livens up one's life.'

They were both silent for so long that he became defensive. 'Well, I mean, look at Djilas. Did you hear him? A real revolutionary, that one. A real, bloody, revolutionary. Where else would I meet such a man? And, of course, there are others like him.'

'You know Djilas, then? And Djerdja?'

'Of course. You know, Stevan, you would like Djerdja. You probably wouldn't agree with his views, but you would like the man.' He hesitated. 'Would you like to meet him?'

Stevan hesitated, but only for a moment.

'Why not?' He shrugged. 'Why not?'

5

As usual when political events seemed headed for the catastrophic, David decided to visit his Uncle Mikhail.

His uncle lived opposite a small park behind the officer's club, only a mile or so from the Ristić apartment. As it was such a beautiful day he decided to walk. He hurried along King Milan Street, his eyes clouded with thought.

Mikhail Ristić would, he knew, be upset and worried about the recent political events in Europe. As always, though, his main preoccupation would be the effect these events might have on his beloved Serbia. A dedicated patriot, the old man was the product of a childhood that had been steeped in the history, culture and traditions of Serbia. Although his family had been quite poor, Mikhail, his brother Nikola, and later the baby, David, had never lacked for someone to tell them again and again the story of the first Karadjordjević, the peasant farmer who had routed the Turks and begun the Karadjordjević dynasty. Nor had there been any shortage of old men willing to sit down with them, play the *gusle*, and entertain them and teach them songs extolling the grandeur and terror of Serbian history.

The Ristić boys had grown up in Plevlje, a country town of Metohija, absorbing the richness of this heritage. When the two older boys had reached adolescence they had separated. Nikola had started along the road that was to take him into the church. He eventually became one of the youngest ever bishops of the Eastern Orthodox Church in Skoplje, Macedonia. Mikhail's path led him into the Serbian army where his outstanding courage and leadership quickly gained him the rank of colonel during the 1912–13 Balkan wars. He became interested in politics during the protracted evacuation of the main force of the Serbian army to the Greek island of Corfu, in 1915.

It was on this island that the Serbian politicians and intellectuals first tried to thrash out the possible political solutions for the future state of South Slavs they wished to create after liberation. The main problem was the form unification would take with their 'enemies-brothers' in Croatia and Slovenia.

Out of several theoretical solutions, David's uncle had favoured that of a federal state based on full recognition, not only of national but also of regional differences. When, in 1917, with victory firmly in sight, the Western Entente had offered the Serbs Vojvodina, Bosnia-Hercegovina, Montenegro and the area of Krajina inside Croatia that had been occupied by Serbs for generations, he had argued fervently in favour of acceptance. He was firmly convinced that such a creation of a Greater Serbia was the only thing that would allow Serbs to defend themselves against the 'endless outside and inside interference' into Serbian affairs.

It was also his firm conviction that the solution which had actually prevailed, that of the unitarian centralist state based on national unification, which would embrace one people, one language and one king, was the cause of most of the problems that had plagued Yugoslavia since the Serbian army had, as anticipated, fought its way back to Serbia through Salonika to liberate all South Slavs as far as Slovenia in the west.

The decision had been made against his advice by Serbian patriots who still harboured the dream of one country uniting all South Slavs, a dream encouraged by the delegation of Croat officials who had approached them towards war's end when it had become clear that Croatia was on the losing side and that harsh reprisals could well be in the offing for the role they had played on the side of Austria and Germany.

He had not been impressed by Croatia's Dr Anté Trumbic's fulsome statement that Serbia, by sacrificing its individuality in order to form a common state of Serbs, Croats and Slovenes, should rightfully be called the Yugoslav Piedmont. Nor had he been in favour of the generous gesture made by the Serbian prime minister, Nikola Pasić, who, in response to a British commander's question as to what should be done with the Croat prisoners-of-war in Dalmatia, had replied: 'Send the Croats home. They are our brothers.'

'Some brothers,' Ristić was to fume when in 1919 the Croats had sent a petition to the peace conference asking for separation from Serbia. 'They didn't even have the decency to wait until their own signatures were dry on the agreement before breaching it!' Later, when Croat terrorists trained in Italy and Hungary had murdered King Alexander and then from Venice used the good offices of the Austrians and the Vatican to spread vicious rumours about the Serbs throughout Europe, his rage had known no bounds. This rage was to turn to immense sadness when the British, fearing to upset the Italian dictator, had blocked a movement in the League of Nations to condemn Italy and Hungary for their part in Alexander's murder. About the Croatians he had shouted: 'Let them go. Let them lose their true identity, their heritage, within the murderous Teutonic embrace. Let them lose their souls as they plot and scheme with their devious masters deep down in the cellars of the Vatican!' But for the British he had only sadness. He had shaken his huge head. 'To grovel as they do in front of that clown, Mussolini. They betray not only us. They betray their own principles. They betray their own people.'

Inevitably though, he would return to the treachery of the Croats. 'Remember, David, in accordance with the Paris peace treaty, we were entitled not only to impose war reprisals, but to draw a new map of Serbian ethnic territories that would have reduced Croatia to its true size. Of course we did not and should not have imposed reprisals, but I can tell you this: we would have saved ourselves endless problems had we taken the territory that belonged to us and left the Croats to stew in their own juice until the Austrians or the Germans or the Hungarians swallowed them up again. The truth is, my boy, they are no longer Slavs. They do not want to be Slavs. God help them. They actually want to be Goths! So we should let them go, but not before claiming the territory we defended against the Turks for five hundred years. We provided a wall against the Turks for all those years for the rest of Europe. That has been acknowledged again and again. Even by the Austrians, blast them!'

A sudden impatience to see and talk with the old man he loved so much made David hurry as he neared the apartment building, and made him take the steps leading to its entrance two at a time. David's Aunt Kaja answered the door, the perpetual expression of anxiety on her thin face dissolving into a tight smile as he greeted her.

'David! Come in, come in. I knew it! I knew you would come. As soon as we heard news of the war I said to your uncle, "Now David will come to see us. Now he will come."'

David laughed and kissed her on the cheek. 'Sorry, Aunt Kaja. I did mean to come before this. But time – I never seem to have time. And it gets worse instead of better.'

'Wait until you reach our age, David. Then you will have all the time in the world. Too much time. But come. Your uncle will be delighted to see you.' She led him rapidly down the hall, at the same time calling to her husband. 'Mikhail! Come and see who is here.' They arrived at the study door just as it opened to reveal Mikhail Ristić, his huge frame filling the whole space, his magnificent head bent from a lifetime of hitting ceilings and door frames, even though a special archway had been built to allow him easy access to his study.

'My boy! Wonderful! Wonderful to see you.' His face lit up as he grasped David in a painful bear hug. 'But where have you been? I had expected to see you before this. When did you arrive back? Early August, wasn't it?'

'That's right, Uncle. I was just saying to Aunt Kaja, I'm sorry to have taken so long, but I've been so busy.'

'Not too busy to visit my old friend Blagoje Nešić, my boy.' The old man winked at his wife. 'Of course, we don't have the advantage of a pretty daughter, eh?'

David smiled. '*That's* how you knew I was back.'

'Yes, yes. Blagoje called in to see me right away. Said you would probably be paying me a visit within a day or so. But...' He shrugged, pushed David away from him and adjusted the pince-nez that sat precariously on his large nose. 'Anyway, you are here now. And you look well. Magnificent! The army agrees with you.'

'Well, I don't know about that,' David gave him a rueful grin. 'Still, I suppose it does keep one reasonably fit.'

'Well, I'll leave you together for a little while. I'll make some coffee.' Kaja Ristić moved briskly to the door, paused for a moment as David gave her a message from his Aunt Draga, then hurried off down the passage.

'Aunt Kaja is looking fine. And you, you too, Uncle. You are both keeping well?'

His uncle nodded absently. 'At our age, as much as can be expected, I suppose. Here. Come here, my boy. Let us sit down. Mother will be in shortly with some coffee. We have a lot to talk about. We are all concerned about the situation in Europe.'

'What do you think will happen, Uncle? Britain, France, will it be over quickly, do you think? Are we going to become involved?'

'Yugoslavia? Of course not. How could our little army stand up against Hitler? I know what we did twenty odd years ago, but today? Until we have solved the problem of unity, and how can we trust Croatia? No, no. We must stay out of it, at least until we have solved some of our own problems.'

'But should we stay out of it? When you think of what has been going on in Germany. When we see what they are doing in Poland. Surely it is our duty? I mean along with the rest of the civilized world, of course, to act?'

'No, no.' His uncle leaned forward in the huge, worn armchair. 'What you must understand is that there is a slavering wolf hovering over the whole of Europe. A slavering wolf! And when a slavering wolf hovers above you and you are virtually unarmed and defenceless, what you must do is stay very still and very quiet. Perhaps he will not notice you. Perhaps he will go away.'

'But if he doesn't?'

As though unable to bear the thought, his uncle sprang to his feet. 'If he doesn't? Then we must fight! With our bare hands if need be. We must take him by the throat. We must–' Alarmingly his face turned a deep red, almost purple.

David jumped up and grasped his arm. 'Uncle. I didn't mean to upset you. Here...' He pushed him gently back into the armchair and hurriedly poured a glass of water from the pitcher on the coffee table. 'Drink this.' As the old man began to speak, he held up his hand. 'No, no. Not a word. Until you have drunk this. Until you have calmed down.'

Grudgingly, Mikhail took the glass, drank half of the water, sank back into the chair with a mortified look, and began to grumble. '"Not a word until you have drunk this" indeed. You sound like my old grandma.'

'Well, according to you, she was a very wise old lady. Not above chasing you with a broomstick when you were disobedient, either.'

His uncle slowly relaxed and finally gave a deep chuckle. 'I concede the round to you, my boy. I concede the round.'

'Should I get you some brandy? And perhaps no more politics for today?'

'Nonsense! I don't need any brandy. As for politics. All I really wanted to say was that we must use our heads, David. For once in our lives we *must* use our heads. After all, is that anything to be ashamed of? Look at the big, powerful countries. Look at the United States. It knows well what Hitler is up to, what he is doing to the Jews, for instance. And what does this huge, powerful democracy do? It throws up its hands! Oh dear me, oh dear me, it says. We don't like what we hear and see. But what has it to do with us? And the Soviet Union? Why, we can't beat Hitler, that old bear says.

So we must join him! Britain? France? *Finally* they have moved, but with what reluctance, eh? Who can blame them? Because of course they know they are virtually unarmed against the most formidable foe of the century. So what I ask, my boy, is simply this. Why should little Yugoslavia pretend it can hold its own against this madman, Hitler? We cannot! It is as simple as that.'

David blew out his breath. 'Well, I'm glad to hear you say that.'

Mikhail frowned. 'You are afraid of the Germans, then?'

David stared at him. 'Afraid? No. I wouldn't be afraid to fight them, if that's what you mean.' He gave a cheerful grin. 'I don't want to get involved for purely selfish reasons, I'm afraid. You see, I didn't tell you before. I want to save a bit more money and take a few more courses at the university. I have decided to leave the bank as soon as I possibly can. I want to open a language school in Belgrade. Not much use thinking about it, though, if we are going to become embroiled in a war.'

'What a wonderful idea! Of course you will make a great success of such an undertaking. Tell me, have you chosen premises yet?'

'Not yet, although I have a few ideas.'

'Well, I tell you, David. Promise you will come and talk to me before you make a final decision, eh? I might be able to help you in that regard.'

There was a movement at the door and Kaja Ristić appeared carrying a large tray of coffee and pastries. David leaped to his feet and took the tray from her.' I hope you didn't go to all this bother for me, Aunt Kaja.'

'No, no. Your uncle always has a snack at this time. Mind you, here, I have made sure to bring your favourite cake.'

David kissed her on the cheek and beamed as she handed him the plate.

'You will be staying for dinner?'

'I'm sorry, Aunt. Thank you, but I promised Aunt Draga I'd be home tonight. We are having a special guest, it seems.'

'A *special* guest? Who could that be, I wonder?' Kaja's eyes glittered with the curiosity of the inveterate gossip.

Mikhail erupted with his deep, rumbling laugh. 'Tell her, David. Tell her and save us half an hour of her trying to get it out of you.'

'That is not so! How can you say such a thing?'

'No secret, anyway.' David took a sip of coffee and replaced his cup. 'It's a friend of Andjela's. Bane Protić. You know him?'

'Bane ... Bane ... he is a student?'

'Was. He's an engineer now. Still looking for a job, though.'

'Oh, yes.' Kaja stirred the sugar in her cup, lost interest.

'Still, you must stay a while, David. Did you know Nikola is on leave? He should be home before long. Stay and have a drink with him.'

'He is home? No. I didn't know. I'd be sorry to miss him.'

Briefly they chatted about the Ristić's only son. The couple adored him, but David was often aware of his uncle's sadness at Nikola's wildness, his carelessness. 'God help us if there are too many officers like you in the army, Niko,' he would rumble, only half-jokingly. Nikola, for his part, made no secret of the fact that his father's stories of the past bored him. 'Life is for now,' he would roar at his cousin David. 'Who cares what happened on the Salonika front!'

'You and I should,' David would snap back. 'Your father is our living history, don't you see that?' Still, he could not help being fond of his handsome, black-eyed cousin who drank too much and chased women too much, but who could undoubtedly charm the birds from the trees.

When his aunt had cleared the dishes away and excused herself to prepare dinner, the two men returned to their discussion about the political situation.

'Did you hear that our own communists are supporting the Molotov-Ribbentrop pact, Uncle? After all that ranting against the Nazis, and now overnight it is no longer the fascists who are the villains, it is the British imperialists!

What cynics. How can anyone believe in them? How can they believe in themselves?'

His uncle gave an amused grin. 'Well, now, son. I thought a while back you yourself were rather taken by our communist friends.'

David laughed. 'Not so much taken by them, as interested in their philosophy. Mind you, I wouldn't at all mind seeing some new kind of economic justice in the world. I believe it is needed, that's why I tried so hard to understand them. But I think the Soviets have demonstrated that communism is not the answer. Besides, they are such a noisy, violent lot, with their shouting, their empty slogans. They seem to me to have no connection with their brains, you know?'

'That's the surprising thing, my boy. That no small number of our intellectuals who supposedly *do* have some connection with their brains, support these communists. Oh,' he went on, holding up his hand as David made to interrupt, 'I don't mean our students. They are young, after all. Their blood boils in their bodies and can only be cooled, it seems, by shouting angry threats against their elders. No, no. What worries me, well, it doesn't worry me, exactly. In the long run they will have no effect on our country, after all. Our people have that much sense, thank God. No, no. Perhaps the correct word is *saddens*. What saddens me is to see so many mature men who are supposed to *think*, support an ideology that whichever way you look at it, seeks to enclose the minds of men within an iron band. Extraordinary! These men use free thought to support an ideology that suppresses free thought. What a paradox! Of course, it is the same thing with the fascists and the Nazis, who also have their so-called intellectual apologists.' He hauled his huge frame out of the chair and began to pace up and down the room. 'What is it that makes men want to imprison the minds of others? It has never worked. Not in the long run, you know. The church tried it for long enough, God knows. Is still trying for that matter. But it has, and it will, fail. Why do they think God gave men minds, anyway? No, no. The church failed, and these bandits will also fail.'

'Well,' David agreed, 'I suppose, as you say, they all eventually fail. But they can certainly set history back a few hundred years.'

'That's it. That's it!' Mikhail stopped the restless pacing. 'God only knows, David, democracy has its failings. Amongst other things, even democracies will try to place a yoke around men's minds if they can get away with it. But under a democratic state there is always that leeway, you see. The yoke can be thrown off.' He gave a deep sigh. 'Yet, so far as the communists are concerned, why I could almost forgive the rest of their nonsense if they really could produce a formula for the withering away of the state. What a paradise *that* would be. Because the sad fact is my boy, no man is really equipped to govern others. An indisputable riddle! Until man has found the answer to *that* one, we are stuck with democracy. It is our only hope.' He adjusted his pince-nez and coughed.

'Well, at least you are in good company, Uncle. From Aristotle to John Stuart Mill. None of them found the answer. They all had to fall back on democracy, even if reluctantly.' He paused and thought for a moment. 'What was it Voltaire said? I think it was Voltaire. *It is to those who master our minds by the force of truth that we owe our reverence*.'

'Voltaire? Yes, yes. That is Voltaire. And remember Spinoza, my boy. Your favourite, if I recall well. Look him up again. You will find that he speaks of freedom being the goal of the state, because, he says, its function *must* be to promote the growth of men's minds. Yes, yes. He said that this growth of man's mind depends upon its capacity for finding freedom, and that a mind locked into an ideology is not capable of growth. Look it up, my boy. You must look that passage up.'

'Spinoza! I heard that name and *knew* that the visitor was either my cousin, David, or old Blagoje Nešić!'

They both looked up, startled, at the loud voice coming from the doorway. David sprang to his feet and went to embrace his cousin. 'Niko! But how good it is to see you again.'

Nikola responded with the deep laugh so like that of his father. 'And you, too, David. It's good to see you again. You will be staying for dinner?'

'No, I'm afraid not. I wish I'd known you were back, Niko, although I don't think I could have done much about it. I promised Aunt Draga faithfully I'd be home for dinner tonight.'

'Well, never mind.' Nikola sprawled out in the chair David had just vacated. 'I'll be home for a few more days. Maybe we can arrange something.'

David sat down on a footstool, facing him. 'So! You are back from the Adriatic. You manage things well, Niko. What a wonderful place to spend the summer months.'

Niko grinned. 'Yes, yes. The army has its small compensations. But still, there is no place like Belgrade, David.'

'Especially if your main preoccupations are women and drink,' Mikhail Ristić rumbled, only half-jokingly.

His son roared with laughter and slapped his hand down hard on his knee. 'Like father, like son, eh?'

'Very funny,' his father responded drily. He retrieved his pipe from the ashtray and lit it. 'Very funny.'

'Nikola!' It was Kaja Ristić, bustling in with a warm smile. 'I thought I heard your voice.' She leaned down to kiss him on the cheek, then turned to David. 'Oh, what a pity you can't stay. It would be nice for Nikola.'

'As a matter of fact I'd better be on my way now.' David glanced at his watch. He had intended to call and see Jack Cohen on his way home, but it was already too late. Yet he must get in touch with Jack somehow. There had been no answer each time he had tried to call his home.

'Not until you've had a drink with us, David.' Mikhail Ristić looked over at him with a smile, then sent a wryly affectionate look in the direction of his son. 'I suppose this scalywag deserves some kind of recognition from his cousin.'

'Well, I'm not sure that he does,' David joked. 'But still, maybe one small drink. Only one, eh?'

Of course it developed into more than one drink. There

was certainly no time to call at the Cohen house and as it was he just made it back home in time to shower, dress, and open the door to welcome Bane Protić.

At the dinner table, he noted with amusement, everyone was being excessively polite. Aunt Draga was at her most regal, Zora was keeping her sometimes vitriolic tongue in check, and Andjela could not have been more modest, more gay, more charming. Glancing over at the handsome young engineer, it occurred to David for the first time that he could be entertaining a future brother-in-law.

Well, Andjela could do worse. From what he could recall, Bane came from a peasant family that owned a few hectares of land in a village south of Belgrade. It must have been a struggle for them to put their youngest son through university, even with government aid, but Bane seemed to have done them proud. Well, in any event, he now had his degree. David supposed a job would eventually materialize. Both he and Andjela were young. A financial struggle for a few years wouldn't hurt them. The important thing was that Andjela seemed to be smitten by him and although he did not seem to have much depth to him he did appear to be a kind and amiable fellow one could certainly get along with if he *did* develop into a future relative.

'David, why don't you take Bane into the living room? You can have your coffee there. And would you like a cigar? We have that box you never touch. We'll join you as soon as we've cleared up.' Aunt Draga was already leading the way into the living room. She stayed a few minutes to pour the thick black Turkish coffee, to check that the accompanying glasses of water were cold enough, and then bustled away.

They settled back comfortably in the large chairs. Bane accepted a cigar and David joined him. He was not a smoker, but it seemed the courteous thing to do to join their young guest, who was sinking back with a luxurious sigh. Talking to him, though, David discovered, was hard going. He showed little interest in and, most unusually for a Serb, no knowledge about, politics. Sports elicited a polite but obviously bored response. Philosophy drew a blank stare. The talk turned to food. He seemed impressed by the fact that it was Andjela who made the delicious *gibanica* served at dinner. David was proud to extol his sister's cooking abilities, but after that he was at a loss. If Bane had any interest in anything, he thought wryly, he is taking care to hide it.

However, just as he was about to call out to one of the girls to join them, the young engineer cleared his throat, leaned forward, and began to talk about the difficulties of finding work in the present economic climate, but of his certainty that he *would* find exactly what he was looking for in the very near future.

'One day,' he said rather self-importantly, 'I am going to have a very good job indeed.'

'Yes, of course. I'm sure you will.' David hesitated, then went on. 'Do you know Alex Miletić? He too is an engineer, as perhaps you know. I should think he might have some excellent contacts. Perhaps I could ask him, or, even better, introduce you to him?'

'Could you do that? Of course I have heard of him. A wonderful man, everyone says. Belgrade's best sportsman.'

'More than that. Everyone likes Alex. He has a wonderful nature and if there is anything he can do to help *anyone*, you can be sure he will.'

David leaned back in his chair, pleased to have made some contact with this rather dull young man. What on earth did Andjela see in him? Of course he was certainly nice looking and he did seem easy going and quite kind. Still, one would think he would bore *any* woman frantic. Not that his sister ever claimed to be any kind of intellectual, but still . . . With an effort he brought his attention back to Bane, who had just cleared his throat and seemed about to make some kind of pronouncement. Of course it was about Andjela. Did David realize what a very charming sister he had? Pretty, too. Lovely hair, lovely eyes. Beautiful skin. Just like a rosy apple. He had admired her from the very first moment they met. Nice to meet such a girl who also seemed to be a wonderful home-maker. Marvellous cook, it seemed.

Did she truly make that cheese pastry by herself? He had always thought his mother made the best *gibanića* in the world. Now he was not so sure.

David smiled. 'Consider yourself lucky Zora didn't make it, Bane. Cooking is definitely *not* her forté. But Andjela? Yes, she is an excellent cook. Always has been, since she was quite small.'

A feeling of tiredness descended upon him, as it often did when he was in the company of someone who bored him. He stifled a yawn, sat up straight to keep himself from dozing off, and came to with a start to realize that Bane was still droning on about the virtues of Andjela. His sister's young friend was gazing at him anxiously and out of the blue David suddenly realized that he was muttering something about marriage. My God, he thought, is he going to ask *my* permission? What a waste of time, my boy. Aunt Draga is the hard nut to crack, although from her behaviour at dinner that wouldn't be too difficult, either. For the first time he realized that there had been a concerted plot that evening to leave him alone with Bane. Although the three women were purportedly clearing up the dinner dishes in the kitchen, all was silent. 'I've been framed,' David thought with an inner chuckle, using a term he had picked up as a child from American gangster movies. With an effort he brought his attention back to Bane.

'So of course,' he was saying, 'the amount of dowry Andjela would bring to the marriage is of prime importance.'

David stared at him blankly. 'Dowry?'

'Of course I know, everyone knows, your father was a very wealthy man. So I imagine he left you all very comfortably off, but as to Andjela's share . . .'

'Dowry? But Bane, I think you are a little behind the times, fellow. This is 1939, not 1919.'

Bane gave him a startled look, then seemed to recover. 'Well, perhaps. But still, under the circumstances. My family is not well off, as perhaps you know, and . . .'

David shook his head firmly. 'As for our father being

wealthy, well, yes, at one time I suppose he was. But he was also very generous. He had a habit, whenever a relative, or a friend, needed anything, needed money, you understand? Well, always they came to my father. And he never turned anyone away. But still, when he died, it was a shock, I must admit, to discover how little there was left.'

There was a short silence. Bane appeared to be at a complete loss. About to make an abrupt and exasperated remark, David suddenly remembered his sister's flushed and happy face at the dinner table earlier in the evening. With an effort he reined in his impatience.

'Look,' he said after a moment, 'I do have a little money put aside.' He went on to explain his plan to eventually open a language school in Belgrade. 'Certainly,' he added, 'if my father *had* left more money I would have preferred not to spend my time working at the bank. But, as it was...' he shrugged. 'But of course that's not your problem. The point is, my sister does have a little money of her own. And I might be able to ... how much is it, exactly, that you were expecting?'

For a moment Bane's face lit up again. He named a figure. David simply stared at him, flabbergasted.

'Good God, man,' he said finally. 'There's no way in the world I could find that much.'

'I see.' Bane slowly shook his head, and his face began to redden a little. 'Please understand, a misunderstanding...' He glanced around the room as though seeking an avenue of escape, and began to mutter something about having been brought up in poverty, and that was enough.

'But Bane,' David protested, 'I know things are bad at the moment. The whole world seems to be in an economic mess. But things must improve. And from anything I have read, our country is better off than most. It seems to me to be simply a matter of time. Time and patience. If you could...'

But Bane was already standing. Perhaps it would be better, under the circumstances, if David could thank his aunt for her wonderful hospitality? Perhaps it would also be better, under the circumstances, if he could explain to Andjela? So embarrassing to have to stay and...

Still bewildered about the whole thing, David found himself at the front door, shaking the limp hand that was briefly proffered. It was only when he was back in the living room facing the little group gathered anxiously in the doorway, that he realized the position Bane had left him in.

'But where is our guest?' Aunt Draga asked anxiously.

'What happened?' Zora was wearing a puzzled frown.

And: 'David! What did you *do*? What did you say to him?' Andjela pushed angrily past and ran down the passage to the front door. She was too late, however. Bane had vanished with the speed of a long-distance runner. 'But what did you do, David? What did you *say* to him?'

He stood there helplessly, struggling for words that would make things easier for his curly-haired, brown-eyed and much-loved younger sister.

6

It was near noon when Stevan wakened. He lay there for a moment, getting his bearings. The apartment was silent. No sound from the kitchen, although an aromatic smell of coffee seeping through to his bedroom indicated that the old Bosnian woman who came in every day to fix his breakfast and clean his rooms had come and gone.

He hauled his long frame out of the wildly rumpled bed and padded barefoot into the kitchen. Sure enough, the table was neatly set with a covered platter that he knew would contain cold boiled eggs, cheeses and an assortment of pastries. It was the coffee, however, that interested him. Pouring a large cupful, he paused long enough to idly stir a heaped spoon of sugar into it, then wandered back into his bedroom, drew the curtains and looked out at a grey, cloudy sky.

The coffee tasted as good as its smell had promised and although the first gulp scalded his mouth, even that by no means pleasant sensation seemed to heighten the feeling of excitement that coursed through him. My God, he thought, it's the first time in my life I remember feeling really *alive.* For that matter it was the first time he had ever really appreciated the feeling of being young. Young in the sense that you felt you could renew.

Incredible to think that a meeting with a man he had never even heard of until two weeks ago had produced this sudden feeling of heightened self-awareness. Djerdja! They had met the previous evening in the back room of a small café near Belgrade University, where he had talked most of the night away. As Dragan had ruefully made quite clear, it had not been that easy after all to persuade Djerdja to meet with Stevan. It was only when Dukić had mentioned that Stevan was about to commence working at the *Politika* that he had evinced any interest; there was the possibility that Dragan Dukić's friend might be able, if only in subtle ways, to promote the cause of the Communist Party through his work with the paper. It was that possibility that had brought Djerdja rather reluctantly to the small café.

He had first of all listened silently while Stevan, feeling oddly on the defensive, had hesitantly spoken of his own reservations about the policies expostulated by the Party, about the contradictions, indeed one might say, opportunism, evident in much of what they had to say. Although, he had added hastily as Djerdja stared at him with piercing concentration, he had been impressed by the address the communist had given to the students just after the German-Soviet pact, and somehow had felt ... he had tapered off then, somewhat ineffectually. The truth was, he was not sure *what* he'd felt. His comments had been followed by an extended silence. By his side Dragan had stirred restlessly, prompting Stevan to further remark rather lamely that some friends of his, Olga and Alex Miletić, had been interested in the Party. When he had also found Dragan helping the communists he had simply wondered what it was that drew so many people who...

Again his words tapered off. Just as he was about to suggest that the meeting may, after all, have been a mistake, that he sincerely regretted the waste of time involved, Djerdja, who had apparently come to some kind of conclusion during his somewhat unnerving and unconcealed assessment of Stevan, began to speak. He said first of all that doubtless the reason Stevan had asked for the meeting was not that he was dissatisfied with the unjust social order under which he was living, but because of his own feelings of inner desolation and emptiness. What he perhaps did not realize was that, in fact, these feelings were inextricably tied to the internal contradictions and conflicts existing in the final phases of capitalistic imperialism. This was all manifested very clearly in Yugoslavia, where the Communist Party was engaged in a to-the-death struggle with the corrupt ruling class. The fact that Stevan did not recognize that his own inner conflicts were deeply rooted in this class struggle was nothing new. It was something that could certainly be corrected by the rooting out of negative elements instilled in him by his bourgeois upbringing. With correct education he could come to realize that the so-called 'contradictions' he had spoken of so far as Party ideology was concerned, were nothing more than necessary adjustments to a shifting history.

So far as opportunism was concerned, why, of course! The Party had never tried to hide the fact that it would use any and every means at its disposal to topple world imperialism, which, of course, was simply another name for capitalism on an international scale and level, the magnitude of which could never be underestimated and the overthrow of which demanded the use of any means that presented themselves, either through the political framework or through the use of revolutionary action.

On and on he talked. Dragan, quite early in the evening, excused himself having undoubtedly, Stevan thought, heard all of this before. For himself, he sat there listening intently, only now and then interjecting a comment or a question. The interesting thing was that he had not experienced one moment of boredom. Djerdja's quietly emphatic manner, his powerful certainty of the truth of the message he carried seemed extraordinarily effective. He somehow made Stevan feel that until this moment he had been observing life through a foggy glass window through which Djerdja's arguments crashed with the force of a thrown brick.

In fact, as Stevan was to relate to Olga and Alex, whom he had invited to his apartment that evening for a late supper, although what Djerdja had said was really no different from the communist jargon he had listened to often enough when he was a student, somehow he had made it more understandable. 'Do you remember, Olga, once in London, you persuaded me to go along with you to a theatre to see a performance of Hamlet?'

'Yes, of course. What does that have to do with it?'

'Well, as you know, I was not too enthusiastic about going. As I reminded you at the time, I had studied Shakespeare at school and I never did quite grasp it. It bored me to tears as a matter of fact. Yet when we saw those fine English actors playing ... no, no, that's not the word ... *interpreting* is the word ... when we listened to them interpreting his language, well, what a difference! And that's how I found it with Djerdja. He seemed to make words that had previously been incomprehensible to me, quite clear. Besides that, he emanates a feeling of excitement that is catching. It is still with me, even though–'

'But he made no kind of apology for the behaviour of the Soviet Union? I mean, how could he excuse that infamous pact?' Alex had listened silently as Stevan described his meeting with the communist. Now he put his supper plate aside and shook his head.

'But didn't Olga tell you their line on that?'

'No, no,' Olga interrupted quickly. 'I wanted him to hear it from you. You are more impartial than I could be.'

Stevan smiled. 'Well, Alex, I suppose from their point of view it does make sense. They believe that in order to bring about the dictatorship of the proletariat it is necessary for them to overthrow not only the fascists, but also the Western imperialists. They have simply joined the former in order to overthrow the latter. When they have achieved this, they will then overthrow the former. It could have gone either way with them, you see.'

'But of course!' Alex sat up straight in his chair and slapped his knee. His pleasant face broke into a wide smile of relief. 'But of course,' he repeated, turned to his sister excitedly. 'But that's it, Olga! That's why Stalin ... what vision! You know, I've said it before and I'll say it again. Stalin is the greatest man of the century! Not only to see things with such marvellous clarity, but to have the iron courage necessary to do what must be done.'

Olga was nodding in agreement. 'Of course you are right, Alex. But you see how close we were to discarding the whole concept of communism, just because we were not able to think things through, and because we had no one knowledgeable to discuss the issue with.' She was sitting next to Stevan on his large, comfortable couch and could not restrain herself from leaning forward suddenly and kissing him lightly on the lips. 'How can we thank you, Stevan? If you only knew how depressed we have both been about this whole business.'

Stevan's chest seemed suddenly too small to contain the wild beating of his heart. It was the first time he could ever remember Olga making such a spontaneous gesture of affection towards him. And he'd known her all his life.

'Well,' he managed, clearing his throat, 'don't thank me, Olga. If I hadn't met Djerdja I'd still be wondering what you and Alex found to get so excited about so far as socialism was concerned. I'll be quite honest, Stalin seemed to me to be simply another dictator.'

'Who can blame you?' Alex was leaning forward now, hands clasped between his knees. 'The entire concept of the perfectibility of man as put forward by Lenin, why that itself is difficult enough to grasp. But then to understand that man's aggressiveness and greed has been caused by unnatural forms of social organization and that this unacceptable behaviour can be corrected by a successful proletarian revolution, well it takes a lot of thinking about, a lot of reading, believe me.' He frowned. 'And when I think how ready I was to give up everything I *had* comprehended the moment I was put to the very first test.' He shook his head sadly.

'You were not the only one, Alex.' Olga gave a rueful pout. 'At least we have learned our lesson. Is it not so? I think it will be a long time before you or I start to second guess Stalin.'

'One thing I still can't feel comfortable with.' Stevan

leaned back in a corner of the couch so that he could face them both. 'You know what Bogdan was saying about the working class? About their being no worse, but certainly no better, than any other class? That seemed to me to make sense. Do you really think our workers could organize and bring about a revolution? I can't see it happening myself.'

'But it's all there in Lenin's *What is to be Done?*' Alex was nodding eagerly. 'Lenin himself came to the conclusion that the working class was not capable itself of bringing about a worldwide revolution. He said what was needed was a group of professional revolutionaries who would take the lead, who would *think* for the masses, who would *organize* the masses. You understand?'

'Wouldn't it be wonderful if *we* could be those revolutionary leaders?' Olga's face was flushed, her eyes shining. 'And they allow women to fight, too. And why not? I could fight as well as a man. Better!' She pulled a face at Stevan, who had begun to laugh. 'All right,' he chuckled, 'you would make a great revolutionary. Which is more than I think I would do. I'm not even sure, you know, that I accept all of these theories. I think it will take more than one night of listening even to a Djerdja to turn me into a comrade.'

'The main thing is Stevan, do you think you could arrange for us to meet him?' Alex was looking at him anxiously. 'Would he be interested, do you think, in anything Olga and I could do to help the Party?'

Stevan shrugged. 'Why not? He seemed to think they could use *me*. Although I'm still not sure I *want* to be used. It's a hard thing to explain. You see, the man emanates such a feeling of *excitement*. Impossible to say I wasn't affected! But I'm still not sure I can accept this ideology, you understand?'

'But what could we do? What kind of work could we do, Alex?' Olga's fine eyes were ablaze with excitement. 'Tell us what we could do, Stevan.' My God, he thought, I think this is the first time in her life she has ever really *looked* at me.

'Well,' he said slowly, 'I gather they need people to distribute leaflets. And also, accommodation. For when their people travel. It is often with a false name, false documents. They prefer to avoid hotels, public accommodation. If they can stay in a private home or apartment–'

'Distribute leaflets?' Olga turned to her brother with a mischievous grin. 'Alex, think of all those nice rich relatives we have who own factories. If we could somehow get leaflets to the workers...'

'If you could do *that*,' Stevan laughed, 'I suspect they might give you a nice new revolutionary medal.'

But neither Alex nor Olga were in a joking mood. Excitedly they began to discuss ways they could help the Party. Stevan listened with a slight smile, as always bemused by the passion of their discussion, as their talk again turned to the inevitability of the coming revolution. Was it really true that man could be remodelled? That he could be forced to subordinate his individual interests and desires to the needs of his society? Would a state based on Marxist ideology really lose its reason for existence and wither away? Was Engels' prediction correct?

Impressed as he had been by Djerdja, entranced as he was by the sight of his beloved Olga curled up in a corner of his couch, looking at him in a way she never had before, he remained inwardly sceptical.

And yet, was it, as Djerdja had seemed to suggest, that the fault lay within himself? Why was it he had never been able to become passionately interested in *anything*? Except Olga, he thought wryly, wondering what Djerdja would think of a man whose only real interest in life so far had been a woman. Not women, but *a* woman, which probably made it worse! He thought suddenly of David Ristić. David, who was so passionately interested in just about everything; whether he was studying, reading for pleasure and knowledge, searching for what he called the 'truth' about things, or simply involved in a particular sport, David was always so completely involved. Stevan had always envied his friend's endless entanglement with life. God, he thought, even Bogdan was interested and involved. Even if it was only with the idea of making money. But no, he rejected the thought quickly. Not fair. Bogdan was also interested in using his mind. He enjoyed reading, enjoyed showing off his knowledge of languages, literature. While he, Stevan, why, even this new job at *Politika* failed to make him enthusiastic. The offer had come out of the blue, and he suspected his father's hand. He had nothing else to do. So!

Alex had begun to talk about Stalin again. His open face was full of light. It's true, Stevan mused, watching him. They are like – who was it who said that? – they are like what one imagines the early Christians must have been.

'At least I've learned my lesson,' the big man was saying. He placed a large hand over his heart. 'I vow to you both, Olga, Stevan, I will never doubt Stalin again.'

It was Olga's turn now. She began to talk about how long it had taken her to realize what an empty, frivolous society she had been born into. How unjust, how empty of values. Quite extraordinary how one could observe these things, yet not really think about them. In fact, had she not gone overseas, made that trip to England, met, quite by accident, some people who were aware of these things, who had drawn her attention to them, why, then she would probably still be as empty-headed as many of her school friends. Never mind that many of them held degrees, what they really wanted out of life, what they had been brought up to believe was their only role in life, was to sit around and simper and wait for some man to save them from spinsterhood. None of them! *None of them* had ever given the slightest thought to the injustice that allows a small group of people to live off the fat of the land by profiting from the labour of others. Talk to them about the exploitation of the masses and all you would get would be a blank stare after which they would begin talking about what silly dress they would wear to what silly ball. There was no doubt about it. It was the rich – and she was shamed to admit she was included amongst them – who were the bloodsuckers of the world. The rich, and the bureaucrats they spawned to construct a more comfortable life for themselves.

'Bureaucrats!' Alex caught at the word like a puppy

savaging a slipper. 'I long for the day when we can do away with them. Honestly, I think I detest them more than I do the rich. What kind of people are they? To imprison themselves in their bureaucratic little cubby holes for the whole of their lives for the privilege of gaining a tiny bit of power over the people they are supposed to serve and for the promise of a tiny pension.' He sighed, gazed at Stevan artlessly. 'I hate bureaucrats,' he reiterated unnecessarily. 'If the coming social order does nothing else, if it only manages to eliminate bureaucrats as the state withers away, then it would still all be worthwhile.'

They both seemed so sure that he now understood everything, that he agreed with every word! 'You see, try to understand. I have trouble with this.' Stevan stood up and began to wander restlessly around his living room. 'You two are such true believers. You accept so readily that communism has all the answers to all the questions.'

'But it is a scientific fact.' Alex got up, moved over to the sideboard, and poured himself another coffee. 'Once you grasp *that*, Stevan–'

'Stevan.' Olga leaned forward and fastened her large dark eyes on him compellingly. 'Haven't you yet grasped the magnitude of what we are talking about?'

The impatience in her voice alerted him to the fact that he was on dangerous ground. 'If only,' he said desperately, 'I could empty my mind of everything I've ever learned. You know the kind of thing, Alex. About our history, about our country, how it was formed. About being a Serb. What it means to be a Serb! If only I could empty my mind of everything and start all over again. Do you understand what I mean?'

Alex gazed back at him with genuine warmth and understanding. 'Of course I do, Stevan. You have hit the nail on the head. *You do understand.* That is exactly what you must do.'

'Do you remember something we learned when we were studying French, Stevan?' asked Olga. 'What book was it? We read that when the French King Clovis became a

Christian, when he was being confirmed, Cardinal Remy told him . . . you remember what he told him?' She smiled, began to laugh delightedly as he nodded.

'From now on burn what you have admired and admire what you have burned.'

'That's it! That's it.'

Alex finished his coffee, placed the cup on the mantelpiece. 'But we must go, Olga. We must be off. Look at the time. We must let Stevan get some rest. He's a working man now.'

He saw them out. Djerdja had told him he would send a note through Dragan when he could see him again, and he promised them he would pass on their offer of help with leaflets. Even perhaps with accommodation, when the old people are out of town, Alex said. The big man shook him warmly by the hand. Olga embraced him lightly and kissed him on the cheek, leaving a soft fragrance behind her that seemed to linger long after they had left.

He had a sudden feeling of panic. Of drowning in deep currents of water that were sucking him into dark unknown depths where it was impossible to fight the undertow. He needed to speak to someone about all of this. But to whom? His father? He would begin shouting about bloody Bolsheviks if he so much as mentioned the word socialism!

David! Of course. Who else could remind him so compellingly that he, Stevan Matić, was not a bloody communist, but a Serb. No one could explain quite as clearly as David what that meant. Yes, yes. He would talk to David. But not now, he thought wryly. Not at 2 a.m. on a Sunday morning. But soon. It must be very soon.

7

The marriage of Alexander Miletić and Jelena Marković took place at the historic church of St Sava in December, just two weeks before the Orthodox Christmas. The early evening candlelit ceremony followed by a reception at the home of the bride's parents was, it was generally agreed, the social event of 1939. It gave a wonderful lift to the winter season. David Ristić was present with his aunt, his two sisters and Irina Mirskaia.

When the speeches and the toasts and the dancing were over, when the fine-looking groom had departed with his beautiful bride for a skiing honeymoon at Planica in the Slovenian Alps, the gossip amongst the matrons of Belgrade centered upon the question of who would be next? David Ristić and that exquisite little Russian girl? Or Olga Miletić and Stevan Matić? That one or other or both of the young couples would announce their engagement some time soon was a foregone conclusion, the matrons agreed, with an occasional romantic sigh and an occasional touch of malice. They all knew of girls who had shown interest in the young men and who were obviously about to lose out in the marital merry-go-round.

David found the opportunity to have a brief chat with Stevan, apologizing for breaking the luncheon appointment they'd had a couple of months previously. Family problems, he said briefly, with a worried glance in the direction of his sister Andjela. But you said you needed to see me, Stevan? It was important? Stevan nodded absentmindedly. No, no.

He couldn't even recall what it was. He had probably just wanted a bit of company that day. It was agreed they would definitely get together soon.

In fact they were not to meet again until they were brought together by another Belgrade wedding. Not a fashionable one, this time. Bogdan Bošković and Rachel Aaron were married at a civil ceremony attended only by the groom's mother and stepfather and two friends of the bride. The point was, a happy but subdued Bogdan related to David by phone, Rachel's parents had not approved the marriage, had done everything they could to prevent it, and having failed, now refused to have anything to do with either their daughter or her husband.

'Otherwise I would have asked you, of course,' Bogdan explained. 'But the truth is, I wasn't sure Rachel would go through with it until it was over.' His voice became exultant. 'But you see it seems she really does love me. Even more than she loves her parents.'

'But Bogdan, that's wonderful news. About time you had a wife to keep you in order. Congratulations to you both. And, look, Bogdan, we must celebrate the occasion. Aunt Draga is going to want to give you a party.'

'Very well, David.' Bogdan's voice became formal, self-important. 'Rachel would like that. We would both enjoy that. But, not too many people, I hope?'

'That's up to you, fellow. Whomever you want. You and Rachel can think about it and let us know. Just the family, perhaps. And Stevan, of course. He will want to bring Olga. Oh, and by the way, would you mind if I ask Jack Cohen? I met him on the street a few days ago. I thought he and his family had left the country. Because of the international situation, you know. But it appears they were simply on a short vacation. They have decided to stay in Yugoslavia, after all. Still, he was looking rather glum. A nice wedding party might cheer him up.'

'Jack Cohen? Of course. And about the others, I'll check with Rachel and let you know. We can decide on the date then, perhaps.'

So for over a week the kitchen in the Ristić apartment was filled from early morning to late evening with the fragrant smell of Aunt Draga and Andjela's baking. Zora was busy with her studies which, David claimed, was just as well, bringing a wan smile to the face of his younger sister. At least it *was* a smile, certainly an improvement on the moody silences interspersed with sudden torrents of tears Andjela had been subject to since the departure of Bane Protić from the Ristić apartment and from her life.

The party proved to be a great success. Bogdan was obviously walking on air. Rachel was pale, but seemed to be quietly happy. Even the shy Jack came out of his shell and joined in with the lively conversation that was always such a feature of Serbian parties. The only thing, David was to think later, was that he never did get a chance to talk with Stevan as much as he would have liked, except to congratulate him on the excellence of the articles appearing in *Politika* under his name. He was, Stevan had replied, surprised himself at how much he was enjoying his new profession.

The war between Germany, Britain and France had, amazingly, seemed to have gone quietly away. All seemed calm. David, who had felt a pang of concern upon discovering the Cohen family had decided after all to 'see it out' as Jack put it, began to think they had definitely made the right decision.

Then on the 9th of April, 1940, the 'slavering wolf' struck again. This time the tiny countries of Denmark and Norway were swallowed up in one devastating gulp. German divisions gathered ready for action along the Western Front. The Luftwaffe's endless waves of aircraft devastated seven allied airfields. The brutal invasion of western Europe was under way.

Oddly enough, the endless talk of war that had flooded Belgrade the previous summer was now strangely muted. It was as though people had simply run out of words and were now compelled to silently observe a horrifying drama that was, however, taking place on someone else's stage. History,

God only knew, had always been particularly brutal to the Yugoslav capital. Now for once it seemed content to pass by the historic city, its hunger satiated temporarily at least by the havoc wreaked upon hapless Belgium, Holland and Luxembourg, sacrificial lambs that seemingly also had to be swallowed before the ravenous beast, Germany, met its match, as of course it must. Not even the Germans would prove invincible when they encountered the impregnable Maginot Line.

So, ignoring all lessons of the past, Belgrade and the rest of the world let out its collective breath and relaxed. The rampage must surely be at an end. Even Hitler must know a brick wall when he ran into one! Hitler, however, was to prove that when facing a brick wall he knew enough to skirt around it or attack it at its weakest point. He stunned the French army by launching his main offensive through the hills of Ardennes. By the middle of May German tanks had thundered through the French Ninth and Second Armies at Sedan. France had crumpled like a pack of cards. The Allied army was in full retreat towards the English Channel at Dunkirk.

Had David Ristić at that time in his life not found himself head over heels in love with Irina Mirskaia, these events would have driven him to spend endless hours with his Uncle Mikhail and his closest friends, discussing the war and the effect it might eventually have on Yugoslavia.

A thousand times he told himself he must find the time to visit his uncle; but there was always a concert at the State National Theatre or a dinner dance at the fashionable Aero Club or a lecture or art show at the Kolarac University that he simply had to attend with Irina; or duty calls to be paid upon the still formidable Madame Mirskaia and her pleasant sister-in-law; or arrangements to be made for Madame to visit his home to meet an equally formidable Aunt Draga, who successfully managed to convey to Anna Mirskaia that while her daughter was undoubtedly a prize for any young man, nevertheless, handsome young men of good family and excellent prospects like her golden nephew, whose father had been one of the best-loved men in Belgrade, and who had as uncles a former speaker of the house and the late patriarch, were not exactly to be found on trees, either.

During summer Madame agreed that Irina could accompany David and Zora on their two-week vacation in the capital of Skoplje, Macedonia, where the Ristić family had once lived briefly.

David had rented a small apartment for the three of them, not far from the square that led to the mediaeval bridge over the River Vardar, a bridge that had withstood the test of time since Greek and Roman feet had tramped across it, since Byzantine merchants had wandered into the town to hawk their wares.

They spent a hectic first week visiting relatives and friends, exploring gingerbread churches, admiring the gleaming domes of the numerous mosques in the Muslim quarter and listening to the eerie cry of the *Hodza*, calling the faithful to prayer. They shopped in the busy market place, lingering over brass urns and samovars and bargaining for embroidered tapestries and silver bangles. They sat in small sun-filled courtyard cafés drinking Turkish coffee and watching Albanians strut by with their little white skull caps and homespun clothing and the Turks, whom Irina insisted looked just like sleek, dark, fez-topped seals.

A few days before returning to Belgrade they borrowed bicycles and toured the countryside, drinking in the lilac-soaked air, lazily cycling by yellow and green cornfields and stopping to admire clusters of wild red poppies.

One evening they stayed overnight at a small twelfth-century monastery that nestled close to the turbulent Vardar. They shared a dinner of grilled fish caught fresh that afternoon from the river with a merry-faced old monk who had a deep love of his province and chattered away about its beauty, its history. Did they know that Macedonia was the birthplace of Philip of Macedonia, father of Alexander the Great? And of Aristotle, the teacher and philosopher who had so much influence on Alexander? David nodded. Zora and Irina smiled, looked wise.

Afterwards Zora tactfully opted to stay at the monastery to admire its crudely-executed but powerfully beautiful frescoes while David took Irina for a walk down a well-worn path flanked by young poplars that led to the river-bank. They sat together on an upturned canoe, watched the heavy yellow moon, and exchanged confidences.

David told her about his Uncle Nikola who, even after becoming patriarch of the church, still found time to visit his younger brother's home on the day of the family *Slava*; of how much in awe he had been of the tall man with the flowing silken robes, golden staff and tall headgear of an Orthodox bishop. His uncle had possessed a long, flowing beard, cheeks the colour of apples and the clear, piercing eyes of a man pure in heart. David would never forget him, nor the shock of learning of his inexplicable death. He had been an apparently healthy man who had sickened and died slowly and painfully over a period of several months of an ailment no doctor had been able to diagnose. Rumours had abounded of rifts and jealousies within the church. The word poison had been whispered by the local peasants, but nothing had ever been proved, no motive found.

In return Irina told him about her Aunt Marya's short and tragic betrothal to a young Russian nobleman who had been killed in a hunting accident just one week before the wedding. She also shyly explained to David why she had been so nervous, had become ill, during the train journey from Belgrade to Skoplje. It seemed that for as long as she could remember she had taken ill every time she had to travel by train. It stemmed, she said, from a recurring nightmare in which she found herself on a train. 'It is always the same,' she explained. 'I am on a train. It is coming from nowhere and in the dream I don't know where it is going, only that I must at all costs get off. Finally it arrives at a station. I try to get off, but before I can it starts up again and it goes back to nowhere, and then back to the station again. It keeps doing that. To and from. Back and forth. It is terrible. In my dream I find I cannot breathe, I become hysterical, I want to throw myself from the window, and I always wake up screaming. It is terrible for Mamoushka and Aunt Marya. It distresses them so.'

'But what can be at the root of such a dream?' David gazed at her, concerned. 'There must be a cause. Such a dream must come from somewhere.'

'Well, the only thing we can think of is that I did experience a terrible train journey once. It was when we left Russia.' Of course, she went on to tell him, she did not remember anything about it. She had been a baby in her mother's arms. Perhaps it was simply that she had heard the story so many times. She hesitated, sighed. 'So *many* times.'

Arrangements for her family to leave Russia had been made by her grandfather, she went on. Although he himself had refused to leave the country at the time of the revolution, claiming that he would prefer to die on Russian soil at the hands of the red 'bandits' than live in exile, he had somehow managed to make arrangements to get his daughter, his son-in-law, grandchild and Marya Mirskaia out of the country. Their journey was to take them on a tortuous route from Moscow to a spot some fifty or so miles from the Polish border. From there they were to be picked up by a farmer from the estate of a certain Polish nobleman the general had known all his life, and driven by dray across the border to safety.

They had all been modestly, even shabbily dressed, and due to the uncertainty of train schedules in the country at that time they had taken a basket of simple provisions it was hoped would last them several days if necessary. The train had been packed to overflowing and they had been warned not to leave their seats, above all not to be tempted to get off the train at any of the numerous stops there were bound to be. Too many passengers during those tumultuous times had left a train and had been unable to get back on, or had simply disappeared, or had found when they did struggle back on board that their seat had been taken by someone else, usually a belligerent member of the newly important proletariat, who was not about to give it up.

Irina sighed and looked up at David anxiously. 'I hope I'm not boring you, David. It is all such ancient history.'

'*You* bore me? Never! Please go on.'

'Well, she began again, hesitantly, the trouble had begun when her mother had brought out their small supply of provisions several hours after their journey had begun. Not that it had been much. Some bread, a little cheese and dry sausage, two large bottles of water laced with a little wine. A large woman, she seemed to be some kind of farm worker, Irina's mother always said, who had been sitting in the opposite aisle with two hulking sons, had leaned forward aggressively. 'Are you not going to share with us, citizen?' She had given a harsh gust of laughter, then snatched the basket from Anna Mirskaia's knees. 'Let's see what you've got here.'

Irina's father had protested, but the aisles were crowded with workers who were already casting resentful eyes at the comparatively well-dressed family who each had a seat, and he had lapsed into silence. As it was, on the third day her father had been unable to bear the situation any longer, and had got up at one of the numerous stops where peasants could be seen selling unappetising scraps of vegetables and fruit, and despite the protests of his wife and sister, had muttered something about at least getting them some vegetables to eat, and left the carriage.

In the clear light from the moon David saw Irina's face contort, and for a moment he thought she was going to burst into tears. 'But this is upsetting you,' he said. 'Tell me the rest later. You don't have to tell the whole story now.'

'But I want to,' she insisted. 'Please let me finish. Then it will be over.'

He reached out, took her hand, raised it to his lips.

'Anyway,' she went on abruptly, 'he didn't come back.' She gave a deep, quivering sigh.

After a moment David put his arm around her, held her gently. 'What do you mean, he didn't come back?'

She sat up straight and seemed to have recovered a little. 'Just that. I mean just that.' There was another long pause and then she began, again, to speak rapidly. 'Of course, the moment he left, Mamoushka says some evil-smelling old man snatched at the bundle she had put down to keep his seat for him, and sat down next to her. She did not dare move. Nor did Aunt Marya. The train began to pull away and they tried to lift the window, to shout, to call for him, but the wayside ... Mamoushka says it wasn't even a station, not a real station, just a place along the railroad tracks in the middle of nowhere. But it was crowded with people and they couldn't see him and they waited and waited but he never came back.'

Now she began to cry. David held her tightly. 'It's all right, my little girl. You are all right now.'

She wiped her eyes and tried to smile. 'I know it's foolish. It's just that even though I was a baby when we left Russia well, ever since I can remember, that train ride has haunted me.'

'Why should it be foolish? Aunt Draga always claims that babies absorb much more than is generally thought, you know.'

'But it seems incredible that I should remember. Although perhaps I don't, really. Perhaps it is just hearing the story told so often.'

'And your father? Did you ever hear what happened to your father?'

She shook her head. 'No. Oh, now and then there would be rumours. We heard a man resembling him was picked up by two men along the route we travelled – secret police, perhaps. I know there must have been hundreds, perhaps thousands, who suffered *that* fate. Then we heard once that he had been seen in Moscow. Someone told us that it was certain he was still alive and living in Moscow. Then we heard that he had been seen in St Petersburg and was living there under a different name. Oh! so many rumours. So many. But we never heard from him again, although we did manage to get word to my grandfather. But then, after he died...'

Her eyes misted over again and a wave of love and tenderness made David reach out and take her in his arms. There was nothing he wanted more at that moment than to take care of her forever.

When they returned to the monastery a short time later they went straight to the small whitewashed bedroom Irina was to share with Zora, who was sitting on the side of her bed brushing her hair. David went to his sister excitedly and took both of her hands in his. 'Zora. You are the first to know. Irina has agreed to marry me.'

Later, before leaving the two girls for the night, he drew Irina outside the door, kissed her goodnight and said sternly: "You are in *my* care now. That means you must not be afraid any more, of trains or anything else. You understand?'

Irina had gazed up at him, eyes soft as candlelight, her pretty face very serious. 'Yes, David,' she answered meekly. 'I understand.'

On the train trip back to Belgrade she sat very close to him, held his hand tightly. But she showed no sign at all of any distress, and was obviously relaxed enough to enjoy the beautiful country the train was taking them through. The green wooded hills, sparkling little streams, the golden meadows with their scattered wild flowers He had never, David decided, felt happier in his whole life.

A few days later he returned to the bank. In the afternoon he spent some time at the rowing club, and then made a sudden decision to call on Stevan who had recently moved to a new apartment on Bitoljska Street. Perhaps they could set a date to have lunch together before David left for Negotin.

He arrived at Stevan's building, checked the list of names in the front entrance, and found his apartment was on the second floor. Full of energy as always, he ran up the stairs two at a time, stood outside his friend's apartment door and had actually lifted his hand to ring the bell when it swung abruptly open. He found himself, hand still raised, face to face with a middle-aged man of about his own height and, oddly enough, with a physiognomy not dissimilar to his own.

It was difficult to say who was the more startled. They stood there staring at each other. David had an impression of pale, blue-grey eyes taking in absolutely everything about him. He began to ask whether he had the right apartment, but then the man, with a barely perceptible nod, brushed past him and he caught a glimpse of Stevan hovering in the background.

'David! I wasn't expecting you.' Stevan seemed actually on the verge of stammering. David looked at him, then turned again to catch a glimpse of his visitor, who was already disappearing rapidly down the stairs. He had a sudden feeling that he was intruding, an extraordinary feeling for him to have in connection with Stevan, with whom he had always felt so close, so comfortable.

'Come in. Come in.' His friend seemed to have recovered from his momentary discomfiture. 'Sorry, David. 'You startled me.'

David slowly entered the apartment, trying to comprehend the reason for the unmistakable feeling of tension in the air, wondering why such a brief encounter with a strange man framed in a doorway could leave such an indelible impression on him. He was astonished to realize that, although he had felt a flash of resentment at the way the stranger had with one quick, shrewd, glance, seemed to have summed up everything about him, he himself could have given an extremely accurate description of Stevan's visitor, from the well-cut if slightly flashy suit right down to what looked like a genuine diamond flashing gaudily on one finger.

He allowed himself to be led by Stevan to one of the large, leather chairs and glanced around the apartment, which was similar to the one Stevan had recently vacated, only half listening to his suddenly voluble friend who was saying how good it was to see him, why hadn't they ever had that lunch they were supposed to have together and as a matter of fact he'd bumped into Bogdan the other day and they'd both agreed...

'Who was that man?' Stevan stopped talking in mid-sentence at the interruption and stared at David.

'What?'

'That man I almost bumped into in your doorway. Who was he?'

'Who was he? Oh...' Stevan gestured clumsily, then shrugged. 'No one in particular.' He ... er ... he has something to do with *Politika*. No one in particular.'

'I see.' David nodded, then shrugged. It didn't really matter. And yet...

Stevan was asking him what he would like to drink. A beer? Or would he prefer some coffee?

'What did you say his name was?' His friend stared at him blankly. 'That man, the one who was just here.' He was not sure himself why he was pressing the point. Did it really matter? Time to change the subject! Which he did. Not, however, before Stevan had suddenly blurted out a name he had never heard before.

'Josip Broz,' he almost stuttered. 'His name is Josip Broz.'

8

The moment David left, Stevan began pacing the apartment in anguish; the sickness reached down into the pit of his stomach.

Finally he called Olga.

'I have to see you. Can you come over?'

'If you wish.' Her voice, as always, was calm and sure. 'But if you prefer you could come here. Her parents had gone to Vrnjačka Banja, she said, referring to a popular Yugoslav mineral spa between Kraljevo and Kruševac in central Serbia. 'Daddy's arthritis is playing up again.'

'It is? I'm sorry.'

'So I'm all alone, really. Except of course for Stana.'

Stevan thought about Stana Radović, the fierce Macedonian hill woman who had been Olga's nurse and who now managed the Miletić household with an iron fist. He was in no mood to encounter Stana.

'If it's all right I'd rather you came over here. I can call one of the restaurants. Have some dinner sent over.'

'Very well.' There was a short silence. 'I take it your visitor has gone?'

'Yes. He left a couple of hours ago.'

'Will he be returning?'

'I don't think so. Not so far as I know.'

'I see. All right, Stevan. I'll be over within an hour.' He began to thank her, but she had already hung up. Olga was not one to waste words.

He went into the small kitchen, opened a cupboard and

took out a bottle of *Sljivovica* and poured himself a small glass. The mere fact that he knew she would be with him before long had already quietened the nausea in his stomach. The brandy finished the job; within ten minutes he was feeling more his usual self.

In fact it took her a little over an hour to arrive. She was hatless, wore a loosely belted white linen dress, and looked fresh, cool, self-contained. 'I've been dying to see you,' she said, kissing him lightly on the cheek. 'What was all the mystery?'

'Mystery?'

She laughed. 'My dear Stevan. Almost ten days ago you called and asked that on no account was I to call or visit you at your apartment, and would I please pass the same message on to Alex. When I asked why, you mumbled something about having an important visitor, and hung up on me.' Her mouth broke into the rare and lovely smile that always simply floored him. 'I was furious, until I realized you were probably doing something for the Party.' She had been standing in front of him with her arms folded in the manner of a school mistress. Now she laughed, settled down in a corner of the huge leather couch and brushed her hair back from her forehead. 'Who have you been entertaining this past week or so? Stalin?'

Stevan weakly returned her smile. 'Sorry. I should have been in touch. I meant to drop by and see you one afternoon, but...' he shrugged. He began to tell her what had happened. She knew, of course, that for the past few months he had been helping the Party by writing propaganda and that he had been involved in the setting up of a printing press for the purpose of producing a weekly paper that would keep Party members up-to-date on the ever-changing ideological stance of the Central Committee.

What he did not tell her was that he was not really happy about his involvement in either of these functions. It seemed to him that he had been drawn into a political web which at first seemed to offer endless pockets of escape, but that in fact tightened around him each time he struggled to extricate himself. There had, first of all, been the undeniably flattering interest shown in him by Nikola Djerdja, not to mention the fact that his relationship with Olga had improved immeasurably. Dating from the evening he had told her about his meeting with Djerdja, he had slowly, almost imperceptibly been drawn into the illegal activities of the Party. First of all, as promised, he had arranged for Olga and her brother to meet Djerdja. Then, swept up in *their* enthusiasm, he had found himself going with them to meetings of the Party cell Djerdja had introduced them into. In common with David Ristić, he had found himself unnerved by what he considered their mad proclamations of loyalty and attachment to the Soviet Union. God only knows, he had told himself, Yugoslavia has its problems, but it is a beautiful, rich, wonderful country, vibrant with its own history, its own sense of wild justice. What did it need to learn from the Russians?

But first Olga and Alex, and then Jelena, who had begun to accompany them to the meetings, had listened respectfully to even the wildest proclamations from the motley group of students, intellectuals and sons and daughters of the rich with whom they had all gone to school and who had greeted them with shrieks of recognition and comradely ardour when they first arrived while the one worker and two peasants looked on. Stevan had begun to ask himself: what is wrong with me? He had great respect for Alex and had always admired Olga's intelligence amongst other things, and neither of them ever questioned even the most obviously inaccurate assumptions of certain members of the cell. As for Jelena, she seemed quite prepared to accept whatever it was her amiable giant of a husband wished her to accept. Added to all this was the fact that he had found once he settled down to his work at *Politika* that not only were several of his colleagues sympathetic to the communist message, but its admirers even included the paper's owner. On top of everything else, he had somehow missed having the discussion with David he had felt so imperative at the time. They had both been too busy with their own affairs and now, of course, any discussion of his problem with his closest friend was out of the question. His involvement had gone too far.

'But go *on*, Stevan. I *know* you have been doing things for the Party. We all have. Don't stop and just stare into your brandy glass now you have come to the most interesting part. Who has been staying here with you?'

'Oh! Sorry.' Startled out of his reverie, he sat up straight, and told her about the visit he had received from Nikola Djerdja. 'He knocked on my door one evening, told me they were rather in a spot. The police were searching for this man, a man who was very important to the movement. It was imperative that he stay in Belgrade for several days, but they were nervous about keeping him in any of the usual houses. There were indications that provocateurs had infiltrated the Party structure and so they needed to ensure that he be installed in the safest possible place. Nikola said he immediately thought of me. He felt I would be the last one the police would suspect of harbouring a member of the Communist Party. He told me, however, that if I agreed to take this man in, he in all conscience must warn me that if the police should find him I could expect to find myself in great trouble, could even face an extended jail sentence.' He paused for breath and gave a deep sigh.

'And? And?' Olga urged him on, her large dark eyes sparkling with excitement.

'What could I do? Of course I said it was all right. He then asked whether I was likely to have any visitors. I told him not that I knew of, that perhaps you or Alex might drop in, so he asked me to warn you both to stay away. He also asked that I give the woman who cooks and cleans for me a week or two off. So, as you know, I called you, and then told Bogdanka to take a couple of weeks off to go and visit her sister.'

He went on to tell her how he had then stayed home alone in his apartment for two nights awaiting the arrival of his important guest. There was neither sight nor sound of him, nor did he hear further from Djerdja. He had just about come to the conclusion that they had found another place for him to hide, when around midnight on the third night there was a loud banging on his door and when he opened it Nikola had rushed in with a companion he brusquely introduced as Mr Kostanjšek. He had then departed without a further word.

'But what was this Mr Kostanjšek like?'

Stevan frowned. 'Well as a matter of fact he rather irritated me that first night. You see I had intended to offer him the couch in the study – after all, all of my things are in the bedroom. But he seemed to assume that the best room in the apartment automatically would be his. He told me he was tired, asked if I needed anything from the bedroom for the morning as he did not wish to be disturbed. So I grabbed a few things to wear to work next morning, and then he simply closed the door and went to bed.'

Olga threw her head back and gave a delighted gust of laughter. 'To each man according to his needs! He must have felt he needed a good bed better than you did, Stevan.'

Stevan grinned ruefully. 'Well, he was certainly not shy about taking it.'

'Was he a worker, do you think?'

'I believe he is an engineer. He was well dressed, and I must say when I returned from work the following evening he proved to be very courteous. And, as a matter of fact, rather used to the good things in life I would say. He had hung his suit in the wardrobe and was wearing a pair of my pyjamas, not to mention my best silk dressing gown! I've never known anyone who seemed to make himself so quickly at home in someone else's apartment.'

'What did you talk about?'

'First of all he thanked me for a note I had left, telling him to help himself to the food I had Bogdanka prepare before she left . . . a note I suspect was entirely unnecessary. He was sitting in this chair, reading of all things the English dictionary I have. He told me he was trying to teach himself the language. That broke the ice a bit because of course I was able to give him a few pronunciation tips. After that we had a drink together and I called a restaurant and had some food sent up. And after *that,* we had a game of chess. He easily beat me. I told him I would get even the following night, and this caused him to laugh until I thought he would fall off his chair. He said the devil I would! Then we both went to bed. It wasn't until the following night that we began to really talk.' He hesitated, wondering, after all, whether he should tell her what was really on his mind. 'Look, Olga, how about a glass of wine? Then I'll send out for some dinner.'

'Why not?'

She watched him with a slight smile as he got up and went into the kitchen. It had been, in fact, the moment that he had poured himself and Kostanjšek a glass each from the decanter he was now looking for that Stevan had realized who the man was. Kostanjšek had still been studying the English dictionary he had been holding when Stevan walked in, had glanced up and peered at him through the round-rimmed spectacles, before removing them and accepting the glass. Stevan had immediately realized why he had seemed vaguely familiar to him when Djerdja had made his brief introduction the previous evening.

The truth was, as he had carefully explained to Kostanjšek a night or two later, that for the past several weeks he had been spending a good deal of time in the dead file section of *Politika,* trying to trace the evolution of the Communist Party in the country. He had, of course, known vaguely that in 1921 the Party had been made illegal in Yugoslavia and many of its members subject to arrest, but from that time onwards police crackdowns on the Party and its membership had run up and down a rather slippery slope. He had simply wanted more information, to better understand the nature of the movement within his country since he had found himself ever more deeply involved in its machinations. So it was only natural that he should happen upon the extensive coverage given to the 1928 trial of six communists who were accused, amongst other things, of the illegal possession of bombs and firearms.

Wide coverage had been given to the trial and the paper had singled out a man called Josip Broz for special attention amongst the accused, quoting his comment: 'I do not feel guilty because I do not recognize your bourgeois court of justice. I consider myself responsible only to my own Party,' as being in strict adherence to the conduct prescribed for communists in the presence of a 'class court'. His photograph, featured next to the article, had shown a clean-shaven man wearing round spectacles placed over slightly protruding ears.

'I'm sorry,' Stevan had said hesitantly to the man he knew as Kostanjšek, 'but I recognized you almost immediately.'

The communist had stared at him with eyes turned suddenly guarded, hostile. He had sunk back deeper in the big leather chair, crossed his legs, rubbed his chin with a capable-looking, broad hand. 'May I ask why you are telling me this?' he asked after a short silence.

'I don't know,' Stevan had blurted out. 'Except that I like you. I want to be honest with you.'

Broz had stared at him thoughtfully, then his eyes had lost their guarded hostility. 'The devil you do,' he had chuckled. 'I like that. I like a man who puts his cards on the table.'

From that moment on they had got along swimmingly. Stevan had found himself even telling him about the doubts he had from time to time about the Party. 'The truth is,' he had said, 'I listen to some of the Party members sometimes and what they say seems to me to be absolute nonsense. If it were not for people like Nikola Djerdja and one or two others...' He had broken off, wondering if he had perhaps gone too far.

Broz, however, had simply nodded. 'Yes, yes. I understand you. But you must learn not to worry about such things. Some of our people do get carried away. But the Party needs them, you understand. You must simply keep our revolutionary aims in mind, the overthrow of the bourgeois democratic party and the installation of a just people's republic. It is not necessary to think about anything else. Let the intellectuals argue amongst themselves, learn from them what you can and don't worry about the rest. It will all crystallize in your mind one day. Don't rush things.'

'Whatever are you doing, Stevan?' He turned with a start to find Olga standing in the kitchen doorway.

'Sorry.' He held up the decanter he had just refilled. 'Bogdanka usually does this for me. I've become spoiled.'

A moment later they were back in the living room, seated, and sipping the pale golden wine. He began to tell her that by accident he had found out the real name of the man who had been introduced as Kostanjšek. 'You know they don't like that,' he said. 'They don't like us to know their real names.'

'So? Just don't tell them you know.'

'But I already have. I told him.'

'What on earth for?' She sighed. 'Sometimes you seem to enjoy making life difficult for yourself, Stevan. Do you think he is going to hold it against you?'

'No, no. I don't think you understand. He was not upset at all. I think he realized how much I liked him. Admired him, even. I wish you could have met him, Olga, you would have been impressed. Even more so than with Nikola. This man, you see, has travelled extensively. He is very knowledgeable. A reasonable man. I was even able to tell him ...' He broke off and looked at her searchingly. 'Tell me, Olga. When we go to those meetings. Some of the things they say, don't you find it hard to swallow? Then there are all of the petty little jealousies, the intrigues. You and Alex never seem to question anything, but I have to tell you, I do. Sometimes I want to get up and walk out. Don't you *ever* feel like that?' He shook his head, sighed. 'All of the inconsistencies, you know. And the shouting. Yet if they could even *agree* with each other I might be able to swallow the rest.'

Olga had settled back in the chair, was nursing the glass of wine, nodding her head. She seemed to understand. He got up and began to pace around the room. 'Although I didn't tell him how much I hate the lying. My God, all of the lying

I've done since I became involved with these people. To many of my friends, to my relatives. Even to my parents. I tell you I don't like it. I feel–'

'You feel exactly the way your bourgeois upbringing has conditioned you to feel!' She searched in the large straw bag she had put down next to her on the couch, found a package of cigarettes and removed one. He leant forward to light it for her, and shook his head as she offered him the packet.

'Of course Alex and I notice the same things you do, Stevan. We are not entirely stupid! But we are both more concerned about the ideological differences than with their petty personal little concerns. Have you noticed? Even the more intelligent ones seem to differ about ideological interpretations.' She drew deeply on the cigarette, slowly exhaled.

He gave a short burst of laughter, sat down opposite her as she gave him a look of inquiry. 'Just something...' he paused. 'Something Kostanjšek told me. He said that when he was in Moscow the current joke about the Communist Party in this country was *two Yugoslavs, three factions*. They were not far wrong, I must say.'

'He has been in the Soviet Union then? Interesting!' She gazed at him thoughtfully. 'You said you told him of your concerns. What did he say?'

Stevan repeated word for word what the communist had said. She nodded. 'Interesting. That is just about the way Alex and I see things. We can't do much about the things we don't like within the Party, but the thing is to always keep one's eye on the main objective. It's easy for Alex. He has this quite absolute faith in Stalin. Of course,' she added hastily, 'we all do. But his is quite, quite exceptional, I think.'

'And Jelena?'

'What Alex thinks, Jelena tries to think. What Alex believes, Jelena tries to believe. Except,' she laughed, 'that she still believes in an almighty God. How she must love Alex!'

She stubbed the remainder of her cigarette out in the big,

brass ashtray. 'Well, this is all very interesting, Stevan. But when you called you sounded rather upset. I rushed to get over here quickly. Is something really wrong? Is it just that now you know this man's real name you are frightened? Or what?'

'Frightened?' He frowned. 'Of course not. No, no. When I called you I *was* upset. I haven't told you the rest. You see, I was expecting him to stay a few more days, but when I arrived home this afternoon he was already dressed to leave. Told me he had a call from Nikola and he would be leaving immediately. He thanked me very warmly for my hospitality. Told me we would most certainly be meeting again and then . . .' He hesitated. His face fell.

'Well?' She was becoming a little impatient.

'Well, he slapped me on the back, told me he was glad I knew his real name, just so long as it remained a secret between us. Of course I agreed, then he opened the door to leave and you'll never guess who was standing in front of it: David! David Ristić.'

'David? Really? How is he? It seems ages since I've seen him.'

'Don't you understand? Kostanjšek was startled, but he simply brushed past him and disappeared down the stairs. But the thing that upset me so much, first of all David asked me who he was and I said he had something to do with *Politika*. That's what I mean about lying. I've never told David a lie before in all of my life, nor he me, I am sure of that. So when he asked me Kostanjšek's name I . . . I don't know . . . all this . . . as you say . . . bourgeois guilt, I suppose . . . seemed to surge up. Before I could stop myself I had simply blurted out his *real* name, God!' He rose and began his restless pacing again. 'Do you realize what I've done, Olga? My first real test with the Party, I suppose. And I failed! You know, I don't think I can go on with this. I'm simply not cut out for it. And as for Kostanjšek, when I see him again, how can I tell him that the moment he walked out of my apartment I let him down?' He stood in front of her now, ran his hand nervously through his hair.

'Well, that's simple enough. Don't tell him.'

Stevan stared down at her. 'Are you mad?' he asked.

She frowned. 'No, I'm not mad. I'm simply realistic. Why do you insist on making this so difficult for yourself? Don't you realize that David probably forgot the name two minutes after he heard it? Why should he remember the name of a man who from the sound of it stood in front of him for a fraction of a second? You are making too much of this, Stevan. Please forget the whole thing. I suggest you simply forget the whole thing.'

He slowly sat down. 'You can say that? When you know how much emphasis they put on, well, you know, on correct behaviour?'

'I also know how much emphasis they place on the fact that comrades should not fall into moods of pessimism and despair. I really think that is your main problem, Stevan. You look at the Party, at its members, and all you see is the nonsense, the confusion. What you *should* be looking at is their *objective*. Forget the means they use to obtain it. Forget the opportunism they exhibit all too often. Just keep in mind the glorious *end* to it all. The creation of a whole new society, a new kind of humanity. How much more meaning that goal gives to life!' Her eyes were shining, her voice soft but full of excitement.

'God!' he exploded in total despair. 'If only I could believe the way you do. The way you and Alex believe.'

She leaned forward, placed her hand on his knee. 'But it's not as though you were a Party member. None of us is. Don't you understand? This is a testing period. For you, Alex, Jelena and myself. Now, if you truly belonged to the Party, then I would advise you to tell this man what happened. Once you belong to the Party well, a certain behaviour, a certain conduct is expected of you. Of us all. It is only when we feel that we can meet that test of strength that any of us are entitled to join. Until then, why, we do the best we can. We struggle to understand. That is all. That is all that is expected of you, or any of us. Do you understand?'

He gave a deep sigh. 'Yes, I understand. I suppose you are right.'

'You see, that man who stayed with you. You mentioned he had been in Moscow. He has obviously been a Party member for many years. So, of course, one would expect a certain behaviour from *him*. But until you have achieved that level of experience, of knowledge, why...' she shrugged. 'You simply do the best you can.' She picked up the glass of wine she had placed on the table, drained it, and held it out to him. 'May I have a refill?' She kicked off her shoes, drew her feet up under her, relaxed. 'Now you can tell me all of the news about David. Is the romance still on? With Irina Mirskaia, I mean.'

He refilled her glass, handed it to her, and nodded. 'As a matter of fact that was one of the reasons he dropped by. It's still unofficial, but I gather they will be getting married some time next year. He's off again on army manoeuvres in the autumn.' He drained his own glass. 'Thank God I'm not in the army reserve.'

She smiled, nodded. 'But you know David. With an uncle like Mikhail Ristić, he could hardly be anything other than a true Serbian patriot.'

Stevan studied her for a moment. 'Well, for that matter, so am I.'

She raised her eyebrows, but decided to let it pass.

'Do you think the war is going to touch us? Heaven knows, the prince regent is carrying on a heavy enough flirtation with Hitler. And why *should* we get involved in any imperialist conflict?'

'Well, let's hope we don't. But according to David the military command seem to be rather nervous. He usually goes on manoeuvres for just a couple of months a year. This time he says he's been called up for an indefinite period. Perhaps even until the new year.'

'Truly?' She began to laugh. 'My God, he'll be furious if he misses out on the club ball. Where are they holding it this year by the way?'

'King Peter's Hotel. No, no. He said he promised to take

Irina and that if all else fails he is sure he can get a few days' leave. I promised him that you and I would join his party. Is that all right? Maybe Alex and Jelena could come too.'

'Why not? I'll ask them. Alex won't be too interested, but of course he'll go for Jelena's sake.'

'And you?' Stevan teased. 'Are you going to come for my sake?'

She pulled a face. 'I will go, Stevan Matić, because whether I like it or not my mother has bought me a flaming red dress to wear to the ball. It's supposed to be for my birthday. And I'm not supposed to know about it yet. So what can I do? Tell me, what else can I do?'

He gave a gust of laughter. 'Not a thing! And I can hardly wait to see you in that flaming red dress. But now, I believe I promised you some dinner? Would you like to eat here? Or shall I take you out somewhere?'

* * *

The two-day pass David managed to extract from his commanding officer had not been as easy to get as anticipated. Still, he did manage to return to Belgrade just in time for the ball.

The evening, however, started out in rather a bizarre fashion. He called for Irina in a large *fiacre* containing his sister Zora, one of her admirers, Svetozar Hajduk, who was a cousin of David's friend Ivo, and Andjela and her escort, a young student whose name David could not quite remember. He ran eagerly up the stairs, and reached out to take Madame Mirskaia's hands in his as she opened the door to him. 'We saw you coming from the window. Welcome home, David. You are looking so well. Come in. Come in.'

He laughed, moved over to take Marya Mirskaia's hand, and bend over it. 'That's about the only thing you can say for army life. It certainly keeps you fit.' He glanced around the by now familiar living room. 'Irina?'

'Now, now. Don't be so impatient,' Madame said somewhat archly. 'She's still dressing. She won't be long.'

He sighed happily, and sat down as asked on one of the high-backed, rather uncomfortable chairs. 'You are both keeping well?'

'Except for a little rheumatism, perhaps.'

'Which I suppose is what we must expect at our age, Anna,' Marya sighed.

'What do you mean at your age? Why, you both still look like girls. Look at you both. Bright eyes and pink cheeks. Just like girls.' David was being quite sincere. The whole world looked beautiful to him that evening, including the two middle-aged ladies now protesting, but not very strongly, in front of him.

'The things you say!' Anna Mirskaia smiled and patted the back of her elaborately styled hair. 'I don't believe a word of it.'

'Well, I'm going to *try* to believe every word of it,' Marya laughed. 'It will cheer me up.'

'What will cheer you up, Aunt?'

David sprang to his feet and turned to face Irina as she entered the room. There was a brief silence as he stared at her. Catching his look of dismay, her smile faded, and she gazed back at him uncertainly. 'Is something wrong?'

'Irina . . .' The trouble was that the girl standing in front of him did not look like his beloved Irina. She was dressed in a clinging, low-cut gown of what seemed to him to be a rather tawdry scarlet. Her beautiful golden hair was piled high on her head in a cluster of coquettish curls, her soft mouth heavily covered with a lipstick the colour of what he thought to be the quite awful dress.

'But, you are going to wear *that*?' he blurted out; he could have immediately cut out his tongue.

'Irina. Irina!' Her aunt followed her as she burst into tears, turned and ran from the room. Madame Mirskaia seemed about to join them, changed her mind and turned back to a still-stunned David.

'But how could you? How could you be so *tactless*.' She all but wrung her hands. 'I knew you wouldn't like that dress. I knew it. But she was so happy with it.' She sunk gloomily down into a chair. 'She loves that colour. But it just isn't her. It just is not for her.'

'But, what can I do, Madame?' David spluttered. 'Please go and tell her I'm so sorry. I apologize. Please tell her she looks beautiful. She will always be beautiful to me. Whatever she wears!' he added unhappily.

'You think that will do any good now?' Irina's mother shook her head. 'I don't know what to do. Really, David,' she repeated quite sharply, 'how *could* you be so tactless?'

'I don't know. I suppose it's, well, I haven't seen her for several weeks. I was so looking forward to seeing her again. And, well, it just didn't look like Irina. She was not the way I remembered her.' He sat down, got up again, and walked over to Madame Mirskaia. 'Please *do* something, Madame. Or tell me what *I* should do. What should I do?'

Madame Mirskaia looked at him with undisguised irritation, then pulled herself together. 'Well, as a start,' she said briskly, 'I suggest you go outside and tell the rest of your party to go on to the ball. Tell them you will join them later. This,' she added grimly, 'is going to take some time.'

And it did.

But as things turned out, Irina's Aunt Marya saved the day. She reappeared in the living room almost an hour later, gently leading Irina by the hand. This time David's exclamation was one of obvious admiration. Irina was dressed in a high-necked gown of soft ivory satin that gave a lustrous sheen to her cheeks. The lipstick had been wiped off and the curls on top of her head had been transformed by the new dress into a softly suitable cascade instead of the awful look of garish coquetry lent them by what David was always to think of as that awful red thing.

'It was to be my wedding dress,' Marya told a silent and chastened David. 'I don't want her to wear it to her own wedding, it has such an unhappy history. But perhaps to this ball?'

They left for King Peter's Hotel a little later, a solicitous

David helping her into and out of the *fiacre* as though she were made of fragile and breakable china.

They entered the ballroom as silently as they had sat next to each other during the trip there. Both seemed lost for words, David miserably wondering what he could ever say to reinstate himself after his inexcusable blunder, Irina exuding an icy courtesy that he was quite sure he would never be able to penetrate.

What saved the day, although he was not to realize it until later, was that when they went to their party, they were confronted by a stunning Olga Miletić who was wearing a gown almost identical to the one Irina had discarded. The difference being that the bright colour that had made Irina look simply wanton, gave an undoubtedly regal air to the taller, full-bodied, dark-haired Olga. Then the gasps of delight that both Andjela and Zora gave as they examined Irina's dress seemed to mollify her a little. For the first time that evening she gave David a tentative smile and, after they had danced, things seemed almost back to normal.

Other impressions were to stay in David's mind a long time after that memorable evening ended. His own sense of surprise at Andjela's animation for one. He was amazed by the flattering attention she was lavishing upon the nondescript young student Zora had produced to escort her to the ball. Until he led Irina out onto the dance floor and met the eyes of a smiling Vera Nešić, who swept past them tightly held in the arms of Bane Protić. David had actually felt a stab of pain for his beloved young sister. He could quite cheerfully have knocked the innocuous Protić down, could only hope that Andjela's bright eyes and flushed cheeks were from the music and the dancing, not from some deep inner hurt he could only guess at.

Then there was Stevan.

They managed to have a brief chat while at the buffet table. Stevan had just returned from Zagreb where he had been for several weeks on assignment. He had written a series of articles about the situation in the province since the prince regent, Paul, had granted Croatia *Banovina* – semi-autonomy. The thing that immediately struck David was the new maturity that seemed to have crept almost overnight into the face of his friend. The soft, almost womanly mouth had hardened. The dreamy brown eyes now had a look of directness. It must be the job, David thought. The responsibility is doing him the world of good.

In any event the evening that had started out so badly had finished wonderfully well. Toying with the pile of food on her supper plate, and sipping a glass of red wine, Irina had suddenly looked up at him, leaned over and whispered she was sorry she had almost spoiled the evening. 'You were right,' she admitted. 'That dress is for someone like Olga. Doesn't she look marvellous? I would have looked so silly beside her if I'd worn mine.'

'No, no,' he had protested stoutly. 'You are much more beautiful than Olga, whatever you wear. But this dress you are wearing now. You look unbelievably lovely. Unbelievably.' Others obviously agreed with him. Compliments flowed towards her. The truth was, she really did look exquisite.

At the evening's end he sent his sisters home with their escorts, and accompanied Irina back to her apartment. They decided there was to be no more delay. Their disagreement earlier that night had taught them a lesson. David went upstairs with her, found her mother and aunt still waiting up, told them of their decision to marry as soon as possible after his return from Negotin.

Anna Mirskaia clasped her hands together and admitted that she wanted above everything else to see Irina settle down in some responsible young man's care and Marya and Irina chatted animatedly about possible wedding dates. David assured her mother he would take great care of her beautiful daughter. He could not promise that he would ever be rich. He was not a man who intended to spend his life in the pursuit of money. But they would certainly be comfortably off. Irina wanted to help him with his projected school. They both wanted to travel before settling down to raise a family.

Soon it was early morning. In an atmosphere of joy and excitement Marya solemnly suggested that in order to celebrate she would prepare them all a hearty breakfast.

'I wish I'd known earlier,' David sighed happily an hour later as he pushed back the plate he'd cleaned of a savoury omelette. 'I'd have brought Stevan and Olga home to celebrate with us.'

*   *   *

After the ball Olga had invited Stevan in for some coffee. They sat then for some time, quietly talking.

'Something's happened to you, Stevan. Since you went to Zagreb. Do you want to tell me about it?'

'Well, I *hope* you've been reading my articles. I've been learning a lot about how the Croats really feel about us here in Belgrade.'

'It's a wonder they didn't skin you alive!'

'Why? I simply stated what they feel themselves. Believe me, Olga, I know that since they were granted *Banovina* things seem to have settled down, but after spending several weeks in Zagreb I am convinced there is no way we will ever reach accommodation with them. They have a hatred of Serbs that is quite irrational. They hate our church, although God knows theirs has interfered with ours more than the reverse. They hate us for fighting the Turks, for fighting the Germans, when they themselves succumbed right down the line. What can you do about such an irrational hatred? Seal them off, is what *I* believe. Forget about *Banovina*, full autonomy is what they want. We should give it to them and let them sit back and wait to be swallowed by Austria or Hungary or Hitler or anyone else. *We* are better off without them.'

'So I read in your articles. They caused quite a stir here, you know.'

'So I heard.'

'But it's not just the articles you wrote,' she said slowly. '*You* seem to have changed somehow.'

'I do?'

She frowned, suddenly impatient. 'Stop playing games, Stevan. I don't like it. Are you going to tell me what happened, or not?'

He finished his second cup of coffee and leaned forward. 'You know about the fifth Party conference that took place in Zagreb while I was there?'

'Yes, of course. Nikola Djerdja was one of the delegates. We are expecting him to give us a report at our next meeting.'

Stevan nodded. 'Would it surprise you to learn that I also attended that conference?'

'You?' She stared at him. 'Impossible. You're not even a member of the Party and furthermore . . .'

'Furthermore I *hope* that I soon will be. I've made application. There's a chance I'll be accepted without too much trouble.'

'I don't understand.'

'It's quite simple. I happened to bump into Djerdja while I was in Zagreb. He made an appointment for me to meet him one afternoon, said he had a surprise for me. Took me to this house, somewhere on the outskirts of Zagreb – I'd hate to have to find it again – but, anyway, can you guess who was there?'

'Stevan! I don't like playing games. Either you tell me, or—'

'That man who stayed with me during the summer,' he broke in hastily. 'You remember?'

'The engineer? The one who impressed you so much?'

'Well, I'm not sure now about the "engineer" part of it. But the point is, Olga, that man happens to be secretary-general of the Yugoslav Communist Party. He is a very special man. He has been trained in Moscow, really knows what he is doing. And, well, to cut a long story short, he invited me to attend the conference with him. He asked me to make a few notes for him, apart from the official minutes and resolutions. You understand?'

'The secretary-general?' Her eyes widened and she began

to bite her lower lip, a habit she had when excited. 'But I have heard about him. They call him Tito! Is that the man? Is *that* his real name? You told me you knew his real name.'

Stevan laughed, exultant at her excited response. 'No, it's not his real name, but it's what he likes to be called. It's what they call him within the Party.'

'But isn't he Russian? I have heard, Alex and I have noticed these past few months, really, that there is suddenly much more activity, even within our little group. Alex heard it was because we now have someone here sent directly by Stalin, but I thought he was just, well, you know how he feels about Stalin. I thought it was just a little bit of wishful thinking. But, is it true then, Stevan? Is it really so?'

'Sent by Stalin? Well, I don't know about that. But certainly he was trained in Moscow. A master propagandist, so Nikola told me. And he speaks quite a bit of Russian but, in fact, he was, I believe, born in Croatia.'

'Oh,' she sank back in her chair, pouted. 'A Croat!'

Stevan shook his head slowly. 'No,' he said, 'no, he is not a Croat. He is a communist. You understand? He is an international communist.'

'Once a Croat, always a Croat. You should know that.'

'For God's sake, Olga. And *you* should know better than that. There are many Croatian comrades within the Party.'

'Oh, very well. I suppose you are right. But, tell me. The fifth conference! What happened?'

'Well, nothing really happened. Just a readjustment to things now that the Soviet Union has signed a pact with Germany. From now on, so far as the Party is concerned, the war is not a matter of democracy versus fascism, but simply a quarrel between two imperialist nations. So of course it follows that Yugoslavia must do whatever is necessary not to be dragged into the war. Especially by the British – you know how they meddle in our affairs. We must remain neutral. It would be unthinkable for us to get dragged onto the side now opposed by the Soviet Union.'

'Yes, I see. Of course.'

Stevan leaned forward suddenly, and grasped her hands.

'Olga. Let's get married. Will you marry me? Right now! Straight away.'

She removed her hands from his in a gentle movement, and sat up straight. 'For heaven's sake, Stevan. What's all this? A proposal?' She smiled. 'When I'm not even in the mood for one?'

'Don't joke about this, please. I mean it. I know you've always thought I, well, you always made it clear enough that you felt I had no idea where I was going in life. But now, Tito, he *likes* me. And one day he is going to play a big role in where this country goes. Believe me. I *know* that. And I intend to be right there next to him. For the first time in my life I see a path I want to follow. And I want you with me. Do you understand?' The tone of his voice, so firm, so sure, faltered suddenly as she stared at him silently. 'Do you understand what I am saying, Olga?'

'My dear, of course I do. But, marriage?' She grimaced. 'How can you say almost in one breath that you want to become a communist and at the same time make such a bourgeois gesture as to propose marriage? Sometimes I really *don't* understand you, Stevan.'

He stared at her, dismayed. 'But what are you saying? That was the *old* Party line. The attitude about marriage, about family. You know that. It is all changed now.'

'Stevan, if I changed my mind as often as the Party does, well, I quite frankly should go mad. What you must do is *appear* to accept their little vagaries, at least outwardly, while *inwardly* retaining your own clear vision of what the Party is all about. And what the Party *is* really all about, well, it is all in the manifesto. Abolishment of private property! Remember? A brand-new society. A *just* society. And ownership of *anything* will be out. Even,' she smiled, 'even the ownership of wives.'

He could only stare at her miserably. 'And yet,' he managed after a moment, 'Alex has married. You say nothing about Alex getting married.'

'Well, Alex and I see things differently sometimes. Besides, you know he couldn't survive without Jelena.'

'Yet if what you say is true, if just a few of those people in say, our own Party cell, if only a few of them have different concepts of what communism really means, then even if we *did* take power, God, what confusion there would be.'

She shook her head. 'No. Not if the strong ones take charge. As of course they will.'

She rose to her feet, reached out and took his hands as he also stood up and stared at her dejectedly. 'Look, can't we just go on this way for a time? There's so much to *do*. One day, perhaps, when we have more time for personal concerns. We will talk about it then. I will consider marriage, or whatever arrangement the Party finally decides is suitable, then. I promise. I really promise you that, Stevan.'

He had to be content with that. But the joy, the excitement he had felt when he returned from Zagreb had evaporated. He felt he was right back where he had started. What the devil was he doing getting mixed up with a bunch of revolutionaries anyway? What the devil did he think he was doing?

9

David had spent the previous evening in Negotin. He had called Irina first of all, then had dinner with some fellow officers, afterwards attending a local dance with them. They all agreed it was best to stay overnight at a hotel instead of cycling back to the various villages where they were billeted in accordance with the orders of the commandant of their 76th Krajinska Regiment. The move was, Colonel Milan Čudina had explained, purely cautionary, designed to ensure that in the event of an attack his units and officers would be dispersed, instead of clustered together in Negotin as they had been during previous exercises.

Not that it seemed likely there *would* be war. Not for Yugoslavia, anyway. Only two days previously, on the 25th of March, 1941, Prince Paul had authorized his prime minister and his foreign secretary to finally, if reluctantly, add their signatures to the Tripartite Pact, thus ensuring that Yugoslavia would remain neutral in the war and continue its regular economic relations with the Axis powers.

Bicycling back to the village of Jasenica, David glumly considered the new direction his country seemed to be taking. It certainly seemed to be leading away from the liberal democratic direction his people had always stood for, but on the other hand, as he knew from his Uncle Mikhail, the government had been warned by foreign statesmen such as the British Anthony Eden and the American Colonel Donovan that it could expect no help from Britain or its allies should it find itself engaged in a war against Germany.

So he supposed it had been a prudent move. He was as aware as the other officers in his unit that the ill-equipped, poorly trained Yugaslav army would stand no chance against modern German tanks. Hitler's military machine could, as one of his friends often said, 'eat Yugoslavia for breakfast if it wished!' Yet there was something about the signing of the pact that stuck in his throat. It was the knowledge that his small country, always so fiercely and heroically on the side of democracy, should now have to be associated with those evil Nazi gangsters.

He gave a deep sigh. But there was no use dwelling on it. Best to look at whatever bright side there might be. At least perhaps it meant that at long last he could return to Belgrade. He missed Irina desperately, not to mention the fact that his boss at the bank, old Eugene Krstić, was no doubt in a fervour of impatience at his continued absence. Not that he could do much. As he had said rather pompously when David had first joined the army reserve, 'Of course your absence from time to time will be a great inconvenience, but we cannot complain when our young patriots wish to prepare themselves to defend our beloved country.' Remembering those words, David could not help smiling to himself. The old devil would be beside himself by now. He had never been absent from the bank for more than two months. This time it was nearly five. But what could any of them do? The international situation had obviously made Belgrade uneasy. There was absolutely nothing that could be done about the situation.

Coming in sight of army headquarters, which had been set up inside an agricultural school midway between Negotin and Jasenica, he slowed down and prepared to salute as he caught sight of the regiment commandant standing outside in the sunlight, deep in conversation with two other army officers. The three of them glanced up as David drew abreast, but instead of returning his salute, they called out and waved for him to join them.

'Yes, sir?' David, half on and half off the bike, nodded at Colonel Čudina with a questioning look.

'Good morning, lieutenant. We were just wondering whether you had heard the news.'

'The news?'

'About the putsch.' As David continued to stare at him blankly, the colonel laughed. 'You have a new government. A new king.' He went on to explain that a group of air force officers led by a General Simović had overturned the government of Prime Minister Cvetković, forced Prince Paul to resign, and declared the young Prince Peter of age and installed him on the throne of Yugoslavia.

It took David a moment to fully comprehend what the colonel was telling him. Then with the force of a raging torrent the blood rushed to his head, and he was immediately swept up in a tide of Serbian pride and nationalism. The news seemed like an explosion in his brain. A putsch! His dear land, his beloved Serbia was not after all condemned to walk hand in hand with Hitler's criminal fascist bastards! With a quick movement he removed his officer's *kapa* and threw it in the air with a wild yell of joy. Drawing his revolver from its holster he fired several shots into the air and cried out at the top of his lungs: 'Long live the king. Long live the king!' Then he threw himself back on his bicycle and careered off madly down the dusty road in search of fellow Serbs with whom he could share his news and his joy. The three officers, all Croatians, watched his disappearing figure with wry smiles, exchanged slightly exasperated looks and turned back into headquarters.

That evening David was back again in Negotin. With him were the Petrović twins, Janko and Vladimir, and several other young Serbian officers. It proved to be one of the noisiest celebrations Negotin had ever experienced. Not only the officers, but all the inhabitants of the small town went wild with joy. Great quantities of wine were imbibed, Serbian national songs sung and historical battles of the past relived and rehashed until finally the great burst of national energy and pride burned itself out in the dancing of the *kola*.

In the early hours of the morning it occurred to David to

put through a call to his Uncle Mikhail. There was not the slightest doubt in his mind that the old man would still be awake. He was right. The phone was answered within seconds and the deep firm voice rumbled down the line. 'It's David,' his uncle said. 'It is David isn't it?'

'Who else, Uncle?' David laughed aloud with excitement. 'I knew you would still be up. I knew it.'

'Who could go to bed with all this commotion? You should be in Belgrade, son. You have never seen anything like it.'

'It's pretty exciting here in Negotin, too. What is happening there?'

'What is *not* happening?' All day, into the evening and even now, the streets have been full of people, rushing here and there, waving our flag, carrying placards. "War is better than the pact" they have been saying.' The old man's voice was excited, proud. David felt more than heard the slight feeling of trepidation.

'Uncle?' He hesitated, then plunged on. 'You *are* pleased? You agree this had to be done?'

There was a moment's silence, then his uncle's voice again came through. The excitement was gone, he sounded subdued, sober. 'Agree? Agree or not, it *has* been done.' Again he hesitated, then said proudly, 'I have been approached, you know. Already. By the new government. They are seeking advice, they said. From the wise old heads, I suppose.'

'Well then,' David could not hide his pride, 'they have surely chosen the very wisest, Uncle.'

'Thank you. Thank you, my boy.'

'What are you going to tell them? Do you know yet what you are going to tell them?'

'Tell them?' A sigh drifted down the wire, making David frown slightly. 'What can I tell them? The people are crying that war is better than the pact, but is suicide better than the pact? Well, they have repudiated the pact. It is done. Now all we can do is try to think of something else that will placate the slavering wolf. We must walk a tightrope. We must perform a balancing act.' Again that deep sigh before he repeated soberly. 'What can I tell them?'

'You will think of something, Uncle.'

'You think so? Let us hope, my boy. Let us pray.'

* * *

The wild jubilation in the streets of Belgrade drew Stevan out. He contacted Alex and with Jelena they rushed off to the Miletić home to insist that Olga join them. Laughing and singing and full of excitement they hurried arm in arm down Njegoševa Street, exchanging snippets of news with the happy crowd around them. Someone said that the German ambassador had been attacked that morning as he drove to church in an open car. Someone else handed them a Yugoslav flag and a placard reading *Our country's honour is saved*, both of which they took turns in wildly waving above their heads. At Alex's suggestion they made their way to the Soviet Consulate on King Milutin Street, only to find it guarded by a double cordon of soldiers. Undaunted, they marched on their way until they found themselves with a large crowd gathered in Kalenic market place where they listened to various speakers shouting themselves hoarse. Excitement reached a pitch amongst the four of them when they recognized Nikola Djerdja as one of the communist speakers. They cheered at the top of their voices as he exhorted the crowd to give full support to the Party now that it was obvious that the country would be looking to the Soviet Union for protection.

During the next few days the new civilian government of Belgrade, having taken over from the military, made a conciliatory gesture to Germany in an effort to ensure the country's survival. While the secretary-general of the Yugoslav Communist Party, Josip Broz, issued an angry statement berating the 'Anglophile elements and provocateurs who had destroyed the German tourist bureau and burned the German flag', and while the general public was still savouring the stirring statement made by the British Prime Minister

Churchill that 'Yugoslavia has saved its soul', they rushed the Yugoslav ambassador, Milan Gavrilović, to Moscow where he was to sign a treaty of friendship with the Soviet Union on the 5th of April.

Nervously they awaited the response to their overtures from Berlin, where an incredulous Hitler, upon first being told of the Belgrade putsch, had accepted the news as the joke it must, of course, be. Upon learning that no, it was no joke, but a verifiable fact, the laughter was to turn to hysteria, to paranoia, to unappeasable fury.

Despite uneasy protests from Foreign Minister Ribbentrop, who wished to at least talk to the new government in Belgrade, who preferred at least an ultimatum, the decision was made.

There was to be no declaration of war. On the 6th of April 1941, with no prior warning, the new barbarians of the twentieth-century manned close to five hundred bombers and dropped hundreds of tons of bombs upon the open city of Belgrade, killing from fifteen to seventeen thousand and inflicting untold thousands of casualties.

On the 7th of April, more fighter bombers and Stukas bore down again upon the helpless city and did their best to bomb it into extinction and to take with it any of its remaining citizens. As a horrified and helpless world looked on, Belgrade suffered. Belgrade burned. Belgrade screamed in agony.

* * *

On the evening of the 5th of April, the quiet dinner in company of Alex and Jelena at their beautiful, spacious apartment in the fashionable Belgrade suburb of Dedinje had turned into an all-night political session during which Olga and Alex passionately discussed various interpretations of Party and ideological unity, while Jelena and Stevan listened quietly, from time to time interjecting with a question, or nodding acquiescence to a conclusion. The gentle Jelena kept them plentifully supplied with coffee. At around six in the morning, however, she laughingly cried, 'Enough is enough! I will make us some breakfast and I don't want to hear one more word about the Party until we have finished every bite!'

Stevan was always to remember that he had just finished his last mouthful of scrambled eggs and drained his coffee cup when the noise began. At first a deep hum that grew quickly louder until the deafening sound made them rush out onto the front balcony, stare towards Belgrade some fifteen kilometres away and gasp with awe and horror at the endless waves of *Luftwaffe* bombers that filled the sky as far as the eye could see. It was such an awesome sight that it took them several seconds to comprehend what was happening as the bombs landed and continued to fall like droppings from an incredibly evil and mindless flock of giant birds gone mad.

'Oh my God!' Olga stood there, her hand flying involuntarily to her mouth.

'Christ!' Stevan yelled. 'It's the Germans. But there's been no declaration of war! We are not at war!'

'Dirty fascist bastards!' Alex waved both fists towards the sky, tears streaming down his cheeks. 'What are they doing to Belgrade? What are they doing to our city?' Jelena stood by his side, tears also streaming from her eyes. Very slowly she bunched three fingers together and made the sign of the cross.

Helpless, anguished, almost beside themselves with horror and rage, they could only stand there watching, listening to the shrieks of the Stukas as they left their cowardly pack to zoom down on a dazed and helpless population and gleefully inflict further terror upon surviving civilians, brutally gunning down any tiny, running figures they could find within their machine-gun sights.

Then from the periphery of the capital came signs that the Yugoslav anti-aircraft artillery had pulled itself together and was bravely fighting back. Giant puffs of smoke were followed by the dying whine of several bombers and Stukas as they hurtled towards the earth, crashing in flames.

Later they were to learn that a total of forty-three aircraft had been destroyed and that fighters from the Sixth Fighters Command had intercepted and brought down several other enemy planes. But that morning all they really knew was that they had to get to Belgrade, had to do whatever they could to bring succour to their suffering brothers and sisters.

It was Alex who quickly took command. Recovering from his emotional outburst he told Jelena and Olga to gather together as much food, water, brandy and blankets as they felt would fit into the new Chrysler given to him by his father-in-law as a wedding gift. Meanwhile, Alex and Stevan hurried over to a nearby villa owned by a wealthy communist sympathizer. Neither he nor his wife were at home, but at least they were able to leave a message with a still stunned manservant that one or both of them would return as soon as possible. They were both aware that the villa contained a secret room with radio equipment linked to communist headquarters in Zagreb. As Alex said, this was the obvious place for Party comrades to gather together to map out a strategy and decide what could be done to relieve the bleeding city and to form some kind of resistance to what appeared to be imminent invasion.

An hour later the four of them were in Belgrade, no longer a city but a raging hell of fire and collapsed and collapsing buildings and black, choking smoke. Dead bodies sprawled in the shattered streets, in doorways, underneath rubble. Screams of agony from the wounded and pathetic calls for help filled the air. Adding to the surrealistic horror of the scene were the barking, yelping dogs of Belgrade, running wildly through the ruins in terror.

There were no first-aid centres, no water and thus no fire brigades, no electricity. A shocked and dazed police force was beginning to gather itself together to bring some order to the devastation, to dig out people from beneath the rubble, to control the unspeakable looters.

Mercifully, the Miletić home had not been hit, although a hysterical Mrs Miletić threw her arms around her son and cried that her husband had not returned from his early morning walk. But there was no time for worry or for the luxury of grief. With the help of a grim-faced Stana Radović, furniture was cleared to allow blankets and mattresses to be piled on the marble or richly carpeted floors and the wounded were brought in, dazed and bleeding, while the women stripped sheets into bandages, raided the Miletić cellar for brandy and made gallons of soup over a makeshift wood fire, all the while exhorting Alex and Stevan to find doctors, find medicine, food, more blankets, more, more, more.

In the afternoon Stevan drove back to Dedinje to see whether any members of the communist leadership had been in touch. Finding there had been no sign of any of them, he promptly set about using the radio facilities himself to contact Tito and found the secretary-general not only available, but in a quite foul mood. 'Where is everyone?' he fumed, his voice crackling with irritation. 'Look, there are things that need to be done. Try to come to Zagreb yourself as quickly as possible.'

He spent a few abortive hours searching for Party members before realizing that they must have fled the city. He immediately drove back to the Miletić home, where Alex agreed he should take the car and try to get to Zagreb in accordance with Tito's instructions.

Meanwhile his friends remained in Belgrade, working frantically to help those who were still alive and to assist in the burying of the dead. Among the latter, he was to learn later, was Alex and Olga's father, Judge Ivan Miletić.

* * *

Shortly after midnight on the 7th of April, 1941, David Ristić found himself still on the move with his regiment, away from Negotin and headed towards the Rumanian frontier. Confusion had been the order of the day. His column had been split into three sections, with no explanation given for the order, although he assumed the intention was to head deep into the Serbian mountains south-west from the Danube river, where guerrilla-type action could be undertaken against the enemy. At 2 a.m., exhausted, they had stopped at a village for a few hours' sleep, and moved on again three hours later, after receiving orders from the battalion commander to again split into even smaller columns and to continue marching, each column following a separate route. David's company was ordered to follow the Danube west toward the port of Brza Palanka. He marched ahead of the column, with a feeling of unease, aware that the order given for his heavy machine-gun company to pursue its own route without an infantry unit accompanying it was against the elementary rules of field tactics he had learned at the officers' cadet school in Bilece. Questions addressed to his commanding officer had been brushed aside. He suspected that, in fact, his superior officer simply did not have any answers himself.

Just before dusk they reached the top of a large plateau overlooking the Danube. Aware that both his men and the horses were exhausted, he called for a short halt and stood for a moment in the strong wind, gazing towards the river that stretched away into the distance.

The high whine of a bomber zooming out of the heavens seemingly from nowhere was so unexpected that the whole company stood gazing up at it for several seconds before realizing that this was to be their first encounter with the enemy. The unit had about two-dozen horses, half of them loaded with heavy machine-guns, the others carrying ammunition. There was no time to disperse, nowhere to hide, no time to prepare the guns for any kind of defence. The plane had plummeted down to a level of about five hundred feet and was approaching them fast. David grabbed a light machine-gun, a Czech *Zbrojovka*, and with a sudden feeling of exhilaration; aware that he was holding a superb weapon of the utmost reliability, aimed it at the plane. The bombs were falling now, at least a dozen of them. 'I'll get you, you bastard!' he shouted. He pulled the trigger, and nothing happened. Impossible! Quickly reloading, he again aimed and pulled the trigger. Again, nothing. It would have been too late in any event. By some miracle the sharp, biting wind they had been cursing shortly before had carried the bombs ahead of them into a deep crevice about thirty metres in front of his column. The deep boom, boom, boom, as they exploded was reverberating through the valley, and the earth was shaking beneath their feet. David turned and looked at the group of forty men gathered behind him and realized with a sense of shock that had he not called for a halt for a few moments' rest, they would by now have been moving through the crevice. They would no longer exist. None of them.

The exhaustion, shock and frustration of the past two days suddenly overwhelmed him. 'What the hell is going on here?' he shouted, waving the *Zbrojovka* in the air. 'Who was the last one to touch this machine gun?' For a moment there was total silence, broken by a tough-looking Montenegrin.

'Maybe it was one of our Croatian officers, sir! Or one of our communists!'

The sheer insolence of the remark shocked David back into the icy calm he had maintained since that first moment of disbelief when he had learned his country was at war. 'You are talking about the king's officers, soldier,' he snapped. 'One more word like that and you will be the worse off for it!'

As he was later to confide to his friend Janko Petrović: 'The worst part of it was that I knew I should have had him arrested on the spot. But how the devil could I when similar thoughts had been going through my own mind for forty-eight hours! The army is riddled with traitors, damn it.'

He had encountered Janko when his unit arrived at the army command in Brza Palanka, just before reporting to the colonel in charge. Janko was as bewildered as David at the confused and conflicting orders they had been receiving. He was also worried about his brother, Vladimir, who had been detached from the company with a small group of men and sent in yet another different direction without any clear instructions as to destination or specific military objective.

'I don't care if every one of the Croatian officers in our army has behaved as impeccably as a Serb,' Janko grumbled. 'When this is all over we have to kick them out. Out of the army, out of the country. They're not worth the worry.'

David nodded. 'And then there are all of the rumours that the communists have infiltrated the army, and are causing a mess. No one seems to know *what* is going on.'

At least Colonel Elezović seemed cheerful, and was able to give David a direct order. 'Keep heading south-west toward Pomoravlje, lieutenant. You will join up with the rest of your battalion there.' David told him about the incident with the machine-gun earlier that morning. The colonel chose to ignore any implications behind his story and concentrated instead on the attack itself. 'Yes, yes. The bastards have been coming and going here since early this morning. You were lucky to escape with your lives. I hope your luck holds, son.'

'Thank you, sir. We'll keep going then. Could you tell me how far the nearest village is west from here? The men need a good rest.'

'You should reach it in an hour.' He held out his hand. 'Take care, lieutenant.'

'You too, sir.' He thought about the information the colonel had given him that in addition to the bombing attack on Belgrade, German divisions supported by Italian, Hungarian and Bulgarian forces had attacked simultaneously from the west, the north and the east and were so far penetrating the country without significant resistance. 'And good luck, colonel.'

Elezović nodded. 'We're all going to need that.'

Within an hour David's small company had arrived at a large, prosperous village set in a beautiful, lush valley surrounded by heavily wooded mountains whose peaks were still dusted with remnants of the winter snow. Mounting his horse at the head of the column just after dawn next morning, David smiled, waved at the small group of anxious villagers assembled to bid them safe journey, and wondered how it was possible that such a beautiful world could be at war anywhere. He gave one last long look at the peaceful scene, then lifted his arm in the signal to move and cantered ahead, gulping in large draughts of the cold fresh air.

By early afternoon they had arrived at a crossroads, where to his relief they met up with other companies of the battalion. Maybe somewhere someone, after all, really knew what he was doing! However, apart from the fact that they were to wait there until their ranks were swollen by further arrivals, no one seemed too clear about their ultimate aim. Confrontation with the Germans? The heavy troop concentration seemed to indicate that a large battle lay ahead of them. Some of the officers, however, thought they would be undertaking guerrilla action.

David again told a group of his friends about the incident with the German plane and the jammed *Zbrojovka*. There was a moment's silence, then they all began speaking at once. It seemed that most of them had had similar experiences on their way to the crossroads. Either guns had jammed, or bullets had proved to be defective.

'Could be anyone! Communists, Croats, or maybe just our own damned incompetent army.' Lieutenant Ljubić, of the black curly hair and fierce moustache, spat. 'We Serbs have too many enemies within our own country. That's what we brought on ourselves when we gave up our dear Serbia for this treacherous Yugoslavia!'

The others nodded grimly.

'God only knows what will happen to us if we lose this war, as we most certainly will. What did those silly bastards in Belgrade think we were going to fight with? Guns left over from the Balkan wars?' A Captain Jović had joined their ranks, paused a moment to add to their gloom, and then walked on.

That evening they received orders to march. For the next few days they continued west, with a continuous concentration of more and more troops joining them from the rear until their battalion ripened into a regiment, a brigade, and finally the whole Krajinska Division with its special attachments and units, including artillery. A great mass of soldiers packed into a narrow valley, slowly on the move.

Although German troops were reported to be pursuing them from the rear there were, in fact, no signs of the enemy. No planes, no tanks, no distant gunfire. On the third day at around 5 p.m. orders were given to blow up an old stone bridge over a deep, wild mountain stream in order to halt the advance of invisible German tanks. It was estimated it would take the enemy several hours to build a pontoon bridge.

No one, however, had expected the heavy German units that lay ahead of their advance. Their artillery unit was positioned about twenty kilometres in front of the division, a mere drop in the ocean for the enemy's modern guns. At dawn the shelling began. The division's command reviewed the situation, which did not look good. Germans ahead and closing in at their rear and the high Homolje mountains flanking them to the left and to the right.

To try to take on the modern tanks and artillery of the enemy would be suicide. The sad fact was that the Yugoslav army was not prepared for this new and deadly kind of warfare. They were facing a foe of tremendous armed superiority. The decision had to be made. The order given.

Surrender!

David was thunderstruck. 'Surrender? To the *Boches*? Never!'

'Why not? Why should we be ashamed?' asked Lieutenant Ljubić. 'Look at the Czechs, look at the French. At least they had some modern weapons to fight with. And did they fight? No! So why should we when we have nothing but obsolete guns and our bare hands and a parcel of bloody traitors within our ranks!' He spat, then fluently and expertly cursed each and every one of the imbecile air-force officers who had got them into this mess with their bloody putsch.

'All I know,' David said coldly, 'is that I am a Serb. I will never surrender.'

'No? What else, then? You are going to fight the whole

German *Wehrmacht* with this?' Ljubić grabbed the rifle slung over David's shoulder and waved it above his head. 'With *this* you are going to bring down the *Luftwaffe*, eh? You are going to stop entire German divisions with this?'

David angrily retrieved his rifle. 'I don't know what I'm going to do,' he snapped. 'But I'm damned if I'm going to stay here to be rounded up by those criminal fascist bastards like some sheep.' He glanced around at the small group that had gathered around them in a circle. 'I'm going over the mountains. Is anyone with me?'

'We're with you, David.' The Petrović twins who, happily, had found each other again, stepped forward and looked around the group.

'That makes us three, anyway,' Vladimir said after a moment's silence.

There was a sudden deep explosion of laughter from Ljubić. He reached out to slap David's shoulder. 'Damned if I'm not going with you, too. Although only God knows why. And that,' he added with a wide grin at the Petrović brothers, 'makes us four!'

They were ready to leave within fifteen minutes. They each took a rifle and some ammunition but otherwise decided to travel light. They sent a message to their immediate superior, Captain Stanković, that they did not intend to surrender. Briefly, David considered trying to speak to the officer in command, the Croatian Colonel Milan Čudina, a man he knew well and considered to be a good friend. But there was no time! German artillery had already reached the outlying houses of the village; a deep rumble informed them of approaching tanks.

Hurriedly he joined his friends as they began to quickly walk towards the base of a steep mountain. They paused only once to look back, and caught sight of the first German tank as it rumbled through to the village square. A moment later Colonel Čudina did, in fact, appear. He wore a wide grin on his face. His arms were outstretched in welcoming, fraternal greeting as he strolled towards the leading tank. Reaching its side he climbed in, slapped the German officer beside him on the shoulder and began to gesticulate, laughing and joking with unabashed pleasure.

It was, David decided, the saddest, most humiliating scene he had ever witnessed. To have to watch, with a deep and bitter sense of betrayal, an officer he had held in deep respect, now greeting the enemy as a long-lost friend; to have to watch as literally hundreds of officers and men of the once proud Serbian army waited quietly to be delivered into the hands of the Nazi gangsters, was almost more than he could bear. Badly armed, badly equipped and lacking in loyal and decisive leadership as they were, nevertheless the Serbian people would have expected them to put up their traditional fierce fight. Thank God, he thought, Uncle Mikhail isn't here to see this. It was the first time he had allowed himself to think of any member of his family since he had learned of the bombing of Belgrade. Now the memory of his uncle filled his mind. It did not occur to him for a moment that anything might have happened to the old man. Whoever or whatever would eventually kill his uncle, it would not be the despised *Boches*! Of that he was certain. But I wonder what he's doing, he thought. I wonder where he is at this moment?

* * *

Early that morning Mikhail Ristić had been summoned to a meeting of the government in order to discuss reaction to the calamity that had befallen the capital and the country. He had agreed with the assessment that the young king should somehow be spirited out of Yugoslavia to prevent the fascist invaders from getting their hands on him. Malleable and impressionable as Peter II was, it was essential that the enemy be prevented from using him for propaganda or other devious purposes. Where Mikhail had drawn the line, however, was at the suggestion that the government depart with him. The government's place, he had thundered incredulously, was with its people, as was the king's had he been older and made of sterner stuff. When the matter had been pressed, when a suggestion had even been made that he accompany them on such a cowardly flight, David's uncle had stalked out of the meeting.

Now he sat alone, brooding, in his study. The Ristić apartment building, although smoke-blackened and devoid of windows, was at least still standing. His wife, Kaja, recognizing his mood, had slipped in with some tea made on the small spirit stove she kept for emergencies, and then left him alone.

After a long period of bitter thought, he rose abruptly from his chair, walked over to his desk and unlocked the middle drawer. For a moment he stood there staring down at the sheaf of loose notes he had taken at the proceedings of the National Security Council that had been called into session in March after the prince regent had held talks with the American Colonel Donovan and the British minister Eden. Hesitantly he reached into the drawer and removed his notes, took them back to his chair, and began to re-read them.

He hurriedly skipped through the reports from Prime Minister Cvetković and the chief of the general staff, General Nedić, both of whom had confirmed the general consensus that Yugoslavia was not prepared for war against the Axis powers and would be unable, particularly in view of the fact that it had been made clear by both Donovan and Eden that no foreign aid could be expected from either the Americans or the British, to organize any serious resistance against possible invasion. Both reports stressed the view that war with Germany would be national suicide. Ristić shook his head, frowned, and found the page where Prince Paul's address to the council began.

> Under the circumstances elaborated here today, we have no other alternative than to sign the Tripartite Pact. Our first duty is to our peoples and to our country, to save them from the scourge of war. The only way to achieve this, at this historical moment, is to avoid provoking Hitler and Mussolini. We are too small

to fight them alone on the European continent. They would swallow us within days and what would that achieve? Nothing, except a national tragedy and occupation by the ruthless Nazis. Our peoples would suffer unnecessarily and nobody would thank us for that sacrifice. Remember! At this stage of the war, the two greatest countries, the USA and the USSR are not getting involved in the conflict. They are watching from the sidelines and waiting for someone else to fight. Thus, we would be lunatics if we should plunge into a war for no other reason than our national pride.

Consequently, we royal regents have agreed to send our prime minister and the minister for foreign affairs to Vienna to negotiate and sign the Tripartite Pact. This Pact will ensure us complete neutrality and preserve the sovereignty of our territory. There will be no provisions enforced upon us to allow any passage of foreign troops through our territory or any other violation of our independence. However, we will agree to continue our economic relations with the Axis powers on a reciprocal basis.

The pattern of these relations will be approximately the same as now. There will be no military commitment on either side, nor any exchange of military information at all. The agreement we have reached is, in fact, far more generous than that imposed by the Axis upon other signatories of the pact.

The most important requirement at this moment is to preserve peace and calm in the country. The government must undertake strict measures to prevent any demonstrations, acts of violence or sabotage by any political group, and particularly by the communists.

With a sigh Mikhail now gazed into space, recollecting the events that had led up to the devastation of his country.

They could, of course, be traced back as far as 1936, the 7th of March, 1936, when Hitler had taken a roll of the dice and occupied the Rhineland with just three battalions, fewer than five thousand men. As the Führer himself had admitted later: 'If the French had marched into the Rhineland we would have had to withdraw in shame and disgrace.' But the French, despite their overwhelming military strength, had hesitated. They had nervously turned for support to the British, seeking assurances that the latter would honour her treaty obligations under the Treaty of Locarno. Leaning back in his chair, Mikhail closed his eyes and repeated softly to himself the subsequent appeal by the French minister Flandin: 'If England will act now, she can lead Europe ... all the world will follow you and you will thus prevent war ... if you do not stop Germany now, all is over ...' The reply from foreign minister Anthony Eden had said it all. He '... doubted if the British people were ready for war ...'

Why was he reviewing all this? He knew it all by heart, anyway. The knowledge he was trying to come to terms with was that his own invitation to attend the Security Council proceedings had come to him direct from the prince regent, whose purpose had clearly been to get the backing of one of Yugoslavia's most respected and esteemed military heroes and statesmen in the signing of the pact. No pressure had been exerted, no request attached to his invitation. Mikhail had known immediately, however, what Prince Paul and Prime Minister Cvetković wanted from him. Why had he not been generous enough to comply with their unspoken request?

Recalling his own unwavering support for the British, he now moved uneasily in his chair. There was certainly no doubt that he had been irritated recently by both British and American interference in Yugoslavia's internal affairs; the threat by the supposedly neutral America to freeze Yugoslav assets in the event that they signed the pact; the infiltration into the country by the British of a group sent specifically to foster discord and revolution amongst the population. Remembering the British government's refusal to ask its own people to show courage against aggression in 1936, he had been particularly incensed by the BBC broadcast of the Serbian-speaking British statesman, Leopold

Amery, asking the Serbian people to reject the Pact, appealing directly to their passion for democracy, their sense of honour, and cynically tapping into their streak of wild romanticism by reminding them of the tradition of Kosovo and stirring up once again ancient feelings of mystical reverence for Tzar Lazar who had preferred a 'heavenly kingdom to one on earth'. Truly, the machinations of the Allies in driving his small country to the brink of ruin had had to be seen to be believed. Their motive? To buy time, of course, but why was it that he, Mikhail Ristić, had taken so long to understand the one constant behind their thinking. It was really quite simple – Yugoslavia was expendable!

Restlessly he rose to his feet and began pacing the floor. The rhetorical question as to why he had not spoken up in favour of the pact, of course, required no answer. It was pride! Damned Serbian pride that would not allow him to express publicly what he well knew in his heart. The pact indeed would have been the only thing that might have saved his country.

Stopping before his chair, he again picked up his notes and glanced at the last few words that had ended Paul's address.

> This is, perhaps, the most decisive moment in the twenty-three years' existence of Yugoslavia. Let us be united and act together, while putting our national interests and independence before any other consideration.

All right, great Serbian hero, Mikhail Ristić, he thought, forcing himself to walk yet again to the papered-over window of his study and peer through a small tear at the devastation that was now Belgrade. *Take a good look. There is the price. This is where your great pride has brought your country.* He stood there for a long time, staring out at the rubble that had once been part of his brave, historical city. Slowly the tears began to trickle down his cheeks.

PART TWO
1941–1942

Often when I have thought of invasion, or when a bomb has dropped near by, I have prayed 'Let me behave like a Serb.'

Rebecca West, *Black Lamb and Grey Falcon*

1

On the 10th of April, 1941, the German 'liberators' marched triumphantly through the Croatian capital of Zagreb to a warm greeting from the cheering population that swarmed the streets to shower them with flower petals. Sitting on the terrace of a café, sipping coffee, Stevan Matić watched the strutting conquerors, listened to the friendly roar of the crowd and fought a violent inner battle to control the bile that had risen in his throat at a sudden memory of Belgrade burning. Between the deep breaths he forced himself to take he stole an occasional glance at his companion, Josip Broz, who was also watching the historical spectacle laid out before them, and wondered what thoughts were running through his mind. Hard to tell. Calm-faced and impassive, the Yugoslav Communist Party leader sat holding an elegant cigarette holder designed, Stevan suspected, to show off the diamond ring of which he seemed so inordinately proud. What, he wondered for the hundredth time, had ever made this man become a communist? Always so beautifully and immaculately dressed, always at such pains to avoid being mistaken for a member of the proletariat, always more than ready to partake of the bourgeois luxuries that Marxist doctrine so virulently repudiated.

A desire for personal power? He instantly dismissed the thought as disloyal, the same way he had tried to dismiss from his mind the memory of Belgrade's destruction. That quick surge of Serbian nationalism had brought with it such inner turmoil that he had had to make an immense physical effort to prevent himself from standing up and shouting his outrage at the patrons of this fashionable coffee place. The incident, he thought, was a warning of the need to discipline his thoughts no matter what violence and havoc such an effort might cause to his inner self. What he now had to remember always, was that thanks to the man sitting so calmly at his side, he was now a card-carrying communist.

Tito had made no bones about the fact that Stevan's acceptance into the Party had been strongly opposed by almost everyone concerned except himself, whose will in such matters, as always, had prevailed. With an almost imperceptible touch of malice, he had described to Stevan how Milovan Djilas, his third in command, had questioned his ability to withstand harsh police interrogation should the need arise; how Marko Ranković, described by the secretary-general as a 'sly but dedicated comrade, the son of a Serbian peasant' had simply, but eloquently, spat; and, what had hurt most of all, outlined in detail the opposition of a man who had attended university with Stevan, Ivo Ribar, who belonged to a well-to-do Belgrade family and whose support Stevan had felt he could count on. Ribar, according to Tito, had described him as something of a lightweight who did not have the intellect to absorb the intricacies of Marxist dialectics and who would never be able to rid himself of bourgeois sentiments and be able to assimilate the strict discipline membership of the Party demanded.

All of this, Stevan understood, had been revealed to him because of Tito's extreme irritation with the Party leadership that had so readily deserted Belgrade when it came under fire. 'What's wrong with them?' he had fumed. 'Don't think I haven't noticed that some of them often displayed incorrect behaviour, but, by God, to learn that they would run under fire! And *they* question *my* judgment about *you*. I can't wait to let them know you were the only one who stood firm when the occasion arose.'

Almost immediately, however, Tito had shown signs of

having regretted letting Stevan glimpse the inner workings of the Party, brusquely dismissing the subject when Stevan had begun to express disappointment with Ribar's expressed opinion about him. 'Better not to talk about such things,' had been the response from Tito, followed by a pointed change of subject.

The knowledge that his application for membership of the Party had almost been rejected did, however, add a touch of piquancy to his attendance at a meeting Tito held a few days later in Zagreb to discuss the Party's response to the savage invasion of Yugoslavia. The meeting had initially been delayed because neither word nor representation had arrived from Bosnia, Montenegro or Macedonia, where most of the comrades had also scattered in disarray when confronted with enemy invasion. When it did finally go ahead *Stari* – the old man – as Tito was often called, began by pointedly commenting on the correct attitude that had been displayed by comrade Matić, who not only stood his ground in Belgrade but had, by setting up a makeshift hospital there, greatly enhanced the reputation of the Party, which might otherwise have been seriously damaged by what he drily referred to as the 'hasty departure' of certain leading communists.

Having got that off his chest, he plunged into a prolonged statement about what he considered Party strategy should be under the present circumstances. Stevan leaned forward and listened attentively as he spoke about the unique opportunity open to the Party to prepare itself to fill the vacuum that now existed at the top lèvel of government. Although he was still awaiting instructions from Moscow, it was obvious that the old machinery of state would be defunct, or, he added, compromised by collaboration with the enemy. The task of the Yugoslav Communist Party, then, was to organize itself militarily in order to be able to attack these *internal* enemies and thus eventually take power themselves. That their task would be made much easier by the alliance between Germany and the USSR was obvious, and spoke for itself.

Members of the Party leadership who had managed to attend the meeting were gathered at a table at a house on the outskirts of the city. The secretary-general's summing up of the situation had been listened to silently. There had been no interruptions and now there seemed to be no questions, no disagreement. Stevan glanced around the table, waiting for someone to pose some of the queries that had arisen in his own mind, but there was complete silence. Perhaps some of the comrades were still stinging – or sulking – at Tito's not-so-subtle hints that some of them had, under fire, behaved with something less than revolutionary fervour. He stirred restlessly on his hard chair, wanting answers to some questions in his mind, but not quite having the courage to ask them. In fact, he would have remained silent had not Tito glanced towards him with those pale, calm eyes, and smiled slightly. 'You have something to say, comrade?'

'Well, no. I mean, what you said about the old machinery of state, about its collaborating with the enemy...' He hesitated, suddenly aware that several cold sets of eyes were boring into him from around the table. Tito, however, nodded encouragement.

'Yes?'

'The fact is, I'm sure *someone*, I mean, of course there will be some kind of resistance group. The whole of our history shows that. So if the Party continues only to attack internal enemies, if we don't do something about liberating the country, surely we might lose an opportunity that...' He pulled up short as the pale eyes resting upon him hardened, turned ice cold. Stevan's voice slowly petered out. He looked rather desperately around the table, but found no help.

'As I just finished saying!' The secretary-general's voice was tight with irritation. 'It is clear that the old machinery of state will be defunct *or* compromised by collaboration with the enemy.' Stevan found that his hands had become suddenly clammy and a light bead of perspiration was gathering on his forehead. His throat was quite dry. During the moment of silence that followed Tito's icy reassertion of the

Party's position he cursed himself for being such a fool as to open his mouth. Why *should* the communists do anything? The Soviet Union, after all, was now a German ally. As for any assertion that others might collaborate with the enemy, he remembered something Nikola Djerdja had recently told him. *There is objective truth and then there is class truth.* He gave a slight cough, moved uncomfortably in his chair, and finally looked up, red-faced, to find that Tito was now regarding him with something like amusement.

'Any more questions, Comrade Matić?'

'No. I mean, no, thank you, comrade.'

At least, he was to console himself later, he had learned a valuable lesson. It was to be a long, long time before Comrade Matić was to open his mouth at any Party meeting unless it was to agree with everything that came out of the mouth of the secretary-general.

* * *

Early in the morning the train stopped at Topcider, a suburb of Belgrade. Word spread quickly through the passengers. The central station had been damaged during the bombardment and had not yet been restored to use.

David left the comparative safety of his train compartment and joined the crowd on the platform, glancing around carefully in order to assess the situation. The place was swarming with German soldiers. They were shouting commands that no one seemed to understand and were occasionally shooting into the air, whether from frustration or a sense of celebration was not clear. He caught sight of some Yugoslav soldiers, prisoners of war, clearing wreckage on the other side of the track, briefly congratulated himself on his own freedom and then, noticing a lone German soldier standing just outside the station holding a machine-gun, quickly made a decision. He pushed his way through the by now slightly panicking passengers who were not sure what they should do or where they should go, and approached the soldier.

'Verzeihen Sie, Ich wohne dort, hinter dem Berg. Wollen sie mir bitte erlauben nach Hause zu gehen?' He gestured vaguely in the direction of Belgrade.

The soldier, a young, fresh-faced country boy with apple-red cheeks stared at him, seemingly at a loss to find himself addressed in his own language by a neatly dressed civilian who was politely asking his permission to leave the station and return to his home which was 'over there'. He looked first left and then right, as though seeking help, then jerked his head up and down. 'Los, Los!'

'Danke viel mahl.' David crossed the road quickly; before the uncertain warrior could change his mind. A short time later he had reached Dedinje, was able for the first time in several months to catch a glimpse of Belgrade. Through the dust and haze that still covered the city he could see that some buildings were still smoking, others lay in ruins.

He stood quite still for a long time, caught in a spasm of such intense grief that he was unable to move, frozen in a time warp of accumulated history that condemned this people and this city to be forever buried beneath the ashes; forever forced to struggle free from ruins brought upon them by barbarian hordes.

With a formidable effort of will he pulled himself together and forced himself to keep walking, albeit in a kind of daze. Without being conscious of any passage of time he found himself passing the army auto-command near Karageorge Park. He hesitated a moment, then continued climbing the steep street leading towards the Hotel Slavia. Everywhere around him buildings lay in ruins. The destruction of Rome must surely have looked like this. For the first time since he had learned that his country was at war he allowed himself, with fear in his heart, to think about Irina, about his family. Were they still in Belgrade? Were they still alive? Could even his indomitable Aunt Draga, his indestructible Uncle Mikhail, survive this devastation? Let alone his tender little Irina, his loving, warm-hearted sisters.

As he reached King Alexander Street the sun came out.

He hurried towards the Belgrade University student home, which was still standing, as was the technical faculty. Breaking into a run he crossed the small park leading into Queen Mary Street, and stopped to breathe a sigh of relief. His apartment building had not been touched. A moment later he was knocking at the door, almost immediately opened by Andjela, who took one look at him and literally screamed with joy. 'David! Auntie, Zora, it's David! David is here!' She flung her arms around him and then he was being assailed from all sides as his aunt and Zora joined her. Kissing him, embracing him, weeping, laughing, they swept him into the living room where he stopped short, breathless and almost beside himself with relief and joy at the sight of Irina. She was standing in front of the large fireplace, her hands covering her mouth as though to keep herself from crying out.

'Oh,' he said, 'thank God. Thank you God. Thank you, thank you . . .'

Later that night he lay in bed, hands clasped behind his head, gazing at the ceiling, trying to sort out his thoughts, trying to map some future strategy of survival for himself, for his family. He had spent the day listening to the experiences of his loved ones, and telling them what had happened to him since he had walked away from his unit and headed towards the Homolje mountains. They had hung upon every word as he described how he and his companions had trudged up the slopes, encountering at first a light covering of snow that had become deeper and deeper the higher they climbed. Cold, exhausted, hungry and slightly apprehensive at the dense wilderness of the mountain, at the mournful cries of wolves that distantly filled the air from time to time, they had stumbled upon a shepherd's hut. Its occupant had proved to be a young Serbian lad who had welcomed them enthusiastically, pressed corn bread, cheese and the dry meat *pršuta* upon them and made up beds of sweet-smelling straw in front of the fire.

They had left at dawn, after gratefully drinking warm

goat's milk, and had pressed payment upon the boy who kept shaking his head, pushed the money away. 'It is war. You are our brave soldiers. You must not worry about paying. You are my brothers.'

'Not pay you? After you have given us food and shelter fit for kings?' Ljubić had warmly embraced him while the others dropped a stack of notes on the straw beds.

'Even more important, you have given us new heart,' David told him.

They proceeded on their way up the mountain with renewed vigour until they reached the summit, where they stood silently, watching the sun break through the mist until it shed its pale light over the whole spectacular view of the Homolje. The war seemed to belong to some other part of the world that had gone crazy and of which they, thankfully, were no longer a part. They were all in a state of exhilaration brought on no doubt by the purity of the air and their own heady sense of freedom.

Reality, however, quickly set in. They could not stay on this beautiful, remote mountain-top for ever. A short conference was held and the decision made to continue on to the small east Serbian township of Krupanj, where they could buy civilian clothes. There they found the townspeople anxious for news and extremely helpful. They purchased new suits, shoes, hats and overcoats, changed at the home of an engineer they met on the main street, packed their uniforms into canvas bags, and left them with him. 'Perhaps we can come back one day to retrieve them,' they said.

From now on, they realized, there was a strong possibility of their running into German units. So they kept their weapons and their binoculars, until they reached the larger town of Svilajnac, at which point their destinations diverged. David decided to try to make his way to Belgrade, Ljubić said he would stay put in Svilajnac for a while and the Petrović twins continued on deeper into the country to try to reach the village of Kosmaj, where they had relatives. They left their weapons and what ammunition they had with

Ljubić, together with their maps, their identification papers, binoculars and compasses. David kept his bank identification and student cards. Neither of the Petrovićs had civilian identification papers with them, but they said they felt safer that way. If they encountered a German patrol they would try to bluff their way through.

They shook hands warmly and parted reluctantly. Their trek over the mountains, their decision not to stand still and wait to be taken prisoner had brought them closer together. None of them knew what lay ahead, but both David and Ljubić promised, if possible, to visit the twins in Kosmaj, while they all assured David they would contact him should they return to Belgrade.

'From then on,' he told his family, 'everything went fairly smoothly. I did a lot of walking, but eventually found a train headed for Belgrade. I had one bad moment when I found a group of German soldiers standing on the station with the crowd, especially when the officer in charge approached me. But in fact he didn't even ask for any identification. Simply wanted to know if I spoke German. When I nodded he told me to ask everyone to behave in an orderly fashion when the train arrived. I did so and everyone quietened down. From then on I had no problems. I hope things went as well for Ljubić and the Petrovićs.'

'A German officer approached you? Why you?' By now they had gathered around the kitchen table and were drinking coffee.

David shrugged. "Andjela,' he replied, 'I wish someone would tell *me* that.' He reached out to again take Irina's hand in his own. 'Even before the war I seemed to spend half of my life being approached by Germans asking me whether I spoke their language.'

'It is because you are fair, David.' Aunt Draga lifted the enamel coffee pot and refilled his cup. 'They see your fair hair, your blue eyes, and...'

'And they say to themselves, "*Mein Gott!* This one *must* be a member of our master race!"'

They all burst into laughter as Zora drew herself up into a military stance and gave the fascist salute.

'But that is enough of what happened to me. Tell me what happened here. I could hardly believe it when I found our apartment building still standing. Most of Belgrade seems to be in ruins. I didn't even dare think what might have happened to you all.'

His family's story, he was to discover later, was similar to that of many Belgraders. When the bombing began they had made the decision to evacuate the city. Aunt Draga had negotiated with an old pensioner who owned a large open cart and two horses. He had agreed to take the family out of the city, although there had been some dispute as to just how far he would take them. Zora had hurried around to persuade Irina and her mother and aunt to accompany them, and they had agreed immediately. 'We must have made a pretty sight,' Zora laughed, 'all of us women huddled in this old cart.'

They had followed King Alexander Street south, crushed by the devastation around them, terrified by the German Stukas that were still dive-bombing the city. The horses had panicked and it had taken all of the old man's skill to keep them under control. The journey through Belgrade had been a nightmare none of them would ever forget. Finally, however, they had reached Kaludjerice where they had been able to rent rooms in a farmer's house for a couple of days. As soon as they learned that the bombing had stopped, that the Germans had occupied the city, they returned to see whether their home was still standing, and whether they would be allowed to return to some semblance of their normal life. They had been as amazed as David to find their apartment building untouched.

'And yours, Irina? Is it still . . . ?'

Irina nodded. 'Not in such good condition as this, but at least it is habitable. And, of course, there had been some looting. But we were grateful to still have a roof over our heads.'

'But my dear child, you always will have, so long as *this*

family has one.' Aunt Draga leaned forward and patted the small hand David was not holding. Irina turned to him, her eyes filling with tears.

'Your family have been so kind,' she said, 'I cannot tell you how kind they have been.'

'Nonsense!' Aunt Draga waved the words away. 'You are David's fiancée. How else should we be?'

'And Uncle Mikhail? Aunt Kaja? Are they . . . ?'

His aunt frowned. 'What a stubborn man! Do you think he would come with us? Never! "The Hun drive *me* out of Belgrade? Don't talk nonsense, Draga," he said. Stubborn man. He was always stubborn. And of course Kaja wouldn't leave without him.'

'But they are all right?' David shook his head, laughed. 'Don't tell me *their* building is still standing too. It seems unbelievable!'

'Oh, yes. It is still standing. Not a window left in it, mind. But still standing. Yes.' Inexplicably and to everyone's consternation tears began to stream down the old woman's face. 'Oh, son,' she wailed, 'what have they done to our beautiful country? What have they done to our beautiful Serbia? Was it our own leaders who brought this upon us? Were they out of their minds? Oh, God, help us! Shall we ever be free again?' There was an immediate rush to gather around her, to take her hands, rub them, to calm her, sooth her. But she could not stop crying. The tears would not stop.

The truth was that their aunt had lived through one too many wars. She had seen Belgrade occupied before, devastated, but never like this. There was nothing any of them could do. They could not stop her tears. She was inconsolable. The tears kept coming. For her country. For her family. For her beloved Serbia.

'It's delayed shock,' Zora said, cool and calm as ever. 'And her happiness at seeing you, David. She has been so anxious about you. It has all been too much for her. Look, take Irina home. There is a curfew, you know. You will have to be back by seven. By the time you return she will be all right. You will see.'

Thinking now about his aunt's tears, David stirred restlessly in his bed, turned over, and slammed his fist into his pillow. 'German bastards!' he muttered out loud. What was it Santayana had called them? Barbarians! That was it. The northern barbarians. And he was right. How dare they reduce his fearless aunt to tears! How dare they bomb Belgrade? How dare they ... it was no use. He must put them out of his mind or he would never go to sleep. Tomorrow he would see his Uncle Mikhail. Talk to him. But first the bank. He had better go first thing in the morning and report to the bank. Still tossing and turning he finally fell into a fitful sleep, only to be awakened at dawn by the sound of tanks rolling past his window. He got up and looked out into the street. Tanks. As far as his eyes could see. They were heading north-east towards the River Danube, in the direction of Rumania and the Soviet Union. Ah, if only they would keep going until they reached Russia! What was it Bora Borović had said? Something about two scorpions in a bottle. He glanced at his watch. Still time for another couple of hours' sleep. Yawning he climbed back into bed and immediately fell asleep.

* * *

David's sisters had told him that the students' home was occupied by German troops, and had marvelled at the fact that he had not been stopped and asked for identification when he had passed it the previous day. In fact, he had been so intent on the question of whether his family had survived that he had hardly noticed the German guards surrounding the building, the line of tanks and trucks outside. He now walked past them with a feeling of bitterness in his heart, once again unaccosted, however, before taking a short cut through Bitoljska Street to reach the centre of the city. He began to grasp the full dimensions of the damage. Buildings that he had walked past every morning on his way to work lay in ruins, completely destroyed or badly damaged by bombs or fire. At least, he thought grimly, it was confirmation that Hitler was completely mad. Occupy Yugoslavia, yes, if his lust for territory, for power, was so insatiable. But why destroy Belgrade? What had that achieved? Revenge? Was the monster that much of a sadist? He shook his head sadly, relieved to find he had at last reached the bank, which, thank God, was still standing.

Once inside, however, his momentary feeling of relief soon disappeared. There was a warm welcome from his colleagues – many of them had not expected to see him again, feeling sure that at the very least he was by now a prisoner of war – but then they began to talk about the fate of their Jewish friends. Many of them had been killed by the bombing in the Dorćol area, where so many of them lived, but the others had already been ordered by the German authorities to gather at registration centres where they were to be enlisted for 'work in Germany'.

'You mean *all* of them? Kalderon? Gedalja? Alkalaj?' He broke off as each name brought forth a row of gloomy nods. 'Oh, God!' Then, hopefully, 'But what about Anna Cukulić? Her husband is not Jewish. Was he able to intervene?' It was the dark-haired Radmila, a special friend of Anna's, who answered for all of them.

'Do you think that would make any difference to the beasts?' Her eyes filled with tears. 'She has gone! Not only that, but it seems they are marking her husband for investigation.' She turned away, began to brush the tears from her cheeks.

One by one his friends returned to their desks. David went into his office, sat down, but could not even glance at the pile of papers in front of him. The faces of all of his Jewish colleagues, many of whom he considered to be among the finest and most intelligent of the bank's workers, rose before his eyes. And then he thought about Jack Cohen. God! Jack lived with his parents quite near Dorćol. And Bogdan! Was it possible the Germans already knew his wife was Jewish? Could they really, in such a short time, have flushed out that kind of information? Was Bogdan still alive, for that matter! He realized he had been so full of relief to discover his own family were still intact he had not even thought about Bogdan. His sisters had told him about the makeshift hospital that had been set up in the Miletić home, about the death of Judge Miletić. He knew that Stevan was safe. Stevan and Olga and Alex Miletić and their mother. But Bogdan. And Rachel! He would have to try to find out what had happened to them before going to see his uncle.

He looked up to find that Eugene Krstić had bustled into his office, mouthing a welcome, spluttering with the events of the past couple of weeks, almost apoplectic as he talked about the problems the bank had and would be facing. It seemed in any event that the decision had been made to close down for a few days. All employees were to be given new identification papers which would be issued in both German and Serbian. They would be allowed to leave the bank to take care of their personal affairs until it reopened at the beginning of next week. In other words, David finally managed to comprehend from the stream of words pouring out of the old man's mouth, he now had three full days to try and put his world together again. Which was just as well. Certainly his thoughts had been in such turmoil that he had not even glanced at the work piled high on his desk.

Feeling more secure with the new papers issued to him by the bank, he decided to walk through the main streets of the city, to try and ascertain the full extent of the damage inflicted upon the capital before trying to find Bogdan.

Grim-faced, he made his way through the ruins. The exclusive Serbian King Hotel that had faced Kalemegdan Park had been completely demolished. The export bank, the Hotel Moscva and the Hotel Macedonia were all badly damaged. The side of the State National Theatre facing French Street severely burned. He counted almost two dozen school buildings that were destroyed or badly damaged. The national library was burned to the ground. The general hospital and several private clinics severely damaged. The area around the Hotel Slavia was almost completely destroyed as was the area around the central railway station. Everywhere he turned he found devastation, destruction.

A great, burning rage began to build up inside him. With an effort of will he reduced it to a smouldering flame and went in search of his friend.

*   *   *

Bogdan Bošković had been rummaging amongst some papers in a damaged safe in his office at the back of the ruined Three Violins restaurant. He was moving what he could salvage to the family's main eating house on King Milan Street. His mother and stepfather had already left the city for their cottage in Dubrovnik. Bogdan was to stay in Belgrade and manage the family interests. Until he looked up to find David Ristić standing in the burnt-out frame of the doorway, he had been relatively calm, although he still could not control the twitch beneath his right eye. David was saying something, asking something about Rachel, and it was then that it all came back. He couldn't say a word. He began to sob.

There had been four of them. Each had carried a machine-gun. They had banged on the apartment door at 4 a.m., and he had rushed, cursing, to open it and stood frozen with fear as one of them had lifted his evil-looking gun and pointed it directly at his heart.

'Bogdan Bošković?'

He had stared at them, the yellow light from the doorway highlighting the lugubrious picture he made in his tousled pajamas, his mouth slightly open, his small eyes blinking with terror. He had tried to answer, but found his dry tongue unable to function. It had been Rachel, following from the bedroom, still tying the belt around her dressing-gown, who had answered. 'Our name is Bošković. What is it you want?'

'You are Rachel Aaron Bošković?'

'That's right.'

'You must come with us. Get dressed.' The officer in charge of the group addressed her in heavily-accented Serbian.

'I don't understand.'

'So it seems. Although the instructions were simple enough. All Jews were ordered to report to the nearest registration centre. Your name was on our list. You did not report as ordered. So you will now get dressed and come with us. Quickly, woman. Quickly!'

'But, you don't understand, sir. My wife is not of the Jewish faith. She is married to me. I am a Serb. Orthodox church!' Bogdan had made an effort to smile ingratiatingly. The officer responded by lifting his machine-gun and pointing it directly at him.

'You wish to accompany your wife, then?'

'Where are you taking me?' Rachel had interrupted quickly as her husband stood staring at the gun, seemingly petrified.

'We are not here to answer questions. Are you going to get dressed? Or do you wish to come as you are?'

Without a word Rachel had turned back into the bedroom and closed the door.

'And don't take long!' he shouted after her. 'We have no time to stand around awaiting the pleasure of a Jewess.'

Bogdan had regained control of his limbs, his voice. 'But you can't just . . .' he ran his hand through his tousled hair, shook his head. 'You must have some papers. There must be some legal procedure. You must . . .' He met the German's pale, unblinking stare. He had eyes like a dead fish.

The bedroom door opened and Rachel reappeared. She was wearing a print dress underneath her lightweight green coat. A silk scarf was tied around her hair. She held her head high and smiled bravely at her husband. 'I'm sure it won't take long, dear. I'll be back soon.'

The officer had laughed. 'Yes, yes,' he said, 'of course.'

'But where are you taking her?'

'You wish to come with us and find out?'

Bogdan had hesitated. Memories of the vague stories he had been hearing about the fate of the Jews, of those who tried to defend them, swam around in his mind. He had opened his mouth to say yes, yes I want to go with her, but nothing came out. Oddly, it was Rachel who now seemed to take command. She had been watching him intently, and now she walked over to him, reached up and kissed him tenderly, forgivingly.

'Why should you? I'll be back soon enough.' She had walked briskly away from him then, sweeping past the four Germans as though they simply did not exist. For a moment they seemed nonplussed, stared after her retreating form with gaping mouths before angrily gathering themselves together to follow.

Within seconds the apartment was empty, silent. It was as though they had never been there. Automatically Bogdan had moved over to the front door, closed it, returned to the bedroom, and sat down on the side of the bed. After a little while he had became conscious of the tick-tick-ticking of the alarm clock that stood on the small table next to Rachel's side. The ticking seemed to fill the room with a roar. Alone ... alone ... alone ...

The enormity of his loss had hit him. He clenched his fists, lifted his arms above his head, and listened as if from a great distance to the sound of his own voice screaming. Rachel, it shrieked like a mad banshee. Rachel, Rachel, Ra-ch-el!

He now became aware of David's hand on his shoulder, aware of his voice repeating over and over, 'Steady Bogdan, steady there. Take it easy, take it easy, fellow.' Take it easy! What did *he* know? Ristić was forcing a glass between his lips now. He gulped noisily at the burning liquid, hiccuped, and at last found his voice.

'Gothic brutes!' he shouted. 'Dirty Huns!' Tears were pouring down his cheeks, his lips were trembling, he was beside himself, incoherent with grief, with rage. 'I begged them,' he screamed. 'I *begged* them to let me go with her. I fought, there were four of them. Four of them, David. With machine-guns. You understand?' He pointed vaguely towards his head. 'They hit me. When I came-to she was gone. You understand? They just took her. They took her away from me.'

'My God!' David was appalled. 'They can't do that. Even in war, surely there is some law. There must be some international law.'

'I went to see them. Next day. At their headquarters. A Colonel Heidler. But he would tell me nothing. Nothing! I tell you, I can't stand it. I stay in the restaurant all day, all night, I can't go back to the apartment, it is so *empty*. I cannot stand being there alone. I can't tell you how I have been suffering. I can't begin to tell you.'

'Look, Bogdan, there must be something we can do. Calm down for a moment. Let me think.'

'Do you think so, David? Do you think you could speak to him? To Colonel Heidler, I mean. He was not an unpleasant man. Not like the ones who took her away. But he would not tell me anything. Just that my wife had quite possibly been sent to work in Germany.'

'There were four of them, you say?' David shook his head in disgust. 'What a nation! Four armed men to take one little Jewish woman.'

'"Take my advice, Mr Bošković!" the colonel said. "Don't ask too many questions. Don't try to cause trouble, or it will be the worse for you. The war will be over soon, in any event. Then your wife will no doubt be returned to you none the worse for her trip to the Fatherland."'

'Cynical bastard!'

'You think he lied?'

'Look, Bogdan, I am on my way now to see Uncle Mikhail. If anyone can do anything, if anyone will know what can be done, it will be him.'

* * *

'I have already done my best, David. Not specifically for your friend Bogdan's wife, but for all of the Jews. It is a disgrace to the German nation what they are doing to these people. Rounding them up like cattle, banging on people's doors at all hours of the day and night. Forcing them to work in the streets, sending many of them out of the country without notifying anyone in authority where they are being sent, what is to happen to them. I tell you I have seen nothing like this in all my life. Never such lawlessness by a so-called civilized nation. Not in the Balkan wars. Not in the Great War!'

'But who is in charge? Do we have any kind of Serbian leadership? Anyone to represent our people? To represent the Jewish people?'

His uncle passed his hand wearily over his eyes. 'I believe they are negotiating with General Nedić to set up some kind of representative authority. He is not too anxious to co-operate, of course. Whoever accepts responsibility to act for our people now is going to be called a traitor later and will get no thanks for it. Nedić is aware of that. But someone must accept responsibility.' He frowned, gestured angrily. 'You know, of course, that the whole government, the ones,' he added sarcastically, 'who saved Yugoslavia's soul! They deserted the country on April the fifteenth. With the young king. All of them. Imagine! They flew to England from the airport in Mostar, in Hercegovina, you know? I tell you, my boy, to first bring the country into this war and then to abandon the people to these brutal Nazis. This is not in the moral tradition of our two great democratic kings. Ah! What a difference if the first King Peter, if Alexander, if either of them were alive to lead us today. What a difference!'

'I walked through Belgrade today. Do you realize what they've done to our city, Uncle? There must be *something* we can do. Is there nothing we can do?'

'Of course there will be something we can do, my boy. But not at the moment. We must wait for things to simmer down. Then we shall see. For the time being let us be grateful to be still alive. Thank God you had the initiative to avoid being captured. You will see. Something will be organized. When it is we will need every able-bodied man we can find.'

'And Nikola? You are sure he has survived?'

The old man laughed. 'My boy, he is still with his cavalry unit somewhere in the Srem. Of course he has survived! He is his father's son, after all.' He placed a large, gnarled hand over his heart. 'His father would feel it *here*, if anything had happened to him. No, no. My Nikola is fine, wherever he is.'

'I must tell Bogdan, then, that for the moment nothing can be done?'

His uncle shook his head, frowned. 'Never deprive anyone of hope, David. Tell him that whatever can be done will be done. Yes, yes. You can tell him that. What can be done will be done.'

So in due course he delivered that message to an eager Bogdan, painfully aware as he did so of the fraudulent sound of his own words. But surely what his uncle said was true? No one should ever be deprived of hope!

Yet by the end of April it seemed that Yugoslavia itself was to be deprived of all hope. Germany had delivered the mortal blow, and now its fascist neighbours rushed to tear off a chunk of the small country's still-warm flesh. Hungary gulped down the whole of the Bačka, while the Italians digested Dalmatia, Montenegro and picked at a Slovenia they were to share with the Germans. The Bulgars brutally snatched at Macedonia and Albania swallowed a substantial portion of Kosovo and Metohija.

Croatia received its reward for taking the German occupiers to its heart. It was now the 'Independent State of Croatia' and had been granted a substantial part of Serbian territory in Bosnia, Hercegovina and Sandjack, under the dictatorship of the criminal leader of a gang of cutthroats – known throughout Europe as the *Ustaši* – Ante Pavelić, who was in the process of 'cleansing' the new state of its 'impure' racial elements. Croatia, he announced, would be purged, not only of the Gypsies and Jews, but also of the Serbs who lived within the boundaries of the state's new territories.

'We shall kill some of these Serbs,' his newly appointed minister of religion, Dr Budak, announced. 'Others shall be driven out. Those who remain will be forced to embrace the Roman Catholic faith.'

In Belgrade these happenings were received with unrelieved gloom, exacerbated by the daily effort of waking up to the continual irritant of watching the brutal occupier swarming around what was left of the city, bullying the workforces that were made up of prisoners of war, Gypsies and Jewish captives. Behind closed doors Belgraders exclaimed to each other that the yellow star the latter were forced to wear achieved nothing except to heap further shame upon the fascist oppressors.

Shortly after his return home, David was wondering whether he would not have been wiser to stay in the mountains. The previous evening he had had a row with Irina. Or, rather, with her mother and aunt. After accepting their invitation to join them for an early supper, he had arrived to find the two older women in a state of pleasurable excitement. It seemed that the elderly couple who rented the apartment next door had been forced to evacuate their rooms for two German officers. Madame Mirskaia had been fearful that their own large apartment might also be requisitioned, but after an encounter with one of the officers had been assured that they would be allowed to stay where they were. Not only that, but the officer had gallantly asked that should the ladies find themselves short of food or other provisions, they should not hesitate to call upon him. 'He was,' she told David, 'charming. Really charming.'

David had exploded and flung himself out of the apartment. Irina had come rushing after him, begging him to return, to remember that her mother and aunt had for many years been alone. It had not been easy for them to survive without the help of a man since they had left Russia. And the German officer had hinted to her mother that the alliance with the Soviet Union was not exactly cast in stone. If the Germans were one day to defeat the communists, well, David was to please remember that her mother and aunt were as devoted to *their* country as much as he was devoted to his. Anyway, she had added tearfully, of course they would *never* approach the Germans for help. Even if they had to starve! Did he truly think they lacked appreciation for the home Yugoslavia had given them? For the warmth with which they had been welcomed? No, no. Whatever shortages of food or anything else that the Yugoslav people were to suffer, Irina and her family would gladly share their deprivations.

She had been so upset, so contrite, so defensive and confused that he could not help relenting. He had bent down to kiss her lightly on the lips, and led her back to the apartment, although refusing to go back inside with her. He would be in touch, he said. He would be in touch.

Then the following morning, on his way to work, he had encountered Otto Schmidt, the caretaker, in the hallway, and had stopped to mention some plumbing problem his aunt was complaining about, only to be interrupted by Mrs Schmidt angrily calling to her husband.

'What are you talking to *him* for?' she had snapped at a rather shamefaced Otto. '*We* are in charge now. We don't have to be at their beck and call any more.'

To top it all off, after finally managing to lose himself in his work for an hour or so, he had looked up from his desk to find framed in the doorway of his office a large SS officer. Startled, he had half risen from his chair before realizing that the confident figure in the hated black uniform was Ernst Halder.

'Surprised, David?' Halder had chuckled, strutting in and slapping him on the back. 'I was just passing by. Thought I would drop in and buy you a coffee.'

Wordlessly, unsmiling, David accompanied him down the stairs to the cafeteria. He was too stunned to do anything else. But a great bitterness filled his heart. Was there not one German who had lived in his country for so many years with a sense of shame? It was even worse in Halder's case. He was a *Volksdeutscher*. He had been born here. This was his country. Did he have no sense of shame at all? Was it possible?

He had sat in front of his coffee listening to the Nazi assuring him in a condescending tone of his continued friendship, and wondered just how much more he could take before exploding. Not too much, he was aware of that. His nature was too open, too spontaneous, and already the effort of biting his tongue was having its effect on his temper both at home and at the bank. No. He could not take too much more. And when he *did* lash out at some grinning, arrogant Nazi face, what then? What would it achieve? What would happen to his family? The Germans were masters at checking resistance by exploiting a man's concern for his family.

Some relief came, however, after Halder had tucked his short military stick under his arm and strutted out, assuring David he would 'keep in touch'. David had immediately been surrounded by his fellow workers. They gathered around, looked at him, but no one spoke.

'Well?' he had snapped. 'And if he had invited any one of *you* for coffee? You would have refused?'

'Of course not, David. We understand.' Ivo Hajduk placed his hand sympathetically on his shoulder.

'But what were you thinking while you sat there, David? We were watching you. You looked so grim. You didn't even eat your pastry.' The plump Radmila tilted her head, gazed at him with her wide black eyes.

'Thinking? I was thinking,' he said slowly, 'of something Nietzsche was supposed to have said. "The presence of a fellow German retards my digestion!"'

For a brief moment the unmitigated gloom of the morning vanished as they all exploded into laughter. The laughter was hysterical enough, however, to merely underline the tension under which they were all living and working.

* * *

David was not sure when it was that he first noticed the

poster. It was nailed to a lamp on the corner of Bitoljska and Vasina Streets, opposite the gaping hole that had once been the Kolarac restaurant. One morning curiosity got the better of him and he crossed the street to read it. He stood there for a moment studying the scholarly face of the man depicted, an officer in the Yugoslav army, before letting his eyes take in the text.

> A reward of 100,000 German marks (in gold) will be paid to anyone who delivers Colonel Draža Mihailović, alive or dead, to German authorities.

What, he wondered, continuing on his way with a slight frown, was *that* all about?

He was to find out just two mornings later. He had joined Ivo for coffee and, remembering the poster, began to tell him about it just as a fellow employee from the cashier's section joined them. Ivo had read the poster, but did not know anything about it. The other man, Djordje Glisić, listened quietly and added nothing to the conversation.

That afternoon, however, as David was leaving the bank, Djordje caught up with him. 'Can I join you?'

'Of course.' They began walking along Vasina Street.

'You were asking Ivo about Draža Mihailović?'

David turned to look at him. Djordje, a tall, bespectacled man in his early thirties had removed his glasses and was polishing them with a large white handkerchief.

'About who?' He suddenly remembered. 'Oh, yes. The officer shown on that poster.'

'He is a career officer in our army.' Two German soldiers roared past them on motorbikes and he broke off to stare after them. Approaching was a group of German soldiers on foot who appeared to be off duty. In any event they were talking and laughing amongst themselves and appeared to be in an uncharacteristic mood of relaxation.

'If anyone stops us, Djordje muttered rapidly, 'we are talking about the experiences of our family during the bombardment. You understand?'

'Of course,' David agreed irritably. That he could not even walk through the streets of his own city freely, talking to a colleague, was infuriating. The group of Germans drew abreast. They stopped talking amongst themselves and stared arrogantly, suspiciously even, at the two civilians. They did not stop them, however, and seemed content as both men drew to one side to let them pass.

'Bastards!' David muttered when they were out of earshot.

'Yes,' Glisić agreed grimly, 'but thank God someone is trying to do something about them.' Rapidly then, in response to David's inquiring look, he went on to explain that Draža Mihailović, who had been stationed with his unit in Bosnia when the Germans attacked, had apparently after some fierce fighting, escaped into the Serbian mountains with a battalion of assault troops. He was now established at Ravna Gora, where he had been organizing a guerrilla force since the beginning of May.

David listened with a sense of rising excitement. 'Ravna Gora! But he couldn't find a better place.' Ravna Gora was part of the Suvobor Range and extremely difficult of access. 'Thank God someone is at last fighting back,' he added.

Djordje nodded. 'But can you imagine his difficulties? With both the country and the army to all intents and purposes no longer in existence, he has one hell of a job trying to get hold of arms, raise money, rally more officers and men to his side.'

'But he must have them worried? If the Germans are offering a hundred thousand marks, in gold, dead or alive, the poster said. He must have them worried.'

'Oh yes.' For the first time since they began their walk Djordje smiled and became mildly boastful. 'I think he *might* be causing them a little lost sleep. Perhaps they are remembering what we Serbs did to them in the past. Not to mention the Bulgars, the Austrians–'

'And to the Hungarians, Italians and Turks!' David was not to be outdone in remembering historic Serbian deeds of the past.

They had by now turned into Bitoljska Street and Glisić paused before crossing the street to continue on his own way. 'I have to leave you here, but I'll tell you what I'll do. I'm going to make an appointment for you to see someone who can give you more information.' He hesitated, stared at David searchingly through his thick glasses. 'That is, of course, if you are interested.'

'My God! Of course I'm interested.'

Glisić gave a faint smile. 'Good. We'll leave it at that, then. As soon as I've arranged something I'll let you know the time and place. Agreed?'

David held out his hand. 'Agreed!'

Now he was standing outside the third-floor apartment of a smart-looking building on Zeleni Venac Street, urgently pressing the bell. He glanced at his watch. Exactly three. He was right on time. A little after five that same afternoon he was on his way home in a state of suppressed excitement.

The information he had received from the tall, good-looking Serb who had answered the door and introduced himself as Stan Perić, had been very much to the point. The first thing Ristić should be aware of was that any connection he might form with the clandestine organization represented by Perić and by the two dark-haired men with him, Nick Marić and Vlada Djukić, could cost him his life. Having made sure he was fully aware of the danger involved, the man Perić who, it seemed, was a major in the Yugoslav army, outlined the organization's function. It had been formed in order to rally support in Belgrade for Colonel Mihailović and to organize a supply of material and arms to his troops. It was also hoped that ten brigades could be set up in Belgrade ready for instant mobilization should Mihailović acquire enough strength and arms to drive the Germans out and take over the capital. Each brigade would be divided into four battalions and have four companies along the same lines as the army. The strength of each unit would depend upon each brigadier.

Reaching his own block of apartments, David ran up the stairs two at a time. For the first time since returning to

Belgrade he felt his old, exuberant self. He had even been able to walk past a German patrol without experiencing the usual tightening around his heart, the usual mouth full of bile. *Just you wait, you fascist bastards,* he had thought almost gaily. That afternoon he, David Ristić, had been appointed brigadier of the First Brigade in Belgrade of the army presently being formed by Colonel Draža Mihailović, God preserve his soul! No matter that Perić had answered his stunned query about the rank of brigadier with a grin.

'You are joining a guerrilla army, Ristić,' he had said. 'For the purposes of recruitment you are a brigadier. If we have to send you out into the field, though, I'm afraid it will be a quick demotion back to lieutenant.' David had laughed, nodded. Well, it was no matter either that the First Brigade consisted of one member, namely himself! By next week, he had assured Major Perić, he would have at least twenty men. By the end of June maybe a hundred. David knew dozens of young men of his own age all bristling with inner frustration at having to watch the arrogant German bastards strutting through their city as though they owned it. Friends he had gone to school with, friends in the rowing club, in his ski club, friends at the bank. First on his list, he was thinking happily, was, of course, Stevan. David had not been in touch with him for some time now, but he knew he must be suffering at the forced inactivity. Then, Bogdan. At last he could do something about his Rachel!

He had by now entered the apartment, which seemed uncommonly quiet. 'Aunt? Andjela? Zora?'

'In here, David.' To his surprise both his aunt and Zora were in the small parlour off the main sitting room, an area they rarely used. They were sitting together on the brocade-covered chairs, sewing.

'What are you doing in here?'

'Sewing!' Zora angrily bit off a piece of cotton and examined the piece of embroidery she was working on.

'Well, I can see that, sister.' David laughed, picked up a chair, swung it around and straddled it. 'Where's Andjela?'

'In her bedroom.' Aunt Draga gave a deep sigh and

gloomily folded up her sewing. 'You're late, David. Have you had lunch?'

'Yes, of course.' He suddenly noticed the tray on the small table in the centre of the room. 'You've had guests, then?'

'Your Aunt Kaja was here.'

'Aunt Kaja?' He hesitated. 'Is Nikola . . . ?'

'Nikola is back in Belgrade.'

'He is? Wonderful!' *Another recruit for the First Brigade.*

'Is it?' Zora scowled. After a moment she turned back to her sewing. 'It seems he has joined Nedić's quislings,' she announced abruptly.

'Nikola?'

'But what else could he do?' His aunt was frowning severely at her niece. 'You know what these terrible Germans are doing. They have been rounding up all of the regular army officers. Sending them to Germany. At least this way Nikola can remain in Belgrade.'

David digested that. 'And Uncle Mikhail? How is he taking it?'

His Aunt remained silent. It was Zora who answered. 'Badly!' She jabbed the needle through her sewing with unnecessary violence.

'Oh, God!' David stood up. 'I'd better go and see him.'

'No, no. Not now.' His aunt reached out and placed a restraining hand on his arm. 'Give him some time by himself. You know how proud he is.'

'And there's something else.' Zora placed her sewing on her lap, stared at David with something like curiosity in her bright dark eyes. 'Aunt Kaja,' she added wryly, 'was absolutely full of interesting news today.'

'Zora! I don't like you when you are like this.' His aunt gave up the pretense of continuing with her own sewing, put it down.

'It seems,' Zora went on relentlessly, 'that they had a visit from Mrs Nešić. She wanted to tell them that Vera is unofficially engaged. She shrugged. 'Not much use making a formal announcement during an occupation. But anyway, she will be getting married quite soon.'

'Vera?' There was an instant's regret, followed quickly by a feeling of relief. Although he and Vera had never discussed marriage he had simply stopped seeing her since he had met Irina and had been feeling vaguely guilty ever since. Now, he thought, he could drop by and congratulate her. Resume normal relations with both Vera and her family.

'Who's the lucky man?'

'The lucky man, as you call him, is Bane Protić!' Zora stood up so abruptly that the piece of embroidery fell from her lap. She bent down and snatched it up.

'Bane? Oh, God. Andjela!'

'Exactly. And Andjela *too* is taking things badly.' Zora marched to the door. 'Men!' she exclaimed, giving her brother a bitter look. 'They have the privilege of running the world, and just *see* how they behave!' She walked out, slamming the door behind her.

'Hey! Wait a minute,' David protested to his aunt. 'What did *I* do?'

'She's upset because of Andjela. She doesn't mean it.' His aunt got up heavily from her chair, sighed. 'But I can't help asking, son. What is happening to our world? What has happened to our happy world?'

* * *

David called on his uncle the following afternoon.

'Nikola did the right thing, Uncle. Would you rather he had just given up, like so many others? Would you be happier if he were now a prisoner of war in Germany?'

'Do not talk to me about Nikola, my boy.'

'But aren't you being unfair? If he had had any alternative. I mean . . .'

'He had an alternative.'

'Did he? Not unless he had already heard about . . .' David hesitated. He did not wish his uncle or any of his relatives . . . to know anything about his own connection with Mihailović. 'Look, Uncle, you will see. Some kind of underground movement will start up. Once he learns about such a movement, I am sure Nikola…'

'There is already such a movement. I told him about it. I offered to help him get to the mountains, join up with some fellow officers who, like you, preferred not to meekly hand over their arms, offer themselves like sheep to the enemy. But it seems he has some whore here in Belgrade. "Why should I fight, when most of the army preferred to surrender?" he asked.' The old man's face hardened. 'He asked *me* that.'

'Do you know where I could find him? I mean without getting in touch with anyone at Nedić's headquarters?' David gave a slight smile. 'I don't *think* they're looking for reserve officers. Not yet, anyway. But I'd rather keep out of the way of officialdom of any kind at the moment.'

'Why? What do you want with him?'

'Nothing. I mean, perhaps I…' He floundered a little. 'That group of officers you referred to. I happen to know a little bit about them.' He hesitated, drawing back a little from his uncle's suddenly keen stare. 'Well,' he went on lamely, 'I did hear something about them at the bank. Perhaps if I had a talk with Nikola I could…'

'And just what did you hear at the bank?'

'Very little.' His answer was a shade too quick. Again he hesitated, then pressed on. 'Just that an army colonel is trying to form a resistance group. He seems to be successful. There are already posters all over Belgrade offering a reward for him.'

'You are talking about Colonel Mihailović?'

David was leaning against the mantelpiece, his favourite spot in his uncle's study. He now moved a little uneasily, reached out and picked up a photograph of his Aunt Kaja, looked at it, replaced it. His uncle was watching him carefully. After a moment he cleared his throat and nodded. 'I think that is his name.'

'You *think* that is his name.' Mikhail Ristić leaned back in his chair, studied him with a slight smile. 'How very much like your father you are, David.'

'Yes.' Glad to be off the hook, David gave him a relieved smile. 'So everyone tells me.'

With a quick movement, surprisingly graceful for such a heavy man, his uncle stood up, walked over to him and placed a hand on his shoulder. 'You have joined Mihailović!'

David gave him a startled look and reddened, furious with himself. This was not the first time his uncle had effortlessly read his mind. *A fine member of the underground I'm going to make!* 'God, Uncle,' he said, 'how do you do it? How do you *always* manage to know exactly what I'm thinking?' The sentence trailed off at the unexpected sight of tears welling in this tough old man's eyes.

'Only let me thank God,' Mikhail said, 'let me thank God that someone in my family is at last behaving like a Serb.'

2

Stevan re-read the leaflet he was working on and sighed. The basics of propaganda were simple enough. You took a small snippet of truth from the larger canvas, embroidered it lavishly with your own message, then released it upon the masses in as simplistic a form as possible. Still, to someone who had discovered that he enjoyed honest writing very much, the process he was now involved in was degrading. *It is a discipline like any other*, Olga had insisted when he had confided his distaste for the job bestowed upon him by the Party. No doubt she was right. And yet . . . he again read the words he had just penned.

> Capitalistic cliques and imperialist agents consisting of Chetniks, police, traitorous officers and others are plotting together to deceive the workers about the intentions of the great and benevolent Soviet Union.

He pushed both paper and pen to the back of his desk, stood up, walked over to his apartment window and stared down into the street. How in God's name was he expected to convince the Yugoslav masses of the virtues of the first socialist republic when the Soviet Union had cancelled its friendship pact and expelled the Yugoslav minister to Moscow in order, presumably, to further cement its own relations with Germany? Neither the citizens of Belgrade nor the Serbian peasantry were fools, although Tito himself had often assured him that 'people forget things very quickly' and 'repeat something often enough and it will be believed'. Stevan was not at all sure about that.

And now there was this business with that damned army officer Draža Mihailović. His band of guerrilla fighters were not only infuriating the Germans, they were causing the Party no little trouble. Because, of course, ever since it had been learned that the Germans had encountered fierce armed resistance from Mihailović's men on the road between Gornji Milanovac and Kragujevac, they had overnight become national heroes. Already the population had named them 'Chetniks' after heroic patriots of the past who had resisted the brutal Turkish occupation. Exactly what Tito had feared! How in the devil did you manage to smear them without enraging the people and goading them into giving even more support than they already were reportedly extending to the colonel and his ill-armed, ill-equipped, but surprisingly effective recruits? As a matter of fact, in his heart Stevan was as proud of them as any other Serb. But that was beside the point so far as his duties to the Party were concerned!

To make matters worse, the Gestapo had now arrested followers of the group who were being accused of trying to organize arms and men from Belgrade, and had already publicly hanged six Chetnik officers in Pozega-by-Uzice, unaware it seemed that instead of terrorizing the population, all *that* barbarous act would achieve would be to stiffen the people's backbone. In a country that for hundreds of years had been occupied by the Turks, stoicism against terror was as inbred as was the nation's pride.

Sighing ruefully he was about to return to his desk when the doorbell rang sharply. Happy to be distracted he opened the door eagerly, and gave a warm smile of pleasure at the sight of David Ristić.

'David! It's good to see you. Come in, come in.'

'I should have paid you a visit before. But you know how it is, always something crops up.'

'Of course. As a matter of fact I saw your sisters in the street the other day. It reminded me that I should pay *you* a visit.' He nodded towards a chair. 'Sit down for a moment. I'll get us a drink.' He hesitated. 'Would you like some beer? I've got some *Bajloni*.'

'Wonderful.' David sat down, glanced around the apartment, and looked up as his friend reappeared with a couple of bottles and glasses. 'You're lucky you still have this place to yourself, Stevan. The Germans have been tossing people out on the streets, grabbing all of the best accommodation for themselves.'

'I know.' Stevan handed him his drink. 'They've already requisitioned the Miletić home, although Olga and her mother have been allowed to stay on the second floor. I've been trying to get them to move in here. I can always find somewhere else to stay.'

'They will be moving in, then?'

He shook his head. 'I don't know. It's Mrs Miletić. Even with Germans billeted there she seems to prefer her own home. Only natural, I suppose. She hasn't got over the judge's death yet. But how about you? Everything all right at home?'

David shrugged. 'More or less.'

Stevan sat down in front of him, still holding his glass of *Bajloni*. 'How are things with Irina? Set a wedding date yet?'

'How can we? Things are pretty much up in the air. Until we know what direction the war will take, until we know how long the country will be occupied.'

'It could be a long time before we find that out. Don't you think it's best to just try to keep on living as normal a life as possible? Why let the occupation interfere with your personal plans? If you can avoid it, I mean.'

David carefully placed his glass down on the table between them, and stared at him in surprise. 'Surely you can't mean that, Stevan? How can anyone think of their own personal lives when every day we are confronted by Belgrade in ruins? Not only that, but have to watch the Jews digging ditches, repairing the streets. Do you know, just on the way here I saw this elderly Jew, he had the face of a scholar, had never, I'm sure, done physical work before, and this fascist bastard was pushing him, bullying him, God. I don't know how long I can stand seeing that kind of thing. I felt I was going to burst.'

'And if you had?' Stevan shook his head. 'They wouldn't only pick you up, you know. As soon as they learned who your family were...'

'I know. I know. As a matter of fact,' he picked his glass up again, stared into it angrily, 'I've been thinking it might be better if I moved out of the apartment. I could perhaps find a room somewhere close to the bank. Then if I ever *do* get into trouble, well, that might offer some protection to the family.'

'Simpler, surely, to stay out of trouble?' Stevan coolly drank a draught of his beer.

David frowned. 'How can you say that? My God, Stevan, you must be unnerved a dozen times a day, just like the rest of us. Can you say it doesn't bother you?'

'Of course it bothers me. I'm simply trying to accept the fact that as there is nothing I can do, nothing either you nor I can do...'

'But if I told you there *was* something we can do?' David leaned forward eagerly, his blue eyes ablaze.

Stevan hesitated, frowned. 'What do you mean?'

'I mean there is a movement right here in Belgrade, the beginning of a movement that can drive them *all* out of our country. Not only the Germans, but the Bulgarians, the Italians, the Hungarians, the–'

'A movement here in Belgrade?' Stevan smiled. 'So who is going to supply it with arms? The British? What a joke! And even if they did, what could some half-baked underground movement achieve against the Germans? Blow up a few more buildings in Belgrade? Just what we need! God knows, the Germans hardly need an excuse to grab innocent people as hostages. I can just see it! We blow up a building that's probably on the verge of collapse anyway, and a dozen civilians will die for it!'

'No one is talking about blowing up buildings in Belgrade.' David's voice was cold with disappointment.

Stevan was instantly contrite. 'I'm sorry, David. As you were saying, we all get unnerved a dozen times a day. But I don't think it would make things better if–'

'But you see, the whole point is, we will not be carrying out operations here in Belgrade. What needs to be done now is to collect funds, materials, arms, for men who are already in the mountains. I know it's risky, but I'm sure it can be done. Look at Nedić's men. Most of them are only half-hearted supporters of the Germans as it is. They're opportunists. If we have the money I have no doubt they will sell us arms. And the Italians! Have you met an Italian yet who would not rather sell a gun than shoot it? It can be done. I'm sure it can be done.'

'For men who are already in the mountains,' Stevan repeated slowly. He leaned forward, suddenly attentive. 'My God. You are talking about that colonel.'

'Yes, of course. You see? You have heard of him yourself.' Excitedly David stood up and began to pace up and down the room. 'Do you understand now, Stevan? Do you understand what this means to our people? To have had to watch as our army collapsed, as so many of our officers and men just lay down their arms and surrendered, what a terrible psychological blow to our people. But now they are becoming aware that not all of our officers were so ready to capitulate.' He stopped his restless pacing and stood in front of his friend, almost beside himself with excitement. 'Even Uncle Mikhail knows about him! Do you know what Mihailović said when told that he must capitulate? That the whole of the Yugoslav army stood ready to capitulate! He said, "Capitulation? I do not know what capitulation is."'

'Is that true?' Unthinkingly Stevan found himself caught up in the fire of his friend's enthusiasm. 'My God! That's the kind of thing Karageorge must have said when he rose against the Turks.'

And a moment later they were, as they had done countless times in the past, loudly reviewing Serbian history, beginning with the brilliant Nemanjan dynasty of the tenth century that had led to the glorious era when Tzar Dusan had ruled over Serbia in the middle of the fourteenth century and whose empire had stretched over two-thirds of the Balkans.

They spoke, then, in hushed tones, of the disaster that had overtaken a successor, Tzar Lazar, whose sacred bones could be viewed even today as they lay in the Vrdnik Monastery at Frushka Gora, where they had been preserved through wars and insurrections and occupations ever since he had been slain by the Turks on the plains of Kosovo, repository of the Serbian soul, which each summer bloomed magically with wild flowers that could be found nowhere else in the world, nourished as they were by the deep red of Serbian blood that had gushed forth so long ago in futile but magnificent defiance of the Ottoman empire.

Ah, they sighed with great reverence, Kosovo. Kosovo! Heart of the mediaeval empire of the Serbs. Revered the more so because of its loss to the Turkish oppressor. Tzar Lazar's death had heralded the dark age of the ferocious and murderous Muslims, but not before their special hero, Prince Milosh Obilić, who had been despatched from the battlefield to surrender to Sultan Murat as the vastly outnumbered Serbs fell in increasing numbers, had salvaged Serbian honour and forfeited his own life by drawing his sword and driving it through the heart of that fat and cynical tyrant, an event commemorated at Serbian schools every speech day on the 28th of June and celebrated ever since in vivid verse, song, and brilliant paintings by their poets and artists.

On and on they talked, reminding each other of various Serbian insurrections, lingering with special pleasure over the exploits of Strashimir Ivo the Black, the Serbian leader who had defied the Turks from the grim mountain of Crna Gora, leaving them frustrated and raging but still unable to breach his stern and impregnable fortress of the mountain, and finally, turning to that fateful day at the beginning of the nineteenth century when the mighty Karageorge had risen up to begin the Serbian national struggle that was to drive the Turkish usurpers out of the Balkans.

By the time they had reached the roles played by their own fathers who had taken part in the counter-attack along the river Kolubara during the Great War and gone on to drive the Austrians out of the country, their voices were hoarse. Still, David could not resist huskily recalling the famous cry by *Vojvoda* Putnik of the Serbian high command that *there is not one free enemy soldier on the soil of the kingdom of Serbia*.

'And all of the western papers referred to our country as "brave little Serbia",' Stevan shouted, rallying. 'That's what my father says.'

They clinked glasses then, and fell at last into a deeply satisfactory silence. David finally roused himself. 'Well, Stevan,' he asked quietly, sitting up straight, 'what do you say? Are you with us?' David beamed. 'As brigadier of the First Brigade in Belgrade of the Yugoslav army, I invite you to join my unit. I don't mind telling you that you will have the honour of being my first recruit.'

'You mean you've already joined this group?'

'Of course. No need to tell you that I immediately thought of you. The first two members of my brigade, I thought, will be Stevan and Bogdan.' He finished off the rest of his beer. 'What an adventure when you come to think of it, Stevan. Remember how the three of us used to dream of one day being as brave as Prince Milosh? How we would bring even more glory to our Serbian nation? Childish nonsense, of course. Yet, maybe we will have a chance to fulfill those young dreams.' He put his glass down and smiled. After a moment, though, as it became apparent his friend had nothing to say, he gave him a puzzled look. 'But you don't seem very enthusiastic.'

'Yes, well, it's certainly something to think about.' Stevan's words echoed lamely in his own ears. He picked up his empty glass and gazed into it in an effort to avoid David's inquiring stare.

'It didn't take *me* long to think about it.'

Stevan smiled. 'You don't have to tell me! You've always been an impulsive fellow. Full of self-confidence. But think about it for a moment, David. First of all, did you know that these bloody fascists have already issued a proclamation about this so-called "leader of the Chetnik bands"? It's not only that they have offered a reward for his capture, they've already hung some men they claimed were connected with his movement. And now they are talking about reprisals against the civilian population. Do you think they don't mean it? You've seen what barbarians they are. What sense does it make to kill them under such circumstances? My God, David, do you really think one German life is worth the life of a Serb? Do you think a German life is worth *your* life? Or mine?'

'Of course not.' David relaxed back in his chair with relief. So *that* was what had caused Stevan to hesitate. 'The point is, you know our people, how disheartened they were to learn how easily our army fell. Well, this action by Mihailović will restore their pride, you understand? So far as reprisals against civilians are concerned, well, they are certainly making threats. If they do begin to harm our people why, I suppose we will simply concentrate on acts of sabotage. We can destroy communications, bridges, tunnels, ammunition depots and so on. Try to harass German units, you know, try to demoralize them. Certainly we intend to try to accumulate arms, we need to defend ourselves if attacked and also to hold them in readiness for when the Allied army begins its offensive in Europe. We are hoping for a landing on the Adriatic coast. Just think, Stevan, of the lives it will save if the allies find here in Yugoslavia a renewed and well-armed army. Just think about that!'

'The Allies? You mean the British? Good God, David, don't you realize that it was the British who got us into this mess in the first place? I thought by now everyone knew they were behind the putsch, despite their shy protests. But of course it was to their great advantage to have German troops tied up here in Yugoslavia!' He grimaced. 'Churchill and his "Yugoslavia has saved its soul!" Do you think he cares a damn about Yugoslavia? He cares about his empire. That is what *he* cares about.'

David laughed. 'My God, Stevan, you sound like General Nedić or the communists.' He became lost in his own thoughts for a moment, not noticing the sudden reddening of his friend's face, the lowering of his eyes. 'You may be right. Have you heard the latest saying going around Belgrade? "There is no connection with our minds", they are saying, "but we are for the British".' He chuckled.

'Well anyway, even in the kind of operations you describe, the killing of Germans will be inevitable, and our people will be decimated. At least there will be that risk.' Avoiding his friend's eyes, Stevan gestured towards his empty glass. 'Another beer, David?'

'No, no. I must be going. But will you give this some more thought, Stevan? You talk about risk. Don't you think our people would much prefer to take that risk than to remain bowed down under this bloody occupation? You are living alone, Stevan. Well, I am not. Do you think I enjoy hearing my aunt, my sisters, crying at night because they have seen an act of brutality in the streets against a Jew or a Gypsy or a prisoner of war? Do you think I enjoy hearing them cry because Nazi boots are tramping through the streets of our beloved Belgrade, because they cannot walk outside without hearing that traitor Nedić shouting through those blasted loudspeakers that they must despise the British who led us into this, and cooperate with these bloody Nazi criminals?'

'All I am trying to say ... look, what really got us into this war? Our Serbian emotionalism! With a little prodding from the British, of course. In a way Nedić is right. I'm not trying to excuse him, you understand, but, for instance, are you aware that he asked the German command to allow his government to deal with the Jewish question? Well, they gave that right to the Croats, but they refused Nedić because they know damned well that there is no anti-Semitic feeling amongst our people. They felt he would be too soft on the Jews, and from their point of view they were right. I'm sure he hoped to spare these people some of the German excesses...'

'You are telling me, then,' David spoke slowly, a little incredulously, 'that we should just leave things in the hands of Nedić?'

'Well...' again Stevan avoided his eyes. 'As things stand...' he muttered lamely.

David left shortly afterwards. They had parted cordially enough, shaken hands, assured each other they would be in touch. Stevan, however, could not rid himself of the memory of his friend's puzzled expression, the hurt he was unable to keep out of the blue eyes that always reflected his feelings so well.

The thought that David Ristić might in his heart consider him to be something of a coward was unbearable. He went into the kitchen and poured himself another beer, but could not swallow it. Restlessly he moved back into the sitting room, stood at his desk staring down at the leaflet he had been working on just prior to David's arrival. What a bunch of bull! Suddenly he was sick to death of it all. What had membership in this bloody Communist Party brought him, anyway? Olga? He wanted her for his wife, but was not any closer to achieving that. Certainly, his friendship with her brother, Alex, had deepened, yet for the life of him he could not share that big man's unswerving faith in Joseph Stalin. He was proud of his relationship with Josip Broz, a singular man if ever there was, and of his friendship with Djerdja. Yet even these relationships at times served to highlight his alienation from his own bombastic father whose admiration Stevan had always secretly craved, and who would be disgusted to find that his only son was involved with people he considered to be a bunch of bandits.

As for the rest there were all the petty jealousies and intrigues and infighting that was perhaps inevitable within such a secret, tightly-knit organization of mismatched men and women. And the lies! He, Stevan Matić, had been forced to tell and to write more lies within the short period of time he had been with the Party than in the whole of the rest of his life.

In fact his life prior to joining the Party suddenly seemed

to him to have been so beautifully uncomplicated, so sweet, so honest, so clean. He thought about the retelling of Serbian history he and David had engaged in that afternoon, of the great heroic giants of their past, and he again experienced that surging of the blood, that wild singing of the heart that was so much a part of the poetry that was Serbian nationalism.

His apartment seemed too small to contain him. Grabbing a jacket he headed for the door, desperately in need of fresh air, of space and movement that might help him contain the inner violence his friend's visit had ignited.

Outside he was reminded that it was a beautiful day. The sun was beginning to fade, but the sky was still lapis blue. It was going to be the kind of evening that had once brought Belgraders out in droves to enjoy their city's numerous café terraces, the bars loaded down with meats and cheeses and pastry delicacies, to sip *Šljivovica* or *Komovica* or *Klekovača*, the rich cherry brandy Stevan himself favoured. Tonight, however, even without the curfew, Belgraders would have remained in their homes, ashamed of and for the Nazi invader who desecrated and defiled the streets of their beloved city merely by their presence.

Within minutes, however, he became oblivious to his surroundings. He strode along the pavement, eyes straight ahead, hands thrust deep into his trouser pockets, a tall, willowy, pale-faced young man with a mass of black curly hair, a well cultivated moustache and rather soft brown eyes. Somehow, he was thinking, he must come to grips with this violent inner turmoil that was having such a strong physical effect on his body, let alone what it might be doing to his mind.

Perhaps the most shattering thing was that he'd thought he had been cured of what Olga so correctly described were his 'internal contradictions resulting from a bourgeois mind and a bourgeois upbringing'. God knew, he'd certainly tried hard enough to rid himself of all middle-class tendencies and had, he felt certain, convinced himself that although he might not like the means the Party used in its pursuit of what he had come to agree was probably a just world revolution, these means were necessary.

And now to discover that an hour or two spent with an old friend – even though he was well aware that personal friendship, even within the Party, was frowned upon and could lead to deviation, factionalism and various other evils – could bring forth such a surge of decadent nationalistic feelings that had obviously been lying dormant within him waiting to leap out and devour him when he was at his most vulnerable. This left him confused, uncertain, but determined that he must find a way to reconcile the conflicting emotions that not only threatened to tear him apart, but were quite obviously deadly dangerous in his situation.

Unthinkingly, more by blind instinct that anything, he paused at a corner of the street prior to crossing the road and was brought out of his deep reverie by a screech of brakes followed by loud laughter. Glancing around he found that a group of German officers had swept past him in a jeep, leaving him enveloped in a cloud of dust. The vehicle pulled up in front of a devastated building a few hundred yards away. They all poured out, still talking and laughing loudly, and proceeded to take snapshots of the building. Like tourists, he thought incredulously. They are taking photographs of Belgrade in ruins as though they were a bunch of primitive tourists. What insensitive bastards they are. What insensitive bastards! He watched as they piled back into the vehicle and it roared away, then walked on, again deeply lost in thought.

When he returned to his apartment at least it was with a clearer mind. The truth of the matter was that he had already burned his boats. It was impossible now to withdraw from membership of the Party. He must stifle these damned doubts that kept surfacing. He must remember always the ultimate aim of the world revolution the Party was working for; the eventual freeing of mankind from the capitalist yoke that Alex had convinced him was impeding the soul of man from soaring to its destined heights. How irrelevant were his own petty concerns about the means used to achieve this dazzling future. So he had to tell a few lies! What a calamity! He almost writhed with self scorn. Hadn't the church been lying for aeons? *What is wrong with lies when lies can be made into one glorious truth?* Alex had said that and Alex was right. He, Stevan, must make up his mind once and for all to rid himself of these accursed bourgeois prejudices and realize that he as an individual had no right to question the absolute truth of the Party's vision and the Party's aims and the Party's methods.

The decision left him feeling calm and resolute. If only he could do something. Now. Make a gesture that would mean nothing to anyone other than himself, but would perhaps put a seal on his own mind about this irrevocable decision. Gradually an idea presented itself. He walked into the bathroom, removed his shaving gear from the small medicine cabinet, and stood gazing at himself in the mirror. Finally he picked up a small pair of scissors and began snipping away at the edges of his moustache. Then on to the shaving soap and, finally, the razor. Within minutes he was staring at a clean-shaven face flecked with small pieces of white foam. Slowly he wiped his cheeks and mouth with a warm, damp cloth, then burst out laughing. What a ridiculous damned gesture! Could anything be more trite? Yet it was symbolic. If only to himself. How he had cultivated that damned moustache. How he had secretly admired it, revelled in the silky luxuriousness that had so distinguished him from the crowd. Well, he thought wryly, staring intently at the pale, youthful face now reflected in the mirror, that moustache might have been only a small part of the poisonous individualism that had been eating away at his insides. Only a small part. Yet with one gesture he had destroyed it. It was a start. Oh yes indeed. However ridiculous the gesture seemed, it was definitely a start.

* * *

Unaware of the turmoil his visit had aroused in his friend, David slowly made his way to the apartment of Bogdan

Bošković. Of course what Stevan had said made sense. And yet he was unable to shake off the sense of disappointment, the psychological let-down. It had not occurred to him that Stevan would not jump at the chance to take part in what, after all, was the beginning of a national uprising against the fascists. Well, at least Bogdan ... he caught himself just in time ... it was obviously foolish to take anyone for granted in this life or death situation. And, after all, could he blame them? It was their lives he was asking them to put on the line. Although, of course, Bogdan *had* been threatening endless and reckless reprisals against the Germans because of Rachel. His reservations about Bogdan, however, proved to be justified.

'But you must be mad! You could get killed. Don't you know they are hanging Chetnik sympathizers?'

David gave a sigh that came from the depth of his being. 'I simply thought if you were even covertly fighting them it would stop you dwelling on Rachel so much. And by the way, I did ask Ernst Halder if he could find out where she is.' His face screwed up in distaste at the memory. He was not a good actor, and the effort of approaching Halder with a pretence of friendship had affected him badly. 'In any event, although he lectured me for an hour on the so-called greed and perfidy of the Jews, he did agree to see what he could find out.' He hesitated, then went on quickly, 'He called me at the bank only this morning. Claimed she had been sent to Germany. Assured me that conditions within the labour camp there were excellent, but wouldn't give me any other details at all.'

Bogdan stared at him greedily. 'But what else? There must be something else. Was he telling the truth? Do you think he lied?'

'I don't know. Who can tell? I also asked him about Jack Cohen. He claimed there was no record of his having been picked up. I hope to God that's true.'

'But why should he say that if it were not true? I mean, if he were lying, wouldn't he say they had both been sent to Germany?'

'That's what I thought. But, I'm sorry, Bogdan, I really have no opinion about it. How can one believe any of these bastards? But I hope what he told me is true. We can only hope.' He got up to go, but was anxiously waved back into his chair again by Bogdan.

'No, no. Don't leave like this, David. I want you to understand my position. It is just that it is not in my nature to become involved in politics. Movements of any kind. I was involved a little with the communists once, that was enough. No, no. It is not in my nature. Also, I don't mind telling you, not all Germans are that bad, you know. Remember I told you about a Colonel Heidler? I went to speak to him after they took Rachel? He has been very helpful indeed. Assured me that wherever she was she would be well treated. Also, listen to this, David. He is going to help me with the restaurant. I mean with food supplies. You know how expensive food is these days. Well, the colonel has promised–' He stopped in mid-sentence at the expression of icy disgust evident on David's face. 'Well, one has to look after oneself these days. What do you expect me to do? Why *should* I join your movement? What would it achieve? What about our army? What is the army for? Why should I fight if our own soldiers don't fight? I'm a civilian, after all. Just a civilian. I...'

David held his hands up to stem the tide. 'Look, fellow, no one can blame you if you don't want to risk your life. But, my God, do you have to collaborate with them? If they let you have food cheaply it's probably because *they* intend to use your restaurant. You must know that. Good God, man, they took your wife, and if half of the stories being told are true...' He hesitated, shocked into silence by the wild look of hatred that glared out at him from Bogdan's frenzied yellow eyes.

'Don't you say that! Don't you dare say that. You yourself just said a labour camp, excellent conditions. *I* know what people are saying! I tell you the colonel assures me these things are not true. Propaganda spread by the British, that's what he told me.'

A great weariness entered David's soul. 'All right, Bogdan. Very well, fellow. I'll see you around.' He turned, walked out of the small sitting room, along the passage and actually had his hand on the doorknob when Bogdan rushed up behind him.

'Have you been to see Stevan?'

'Does it matter?'

'Yes, yes. It matters.' The small eyes were secret, cunning. 'There is something you should know. Stevan is very close, these days, to the communists. Did you know that? If I were you I wouldn't tell *him* too much about your underground movement. They *are* German allies, you know.'

'Stevan? You lie!' He swung around and lashed out with his fist in a fury of anger, frustration. Luckily for Bogdan he was almost out of reach and the iron knuckles just grazed his chin, sending him reeling against the wall.

'But it's true, David. I tell you it's true!' The words followed him down the hallway, out onto the street and echoed in his dreams that night when he fell into a nightmarish and fitful sleep.

3

'People of Germany! National Socialists! The hour has come. I have decided today to lay the fate and future of the German Reich in the hands of our soldiers. May God help us in this fight.'

The Ristić family listened to the Belgrade announcer's translation of Adolf Hitler's historic words with a mixture of excitement and apprehension. What would it mean for Yugoslavia?

'Do you understand, Aunt?' David asked. 'They have attacked the Soviet Union on the whole front, from the Baltic sea to the Casper Lake. That man *must* be mad. Hitler is a madman, I tell you.'

'But what will it mean for us? Will they leave Yugoslavia now, do you think? Surely they will need every last soldier they have. Surely they will leave?'

'Who can tell? I hope so. But in any event, Aunt, sisters, remember this day, the twenty-second of June 1941. I predict it is the beginning of the end for that madman.'

Was it his imagination? Wishful thinking? Imperceptibly over the next few days the faces of the German invaders in the streets of Belgrade seemed to David to have become grimmer, worried, and showed signs of strain. I wouldn't like to be in their skins today, he would think cheerfully as he passed them in the streets. Not today, not tomorrow, nor any day in the future.

His work with the underground movement in aid of Colonel Mihailović and his Chetniks continued unabated.

Since his encounters with Stevan and Bogdan he had successfully recruited a number of friends and acquaintances into his brigade, enough of them to earn him pleased compliments from the Belgrade command.

Second, Third and Fourth Brigades had also been formed and he had met each brigadier, although they had been introduced to each other by their code names, David's being Pera Savić. Although Major Perić was extremely pleased at the rate at which his brigade was growing, David did not mention that, in fact, he probably could have by now doubled his recruitment. But the bitter memory of the hesitant Stevan and the cowardly Bogdan had made him extremely cautious about whom he should approach. To complete that disappointment, he had also managed to contact his cousin Nikola, and had been disgusted by his point-blank refusal to even consider leaving his comfortable post with General Nedić and his collaborators. Mihailović was crazy, Nikola had said contemptuously. For whom did he think he was fighting anyway? As for his father, the old man would get over it one day. He had no alternative.

David had also come to accept the fact that Stevan had somehow thrown in his lot with the communists. He was not sure how he knew this with such certainty, but he did. It was not only that Stevan had not kept his promise to get in touch. There had been other subtle signs, made obvious by Bogdan's revelation. David handled this deeply bitter awareness by simply refusing to think about it.

There were, however, odd moments when the knowledge sneaked up and hit him from behind, as it were, leaving him feeling frustrated, cold with anger. Such a moment came one day when he stopped to read a proclamation issued by the Yugoslav Communist Party calling upon the people of Yugoslavia to realize that the struggle of the Soviet Union was *their* struggle, calling upon them to take up arms, under communist leadership, against the suddenly vile fascist invaders. *Fascists, who like mad dogs are attacking the Soviet Union, our dear socialist fatherland, our hope and our beacon.*

The 'Second Imperialist War,' he noted ironically, had overnight become the 'Great Fatherland War, the People's War for Freedom and Democracy'. What cynics! What bandits! After a brief, anguished recall of Stevan's inexplicable betrayal, however, he again put his friend out of his mind by the sheer force of his not inconsiderable will.

Hitler's launching of a new front and the local Communist Party's instant volte-face concerning the war and the occupation of Yugoslavia had mercifully, if temporarily, drawn a veil across the trickle of information that had begun to reach Belgrade about the new Croatian government's treatment of the large Serbian population within Bosnia and other areas now under its control. The whole of Serbia had, of course, listened with anger and astonishment to Mile Budak, minister for religion of Croatia's new 'Independent State', as he had declared that: 'We will kill all Jews and Gypsies. The Serbs will be dealt with differently. One-third will be killed, one-third expelled, one-third forcibly converted to the Croat Roman Catholic religion.'

Well, it was a well known fact that the Croat Nazis – the mad *Ustaši* – were totally irresponsible as well as murderous. They had, after all, been trained by the treacherous Italians in the art of assassination, and had cruelly murdered the Serbs' beloved King Alexander. And yet, human beings were human beings. It was impossible to believe that all this was meant to be taken seriously. It was simply bluff and rhetoric.

Until, out of the blue, gruesome confirmation. Dozens of hacked and mutilated bodies began floating down the Sava and Danube rivers, often with brutal and inhuman messages pinned to their bits of clothing. *Serbian meat for King Peter,* some of them said, *destination Belgrade*. And then, unbelievable horror. A group of children playing on the river-bank had found the bodies of a family group that had been hideously mutilated and dressed up as a bridal party before being despatched down the Sava. The children were reported as being hysterical, still under sedation.

Rumours that had begun as an overnight trickle turned into an irrefutable flood. It was well-known that mass arrests of Serbs had been made in Zagreb, Sarajevo, Mostar, Banja Luka, Travnik and Dubrovnik, almost immediately after the *Ustaši* criminal Ante Pavelić had been installed as *Poglavnik*, head of the new Croatian state. Now a stunned Serbian population learned that these mass arrests had turned into mass murders of the most grisly and bestial kind. In some cases, it was understood that even the brutal Germans had seen fit to intervene, so ugly, so unheard of, were the crimes. Was it possible that the Catholic church was standing by and allowing this butchery? Uneasily it was recalled how warmly Archbishop Stepinac, the Roman Catholic archbishop of Zagreb, had welcomed the new order in Croatia, remembered how he had immediately written an open letter to his clergy, referring to the German 'liberation' of Croatia, putting forth his view that: 'these events have fulfilled the long dreamed-of wish of our people'.

David went to his next meeting of the underground movement in the hope that Stan Perić would give some assurance that the grisly reports were somehow wrong, somehow grossly exaggerated, even those that had slipped through from a few concerned Catholic priests, who claimed to be reluctant and horrified witnesses of the butchery being inflicted upon the Serbs. The meeting that evening had initially been arranged to deal with the setting up of a small printing press which it was hoped would enable information to be disseminated more easily between the brigades. When he arrived, however, it was to find such a grim mood prevailing that after glancing around to find he was the last to arrive he had turned to Perić. 'What is it? Is something wrong?'

The major frowned, passed his hand through his thick head of hair, and abruptly handed him a bundle of papers he had been holding. Puzzled, David sat down, again glanced around at the circle of stern faces, and began to read.

It was a . . . report? Reports? Affidavits? No. His mind searched for words, for answers. Why had Perić given him this? Something to do with the Spanish inquisition? It spoke of Catholic priests who…

God no! It must be something … literature? One of Dante's circles of hell? He blinked, shook his head. Women, children, Serbian *women and children, stuck on poles alive … fires built on their bare chests … boiling water poured on live victims before mutilation … eyes dug out of live victims … ears amputated … noses and tongues sliced off … arms … legs … broken … heads spiked … children thrown into fire or scalding water and then…*

He groaned out loud and gazed up at Perić who grimly indicated he must read on.

There were other things, said one anguished affidavit signed by Prvislav Grizogono, Croat Roman Catholic and member of the Yugoslav diplomatic corps, minister to Czechoslovakia, minister to Poland, and addressed to Archbishop Stepinac, that are simply unprintable. These blasphemous atrocities must be stopped!

'Each night,' read yet another affidavit, this one signed by Dr Theodore Lukac, Roman Catholic Croat, director of the district hospital at Mostar, 'Serbs were bound and taken to the Orthodox church at Glina where they were murdered with knives. The corpses floated on the blood and the Ustaši *ghouls boasted gleefully that they "walked in Serbian blood up to their knees".' The killing at Glina, the doctor bleakly added, had gone on for a period of 'one night and eight days'.*

There was more.

Ustaši *surprise attacks on Serbian villages. Children and babies forced to watch as their fathers were tortured, their mothers raped and* then *tortured until, mad with shock and hysteria, it was time for the torture of the children until … merciful death.*

David carefully placed the papers down on the table in front of him. 'I can't,' he muttered. 'I can't … read … any more…'

'Keep reading,' Perić almost hissed. 'It is your duty *as a Serb to read this. Every Serb must read this.'*

He hesitated, then dully picked the reports up again.

They named names.

Names of murderous Ustaši *Catholic priests. Bozidar Bralo, dancing in his cassock around the bodies of tortured Serbs, in one hand a knife, in the other a cross. Nicolas Pilogrvić of Banja Luka, guilty of terrible crimes before God. The Franciscans Joseph Vukelić, Zvonimir Brekalo, Justin Medić, Hinke Prlić, the Jesuits Lipovac and Cvitan, all joining with the* Ustaši *in their savage rampages, blessing them while they committed acts of murder or torture, forgiving them their sins as they danced in Serbian blood. The priest, Dyonisius Juricev from the pulpit of his church: 'It is no longer a sin to kill even a seven-year-old child who violates* Ustaši *laws. Although I wear clerical garb, I must use the machine-gun as well'.*

The priest Bozidar Bralo who took part in the massacre of two hundred and eighty Serbs in Alipasin Most, then danced a 'merry jig' with the Ustaši *monsters around the mutilated corpses. The priests Ilija Tomas and Marko Hovko gleefully joining in with the* Ustaši *in the monstrous murders of five hundred and sixty old men, women and children, each a Serbian soul, in Predilovci and Surmanice, Hercegovina.*

Serbs, Serbs, always Serbs, forced to embrace the Catholic faith or to die a thousand deaths. Hot needles under fingernails, salt poured into gaping wounds, Ustaši *who with guttural shrieks would delight in cutting off ears and noses of their still-living victims, gouging out their eyes to be strung like necklaces around their necks or to be added to the* Poglavnik *Pavelić's gruesome basket of 'Serbian eyes'.*

The concentration camps. Jasenovac, presided over by the pathological Franciscan monk Miroslav Filipovic-Majstorović, known to the briefly-surviving inmates as 'Father Satan'. His murderous assistants, Fathers Brkljanić, Matković, Matijewić, Brekalo, Celina, Kipova . . . the list of names was endless. The Franciscan seminarian Brzica, who boasted that alone one night he had decapitated nearly fourteen hundred Serbs, using his 'special' knife.

'No!' David almost shouted. 'That's enough. It's enough.' He flung the papers down and glared at Perić.

'All right,' the major agreed softly. 'Now we all know. Now we are all aware. Let us discuss our strategy.'

* * *

'No, Aunt,' he said later that evening. He pushed the plate of food she was pressing upon him away. 'I'm sorry. I suppose I ate too much for lunch,' he added lamely as she frowned and shook her head in distress. She knew something was wrong. As always, food was her only remedy. The only way she thought she could help. He rose to his feet and kissed her cheek. 'I'm sorry,' he said, and added, 'I need to catch up on some study, Aunt. I think I'll go to my room.'

Once there he began to pace. He could not rid himself of the terrible pictures the reports had drawn indelibly on his mind. To make matters worse, after an hour of intensive discussion with Perić and the other brigadiers, he had come to realize that there was little he or they could do. As always, the problem was weapons. They had managed to collect some money and buy or steal a few out-of-date machine guns and some ammunition. It had all been despatched to Mihailović's forces in the field. But the *Ustaši* thing! The Croats were by now as heavily armed as the Germans and the Italians, in addition to which they were protected by the criminal occupiers. He flung himself on his bed, arms folded behind his head, gazed up at the ceiling, jumped to his feet again, resumed the restless pacing. Around 11 p.m. his aunt and sisters knocked on his door and bid him goodnight. By midnight he could stand it no more. Damn the curfew! He reached into the back of the wardrobe, pulled out an old raincoat and patted the pocket where he had planted a revolver 'just in case'. A few minutes later he quietly left the apartment. His mind was quite feverish. If he bumped into a German patrol he decided grimly, again patting the comforting weapon in his pocket, so much the worse for them and to hell with the consequences.

It was Kaja who answered the door, Mikhail Ristić hard on her heels, still tying the knot of his old dressing-gown belt, night cap slightly askew on his ruffled hair.

'David! But what is it? Something is wrong? The family?'

'No, no, Aunt. Nothing. It's only, I'm sorry, but...'

'Come in, then. Come quickly.'

'Uncle Mikhail? I have to talk to you. I'm sorry.'

'It's all right, Kaja. It's all right. You could bring us some tea. Perhaps a little brandy.' He gently waved his wife away, took his distraught nephew's arm, led him into his study, pushed him down into a chair, sat opposite him, and listened.

The story tumbled out somewhat incoherently, in fits and starts, in short half-sentences. 'You understand, Uncle? It seems even Mihailović is not able to help. Oh, he has sent what officers he could spare to Bosnia. Captain Bosko Todorović – I'm sure you have heard of his exploits – and another of our bravest men, an officer called Dangić. But the problem is, *always*, lack of arms, ammunition. They have been instructed to organize the remaining Serbs in the area to somehow form into units, to help them defend themselves by any means available, but Uncle! If you could just *read* these reports, affidavits, *everything*. There is no doubt about their authenticity. I can assure you there is no doubt.'

Mikhail raised one hand. 'No need to assure me about these outrages. These terrible outrages. No, no, son. I know all about it. I know,' he paused, cleared his throat. 'I know more than any man should *have* to know about these bloody *Ustaši* ghouls. I had hoped, well, I knew I had to tell you sometime. I was just waiting for the right time. Stupid of me. I should have known you would learn. But I know what you have had on your mind. I know that every morning you get up you could find the bloody Gestapo on your doorstep. You know what they are doing to anyone caught helping Mihailović! I just wanted ... but I should have told you. I should have told you everything.'

'But what is being done? Is anyone doing anything? Our government in exile? Our Allies? Our church?'

'Ah. Our church.' The old man sighed heavily. 'Under siege. Under total siege. Those ghouls, they are burning down all our beautiful churches; often filling them beforehand with innocent Serbian victims. They have embarked upon wholesale torture and murder of our priests. What they did to the Orthodox Metropolitan, David: Desitej, you will remember Desitej. I took you once to meet him. Mad! He has gone mad because of what they did to him.

'Our Bishop Platon of Banja Luka, our Petar Zimonjić, our Bishop Sava. All gone. Murdered! Tortured! Murdered in the most savage, the most...' His eyes filled with tears. He shook his huge head.

David sat quite still. A terrible feeling of doom, of hopelessness, seeped through him. 'The Muslims?' he whispered after a moment. 'Are they?'

'Same as the Croats. A few protest. Most avert their eyes in fear and terror, no doubt. Some, who learned too well from the Turks join with the unspeakable *Ustaši*.'

'Our Allies?' He had recovered his voice and now spoke too loudly.

'They say we exaggerate.'

'Our government in London?'

'Is deeply concerned, but the Croat contingent denies everything.'

'Nedić?'

The old man nodded, brightened imperceptibly. 'Has protested with great vigour to the Germans. Has demanded that Bosnia at least be placed under the authority of the Serbs. Quite obviously, under Nedić, the brutality would stop, at least in that area. Yes, yes, he has protested with great vigour to the Germans. What an irony! Do you understand the irony, David? Our one hope is the Germans. The Germans and the Italians. Our loathed enemies. You have heard of General von Horstenau? The German plenipotentiary for Croatia? You have of course heard of him. He has made it clear to Nedić that he considers the Croat behaviour unacceptable. Bestial and totally unacceptable. "These people", he has written, "these people should not be allowed to govern themselves". He has apparently repeatedly protested, even to Hitler himself, about what he correctly calls these "grotesque atrocities" which he feels are a blot on the "good name" of the German army. What an irony! He fears for the good name of the Germans. One must laugh out loud!'

'And the Italians? You said the Italians?'

'For some time now we have been advising the Jews to make their way to Italian-occupied areas. Many of them are refusing to hand them over to the Germans. Not the fascists, though!' He leaped to his feet in fury. 'That bloody fascist government which has been evicting Serbs from our beloved Kosovo and bringing in all those blasted Albanians. No, no.' He calmed down, took a deep breath, sat down again. 'But the Italian soldiers, you understand? The simple Italian soldiers who, thank God, seem to retain a human heart. They have saved, well, we will never know, thousands, tens of thousands of our Serbian people, our children? They cannot stand to see what those murderous ghouls do to the children. They have, in Banja Luka, Mostar, in Lika, they have saved God knows how many Serbs and Jews. And now, of course, our Serbs are fighting back. At first, it seems, they were so stunned, so disbelieving. Whatever our differences they have always, as you know, considered the Croats to be our Slavic brothers, but now resistance has begun. They took a stand at Gračac; were so effective that the Croat murderers had to send for help to the Italians. The Italian Sharpshooters Regiment arrived and were so revolted by the evidence that lay all around of the torture of women and children that they, well, they turned their guns against their own allies, the Croats. Yes, yes,' his eyes lit up. 'They turned their guns upon the Croats!'

'My God! We must be grateful to the Italians, then? But then, the Vatican! Surely the Vatican. If its own priests are involved...' He hesitated then, remembering the total silence from the Vatican when the Croats had been proclaimed an independent state and immediately announced: *We will kill all Jews and Gypsies. The Serbs will be treated differently. One-third will be killed, one-third forcibly converted to our Catholic religion and one-third will be expelled.*

A look of intense disgust passed over Ristić's face. 'The Vatican,' he said icily, 'has been approached.'

'Yes, yes. And?'

'And these reports, they say, are greatly exaggerated...'

'They don't know, then? They are not informed?'

'They know.' In the dim light from a shaded lamp his uncle's feature's hardened. David had never seen him look so grim.

'But, but, men of God! How can they? They are not of our faith, but surely, they are men of God? How can they allow ... allow...'

'How can they allow their own priests to carry a crucifix in one hand and a murderer's knife in the other?'

'I cannot understand. How can it be explained?'

From the depth of his being Ristić produced a deep sigh. He stood up and moved to take the tray from his wife who had appeared in the doorway. 'Thank you, Kaja. You run along to bed. I'll be with you shortly.'

'David will stay the night? The curfew. It's so dangerous, so...'

'Yes, yes, of course he will stay. You just run along to bed. I'll be with you soon.' He poured a dash of brandy into a cup of steaming tea and handed it to his nephew. 'I don't know, son,' he said quietly. 'Perhaps it is simply that when a church grants itself the power to forgive any sin, then, why, any sin becomes possible. Perhaps it is as simple as that.'

During the silence that followed he sat down again. 'Remember,' he reflected, 'many of those affidavits you saw were from Croats. Men who are just as horrified as some Germans and the Italians. We must remember that.' Another deep sigh then, briskly, 'Well, now drink your tea, son. You will stay here for the rest of the night, of course.'

'And tomorrow? I paced ... paced my room for hours before coming here, Uncle. I felt something in my blood bursting to get out, my skin could hardly contain what I felt, you understand? How do I carry on with this knowledge? How do I contain it?'

'It is the special trial of the Serbs, David. Our skins must contain, deal with, so much history. Sometimes there is simply too much to contain. Our knowledge and our despair literally burst out of our skins. And now! We have this extra burden. But we *must* contain it. *You* must contain it. The safety of your family depends on this.'

'I know,' David said bitterly. 'But *how*. How do I . . . ?'

'You quietly tell yourself, son. You quietly tell yourself that one day, one day, all of these murderers and ghouls will face the rage of the Serbs.' He sprang to his feet, and his towering figure loomed over the room. In the flickering light his face was suddenly that of a terrible avenger. 'Oh, yes. You will remember this, son. One day they will all – *all* – have to face the terrible rage of the Serbs!'

* * *

The Yugoslav Communist Party did not hesitate to spring into action at the call to arms from their socialist fatherland. Instructions from Moscow were brief and to the point. They were to organize partisan detachments immediately in order to alleviate the struggle of the Soviet people.

Easier said than done! However, they were offered spontaneous and brotherly help from the Chetniks already in the field who were under the command of an experienced and courageous leader whose name had already become a legend to the Serbian people.

From his headquarters at the villa in Dedinje from where Stevan had first contacted him after the bombing of Belgrade, Josip Broz listened to a report concerning the growing reputation of the Chetnik leader. 'What kind of man is he?' No one really knew. He dismissed them with an impatient wave of the hand. 'Ask Comrade Matić to find out, then.'

Stevan, who had lately become in turn resentful, amused and finally flattered at the new tendency of the secretary-general to use him as something between a valet and a secretary, set about gathering what information he could about the guerrilla leader, eventually submitting what he had discovered in the form of loosely written notes, which Tito asked him to read aloud.

Colonel Draža Mihailović, Stevan began, was a well-trained military commander who had begun his career at the Belgrade Military Academy. Prior to the outbreak of the 1914–18 war he had received two decorations for acts of bravery during the Serbo-Turkish war. He had distinguished himself further during the Great War, receiving several more decorations including the coveted White Eagle. During the 1920s he had taken courses in the French army after which he had been promoted to staff officer. He had served as professor of tactics at the higher college of the military academy before being appointed military attaché in Sofia and, finally, in Prague.

Mihailović was well-known as a bitter anti-Nazi and anti-fascist. He had anticipated the attack on Yugoslavia by Hitler and had submitted a report to the Yugoslav general staff outlining a course of action which would involve abandoning the indefensible northern frontiers and concentrating forces in the mountains, well out of reach of the formidable German Panzer divisions. His book on guerrilla warfare was considered by many of his fellow officers to be the definitive work on the subject. He was married.

Stevan, nearing the end of his report, looked up. 'Two children,' he added cheerfully, 'if that is relevant.' He waited expectantly for some comment from the communist leader. All he received, however, was a distant look from the pale blue eyes.

'Mmmm . . .' Tito muttered, and lowered his eyes to some papers on his desk in what appeared to be a gesture of dismissal. He looked up again quickly, however, as Stevan rose and prepared to leave with the report still in his hand.

'Leave those notes,' he said sharply. 'Leave them with me.'

* * *

A week or so later Stevan was again with the communist leader who, this time, was unabashedly in the grip of one of the mercurial rages that seized him from time to time. It had to do with the recent and quite extraordinary uprising against the Italians in Montenegro. Led by several Chetnik officers including, Stevan noted with a start, two well known Montenegrin Chetniks who were acquaintances of his, Bajo Stanishić and Captain Pavle Djurishić, the guerrillas had assaulted the Italian garrisons, taking town after town until, a few days later, the occupying army held only Cetinje, Podgorica and Niksić.

Having firmly secured the area, however, the Chetniks had brought in the less experienced communist groups to hold the towns, and had themselves withdrawn to regroup in other areas of the country. Whereupon, Stevan learned from an irate Tito, the partisans, under the leadership of Milovan Djilas, who had been despatched from Belgrade by the secretary-general to take charge of the situation, had immediately tried to replace local authorities with communist sympathizers. Upon encountering fierce and hard-headed resistance to the installation of this 'new regime' by the local population, Djilas had responded with what a tight-lipped Tito referred to as 'harsh, sectarian and incorrect behaviour'. *My God*, Stevan translated to himself, *they have been liquidating the Montenegrin authorities!* Undoubtedly, from Djilas' point of view, this would amount to no more than using violent revolutionary methods to wipe out the bourgeois democratic leadership. However, as Tito had immediately and furiously realized, what was needed at this point in the revolution was the cooperation, not the alienation of the population.

A call had gone out from Montenegro to Mihailović, asking him to 'come back and save us from these communist madmen'. By that time, however, it was too late. The Chetniks were in the grip of their perpetual shortage of arms. The Italians had returned with the help of large sections of the population who claimed to prefer *their* occupation to that of the 'bloody Bolsheviks'. The latter, lacking experience, coordination and the goodwill of the people, had been forced to withdraw.

'Must I be everywhere?' Tito fumed. The experience

taught him something, however. 'I am going to leave Belgrade. Join the troops in the field.' With a lightning change of mood he rubbed his hands together almost gleefully, chuckled, and appeared very pleased with himself at the decision.

Stevan had looked at him eagerly. 'Take me with you?' he almost pleaded. 'Will you take me with you?'

Tito's chuckle deepened into a roar of laughter. He slapped him on the back. 'By God I think I will!' he said. 'Yes, yes. I think I will.'

* * *

The initial exhilaration David had felt upon joining the Belgrade underground movement was fast disappearing beneath the weight of personal problems. Two incidents at the bank also helped heighten the feeling of gloom that had descended upon his usually optimistic nature.

The first came when he reported to work as usual one Monday morning and was told that Djordje Glišić, the colleague who had introduced him to the movement, had been arrested by the Gestapo at his home during the weekend. Glišić's wife had already been in to see Eugene Krstić, who was rushing around, wringing his hands and muttering threats against the German barbarians, almost in tears at the knowledge that there was nothing he could do.

David was overcome by a wave of anxiety and depression, exacerbated by the knowledge that he himself had inducted into the movement several colleagues, including Ivo Hajduk and Bora Borović. The only consolation was that neither he nor Djordje knew which fellow employees the other had drawn into the movement.

It was not only the deep concern about Glišić and his treatment at the hands of the notoriously brutal Gestapo, but the knowledge that his betrayal may have come from someone at the bank. God only knew, there were a number of *Volksdeutschers* who worked there still, but both he and Djordje had been extraordinarily careful about whom they approached. Could it be one of the communists? Surely not since the invasion of the Soviet Union!

As though to prove the latter point, the following Thursday brought the second shock that plunged him into even deeper despair. He had removed a file from his office in order to ask Vera Kojić to complete some statistics for him, and was standing at the side of her desk, explaining what he needed, when two Gestapo officers entered the bank.

There was an immediate hush from employees and customers as they crossed the marble floor and stood for a moment behind the cashiers' counter, letting their eyes roam over the whole scene before insolently pushing open the door leading into the main office. Without the slightest hesitation they strode towards Vera's desk. With a lurch of the stomach David realized this was it! Desperately he looked around for some kind of weapon. Damn them, they weren't going to take *him* that easily. Through the rush of blood pounding in his temples he suddenly understood that they were not even glancing in his direction. Instead they stood in front of the desk looking down at a desperately pale Vera. The older of the two stared at her coldly.

'Are you Vera Kojić?'

'Yes, I am.' A soft, dry whisper.

'What?' A shout!

'Yes, I am Vera Kojić.' She had regained her voice, which was now unnaturally loud.

'Good! You will come with us.'

Without a word she stood up, picked up a few things from her desk, put them in her bag, and then placed herself between the two beefy bullies like an obedient child.

'Wait a minute!' Two pairs of cold blue eyes swung around to observe David. 'This young lady is an employee of the bank. You can't just ...' For the first time his use of fluent German had no effect except, he realized later, to perhaps have saved *him* from further investigation. They simply ignored him and nodded to the by now obviously trembling girl to start walking.

Before she did, however, she turned and gave David a look of such cold contempt that he stood rooted to the spot. *Impossible! She thinks I…* To add to his feeling of despair and indignation, he began to feel that some of his colleagues were looking at him askance. *Do they really think… ?*

Nor was there any cheer to be found at home. Zora, in her last year of medicine and trying to study under less than perfect conditions had become irritable, and had her nose forever poked into a book. His aunt was distracted, vague, and worried about Andjela, who since learning about the betrothal of Vera Nešić and Bane Protić had become by turns tearful and moody. All at a time when he was trying to think of an excuse to move out of the apartment in case, like Djordje, he should eventually be apprehended by the Gestapo.

Then there was Irina. He had, he knew, been neglecting her. Most of his spare time had been spent in recruitment or at meetings for the movement. Between that and the curfew there had been precious little time for anything else.

The following week, however, the news Stan Perić had for him raised his spirits. In eastern Bosnia, under the leadership of small groups of Chetniks, the *Ustaši* were at last being driven back, 'into the dirty, sleazy holes from which they crawled', Perić said with obvious satisfaction. Units had also been formed in Hercegovina, Central and Western Bosnia and Lika. All led by army officers attached to Mihailović, or by local leaders drawn into the Chetnik movement. Perić was also able to assure him that Djordje did not know which employees of the bank David had recruited.

'He doesn't even know for sure whether *you* are with us. Yes, yes. He directed you to us, but that was the end of his involvement, you understand. We do what we can to protect you all,' he added. 'God knows, it is little enough, but yes, we do what we can.'

David returned home in a more cheerful frame of mind

than he had enjoyed all week, to face a new blow that all but stunned him.

After serving him a light lunch in a silence that David, busy with his own thoughts, had been grateful for rather than recognizing his aunt's deep sighs and lack of customary chatter as being a forewarning, she handed him a letter from Andjela who had been spending the past week with relatives some hundred kilometres outside Belgrade. His sister had never reached the village. She had instead, it seemed, eloped. With a man David neither knew nor had ever heard of.

'But of course you know him.' Aunt Draga picked up a table napkin and began fanning herself furiously with it.

'I tell you I don't.'

'Yes, you do. Don't you remember the ball you took Irina to? He was Andjela's escort.'

Vaguely a rather nondescript face rose up in his mind. '*Him*? But...' He searched his memory. 'I thought he was only a student. And a poor one at that. Besides which,' he said loudly, filled with anger, 'I don't even remember his name!'

'Of course you do. It's...' She repeated the name for him. He was in no mood for it to register.

'How can she have done such a stupid thing?' He pushed his chair back from the table and began pacing up and down the room. 'Just to get revenge on Protić, or what? What a stupid thing for her to do.'

His aunt leapt to her niece's defence, which angered her nephew even more. The final word, however, was given by Zora, who had arrived home an hour or so after David.

'I know him. He's a medical student,' she said briefly. He is poor, but reasonably kind, I think. And she had to marry someone. You know all Andjela has ever wanted to do is marry and raise a family. And she's a one man woman. If she can't have Bane Protić does it really matter whom she married? So long as he takes care of her, treats her well, gives her children.'

While her pragmatic comments did not put an end to the

family discussion, they at least quietened things down. They re-read Andjela's letter. She begged them to forgive her for not letting them know her intentions. She had not wanted any fuss. Her new husband might be poor, but surely that was better than someone who placed money above all else, she wrote, in a brave but pathetic allusion to Bane Protić. She also hoped the family would welcome them both when they returned, and would agree to their sharing the apartment. As they all knew, it was impossible now to find inexpensive accommodation in Belgrade.

'There goes my bedroom,' Zora sighed. 'I suppose I'll have to move in with you, Aunt Draga.'

For the first time David began to see a ray of light in the situation. 'Perhaps not,' he said slowly, realizing this was his opportunity to find other accommodation and put a little distance between himself and his family for their own safety. 'Maybe not.'

The following Sunday he accompanied Irina, her mother and aunt, to a service at the Orthodox church that was close to their apartment building, afterwards returning home with them for lunch. Since he had stormed out of the Mirskaia apartment all those weeks ago when Madame Mirskaia had so fulsomely praised the German officers now living next door to them, relations with the three women, even Irina, had become more formal and unnaturally polite.

Today, however, he sensed something in the air. Madame Mirskaia fussed around, anxious that his wine be chilled just so, that he relax in the most comfortable chair, that he take a second helping of the creamy dessert Irina herself had concocted. After coffee Irina nestled at his feet while Marya produced a balalaika and began to delicately strum the rich, mournful Russian melodies that were so close to, yet different, from Serbian music. It lulled them all into a rather pleasurable mood of romantic melancholy. David leaned his head back on the chair and closed his eyes. Madame Mirskaia sighed. Marya placed the balalaika to one side and smiled sadly. Only Irina still seemed restless. After a little while she got up, went into the kitchen, and returned with delicious hot tea served in delicate china cups with thin slices of lemon adding to the spicy smell.

They began to chat about the high cost of food, and then, significantly, about the brutality of the German occupier. Irina had arrived home from shopping in tears only a few days ago, having heard that several dozen Jews had been taken outside Belgrade and shot by the Gestapo.

'Rumours, rumours, Madame sighed. 'Who knows if they are true?'

'With the Gestapo you can believe anything,' David scowled, thinking of Djordje and Vera.

'And your aunt? And your sisters? They are well?' Madame quickly changed the subject.

'As can be expected.' David shifted a little uncomfortably in his chair. Well. They had to be told. Briefly he gave them the news about Andjela.

Sensing that he was not happy about his sister's impulsive act, the two older women made soft, noncommittal remarks. Irina took his hand and held it against her cheek.

'But you say,' Madame said thoughtfully, 'that they will be living with your family?'

David nodded. 'They will have the large room Zora and Andjela have shared. Zora can have mine. As a matter of fact I've been thinking about moving out, anyway. I have been looking for a small apartment, a room even, closer to the bank,' he added lamely, aware that he could not really live much closer to his place of work than he already was.

It was then that he discovered what was on the minds of the two older Russian women. Irina had told them of the decision to postpone their wedding plans until they could see further into the country's future, particularly because with the sky-high cost of food and the difficulty in finding decent apartments in Belgrade since the occupation, David's savings account would soon disappear and with it their dream of opening a school together.

Madame Mirskaia now suggested that they set their wedding date. She and Marya had been talking things over. They were sure they could get a pass from the German authorities that would allow them to travel to Dalmatia where they had a friend living on the Adriatic coast. They could stay there for two or three months during which time David and Irina could have the apartment to themselves. And when they *did* return well, would it be so different for David, living as he had been with three women, asked Madame a little archly?

David stared at them, as startled as Irina appeared to be. After a moment she began to laugh. 'Why Mamoushka,' she said, 'I believe you are trying to marry me off.'

There were laughing protests, some jokes. But by the time David left it had been agreed that he and Irina would discuss the suggestion alone together some time the following week. The thing that stayed uppermost in his mind as he slowly walked home was Irina's aunt leaning over to say softly, 'Her mother and I are anxious about her, David. She has been having that nightmare again. About the train, you remember? We thought it had stopped after that trip to Macedonia with you and Zora, but...' She had broken off with a graceful shrug of her shoulders as Irina and her mother returned from the kitchen where they had taken the tea things.

Darling, sweet little Irina. He felt a surge of tenderness towards her, an intense longing to relive the early days of their courtship, before this damned war had raised so many barriers to their happiness. Her mother and aunt were obviously both worried about her, anxious that her future be secured, that she settle down with someone responsible who would take care of her. Both women had been so kind to him today, so careful not to offend. They must both be elated by Hitler's steady advance into their beloved Russia, must hope this meant they could one day return to the home they loved so dearly. Could he blame them for that? In any event they had said not a word about it today, and had made it clear how thoroughly they condemned the brutal occupation of *his* country.

He had reached his apartment building, ran quickly up the stairs, and let himself in, pleased to find that his aunt and Zora had not yet returned from their visit to some nearby friends. He needed time to be alone, to think. The window of his bedroom was half open, and from the student's home the Germans were blaring out that damned song they played over and over, 'Lili Marlene'. Had no one composed any other song for them? Abruptly he slammed the window shut and lay back on his bed, arms clasped behind his head, gazing up at the ceiling.

What if he should withdraw from the Mihailović movement? A fairly simple thing to do. He could explain to Stan Perić that he wanted to get married, that he could not in all conscience subject his wife to the anguish Mrs Glišić had been put through. He frowned, thinking about the way Lina Glišić had been haunting the bank since her husband's arrest. A small, dark woman with fine eyes and olive skin she seemed unable to accept the fact that such an august institution as the State Mortgage Bank could have no power over the fate of its employees. She had, in fact, been driving Eugene Krstić out of his mind. He had, finally, asked David to accompany him to Gestapo headquarters, to try to find out what had happened not only to Glišić and Vera Kojić, but to other Jewish and communist employees who, like them had been taken away for no reason anyone could see. The trip had, of course, proved fruitless. The following day David had of his own accord again gone to see Ernst Halder, pointing out that the people who were disappearing in such large numbers from the bank were, in fact, Halder's ex-colleagues. The SS man had, however, turned sullen, threatening even; had hinted that David's interest in the fate of 'Jews, communists and other subversives' could cause him a great deal of difficulty. In which case, Halder made it clear, David could most certainly *not* rely on his further friendship. 'You always showed such an interest in our language. I thought you were our friend,' he scolded, shaking his head more in sorrow than anger.

Bastard! David thought now as he had then. The point was, should he stay in the movement? He had not only himself to think about. Should he be picked up there would most certainly be repercussions for his family. And if he married Irina now ... but, no. Impossible! How could he withdraw after having recruited so many men himself? Many of them married. Some with small children.

On the other hand, he thought wryly if not really seriously, there was the point of view offered by Bogdan Bošković. David had found him waiting outside the bank a few days after their row, and Bogdan had insisted that they lunch together. Sitting in a small out of the way restaurant on Bitoljska Street, David had listened as Bošković delivered something that was part lecture, part self-justification. 'You are not trying to understand my viewpoint,' he whined. 'But let me just ask you this, David. For whom and for what are you asking me to risk my life? *Pour qui et pour quoi?* as the French wisely say. Our people? Well, the Germans are not treating them so badly, you know. So long as they stay out of trouble. And in any event, since when have the people of *any* country been grateful to those who die for them? Take a look at history. It's the *winners* they are grateful to! And at this stage of the war, who is to know who will be the winners? The way I look at it, if it is the Germans – and at this point they certainly appear to be – then I can only do both myself and Rachel good by remaining on good terms with them. If, on the other hand the British, say, should prevail, then there is nothing to stop me from becoming friendly with *them*. But why should I fight for them now? After all, you know, they are the ones behind that damned putsch, the one that caused all of this. That's a well known fact.

'Or are you telling me I should fight for our government? The one that landed us all in this soup and then ran away to its sponsors and left us all in the lurch? I tell you, David, it does not make sense what you are doing. What you are asking *me* to do. It does not make sense.'

'It may not make sense to you, Bogdan, but you mention people being grateful only to the winners of a war. Perhaps you are right, but I think if you look a little closer at history you will find they are far from grateful to people they perceive to have been collaborators. And you, fellow, are dangerously close to–'

'A matter of timing, David. You see, one must simply know how to see the writing on the wall. If one sees the Germans, for instance, beginning to lose, then one perhaps slips out of Belgrade, lies low for a little while, then joins the winning force. As for the carnage that always follows anyone's victory, it is my firm belief that as many innocent fellows die as do true collaborators. More, in fact. They are not so *aware*, you see, of how the world operates.'

David pushed his plate away, sat back in his chair, swore fluently for several seconds, and then burst out laughing. 'My God, fellow,' he said, 'I knew you were always ... but I swear I never realized just how opportunist ... just how opportunistic you really are.' He shook his head. 'You are so bad I can't even get really angry with you.'

'Opportunistic?' Bogdan was genuinely hurt. 'How can you say that? No, no. I am not an opportunist. I am a *survivor*. I intend to survive. What else do we have in this world other than our lives?' Oddly, his long, greyish-coloured face took on a look that was close to dignity. 'My philosophy, you see, is that it is our duty to preserve the life we have been given. In all honesty, David, if you truly think about that, can you disagree?'

'I suppose not,' David said slowly, '*if* you are prepared to pay the price.'

'Price? What price?'

'The price, fellow, of living inside one's skin. That is the price!'

The bedroom had become extremely warm and stuffy. Getting up from his bed David reopened the window with a sigh. What a choice! Listen to that blasted song for the thousandth time, or stifle. Yawning, he lay down again. The next thing he knew he had awakened to find his aunt fussing over him. 'The window wide open and no cover over you. You will catch your death of a cold,' she scolded.

At least he felt refreshed. So far as his problems were concerned he would talk to Irina about setting a wedding date. He had arranged to pick her up after work on Wednesday and take her to lunch. Once that decision was made he would face each problem as it arose. Following his still grumbling aunt into the kitchen, he switched on the radio and then suddenly grabbed her around her ample waist and began to dance comically to the grimly martial music that blared forth. Drawn by the noise, Zora joined them and began to giggle at the sight of her struggling aunt who, as always, was caught between indignation and pleasure. Her laughter proved infectious. Soon the three of them were laughing together until the tears came. Finally, Aunt Draga, wiping away at her eyes with her apron, produced three mugs of coffee. They sat around the kitchen table and reminisced about the happy past.

* * *

Tito had been as good as his word.

By September Stevan had left his apartment in Olga's hands and had joined the communist leader at his headquarters in the mountain hamlet of Stolice in central Serbia. The extent of the Chetnik guerrilla operations had come as a surprise. In the short time the Mihailović insurgents had begun to organize, only the larger towns remained in the hands of the Germans within Serbia. The villages and hamlets were firmly controlled by the Chetniks, who were gradually drawing small groups of partisans into the action. A few communists had already helped the Chetniks in acts of sabotage such as derailing trains, ambushing enemy convoys and blowing up bridges and ammunition dumps.

With only the slightest mental hesitation, Stevan assisted Tito in drafting a highly exaggerated message for Moscow concerning communist participation in the action initiated by the Chetniks. 'Partisan operations in Serbia,' it said, 'are assuming to an ever greater extent the character of a national uprising. The hamlets and villages are all in the hands of the partisans'. This fulsome piece of propaganda having been disposed of, the message got down to more accurate and urgent business: 'Our great need is for arms – please let us know if you can supply us with arms'.

Later, Stevan lit a cigarette and went for a stroll through the tiny village, taking in deep breaths of the glorious mountain air. He passed by a small group of comrades who had gathered near the square, and felt a sharp stab of loneliness as they stopped talking and nodded a polite greeting to him, waiting until he was well past before resuming their conversation. Resentment of the fact that he, a comparative newcomer to the Party, should be favoured with such a close relationship with Tito was, he supposed, natural enough. It certainly had not worried him when he was in Belgrade. Had been, rather, a source of amusement. Here in this isolated mountain village, however, things were different.

In fact, although the partisan leader seemed to enjoy having him around, and certainly made use of whatever talents he had, either in writing propaganda, taking notes, or digging out facts and figures for him, Stevan had become aware that Tito was not a man who would or could get close to anyone. Lately, in fact, he had taken to treating the younger man much as an impatient priest might an obedient but slightly irritating acolyte.

He reached the outskirts of the village and stood there for a moment finishing his cigarette. If only Tito would agree to at least let Alex Miletić join them. Thinking of the way Olga's brother had approached him, so humbly, to ask whether he could get Tito's permission for him to accompany them to the mountains, Stevan felt a stab of remorse. God only knew, Alex was a far better communist than he, Stevan, would ever be. And yet Tito, when Stevan had approached him, had shown no inclination to grant the big man's wish. 'We need people in Belgrade,' he had said vaguely, and had given an impatient gesture of dismissal when Stevan had tried to pursue the subject.

With a deep sigh he ground out the butt of his cigarette. Best not to think about these things. Better to turn in, have an early night. Tomorrow he was scheduled to accompany the Secretary-General on what he had referred to as an 'important' trip. God only knew what that meant!

Breakfast was early. Bread and cheese and bitter coffee. He stood around for a couple of hours in the chill mountain air, stamping his feet, rubbing his hands, exchanging a few words with the dozen or so other comrades gathered in a group waiting for Tito. Who, when he did finally appear, offered no explanation for the delay. But at least Stevan finally discovered where they were going.

'To see that army fellow.' Tito said shortly. It took a moment for Stevan to comprehend, and then his heart began to beat rapidly. My God! We are going to see the legend! He took a deep breath to calm himself. Best to make sure. 'You mean, he hesitated, then began again carefully. 'We are going to Western Serbia, then?'

'Yes, yes.' Tito waved an impatient hand. 'To the village of Struganik. To see that fellow Mihailović.'

* * *

Belgrade! In ruins, but still his city, a city like no other; a city that he loved dearly. David Ristić walked through its torn streets in something of a daze. There had been the urgent summons from Stan Perić. The hurried visit to the third floor apartment on Zeleni Venac Street. Djordje Glišić, he had learned, was dead. He had died with great courage, revealing nothing under torture, the major had said. Yet someone within the movement, low and treacherous as a snake, had been giving vital information to the special section of the Gestapo that had been set up to deal with the Mihailović threat. Several staff officers had been arrested, one of whom had been shot, the others deported to concentration camps in Germany. There had been a devastating round up of Mihailović sympathizers, many of whom were now in concentration camps at Banjica and Dedinje and Sajmiste. Brigadiers of the Second and Third Brigades and the wild-eyed young leader of the Fourth, had been rounded up and Perić was still awaiting news of their fate.

Tortured? Shot? In a concentration camp in Yugoslavia or Germany? He would eventually find out. He had his sources. For now the problem was David. God only knows how they missed you, Perić said, but they could catch up with you at any moment. We have to get you out of Belgrade. Into the mountains.

Catapulted into a situation over which he had no control, David walked the city streets until he had calmed down. His mind, now icy cold, took over. The personal problems – Irina, his sister Andjela, even details connected with his underground brigade were all swept away by an onrushing historical tide. If he had to leave Belgrade for an indefinite period there were things that had to be done. Methodically, he set about doing them.

A brief scene with the moist-eyed Eugene Krstić, who had long ago, it seemed, guessed. The warm and emotional shake of the hand. The rush to put together a salary package containing every conceivable penny the State Mortgage Bank could owe him for every last hour's work, for holiday pay, for future holiday pay. Whatever was in the envelope might have to last his Aunt Draga for a long time.

An affectionate, loving goodbye to an aunt rigid with worry, starry-eyed with pride. The warm embrace from Zora, who had dissolved into tears, the biting tongue silenced.

The tearing scene with Irina. Beautiful little Irina on her knees, her arms clasped around his legs, her cheeks pressed against his thigh, begging him not to leave her, at least to take her with him. She could not face this cruel life without him. She would die! The piercing ache of his heart at her tears. The whispered exhortations for her to be brave. She must never give up. He would be back. Perhaps even after a few weeks when this present crisis had passed. She must believe that. He would come back to Belgrade for her one day.

And now this hurried walk to the designated spot where he would be picked up by motorbike and taken into the mountains.

'And my destination?' he had remembered to ask the urgently pressed Major Perić.

'Destination? Why, to our headquarters. To our headquarters in Ravna Gora.'

4

The legend turned out to be something different from the larger than life figure Stevan had expected.

Sitting well on the outskirts of Tito's group of advisers as he was, he had an excellent opportunity to observe the Chetnik leader. Slightly built, but wiry, with a black beard that half hid a pleasant, rather shy-looking and scholarly face, the 'army fellow' facing the communist leader across the large table looked, in fact, more like an itinerant professor than the Balkan Eagle, the Robin Hood of Serbia, the White Hope of the Allies in the Balkans, as he was being hailed in the world's press.

The two leaders were now eyeing each other cautiously. Their initial negotiations, however, had been cordial. Both shared similar problems, the main one being the sparsity of arms. An agreement had been reached on collaboration in the field and the division of all arms taken during action by either side against the enemy.

Courteously, but firmly, the colonel now broached a problem that had been brought to his attention by several villages. It seemed that partisan groups had been entering certain areas, evicting local authorities by force, and setting up new bodies called National Liberation Committees, under the leadership of members of the Communist Party. He pointed out that his own officers had been instructed that they must at all times respect the local autonomy of the municipal authorities. It was not only a matter of this being the right thing to do, but, quite obviously, no guerrilla movement could survive for long without the cooperation of the population, especially in the country areas. He therefore suggested that in future the local autonomy of all administrative and political functions in the villages and towns be respected by both sides. Personally, other than hoping that after the war a plebiscite would be held in the democratic tradition of the people with respect to the future of the country, he entertained no political ambitions. He was simply an army officer who considered the most pressing issue facing the country at the moment to be the eviction of the enemy from all areas of Yugoslavia.

Another matter he had been asked by village representatives to deal with was that of recruitment. Complaints had also been received that young men were being forced to join communist units against their will. He himself had been accepting volunteers only. He hoped agreement could be reached that in future any young men approached should be given three options. They could refrain from volunteering if they wished, or they could be offered the choice of joining either a Chetnik or a communist group.

Rather to Stevan's surprise, and to the colonel's obvious relief, Tito accepted both suggestions quite readily. It appeared he had something else on his mind. It was his understanding that the Chetniks now occupied the township of Uzice in the West Morava Valley. Uzice not only connected the rail and road communications of Western Serbia, but he believed there was a small munitions factory there. He felt this would be an ideal site for his own headquarters. It would also in his opinion be a more suitable locale for coordinating his own actions with that of Colonel Mihailović. Any munitions produced in the factory would, of course, be equally shared with the Chetniks.

The tension that had been evident on the colonel's face during the lecture he had so sternly delivered disappeared. A man was suddenly revealed who much preferred agreement and conciliation. Uzice? Of course. He would be delighted to cooperate in any way possible. A lively discussion followed concerning the transfer of the town to the communists before the talk again took on a tone of ruefulness concerning their mutual lack of arms.

Would it not be possible, Tito asked, for the colonel to make an approach to General Nedić, who had recently been appointed prime minister by the Germans, and who must surely have access to a large assortment of arms and ammunition? It was his understanding that the attitude of General Nedić towards the occupation was at the best ambivalent. Certainly the Germans did not trust him as fully as they did his counterpart in Zagreb, Ante Pavelić. Perhaps Nedić would not be adverse to...

He hesitated as Mihailović began to laugh, to shake his head. Behind the steel-rimmed glasses his blue eyes were dancing merrily. Still chuckling, he began to explain. It seemed that when General Nedić was minister for war under the previous government, Colonel Mihailović had been something of a thorn in the general's side. While Nedić did in all probability resent the German occupation of his country, he had certainly not been averse to fascist theories, and had entertained the belief that the route Yugoslavia should take should be that of neutrality with the Germans. These ideas had, of course, clashed with those of Mihailović, who had, in fact, mistrusted and disliked the Germans since the First World War. What could you think about people who displayed such reckless disregard for human life? And their expansionist aims had been clear to him for many years. It was for that reason that he had spoken and written about the need for modernization of the Yugoslav army, and had predicted the need for guerrilla warfare should the Germans invade. This outspokenness had, in fact, led to Nedić's placing him under house detention several times. He had also incurred the general's wrath by forbidding anyone under his command to attend any kind of pro-fascist meetings, an action that had led to his being placed under arrest and again held in detention for a further ten days.

'So you see,' he chuckled, 'even if the general does have

arms to spare, I'm afraid I would be the last man to have access to them.'

The meeting finished shortly afterwards in a cordial and friendly atmosphere. Tito was obviously delighted at the concession he had received with regard to Uzice. The Chetnik leader, too, seemed well pleased at the assurances he had received of mutual cooperation.

It was to be several days before Stevan had a chance to gauge the communist leader's reaction to the colonel. Once returned to Stolice, Tito had been busy with meetings with Central Committee members who had come, at his request, from all over the country in order to take part in a policy conference. Stevan had taken notes at some of the meetings while Zdenka, an attractive but shrewish young comrade whom he had come to realize was to the communist leader far more than her designated title of 'secretary' would indicate, handled others.

He had just finished clarifying some of his notes with Tito concerning the decision that had been made not only to set up separate partisan commands in Bosnia, Croatia, Hercegovina, Slovenia and Montenegro, but to evict or liquidate local authorities and establish National Liberation Committees under communist leadership wherever possible, in direct abrogation of the agreement reached with the Chetnik leader. The decision, made at a meeting Stevan had attended, had been clear enough. The fact that he found it necessary to confirm it with Tito, he thought with a sigh, was another indication that he was still indulging himself in that abstract luxury of the bourgeoisie, an individual conscience. Closing his notebook, he was about to leave when, as though reading his thoughts, Tito gave him a shrewd look and asked what he had thought of 'that Chetnik fellow'.

'Why,' he said, taken by surprise, 'I thought he was a very decent kind of man. Very decent.' The thought followed immediately: *My God! What made me say that? He's not going to like that*. 'What did *you* think of him?' he asked quickly.

The secretary-general remained silent for so long that Stevan decided he had either not heard his question, or was choosing to ignore it. It came as something of a shock when Tito suddenly looked up from his desk and glared at him furiously.

'He's supposed to have all those medals,' he replied loudly. 'If he has all those medals, why wasn't he wearing them?' Angrily he began to forage amongst some papers. Startled by his explosive vehemence, Stevan sat quite still, unable to draw his eyes away from the communist leader's hands, which were visibly trembling.

A week later they were in Uzice. As promised by Mihailović, the Chetnik unit had evacuated the township, handing the munitions factory and even a small printing press over to the partisans. One of Stevan's first tasks had been to find and set up a suitably impressive location for Tito's headquarters, which he did at the local bank, over the vociferous protests of management. Tito seemed pleased with the bank's offices and was, in fact, more relaxed and at ease than he had been since the decision had been made to leave Stolice.

Even Zdenka the shrew seemed more amiable, Stevan thought, as he answered a summons from the communist leader late one afternoon. At least she did not snap his head off when he appeared at the bank at the appointed time, but merely scowled and nodded for him to go in.

Tito was all smiles. Elements of the township's local government who had loudly protested against the complete takeover of Uzice by the communists, claiming that this was not what the Chetniks had intended to happen, had been summarily dealt with that morning by the newly set up 'people's court'. Labelled collaborators and traitors, the more 'dangerous' elements had already faced a firing squad and it was anticipated there would be no more stirring up of the local population against their communist liberators.

Getting up from his desk, Tito began pacing up and down, rubbing his hands together, discussing surrounding areas where it was intended to set up further National Liberation Committees, finally pausing to stand at the window where he gazed out at the main street before turning back to Stevan who had been sitting quietly in front of his desk.

'And so, Comrade Matić! Now that everything here is settled, how would you like to make a short trip to Belgrade?'

'Belgrade?' Stevan stared at him uncomprehendingly.

Tito returned to his desk and sat down. 'I've been thinking about that request of yours. To invite your friend – what was his name, Miletić? – to join us here. You say his wife is a nurse?'

'Alex? Jelena? She's not a certified nurse, no, but she has done voluntary work at the Belgrade hospital.'

Tito nodded absentmindedly. He picked up a ruler and began to turn it over in his hands. 'I can foresee the day when we will be needing engineers. You said he was an engineer?'

Stevan leaned forward eagerly. 'One of the best. And I know they would both be–'

'Useful. Yes, yes. I can see where they might both be extremely useful.'

Stevan had been about to say that they would both be ecstatic at the thought of joining the partisans in the field, but no matter. He leaned forward again, and again was forestalled.

'And then there was that young woman you introduced me to. Damned attractive.'

'Olga. Alex's sister.' A feeling of joy began to pulsate through his veins. God! How he had longed . . .

'Intelligent, too, I noticed. Don't think I didn't notice that.' Tito nodded thoughtfully. 'I've been thinking. A woman like that. She could be very useful to us in Belgrade. We could do with someone like that in Belgrade.'

The excitement receded. Stevan felt flat, empty. 'I don't see how Olga could do much for us in Belgrade,' he answered slowly.

'But you said she speaks foreign languages?'

Stevan nodded. 'English, French, German. She has travelled quite extensively. So she was in a position to perfect them, you see.'

'And you said she has some German officers billeted in her house?'

Again he nodded, puzzled, uncertain.

'Well then all the easier for her to make friends with one of them. She could get us information about their troop movements, and equally important about Chetnik movements. And she can ascertain what they know about *us*. Her help could be invaluable. Invaluable!'

'I . . . see.'

'So that's settled! You can leave for Belgrade first thing in the morning. You can take your time. No need to rush back. It might take a few days to arrange things. For your friend Alex and his wife, I mean. They will return with you, of course. He stood up to indicate the interview was at an end and held out his hand.

'I probably won't see you before you leave. But drop in here early tomorrow morning. Zdenka will have some instructions for you to pass on to . . . what was her name? Olga! Yes, yes. Zdenka will give you the instructions.'

Quite calmly Stevan allowed himself to be dismissed. Quite calmly he walked out onto the main street and nodded to a small group of comrades who were gathered around a motorcycle one of them had 'requisitioned' from a local merchant. They were arguing and joking about who should be the first to try it out. Stevan hesitated for only a moment, then pushed his way through them, threw his leg over the saddle and before they could even grasp his intent had roared away in a cloud of dust, leaving them cursing and yelling loudly as they were forced to leap out of his way. Their indignant cries faded into the background. Blindly, he roared along the main street, then made a sharp turn left. Through a haze of red he heard more shouting voices, and automatically swerved to avoid a horse and cart. Images floated through his mind. People stopping to stare. People waving and calling out. Everything seemed to be happening very slowly. A kind of slow motion.

Some time later he found himself in the grounds of the local high school. He circled slowly around the large area, then something seemed to click in his mind. It was here the comrades had set up a small gymnasium for themselves. A little later he was in the locker room, shrugging himself out of his light, woollen jacket. Then he found himself in the deserted gym standing in front of the punching bag. Quite tenderly he began to jab away at it. Presently an image imprinted itself, though imperfectly, upon the bag. It was the face of a man. Broad, good-looking, blue-eyed. A respectable, middle-aged bourgeois face that somehow inspired confidence.

Bastard! The gentle jabs became faster and turned vicious. He was punching now in a blind rage. Who in the hell do you think you are? *And you said she has some German officers billeted in her house? Well then all the easier for her to make friends with one of them.* Just like that! If he wanted some kind of bloody Mata Hari in Belgrade, why not send that shrewish little bitch, Zdenka! But, of course, that might leave Comrade Josip Broz without one of the vital comforts of home, might it not? He punched at the blandly smiling face with all his might. Who did this Croatian bandit think he was, anyway? A peasant! A peasant who had risen in life to the lofty heights of a metalworker. Engineer, shit! Whom did he think he was fooling, anyway?

The intense emotion that had raged inside him subsided quite suddenly and with it went the violent burst of energy, leaving him feeling so weak that he collapsed against the punching bag, leaned his face against it, feeling the sweat mingle with the tears of rage coursing down his cheeks.

Drained, he slowly dressed, walked out into the yard and remounted the motorcycle. He rode back to town and returned it to its previous 'owner'. The comrade who lay claim to it took one look at his face and accepted it back without a word.

The next morning he found he could even smile at his

own reaction. So Comrade Stevan had had a tantrum! Interesting. And, in any event, it had all been over nothing, really. He would, of course, relay Tito's message to Olga. He could imagine her reaction! How she loathed those Germans who had intruded into her home. He made a sudden vow. Whatever biting words Olga hurled at him would be returned word for bitter word to the secretary-general. There would be no glossing over. Broz would find out for himself the reaction of an intelligent upper-class Serbian woman to his dirty little plans.

With a jaunty step he entered the bank building and accepted the envelope Zdenka held out to him with an ironic smile. He really could hardly wait to return with Olga's reply!

* * *

'Welcome to Ravna Gora, Lieutenant Ristić.' The colonel held out his hand. 'I understand you are the nephew of Mikhail Ristić!'

'That's right, sir.' David saluted, gave a slight bow and accepted the proffered hand.

'A fine patriot. I have long been an admirer of his.'

'If I may say so, sir, he is very proud of what you are doing.'

Mihailović nodded, gestured towards a chair and returned behind the desk that had been set up for him in the village meeting hall. 'So. You had to leave Belgrade in rather a rush?'

'I'm afraid so, sir.' David hesitated, then plunged on, aware that he might not have too many chances to speak personally to the Chetnik leader. 'I'm still rather worried about the rest of my brigade. I know Major Perić said that a new brigadier would be appointed, that the men were in no immediate danger, but . . .'

'I understand.' The colonel nodded sympathetically. 'Let me assure you, lieutenant, if Major Perić said that, then there is indeed nothing to worry about. For the moment, in any event.'

'Thank you, sir.'

'I also understand you have requested an immediate posting to one of our units in the field.'

'If it is possible, colonel. You see,' he hesitated, then rushed on, encouraged by the keen, sympathetic attention Mihailović was giving him. 'I suppose it is all the inaction in Belgrade. Just waiting, worrying. I feel the need to move. I feel the need to be involved in some action.'

'I'm sure your wish will be granted.' For a brief moment the blue eyes behind the glasses glinted merrily. 'Perhaps more quickly than you realize. However, before we give you a posting, there is one small task I would like you to perform for me.'

He went on to explain, not without an expression of pride, that he had received word from the British that they were sending a special mission to Ravna Gora, presumably to discuss coordination of action against the Axis forces. The officers were being despatched via a British submarine to the southern Adriatic coast of Montenegro. 'They should be arriving any time now,' Mihailović said. 'Of course, I understand the British officer concerned is to be accompanied by two Serbian general staff officers from London, but I believe you speak English?' As David nodded, he went on. 'Then I would prefer you to stay with us here at headquarters – at least until we are quite sure there will be no difficulties understanding each other.' He gave a slight smile that developed into a chuckle. 'Who knows, lieutenant, we might even be able to show you a little action before they arrive.'

That night David discovered the meaning behind that somewhat mischievous chuckle.

Tossing and turning restlessly in the quarters he was sharing with a dozen other officers in the village school, he was brought sharply awake by the sound of sporadic gunfire coming from the outskirts of the village.

He was on his feet in an instant, as were the other officers. 'Oh Christ,' exploded the tough Serbian lieutenant who had spent the evening showing David the ropes. 'Those German bastards. What I'd give for a decent night's sleep in one place.' Muttering and cursing with the rest of them, David was further infuriated to discover that it was not possible to stay and fight.

'Not enough ammunition,' Lieutenant Mirković explained briefly. 'The guard will hold them for as long as possible, then try to get away before dawn to join us. Here, come along, quickly!'

The evacuation that evening went smoothly. The bearded Chetniks had perfected the art of silently fading into the mountains, blending in with the trees. By the following morning they were ensconced in another village. The villagers were warmly welcoming, especially towards Mihailović, whom they obviously adored. Old women rushed out with small bouquets of flowers or baskets of fruit or cheese. The children danced around him calling out excitedly '*Čiča*! *Čiča* is here.' The Serbian term, roughly meaning 'good old man' was a little premature for the middle-aged colonel, David reflected with some amusement, but he apparently enjoyed it. Laughing and teasing, he held out his hands to them all, obviously delighted with the reception. It was a village that had offered them hospitality several times before and in no time a makeshift office had been set up for him, and quarters apportioned out to the officers and men.

David sat with Lieutenant Mirković around a small fire and waited ravenously for his share of the aromatic bacon being cooked by a tiny Montenegrin called Toma. Over a heaped plate of bacon and bread he listened as Mirković explained that the events of the previous night were par for the course. Gulping down a mug of bitter black coffee he learned that, in fact, only a few nights previously Mihailović himself had nearly been captured. He had insisted upon returning to a village to retrieve some documents listing various villages that had offered help to the Chetniks and had escaped by the skin of his teeth when the enterprising villagers had simply buried him beneath a mound of leaves. The lieutenant finished the story, then belched loudly, causing the cook Toma to glance at David and give a comical shrug before scurrying off with his large frying pan.

During the following week they were under constant attack, and were constantly on the move. The Germans seemed always on the verge of capturing the Chetnik leader, and were often but two paces behind. His genius in eluding them and then using his small supply of arms and ammunition to cause maximum damage to their supply lines or communication systems infuriated them.

Two representatives of the British mission did finally arrive after a rugged trip through the rough and rocky mountains of Montenegro. David was to find that his services as an interpreter were not, after all, required. The mission was, in fact, a joint endeavour of both the Yugoslav government in exile and the British government. One of the officers, a Major Lalatović, was a Serb. The British officer, Captain Hudson, spoke the Serbo-Croat language.

David was present, however, when Colonel Mihailović exploded in an uncharacteristic burst of anger after discovering that the party had first of all made contact with Tito's partisans; that two members of the group had stayed with the communists in order to monitor their activities; and that the intention of the mission was to press him to undertake large-scale operations and to coordinate such operations with the partisans.

With an obvious effort he then swallowed his irritation and began to explain patiently that the country was occupied by over twenty fresh and well-equipped enemy divisions. Not only Germans, but Italians, Hungarians, Albanians, Croatians, Bulgarians and so on, plus several specialized SS divisions, police units, and last but certainly not least the Gestapo, with its intelligence units that were spread throughout the country. To undertake large-scale operations against all these enemy forces was, quite simply, impossible, given the lack of arms, ammunition, medical supplies and even something as basic as uniforms or the warm clothing and footwear that would be so necessary with winter looming.

So far as the partisans were concerned, a further meeting with the communist leader, a man who called himself Tito, had been arranged. Here, too, there were many difficulties, the main one being that the partisans had tended to break most of the commitments they had made during the first meeting. Mihailović carefully explained that he had been forced to meet with several delegations from villages the partisans had plundered. Not only that, but in many instances they had liquidated local authorities and set up something they called National Liberation committees under communist leadership. He pointed out that it was his own policy to insist that his people scrupulously pay for any food or other goods received from villages or townships they entered and to abide by the rules of the local authorities. He felt it was hardly necessary to point out the difficulties of trying to coordinate action with a group whose tactics were so dissimilar to his own.

In any event, he said with a sigh, he would again try to clear the problems up with Tito. He considered it essential that there be some coordination between the two groups, if only because the enemy was threatening to institute severe reprisals against the population for any Germans killed or wounded by any of the guerrilla forces. Protection of the people must, of course, be given first priority. It was more essential than ever that all action taken should be carefully considered with regard to its effectiveness in immobilizing enemy forces. Emphasis should continue to be placed upon acts of sabotage, destruction of communications and war supply depots, harassment of troops and similar tactics. Anything else could lead to the total annihilation of the Serbian people. Conservative estimates indicated that thousands of Serbs – men, women, children – had already been murdered by the *Ustaši* in Croatia and Bosnia. Every effort must be made to protect innocent civilians from further acts of genocide by members of the Axis forces.

Frowning slightly, seeming almost to have forgotten those around him, the colonel worried aloud about isolated acts taken by inexperienced partisan groups that could lead to severe reprisals. A way must be found to draw them into one disciplined unit that would be ready to rise up immediately upon an Allied landing in the Balkans. Meanwhile they should unite in harassing and impeding the enemy without giving them an excuse to brutalize civilians.

It was difficult to read Hudson's reaction to Mihailović's assessment of the situation. He did, however, indicate that he would recommend that an effort be made by the British to help with supplies, which seemed to be enough to galvanize the colonel.

Later that evening he gathered his officers around him to tell them the good news. Once the British understood the situation, he exulted, arms and ammunition were sure to pour in. 'Do you understand? Do you realize what this means?' The intelligent eyes sparkled. 'Do you understand?' he repeated. 'Now the battle can really begin.'

5

David was fast learning the frustrations of operating as a guerrilla force with inadequate arms and ammunition. There had been the exhilaration of taking part in the attack on the town of Shabatz. Out-armed and out-manned as they were, nevertheless the Chetniks had half of the town in their hands until fresh and superbly armed German reinforcements made the odds so overwhelming that Mihailović had been forced to order the retreat.

Things, of course, might have been different had the promised British aid turned out to be more than a few old Italian sub-machine-guns and an inadequate supply of assorted munitions. On the other hand, Shabatz had taught them the intense pleasure of letting the fascist bastards know that the whole of Serbia was not exactly remaining passive under their occupation. There were also the encouraging reports Mihailović was receiving from his commanders in the field, indicating that Chetnik forces were, in fact, liberating and holding large areas of the country. The Germans were discovering what their forefathers could have told them; the Chetniks made up in ferocity what they lacked in arms.

The response from Belgrade, however, was more horrifying than anything they could have imagined, even from the barbaric Germans. The morning Mihailović gathered his officers together to discuss the decree that had been issued under direct instructions from General Keitel, supreme commander of the *Wehrmacht*, consternation and disgust were discernible in every man present. From now on, the colonel said gravely, for every German soldier killed by the rebels, a hundred Serbian hostages would be immediately executed, for every German wounded, fifty Serbs would die. 'What kind of army do they have?' asked one officer. 'Do we frighten them so much that they have no other recourse than to murder civilians?' He shook his head in disgust. 'I thought the Germans at least had some sense of honour, but these ... they are as bad as the Turks.'

Mihailović nodded. He seemed tired, a little depressed. 'One wonders, gentlemen, if we will ever be rid of the Turks! Of course, we know they have been taking our people in Belgrade. There have been executions, as you all know. Many in our movement have been sent to labour camps in Germany. That one can understand. Anyone who joins us knows the risk he takes. But when it comes to civilians, that is another matter.' He placed his hands flat on the small table he used as a desk and studied them for a moment before looking up. 'The action the enemy is taking is barbaric and surely repugnant to all civilized men. But it must be dealt with. In future we must ensure that there is no indiscriminate killing of Germans that would prompt these barbaric reprisals. God knows, our people have – are – suffering enough. Of course, where it is possible to ensure that an area can be liberated and that we will be in a position to offer protection to our people, that is another matter. Also, it goes without saying, acts of sabotage will continue. Under these new and terrible guidelines, however, the emphasis must be on ultimate disruption to the enemy on all fronts, but within bounds that will safeguard the population.'

Shock, however, was to follow upon shock.

Sitting around a fire with Lieutenant Mirković and two other bearded fighters several weeks later, David learned that the partisans were ignoring Mihailović's instructions that no action must be taken that would endanger the population. As a result of what Marković called 'senseless, useless and indiscriminate action taken by those bloody Bolsheviks', an appalling price had been paid. Thousands of civilians executed in the Maćva area, an estimated five thousand killed in the town of Kraljevo, while in Kragujevac the price paid had been the lives of some six thousand males, including three classes from the boys' secondary school. The children had been led out to be slaughtered with their masters.

Barbarians! Murderers! Child killers!

The outrage felt against the Germans was fully matched by the incredulity and indignation at the irresponsible actions of the partisans. 'What kind of men are they?' David cried, while Mirković cursed steadily and expertly and their two companions muttered in their beards and shook their heads.

'Could we expect otherwise?' asked the man called Salko. 'We shouldn't be dealing with those devils in the first place. Godless communists! What else could we expect?'

'Godless?' asked his friend, a red-haired man from Slovenia. 'But you know how it was. None of us took them too seriously. Even my old mother, dead now since last year,' he said, crossing himself, 'used to pray for them. "They are against the fascists after all", she used to say, "They only pretend to be Godless. They are just boys playing games". She used to feel sorry for them,' he added, 'always being chased by the police.'

'Some boys,' Mirković snapped. 'And they weren't exactly against the fascists when Stalin signed his dirty pact, were they? I tell you we should never have had anything to do with them in the first place. Even when they were supposed to be fighting side by side with us, more often than not our commanders reported that the cowardly bastards were retiring from their positions, exposing our men to enemy attack from the rear. Our colonel did not know what to believe at first, but he received too many similar reports for it not to be true. Then we had word from Ljubovija and Kragujevac. In both cases the bastards offered cooperation, then took our men by surprise and disarmed them, made off with their arms. I tell you, we are dealing with devils here. As bad as the Germans, mark my words.'

'But surely Mihailović is going to do something?' David asked. 'If they behave in such a barbaric fashion, and if they are being so reckless with the lives of our people, how can we continue to associate with them?'

Mirković nodded. 'He has arranged for another meeting with their leader.' He stared at David. 'But you should know that. Your name was posted as one of the officers who will accompany him. You haven't seen the notice?'

David was already on his feet. 'Is it true?'

To his intense delight it *was* true. It was the first indication he had had since he sat in on the meeting with the British mission that Mihailović remembered him. Maybe, he thought with a feeling of excitement, it was also an indication that soon he would be given a posting to a permanent command.

In any event it would be extremely interesting to see this man called Tito, the communist leader he had been hearing about. For the first time in months he allowed himself to think about Stevan Matić. Was he still in Belgrade? Just how close had his connection with the communists been? Perhaps it was, after all, a mistake. Who could trust Bogdan? Yes, yes. If only he had gone back to see Stevan he was sure he would have found it to be all a mistake. They would have had a good laugh about it. And today, who knows, Stevan might have been right here by his side. He spent the rest of the evening thinking about his friend. I wonder, he thought, what he is doing right now?

* * *

Stevan arrived in Belgrade by train early in the morning and decided to check in at his own address before trying to contact Alex. It was the low, brass bowl of flowers in the centre of the coffee table that gave him his first intimation of her presence. Flowers, and on the mantelpiece several pieces of fine china and a photograph of Judge Miletić and his wife surrounded by a cluster of snapshots of Alex and Olga that must have been taken some time in the 1920s, together with more recent photographs of her brother's wedding. Above the fireplace, his large and bloody painting of the Battle of Kosovo had been replaced by an oil painting of Skopska Crna Gora, the range of Macedonian hills that were the home of Olga's sullen but fiercely protective nurse, Stana Radović.

He walked into the bedroom and found in the scatter of richly embroidered pillows thrown across his plain white bedspread, in the delicate perfume that hung lightly in the air, further evidence that she had taken him up on his offer to move into the apartment.

There was no sign that either her mother or Stana had accompanied her. The small room designated as guest room and/or study remained unchanged. The kitchen at first glance showed no sign of her presence, until he opened a cupboard and found two sets of delicate china had been added to his own motley collection of mismatched mugs and plates. The refrigerator, he discovered, now held a variety of fresh meats, cheeses and salads, instead of the piece of stale cheese and bottles of *Bajloni* he had left behind.

He stood there staring at the contents for a moment, closed the door, and turned to find her standing in the doorway watching him, a slight, enigmatic smile on her lips.

'My God, Olga! How did you get in? You gave me a start.'

She tossed her head back and laughed. 'What a fine partisan you must be! Just imagine. If we were out there in the field I could easily have...' She moved to the sink, picked up a large kitchen knife, and drew it across her throat. 'And that would have been the end of Comrade Matić!'

'Thanks very much,' he said drily. 'A wonderful welcome home. And you still haven't answered my question. How did you get in? I should have heard you open the front door.'

'But I did not have to open the front door, comrade.' Her dark eyes began to dance. 'You left it wide open, for me or for anyone else who happened to be passing by.'

'Oh God!'

'Exactly.'

She was wearing a cream-coloured pleated skirt with a matching, loose-fitting sweater. The black hair was shining as ever, the fine eyes still sparkling. But there was an indefinable difference about the way she was watching him, something he could not quite put his finger on.

'You'll never believe this. It's quite extraordinary.' She was carrying a small paper package that she placed on the kitchen table as she sat down and motioned him to sit opposite. 'I knew you would be here today. I knew it! If you don't believe me...' She opened the package and revealed half a dozen of his favourite cheese pastries, still warm from the bakery.

'Witch!' He reached out and picked one up. 'It's that old nurse of yours. She's been teaching you black magic. Don't think I didn't notice that painting above the fireplace. Even when she's not around she makes sure you have something to remind you of her.' Olga laughed, got up and filled the coffee pot with water, added some heaped spoons of coffee, placed it on the stove and sat down again.

'Poor Stana. I believe you are afraid of her. Yes,' her eyes began to dance. 'I believe you have always been afraid of her.'

'Who wouldn't be?' He swallowed a piece of pastry. 'Those hooded eyes. Like a hawk! And ever since I can remember she has watched me with them as though I were a Turk. If I even got within a yard of you!'

She began to laugh, and shook her head. 'You exaggerate. How you exaggerate. You always did.' Incredibly, her eyes began to mist. Stevan, about to pick up another pastry, stared in amazement as a solitary tear rolled down her cheek.

'Stevan,' she said briskly, almost accusingly, 'why didn't you tell me I felt this way about you?' She reached out, touched his face, withdrew her hand. 'Why didn't you tell me?'

'What did you say? What was that you said?' He almost shouted it. A powerful feeling of exultation surged through him. 'My God, woman,' he exploded loudly, 'I've only been *trying* to tell you since you were ten years old.'

She began to laugh again then to cry. The coffee boiled over. The remainder of the pastries cooled, forming small grease spots on the paper.

Time dissolved.

Then, magically, they were lying together amongst the scattered pillows that had been so beautifully embroidered by Stana Radović. A long time later she was telling him that she hadn't realized until he left Belgrade with Tito. It had been then she had begun to miss him. Wildly. Desperately. It was incredible just how much she had missed him. It was *then* she had realized...

She sighed, yawned, snuggled closer.

Much later, he asked, 'Is it true? Did you really know I would be back this morning?'

'Yes, it's true.'

'But I don't understand.'

'Nor do I.' She sat up, leaned on one elbow and looked down at him. 'And yet I knew.'

They talked about their childhood, about the time they had met in London. She didn't know why it had taken so long for her to discover that she loved him. Then she sat up again. 'Yes I do.'

'What?'

'I know why it took me so long to discover.' She was very serious. 'It was what Stana always said about you. Do you know what it was?'

'No. Nor do I wish to!'

'She always said "He doesn't know in which direction he is going, that one".'

'I knew it would be complimentary.'

'No, no, Stevan. Don't you understand? She was right. It was after you joined the Party that you changed. You are much more mature now, do you know that?' She leaned down and traced the area above his lips where the famous moustache had once resided. 'You see,' she said tenderly, 'you don't even have to hide behind those whiskers any more.'

'The Party! How far away all that seems.'

She gave a contented sigh and lay down beside him again.

A long time later they got up. Olga heated soup, made toast. They sat in the kitchen talking, talking. They had known each other all their lives yet it seemed as though they had never before had a chance to exchange thoughts, dreams, plans for the future. Stevan had completely lost track of the hours.

When he awakened for the second or third time daylight was flooding the bedroom. Olga must have been up and drawn the curtains. From the bathroom he could hear a soft crooning. He glanced at his watch. Almost 8 a.m. He had been home almost twenty-four hours.

When she appeared in the doorway, fully dressed, he beckoned to her. Laughingly she shook her head. 'Oh, no. You must get up, you lazy creature.' He sat up, protesting. 'But what are you dressed for? Where are you going?'

'To get us some breakfast.' She nodded sternly in the direction of the bathroom. 'It's all yours, and we will talk later, yes?'

Before he could even protest she was gone. He heard her moving around in the kitchen, so with a resigned sigh and a yawn he rose from the bed and made his way to the tiny bathroom.

'I have to go home, you see.' They had finished their omelettes and were sitting in the living room over their second cups of coffee. 'Mother was expecting me yesterday afternoon as a matter of fact. I know she'll be worried. And, of course, it is going to take time to tell her about us. To try to explain about the Party. To explain the reason I must be with you.'

He put his cup and saucer down carefully. 'With me?'

'Yes, of course. That's why you returned to Belgrade, isn't it? To take me back with you?' She smiled. 'To think I haven't even asked you about Alex and Jelena. See how selfish you have made me! Will it be all right now? For them, too, I mean.'

'Alex and Jelena.' He repeated their names slowly, as though just coming out of a dream.

'You said you would try to persuade Tito to let them join you, don't you remember? To let the three of us join you.'

'Of course.' He nodded. 'He did agree, I mean, so far as Alex and Jelena are concerned. He . . .'

She was studying him with a slight frown on her face. 'What is it?' she asked quietly. He did not answer. 'He did not give permission for *me* to come. Is that it?' She had been sitting in the big leather chair, feet curled under her in her favourite position. Now she straightened up, swung her legs back onto the floor, and sat there primly, like a child behind a school desk. 'Is it because we are not married?' she asked. Immediately shook her head. 'No, how can it be? Judging by all of the rumours *he* would be the last one to insist on marriage. Party rules or not!'

'No. It's not that. He . . .' Impulsively he turned, picked up the jacket he had thrown loosely over the back of his chair, removed an envelope, and handed it to her.

With a puzzled look she again searched his face, then with a light shrug she opened the envelope and scanned its contents. Then she sat very, very still.

After a long moment he gestured abruptly. 'Of course, I know what you . . .'

'You know what's in it?'

He nodded miserably. 'Of course I knew that you would reject the idea out of hand. That you . . .'

He again broke off in mid-sentence as she raised her head and stared at him. 'And did you tell *him* that?' There was something in her voice that precluded any answer at all. 'Did you tell *him* that?' she repeated slowly, staring at him steadily, unable, it seemed, to take her eyes from his face.

Helplessly he returned her stare, unable for the life of him to say one word. Slowly, though, his face began to redden.

* * *

The meeting took place quite close to Ravna Gora, at the village of Brajići.

As a junior officer, David kept tactfully on the outskirts of the group that accompanied Mihailović, which was just as well, he decided later. The shock he felt on first seeing the communist leader, the fellow they called Tito, must have shown on his face. He recognized him immediately as the man he had met leaving Stevan's apartment all those months ago. There was no doubt about it. Good God, even in this mountain village setting and dressed in what he supposed was meant to be some kind of rough uniform, the man looked like nothing less than a successful if somewhat dandified bank manager or merchant. For a brief moment he wondered what would happen if Tito – he could not remember the name Stevan had given him, although he was sure it was not Tito – recognized him. Would he ask after Stevan? Should he, David, ask after Stevan? The jumble of thoughts ran around his mind as preparations were made to gather around the large table supplied by the villagers.

In fact Tito did not really seem to notice anyone other than Mihailović. The latter was in an uncharacteristically grim and determined mood. With little emotion he flatly laid out his list of complaints to the communist leader.

Firstly, he referred to the agreement that had been made when the Chetniks handed over the township of Užice to the partisans, that an equal share of the production from the munitions factory be allocated to Chetnik units. The fact was that out of the several thousand rifles that had been produced, only about five hundred had been received by his men, the vast majority of which had proved useless, since they were without bolts. In addition to this, a stream of complaints had been pouring into Chetnik headquarters at Ravna Gora from villagers and townspeople in areas that had been handed over to the partisans by Chetnik units. Far from feeling liberated, these people had complained bitterly about the authoritarian methods used by the communists, and about their predilection to usurp the authority of local leaders in a tactless and often violent way. Mihailović reminded the communist that, in accordance with instructions he had personally issued, in districts occupied by Chetniks, partisan groups were at all times treated as equals, whereas in areas held by partisans Chetniks had often been disarmed as though *they* were the enemy, and in any event had been granted no status whatsoever by the communists. This was in direct violation of the understanding reached at the previous meeting. Pointing to areas such as the township of Gornji Milanovac on the River Danube, which was held by Chetnik forces, the colonel said that in his opinion this was the ideal situation – the communists had been granted equal authority by the Chetniks, and the result had been excellent and mutual cooperation of the kind that had initially been envisaged.

Mihailović went on to give an endless list of instances where partisans had refused to allow recruits a choice of joining the Chetniks, whereas his people had followed his strict instructions that each man must be offered the choice of joining either the Chetniks or the communists. His commanders were not fools, they could not be expected to accept this kind of situation indefinitely. He then listed several complaints also received from his commanders in the field that partisans had often withdrawn from joint action taken against enemy forces, leaving Chetniks in very vulnerable positions. He stressed that these reports had been received from commanders who were far apart in the field, yet the pattern of events was strikingly similar. It was the common view that the intention was to force the Chetniks into expending all of their ammunition, while the partisans conserved their own.

In a more conciliatory tone, the Chetnik leader went on to say that he realized the difficulties involved in controlling units in the field, where different interpretations could be given to orders emanating from headquarters. But in view of the overwhelming number of complaints he had received, not only from his own men, but from villagers and townspeople themselves, it was his strong hope that the communist leadership would address itself to rectifying these abuses of the mutual agreement that had been arrived at in Struganik.

As the communists stared at him silently, he went on to say there was an even more important matter that should be discussed. This was the savage reprisals that were being carried out against the civilian population for each German soldier killed or wounded in action. Painstakingly, he listed action taken by partisans that had achieved little other than the killing of a few enemy soldiers, but that had brought terrible reprisals against the population. In particular he referred to a senseless action by the communists that had led to the brutal murder of so many children in Kragujevac. He then went on to outline measures to ensure that action not be taken unless there was a specific military objective of importance or in instances where the people could be both liberated *and* subsequently protected. There were, of course, also limitless opportunities for acts of sabotage that would keep the killing of the enemy to a minimum, but cause him grave damage. To continue in the manner the partisans had adopted would only cause more senseless killing of civilians, the burning of villages and other brutal reprisals.

He finished his statement by gravely emphasizing that if they could find no other grounds for agreement, it was essential, for the protection of the population, that they find agreement in this area.

Now it was the communists' turn, and their leader, too, was impressive.

He launched into a strong denial that any of his men had ever withdrawn from battle leaving Chetniks in vulnerable positions. Oh, no. Quite the contrary! That, in fact, was what Chetniks were doing to *his* men. And what was all this cooperation the colonel was talking about? Quickly he reeled off a list of names of certain Chetnik officers who had offered anything but cooperation. He would be more impressed by the colonel's sincerity if he were to dismiss these obviously incompetent men, so-called officers, who, according to reports received by *him*, had acted in a quite cowardly fashion in the heat of battle. Also, there had been instances where Serbian officers had refused to cooperate with Croatian partisans in the field. What an insult! Were his brave partisan soldiers to be compared with the *Ustaši*?

So far as the complaints concerning the rifles from Užice were concerned, he dismissed these with a contemptuous wave of the hand. Were his men supposed to stop and examine every bolt and nut that left the factory? They had far more important things to do, of that he could assure the colonel. As for the killing of civilians was concerned, it was obviously an exaggeration. Did the colonel believe all the propaganda the Germans were spreading?

Except for a tightening of the lips, a slight reddening of the face when Tito referred to his officers' cowardice in the field, Mihailović sat silently through this tirade. When it had finished, however, he again began to speak.

It was difficult, he said evenly, to accept that trained army officers who had shown extreme courage when the enemy first entered Yugoslavia, who had each one fought fiercely and bravely before retiring to the mountains to continue the fight, instead of laying down their arms in surrender as so many had done, would suddenly and inexplicably display cowardice.

With regard to Serbian officers refusing to accept Croatian partisans into their units, this was possible, and he would certainly look into it. One must remember the unspeakable brutalities that had been perpetrated upon the Serbian population in Croatia and Bosnia, and realize that some officers might entertain feelings of hostility towards Croatians, all of whom were most certainly not *Ustaši*, an attitude that he, personally, strongly disagreed with as being short-sighted and unfair. He would certainly look into this matter, he repeated.

But again, speaking with all of the conviction he possessed, he stressed the need for caution in carrying out any action that would rebound against innocent civilians. This was not an honourable way to conduct war. That the Germans had chosen to reveal themselves as barbarians in this matter was all the more reason why the Yugoslav army should act in a civilized and honourable way. He begged the communist leadership to consider the consequences – the extremely severe and brutal consequences to the people – that could result from ill-considered, ill-conceived and, ultimately, ineffective action carried out by random groups of undisciplined guerrillas.

The meeting broke up shortly afterwards. An uneasy truce seemed to have been reached as both parties agreed that collaboration between them was essential. As Mihailović put it, only the enemy could benefit from any breakdown in their mutual cooperation.

David had followed the proceedings with an intense and concentrated interest and a feeling of pride in the quiet determination and decency shown by his commanding officer. On the trip back to Ravna Gora he fell in behind Mihailović and one of the senior officers, turning over in his mind the comments of the communist leader and the colonel's response, seeking answers to a dozen questions that had presented themselves. Almost unconsciously Mihailović's quiet voice penetrated his thoughts. The colonel was wondering out loud whether it was possible that Tito did not really know what had been going on with his own partisans in the field? 'After all,' he mused, 'he is not an army man. He is a civilian we must remember. Perhaps he has not yet managed to establish discipline, control.'

'I would say he was pretty much in control,' replied the major, an elderly staff officer who had come out of retirement to join Mihailović in the mountains. 'I noticed none of the others had much to say. They all looked to him.'

'That's true. He certainly *seems* responsible enough.' They rode on in silence for a few more moments before the colonel again turned to the other officer. 'Was that your impression? What *was* your impression of the man?'

There was a brief silence.

'My impression,' the major finally replied, 'was that far from being a communist, there goes a man who would be king.'

The rest of the conversation was lost to David as he experienced a surge of memory that blocked out everything else; the voices, his companions, the biting air of the mountains.

It had been just prior to Stevan's departure for London. He had joined David, Bogdan and the former's sisters on a picnic in Koshutnjak Park. Returning home, they had been about to cross a pathway when they heard the sound of several approaching horsemen. Turning, they recognized a unit of the king's horseguard, resplendent and glittering in their blue jackets, red breeches and cockaded black astrakhan *Śubare*. They were escorting the slight, upright figure of the heir apparent, young Prince Peter.

Both girls had given exclamations of delight, but it had been Stevan who had instantly reacted. Tearing off his cap, he had waved it excitedly in the air. 'Long live the king!' he had shouted. 'Long live the king!' Startled, David had stepped back off the pathway, straightened himself up and saluted smartly as the horsemen cantered by. The young prince had turned and slightly inclined his head, before they all disappeared around a bend.

Stevan! The quintessential Serbian patriot! What had happened to him? What in the name of God had happened to him?

* * *

Stevan had returned to Užice from Belgrade, together with Alex and Jelena. After settling them into a tiny apartment in one of the back streets of the town, he made his way to headquarters to report back and see if the communist leader could make time to meet his friends.

Zdenka was as uncooperative and ill-tempered as ever, but after drawing from her the information that Tito had just a few days previously returned from a meeting with the

Chetnik leader, he finally persuaded her to make an appointment for the following morning around ten, although she would not promise that Tito would, in fact, find the time to see them.

Stevan arrived some fifteen minutes before the appointed time, and had just sat down to await the arrival of Alex and his wife, when Tito poked his head out of his office, saw him, and invited him in.

The secretary-general was, surprisingly, in a towering rage. He motioned Stevan to sit down and then launched into a tirade the moment Zdenka closed the door behind them.

'You were lucky you didn't have to come with us to that meeting,' he snapped as he stalked up and down the office. 'You wouldn't have believed it! That moralistic, bourgeois little colonel! Pretending to be so concerned about civilians! Complaining to *me* about protecting the people! What does he think? That we should be the only ones to risk our lives? We should be the only ones willing to die? Who does he think he is? Why shouldn't the people die with us? What's so special about *their* lives I would like to know!' He prowled around the room like a caged tiger, continuing for a full five minutes in that vein before finally calming down and settling himself behind his desk. 'Well,' he finished ominously, '*he'll* find out!'

He began to talk of other things. 'So you are back! Everything went well? Have you found accommodation for your friends? I'm looking forward to meeting them. Alex Miletić! Yes, yes. I have heard of him, you know. A great sportsman. The kind of man we need on our side.'

Stevan nodded. 'He's certainly looking forward to meeting *you*. He's been waiting to join you for a long time now.' Tito gave a slight smile. His ferocious mood of a moment ago seemed to have disappeared. 'And what about your other friend? Olga, that is her name?' The blue eyes took on a slightly malicious look. 'You gave her my message?'

'*And did you tell him that? Did you tell him that?*' Her voice rang so clearly in his ears that he gave a start and almost looked around, expecting her to appear behind him. It all swept over him again. That quiet little scene. His subsequent insistence that she forget that message. That she return to Užice with himself and Alex and Jelena and the devil take Tito and his insolent presumptuousness. Nothing had moved her. Not his protestations of love, nor his shouting, not his soliciting of help from Alex and Jelena. 'Just tell your Tito that I received his message,' she had said.

Not, of course, that she would do anything about it. Apart from anything else, my God, how she loathed the Germans. It was just that she had made him feel ... did she think she was living in the nineteenth century? Just because her father would have soundly thrashed the communist leader had he received a similar request about any decent Serbian woman, and from what Stevan knew about his own bombastic father, Tito would probably now be a dead man in similar circumstances! But, damn it, this was the twentieth century. Besides, *she* was the one who had wanted to get mixed up with the communists ...

'I asked if you gave her my message.' Tito was frowning now, impatient. The door opened behind him. He heard Alex's voice, a soft murmur from Jelena.

'Yes,' he said evenly, avoiding the other man's eyes. 'I gave her your message.'

And then there took place a short, rather ludicrous scene when Zdenka, having ushered Alex and Jelena into the office, refused to leave. The reason was obvious. Like all men meeting Jelena for the first time, Tito seemed unable to draw his eyes away from her face. Alex stood there smiling slightly. He was used to this reaction and had long since ceased to worry about it. The truth was that although Jelena had a rather plump, chunky figure, her face was one of unsurpassable beauty. Smooth, serene, a perfectly structured setting for the warm brown eyes with their lush dark lashes and the brilliant, dazzling smile that revealed strong, white, perfect teeth.

'So you're our new nurse,' Tito murmured with a warm smile, suddenly all charm. 'Come in, come in. Sit down.' He turned to Zdenka, who was still hovering behind them with a sullen look on her own attractive, Gypsyish face. 'You can bring some tea,' he said curtly.

For a moment Stevan thought she was going to pick something up and throw it at the secretary-general. She made an abrupt movement, dark eyes flashing fire, then suddenly turned on her heel and stalked out, slamming the door loudly behind her. Tito appeared not to notice. Courteously he sat them down around his desk, joked about his own clumsiness in sport compared to Alex's well-known prowess, slapped Stevan on the back and made flattering comments about his general helpfulness.

Within five minutes the door opened and a young girl appeared with tea and a tray of small pastries. The raging tiger of ten minutes ago was suddenly a genial and charming host. He sat behind his desk warmly beaming.

'Well,' he said happily. 'Isn't this nice? Now we can have a little chat.'

6

On the 21st of November 1941, major clashes were reported between the Pozega Chetnik units and the Užice partisans.

'We have exact knowledge of their movements,' Tito announced the following day. 'I have ordered a full-scale attack. It will take place tomorrow morning at four a.m.'

'My God,' Stevan said anxiously to Alex, 'does he know what he's doing? Isn't it enough that we are occupied? Does he want to precipitate a civil war?'

They were sitting in the tiny kitchen of the Miletić apartment. Alex was at the head of the small wooden table, working intermittently on some bridge specifications. Stevan sat at the other end, and between them Jelena contentedly shelled a bowl of peas. Alex looked up from his papers, removed his glasses, and considered the problem in his usual slow and methodical way.

'Here,' Jelena said, handing Stevan a small dish of plump green vegetables, 'you can shell some for me.'

'Yes,' Alex said finally. 'I think he knows what he's doing.' He tried but did not succeed in keeping a note of excitement from creeping into his voice. 'He has begun the revolution!'

Stevan stared at him. 'The revolution? In the middle of an enemy occupation?'

'What better time? The country is in chaos. You know as well as I do that in normal times, well, you know the strength of the Party before the invasion. A few thousand. A tiny minority.'

'Yes, but...' He grappled with the enormity of the proposition. 'But my God, Alex...'

Jelena frowned. 'I wish you would stop taking the Lord's name in vain, Stevan.'

'Yes. But, my God, Alex. You know yourself, since we established contact with the Soviet Union, their instructions have been that we must cooperate with the Chetniks. They know we don't have the support of the people. In fact they keep insisting that we play down the fact of our communism. You know that as well as Tito does.'

Alex nodded. 'Yes, but we must take into consideration that our brothers in the Soviet Union do not fully grasp the situation here. Stalin, in his wisdom, has realized that the Russian people have not yet fully embraced the ideology that is leading them out of their backwardness. We must remember, after all, that their hearts and minds have been firmly in the grasp of the church for endless generations. They cannot be expected to change overnight. So, in the Soviet Union it is necessary to ask the people to fight, not for socialism, but for Mother Russia. It is a sign of Stalin's greatness that he is even allowing the cooperation of the church. It is only natural that our Soviet brothers, therefore, assume that the situation is the same here in Yugoslavia. And up to a point, they are right. But they have not grasped the one essential difference: here we do not hold power. Nor, during normal times, would we have any chance of grasping it. Our people, as you know, have their minds set on democracy. They do not realize that all *that* means is that they are ruled by a greedy bunch of capitalists who manipulate weak politicians and rob the people of their rightful heritage. No, no. I think Tito is right. Once we grasp power, our Soviet comrades will recognize that.'

Stevan picked up one of the peapods shelled it and absent-mindedly popped the contents into his mouth. Jelena sighed and reached out to slap his hand. 'I asked you to shell them, not *eat* them. You are as bad as Alex!'

'Well, Alex,' he said. 'I suppose you are right. I trust your opinion. You know that.'

The big man replaced his glasses and frowned. 'But you must learn to trust our leader, Stevan. Remember, he was the sole survivor from all of the Yugoslavs who were executed in Moscow during the great purges. Do you know what that means? It means he holds the absolute trust of Joseph Stalin. And *that* means, as far as I am concerned, that he has the absolute trust of Alex Miletić. Do you understand?'

Stevan nodded, a little shamefacedly. Before he could prevent it, however, one of those treacherous thoughts that he was trying so hard to eliminate popped into his head. *Was it because he held the absolute trust of Stalin? Or was it, as some whispered, because he had been willing to betray all of his comrades in order to ensure his own survival?*

Quickly he pushed the thought from his mind. 'Here,' he said, taking the big bowl from a surprised Jelena, 'give me that. I will shell them in double-quick time, and you will see that I won't eat so much as one little pea, just to set an example to your husband!'

Alex grinned and returned to his papers. Jelena laughed, got up from the table and began to busy herself with preparations for dinner.

It wasn't until later that Alex said what had been on his mind all evening. They had finished the large steaks and were sitting in the small room that served as bedroom and living room, drinking coffee, when he managed to mutter, 'I haven't told you before, but David Ristić, did you know he is with the Chetniks?'

'Oh, Mother of God! It will come to that then? Serbian brother against Serbian brother?' Jelena began to cry, silently. She got up quickly, gathered the cups together, and took them into the kitchen.

Alex watched her leave the room with a slight frown on his open, craggy face, then turned back to Stevan. 'I'm sorry, Stevan. But, of course, our personal feelings ... what are our personal feelings in the face of grave historical necessities?'

Jelena emerged from the kitchen. 'Sorry,' she said, with

that heartbreakingly lovely smile. She rested one hand lightly on Stevan's shoulder. 'I promised a neighbour I would mind her children for an hour or so. She wants to visit a friend. I'm sure I'll be back before you leave.' She leaned down to kiss her husband's cheek.

'We've been here for such a short time,' Alex said fondly as the door closed behind her. 'And already she is doing things for the people.'

Stevan watched him silently for a moment. 'Should she be here, Alex?' He hesitated. 'Things are rather quiet at the moment, but they are obviously going to get very rough.'

The big man nodded. 'I thought about it. But how could I in all conscience leave her in Belgrade? She has every right to take part in the greatest revolution mankind has ever seen. I have no right to deprive her of that. Besides . . .' he smiled almost shyly, 'it is, of course, a great joy for me to have her here.'

'I understand. But . . .' He hesitated.

'What is it?' Alex rested his head in one large hand and studied him. 'Say what is on your mind, Stevan.'

'Well. I suppose it's none of my business.' He frowned. 'Yes it is! I am fond of both of you, you know that. It's just, does she really believe in the revolutionary cause? She was always so close to the church. Has she really given up her religion? It seems to me not.'

The big man drew his pipe from his pocket, lit it and sat holding it and staring into space. Finally he looked directly at Stevan. 'I've tried to explain to her. There is really no conflict between what the man Jesus Christ taught, and what Marx taught. The former brought the message, at the right historical moment, that men must love each other as brothers. Marx brought a different message, at the right historical moment, that men must treat each other with fairness, with justice.' He placed the pipe in his mouth, sucked on it contentedly for a few moments, then withdrew it and continued. 'Consider the parallels. They tell us God gave his only son to save mankind. And Jesus left behind his disciples. Now Stalin, Marx's own most brilliant disciple, has given not only his own comrades … think of those trials, think how it must have wrenched his soul to sacrifice his own close brothers in the revolution, to send them one by one to their deaths. What iron compassion! Where did he find the strength? Not only his own close comrades, but his own people. And for what? Himself? No! For the sake of world revolution. For the sake of the world proletariat!

'Jelena understands that, I think. Although it was not easy to teach her at first. But now she understands that it is still possible for her to believe in this God of hers, without submitting to the blackmail of the church. She has admitted, in any event, that it was really the pageantry that drew her to the church. She always believed in her heart that she had direct contact with God. Now she realizes that, in fact, the church has little to do with Christ's teachings. It has simply used his words to grasp power for itself. Well, now Marx has left us his disciple who has taken the first step in returning all power to the people.'

He glanced down at his pipe, found it had gone out, removed matches from his pocket, relit it and gazed earnestly at Stevan. 'You understand?'

'Of course.' *Understand what? Stalin and Jesus Christ? Is Alex mad? Or am I mad? Or is it simply the whole world that has gone mad!*

They talked for an hour or so more. About the implications of Tito's orders to launch a full-scale attack against the Chetniks. About what the reaction from Moscow might be. About the problems with the perpetual shortage of arms. Stevan left shortly after Jelena returned.

It was a cold night, with a blustery autumn wind. He thrust his gloveless hands deep into his trouser pockets and bent his head a little against the buffeting of the wind. Nothing Alex had said made sense to him. Surely by now *everyone* knew that what Stalin had done was concentrate more power in his own hands than any of the tzars ever had. Yet when he had hinted as much, the big man had stared at him in surprise and pointed out that of course it was necessary to initially rule the backward masses with an iron hand, until they reached the necessary state of evolution that would allow them to take the responsibility into their own hands. Alex, like all of the comrades, had an answer for everything!

Then why didn't it satisfy him?

Impatiently, silently, he swore at himself. For better or worse, he had thrown in his lot with the revolutionaries. As he had told himself a hundred times, it was too late now to retreat. But how much simpler things would be if he could only accept their truth as *they* all seemed to accept it. On the other hand he *was* making progress. The questions still kept leaping unwanted into his mind, but the effort of suppressing them was becoming easier. Unless you want to go mad, he reminded himself, you must learn simply to accept. Stop the questioning. Just accept. He had reached his own quarters, and he turned into them with relief. That was the answer.

Accept, accept, accept!

* * *

'We have to accept the situation. Unpalatable as it is, we have to accept the fact that we not only must cope with the Germans and the Italians and the Croats and the Bulgars and the bloody Albanians, but now we must fight a civil war.'

Although Mihailović's officers had known for some time about the occasional skirmishes between Chetnik and partisan units, it had been hoped that if agreement could be reached by the leadership of both factions, things would settle down. Now the communist leader had thrown down the gauntlet! The main issue in his mind, it was clear, was not to drive the enemy from the country's soil, but to take advantage of the situation and to cause even more internal chaos in order to grasp power for his party.

It was a bitter pill to swallow. Serb against Serb? Unthinkable. Unnatural. They sat around the camp fires talking, talking, talking. Arguing. Shouting. But it always came down to the same thing. In addition to everything else this was civil war. Accept it they must. If the treacherous communists were so power mad that they could not decently wait until the invaders had been routed, there was not a thing that could be done about it. Except what their ancestors had always done. Fight, fight, fight.

That the fight was succeeding beyond their wildest hopes was verified when in the middle of November their leader was asked to meet with a delegation from the German commandant for Serbia in order to discuss a truce. Wild rumours spread through the Ravna Gora headquarters. The Germans would offer to withdraw! Impossible? No. It was no secret that their Soviet adventure was beginning to cost them dearly. It was no secret that the German units tied up in Yugoslavia by the sheer ferocity of the poorly equipped and often almost completely unarmed Chetniks had been forced to seek reinforcements from the *Wehrmacht*. Nor was it any secret that the response, as broadcast throughout the country by the German puppet, Nedić, had been the draconian measures against civilians ordered by Keitel from Berlin. The measures might have slowed down Chetnik activity, but they had certainly not stopped it. Fewer Germans were being killed, more were being taken prisoner, used for barter against the lives of civilians. So perhaps the enemy was going to act with intelligence for once and realize that the fighters of Mihailović would never give up. Never!

Their optimism was short-lived. After a long night spent with a German delegation in the village of Divci on the 13th of November, Mihailović returned with the news that there had been no offer of withdrawal by the enemy. Instead he had been harangued for hours about the futility of his struggle against the mighty *Wehrmacht*. His response had been to demand the complete evacuation of all enemy troops from his country. It was his intention, he had told them, to rid Yugoslavia of both fascists and communists. If they were prepared to discuss their own evacuation from the country he would be prepared to stop his harassment of their troops within a short time limit to allow for withdrawal. From what he had heard of their problems in the Soviet Union it would certainly be in their own interests to leave Yugoslavia, in which case he could direct all of his forces against the communist threat. The German response had been frigid. The meeting had proved to be futile.

David Ristić was still waiting for a posting to a unit he could consider his own. The frustration of feeling he did not really belong at headquarters, however, had been somewhat alleviated by recent action. A week or so prior to Mihailović's abortive meeting with the Germans, a cry for help had been received from a village on the perimeter of Ravna Gora. A unit of German soldiers had arrived there in search of Chetniks and were brutalizing the villagers. There had been shootings, executions and assaults upon women. The village church had been razed to the ground. David had immediately been ordered to take twenty men and liberate the village.

He had led the attack at dawn. He led it with a bloodthirsty yell that seemed to come deep from within; that had frozen the Germans in their tracks and galvanized his own men into similar unearthly shrieks that reverberated in the ghostly morning air as though the spirits of their ancestors had risen from the earth to once again hurl defiance at the Turks. To add to the eeriness of the scene a storm that had been threatening for hours broke. The thunder of Zeus mingled with their blood-freezing cries. Lightning zigzagged through tall pines and lit up the staring faces of dead German guards, the Aryan Turks, throats gashed from ear to ear, and then followed the hurtling figure of a young, golden-bearded avenger who leapt effortlessly over fences, machine-gun spitting fire, the vengeance of his ancestors still pouring from his throat in a primeval, remorseless scream of retribution.

Later, reliving the whole scene in his mind, exulting in the knowledge that his men had followed him unhesitatingly, he had thanked God that he had known when to stop. At precisely the right moment an ice-cold directive had entered his mind, warning him that it was necessary to take prisoners, that prisoners were an insurance against further enemy vengeance being taken against his people.

The villagers, in the by now strong morning light, had gathered around with welcoming cries. *Dobro Došli Braćo, Dobro Došli Braćo,* they cried. Welcome brothers! Adding proudly, we knew our colonel would not fail us. We knew he would save us from these barbarians!

They had returned to Ravna Gora in triumph, herding their sullen group of prisoners and bearing fresh milk, cheese and fruit from the villagers, David proudly wearing a German Luger strapped to his waist that was to stay there throughout the rest of the war. From that moment on the men had begun to refer to him as 'Lieutenant Lightning'.

To David's amusement these events were also followed by an almost imperceptible change in Lieutenant Mirković's manner towards him which, although correct in his rough way, had only just hidden an air of forbearance that he seemed to harbour towards any junior officer who arrived at headquarters and was turned over to him for initiation into the uncertainties of Ravna Gora. Mirković was a stocky bear of a man with a stubbly black, grey-streaked beard and small green eyes. Because of the role allotted him of initiating the newcomers, the men had nick-named him *Baba*. David had roared with laughter when he first heard the name. No one less like a grandmother than the ferocious Serbian officer who resembled a bear, swore with a fluency and imagination that put even the peasants, champion swearers all, to shame, could be imagined.

They walked together one bitterly cold November night shortly after Mihailović had returned from Divci. In his rough way, Mirković congratulated David on his coolness in taking German prisoners. A veteran of the assault upon the fortress of Visegrad earlier in the year and of fierce fighting that had taken place in Valjevo, Sabac and Kraljevo, most of his close friends were in Bosnia. He spoke with emotion about the courage of the Chetnik commandants whose names were already beginning to resound throughout Bosnia as they took town after town: Foća, Vlasenica, Srebrnica, Kalinovik, Rogatica, Pale, Han-Pijesak, Čajniče, Goražda, Rudo, Prača, Ustiprača, all wrenched from the *Ustaši*, the Germans or the Italians by such leaders as Jezdimir Dangić, Boshko Todorović, Milosh Momchilović, Leka Damnjanović, Rista Cuković and Dobrica Cukić, whose names, he assured David, were destined to resound through future Serbian history. Then there was the peasant Chetnik leader, Radivoje Kerović, who had sprung up to defend his people against the *Ustaši* butchers. Future Serbs would link his name with the peasant Karageorge – Black George – who had led his people against similar barbarities of the Turks.

'The trouble with me,' Mirković confessed, 'is that when I go into battle I cannot stop to think of prisoners. My heart and my head fill with blood. I think what has been done to our people by barbarians of the past and what is now being done to them by these new savages. Yes, yes. I hear the loud cries of our ancestors and all I can think is kill, kill, kill.'

'Hector!' David mused.

'What?'

'Hector. From the *Iliad*. You know? On the battlefield. He fought with an inhuman rage. With a great rage.'

Mirković gave him a sharp look, hesitated, shrugged. 'Whatever that means,' he snapped, 'the point is that we need prisoners now, more than ever, to use as barter.' He spat. 'Filthy German dogs! That's all they are worth. To be used as barter.'

David nodded. 'I know. I was lucky, that is all. Suddenly something told me when to stop. When to stop the men, to take prisoners. But I understand what you are saying. Once that rage grips you, it is a terrible thing.'

'Still, it would be more terrible if it didn't grip us! But talking about prisoners, that dirty communist bastard, Tito, isn't that what he calls himself? When we handed Užice over to him so readily, did you know we also handed most of our prisoners over to him too? At his request! Now *he* can use them. Probably to save the hides of those treacherous black Bolsheviks of his. I tell you, sometimes I wonder whether

Čiča is not too innocent to lead us in this dirty endeavour. Sometimes I think we need someone as black-hearted as the communists themselves. You know how it is, it takes a wolf to know a wolf.'

David laughed, shook his head. 'Then why fight at all? Maybe Mihailović is not as flamboyant as, say, our Karageorge, but he does stand for everything decent in our country. And surely that's what we are all here for? To rid ourselves of these damned fascists so that we can get on with our fledgling democracy?'

Mirković grimaced, then chuckled and slapped him on the shoulder. 'And here is another innocent,' he said. 'Well, Lieutenant Lightning, I hope you are right. I hope both you and the colonel are right.'

* * *

Some two weeks later David was wakened early in the morning by the sound of mortar shells and gunfire. Startled, he leapt up from the bundle of straw he had been sleeping on, rushed out, and discovered that a full-scale attack had been launched against their village headquarters.

So began the German command's most concentrated effort yet to dislodge the Chetnik hornet's nest whose occupants kept swooping down from mountains and out of caves to sting the mighty *Wehrmacht* tail, to taunt and irritate and in many instances paralyse the impregnable forces of the Thousand Year Reich.

Like a plague of insects themselves the Germans swarmed through every village, searched every ravine, every hill, every cave, almost, it seemed, looked behind every tree. With their usual disregard for life they killed. Chetniks, villagers, men, women, children. When they were not killing they were threatening. Then they burned homes, destroyed livestock, defiled churches.

In their furious wake they left death, destruction, broken homes, broken lives, broken hearts. Dead people, dead animals, dead villages. But they could not find Mihailović!

His orders were quite simple. Withdraw, withdraw, withdraw.

And along every step of the way villagers rushed out to help, to warn, to hide, to feed. They directed the beleaguered guerrillas to hidden places, caves and valleys that only they and their ancestors knew. They smiled stupidly at the Germans and shook their heads and said they knew nothing, nothing, nothing. And they did nothing, except perhaps to point in the wrong direction, into a trap.

For which acts they often died.

Under siege, *Čiča* was calm, decisive, orderly as ever. The only time David was to see him falter for one brief moment was when he received news that the Germans had captured his old and good friend, Major Aleksander Mišić, who had been with the Chetnik forces south of Valjevo. Encircled from four sides the guerrillas had been trapped by the German 342nd Division, which had succeeded in killing a dozen officers and soldiers and had executed some five hundred civilians suspected of supporting them. The Germans had also captured what ammunition the Chetniks in the area had, together with their short-wave radio transmitter.

Mihailović momentarily wilted, and General Bader, German commandant in Belgrade, noisily trumpeted forth his triumph.

What consolation came was from the fact that through the British military mission, contact had been established with the Yugoslav government in London. Word that Mihailović had been promoted to the rank of major-general and that financial assistance could be expected to follow came through at a time when Chetnik spirits were at their lowest.

Swiftly following on that news, which brought with it the heartening reminder that the outside world continued to watch their struggle and they did not fight in isolation, came word that Colonel Keserović, another army officer who had refused to capitulate to the Germans, but had gathered together a guerrilla unit of some four hundred men and then agreed to operate under the leadership of Mihailović, had survived several military assaults against the enemy, and had decided to 'wait the winter out' in the village of Kriva Reka on Mount Kopaonik.

The Chetnik leadership regained heart, even though the Germans had plundered their way throughout Ravna Gora, confiscating all the food the peasants had been unable to hide. In what was to be called 'the winter of the century', they withdrew to West Morava Valley. Cold, hungry, still fierce as starving wolves, the Chetniks hunkered down and waited for spring.

* * *

In Užice the partisans came under similar attack, which forced them to withdraw. But, unlike the Chetniks, they were forced to face the full fury of the German onslaught without help from the people. For the first time the motive behind the warnings from Moscow not to try to force their ideology down the throats of the people, to present themselves as a national movement, to cooperate with Mihailović, became only too bitterly clear.

Their policy of liquidation of 'class' opponents under the patent guise of their being 'Fifth Columnists and enemies of the people' in retrospect took on the aspect of a fatal mistake as they were relentlessly forced out of Serbia, into the barren mountains of Sandžak and into eastern Bosnia, harassed every inch of the way by strong German forces, lacking arms, lacking military expertise, food supplies, encountering townspeople and villagers who sullenly denied ownership of any food, who treated them, in fact, as bitter enemies, hated every bit as much as the Germans.

Chaos and despair reigned.

The change in the confident, all-knowing and all-wise Josip Broz, alias Tito, was startling. The man who had always so readily made decisions, issued orders, known exactly what to do, was now desperately seeking advice from subordinates. Where should they go? What to do next? The movement was finished! Fatal mistakes had obviously been made. His had been the decision to ignore instructions from Moscow, he readily admitted. For that mistake the partisans were now paying bloodily and dearly.

When the Germans overtook and massacred their wounded, Tito's final collapse took place. He accepted full responsibility. He would, he declared, resign the leadership.

A shocked Party, hungry, frozen, in a state of black despair, looked into the future without him, and decided it could not possibly be more stark.

His resignation was refused.

7

During the long bitter march out of Serbia, Stevan had made a silent vow to take Jelena under his protection should anything happen to Alex. He was quite sure she would soon collapse under the strain of battle, cold, hunger and fatigue. He blamed himself bitterly for her presence. It was, of course, different with Alex. He had had some idea of what he might be in for. But Jelena!

In fact, she proved to be surprisingly resilient. Under her husband's proud eye she plunged into her duties with the wounded with the fierce protectiveness of a tigress nursing her young. With pathetically few trained medical personnel available, she did her part, darting amongst the sick and the dying, doing whatever was humanly possible without medical supplies, adequate food or warm covering for the former, comforting the latter, sometimes just by a touch of the hand, a hardly perceptible caress of the forehead. She was indefatigable. While the shortage of food slowed others down, the only sign of hunger she gave was an unnatural glittering of the eyes; otherwise there was this feverish activity, an inability to stop, to slow down, to rest.

When they finally came to a halt in the small Muslem hill town of Rogatica in eastern Bosnia, however, she suddenly collapsed with a burning fever. Alex was distraught. Tito made his concern known. Even Zdenka asked from time to time how the patient was doing. For several days she seemed to hover between life and death. Then, one morning, she opened her eyes, called softly for Alex, closed them again and slept peacefully. When she awakened she was able to swallow several spoons of chicken broth and after that her recovery seemed almost instantaneous.

As Jelena had collapsed and recovered from an undiagnosed fever, so did Tito seem to recover from the psychological collapse that had accompanied that ignominious flight through the Sandžak. The fact that the Central Committee had refused to accept his resignation undoubtedly had a great deal to do with the vigour with which he bounced back and resumed leadership.

Zdenka had also been laid low by flu, and Stevan found himself once again called upon to assume duties that lay in the misty realm between secretary and messenger boy. He took down messages to be signalled to Moscow which gave no hint of the retreat from Serbia; of the fact that Tito's forces were now fewer than four thousand. Instead they told of the glorious battle that had been fought in the township of Užice; of the craftiness and guile that had been used to entice the enemy into the barrenness of the Sandžak; of the impenetrable and heroic stand the partisans had taken in order to hold Rogatica. With all the urgency that words could convey Tito requested arms and supplies. *We await your aircraft day and night* was the constant message. There was no response from Moscow.

Undaunted he ignored the Soviet's previous instructions to set up only 'national' units and once again proceeded according to his own blueprint, forming the 'First Proletarian Brigade' under the command of Koča Popović, rebel son of a Serbian millionaire and hero of the struggle in Spain. At the same time he made contact with the Croat partisans in eastern Bosnia who were under the command of Slavisa Vajner. The news he received from the Bosnian comrades did not please him.

Vajner informed him that, of necessity, collaboration with the Chetniks still existed. The latter numbered about twenty thousand and were under the experienced leadership of Majors Dangić and Todorović. The bitter truth was, there existed mass turmoil within the partisan ranks. Whole companies and battalions had been deserting in order to join the Chetniks, who were extremely well trained and better armed than the communists. What he did not say, but what Tito was able to ascertain, was that one reason for the desertions stemmed from the same problem that had unnecessarily arisen in Montenegro under the leadership of Milovan Djilas.

Furiously he waved a copy of a letter he had received from Eduard Kardelj, his second in command in the Politburo, under Stevan's nose. The letter had been written by Lola Ribar, secretary of the Communist Youth Alliance of Yugoslavia and had also, apparently, been addressed to the Central Committee of the Communist Party for Croatia. In it, Ribar complained bitterly about what he called the 'false criterion' used in the liquidation of 'Fifth Columnists and enemies of the people', a criterion, as was all too obvious to the population, that was used by communists more to liquidate 'class enemies' and to settle old scores than to eliminate fascist enemies. In Hercegovina, he wrote icily, when the communists took over they instituted a reign of terror through their military leadership. This harsh sectarian attitude was doing nothing to convince the people they must support partisan leadership. On the contrary, he fumed, it was driving them by the thousands into the waiting arms of the Chetniks.

'They are taking an incorrect attitude,' Tito agreed. 'It is the same old story. Djilas did it in Montenegro. And what happened? The people there were also driven into the arms of the Chetniks.' He put the letter down and peered at Stevan over the top of his glasses. 'I tell you,' he said solemnly, 'we have arrived here in Bosnia just in time. We have arrived at two minutes before midnight!'

Then on the 15th of January the Germans, with support from the Croatian home guard and *Ustaši* divisions, launched a strong offensive against both the partisans and the Chetniks in Bosnia, and once again the partisans found themselves on the run. Comforted by news that the Chetniks were also suffering heavy losses, Tito fell back with his forces from the main road of the German penetration and managed to cross the Sarajevo-Višegrad railway and make his way to the mountains to the south, finally stopping in the small east Bosnian town of Foča on the River Drina. There he received news from his commander in the field, Svetozar Vukomanović, that although it was true that the Chetniks had suffered heavy losses, they had 'demonstrated more strength than the partisans'. His report went on to tell what Tito again angrily referred to as 'the same old story'. The Chetniks, with their military expertise and the support of the population that had enabled them to organize an effective intelligence service, were already slipping back into their former positions.

Still, at least one heartening event took place in early February. Direct radio contact was established with Moscow. Pleased, optimistic Tito sent off a stream of messages concerning the heroic resistance of the partisans in the field, stressing the discipline and sacrifices that had been evident during the retreat to Foča. Small, swift and brutal skirmishes that had, in fact, decimated the partisans, were raised to the glory of mighty battles. All of which were won! So impressive had these heroic actions been, it was stressed, that every day the proletariat were rallying to the banner in droves! With help from Moscow in the form of arms and other supplies, hundreds of thousands more would rally to the cause.

After a short delay the return messages began to arrive. Disconcertingly, Moscow seemed to be more concerned about the fact that their man in Yugoslavia was perhaps becoming a little too self-important than about the heroic resistance of their brothers in Bosnia. *Why did he call himself Tito instead of Josip Broz? Do not form proletarian brigades. The national nature of this uprising must be stressed. Have you established contact with the Chetniks? If not, do so immediately and place yourself under their command. Do this immediately.*

It fell to Stevan's uneasy lot to deliver the communiqués

to the communist leader. Tito, however, remained undaunted and continued to send messages stressing the role played by the partisans in the national uprising, requesting arms, supplies, ammunition.

He did not neglect what were, perhaps, more important matters. There was the problem that the Chetniks, as was the case in Serbia and Montenegro, were still enjoying strong support from the population in Bosnia. Unlike the partisans who, if they did 'liberate' an area, immediately set about forcing their harsh political ideology on the masses, liquidating those whom they decided were class enemies, or those who 'were or had been enemies of the Communist Party' and arbitrarily taking control of food, housing and livestock, the Chetniks, under direct orders from Mihailović, took no political stance and paid for any food or other provisions they needed.

On the 8th of February 1942, therefore, Tito despatched a strong message informing all units that they must coordinate their action for the purpose of clearing the whole territory of east Bosnia from Chetniks and Chetnik influence. This meant that the main action should be directed towards Drina and not towards the external enemy in Sarajevo and around the Bosnia river. To Stevan's inner mortification Tito also approved the action taken by the Croatian communists and some advancing units of the Montenegran Proletarian Brigade in concluding an agreement with the *Ustaši* not to fight each other, but to concentrate their efforts on eliminating the Chetnik forces, or at least forcing them back into Serbia where, hopefully, the Germans could finish them off. This having been done, he seemed to regain enough heart to again contact Moscow.

There was, he radioed in the middle of February, a safe site near Žabljak at the foot of Mount Durmitor where partisans could be despatched to pick up any supplies dropped by parachute. It was not only that the arrival of Soviet parachutists would have an enormous moral and political effect, but if they received enough equipment, he went on optimistically, he could mobilize another hundred thousand men.

Miraculously, their Soviet comrades, perhaps simply worn down by his persistence, agreed to 'see what can be done'. Jubilation reigned in the camp. The honour of leading the reception party who would greet their fraternal Soviet comrades and lead them back to the camp where a wonderfully warm welcome awaited them was given to Moša Pijade, Tito's old friend and comrade who had shared his 'university' days in prison and who, it was whispered, had taught the communist leader all that he knew about Marxism.

The strongest men would be needed to accompany him in order to cope with the journey back, loaded down as they would be with supplies and ammunition that had to be carried uphill in an area where they would sometimes be knee-deep in snow. Alex, of course, was amongst the first to be chosen. He was overwhelmed, almost in tears, as he hurried to tell Jelena and Stevan.

For a month they waited. Bitterly cold, hungry as wolves, but full of optimism and hope, they waited on a freezing mountain plateau for allies who never came, before Tito quietly recalled them. Alex was in a mood of dejection that even the loving ministrations of Jelena seemed unable to lift.

'Can you imagine,' he asked Stevan, 'if they cannot keep their fraternal promise to us, can you imagine what *they* must be going through?' This time, in fact, tears did come as he considered the horrors the Russians must be suffering. 'We shouldn't have asked them for help,' was his conclusion. 'They are obviously fighting for their lives. We should never have added to their burden.'

Tito said little. In direct defiance of the instructions from Moscow he did, however, form a Second Proletarian Brigade, and then a Third, Fourth and Fifth. No matter that each 'brigade' consisted of a few hundred poorly armed, poorly trained men. Who was to know? Who was to count?

And then he plunged into the problems facing the movement in Bosnia. Relentlessly he pressed the partisan forces to 'the liquidation of Chetnik bands and the reorganization of peoples' authorities'. Under his firm insistence, partisans were soon fighting 'shoulder to shoulder' with the *Ustaši* against Chetnik forces under the command of Major Dangić.

Privy as he was to the inner machinations of the Party leadership, although not really a member of it, Stevan became increasingly uneasy about the direction the partisans were taking. He and Alex had established the custom of taking a short stroll together in the early evening before sharing their meagre rations with Jelena and, without intending to do so, he found himself during one of these walks pouring out all his doubts to the big man.

'God,' he said, 'I think I could even swallow collaboration with the Germans, certainly with the Italians, but the *Ustaši*?'

Alex removed his cap, so proudly adorned with the red star, and ran his hand through his hair with a worried expression. 'It is best,' he said uneasily, 'not to talk about these things.'

'But for God's sake, Alex. To whom *can* I talk, if not to you? God only knows. I swallow enough, we all swallow enough. But the *Ustaši*? We are Serbs, you and I, damn it. Have you forgotten we are Serbs?'

Miletić's face closed. 'That is nationalism, Stevan. And you know as well as I do that in the interests of the world revolution, nationalism is a luxury we cannot afford.'

'But the whole point ... don't you see how stupid it all is? Do you know, Alex, if we, well, if we did what Moscow keeps telling us to do, if we would just honestly fight alongside the Chetniks, and then go to the people after the war, I know we would have a good chance of gaining power. Provided, of course, that Tito manages to restrain the madmen amongst us who are alienating the population. The truth is, you know, Tito is not a good military commander. Sometimes I really don't think he knows what he's doing in that area. But he *is* a damned good politician. The way he handles people, manipulates them if you will. I am sure he could lead us to power in a decent way. If only we could begin to *behave* decently. And, my God, think of the lives we could save. Think of the people who are dying just because we refuse to stop and think!'

They had stopped next to a huge fir tree, although Stevan, carried away with his line of thought, was completely oblivious to their surroundings. Alex, though, glanced around anxiously before taking him firmly by the arm.

'Stevan. For God's sake, please stop talking this way. Don't you understand? It is not for us to judge. You should not be thinking this way. Tito is our leader. He has the blessing of Stalin. And if what we have to do sometimes is distasteful to us, think of what Stalin has had to do. Not for himself, not for his own country even, but for the liberation of the world's proletariat! Can we do less? You and I, I am the first to admit it, we are not yet truly developed politically. Until we are, we *must* have faith in our leaders. We must have faith in Tito.'

'Even when he acts against Moscow's instructions?'

Again the big man stirred uneasily. 'The instructions he receives from Moscow might not truly reflect Stalin's wishes. Who knows? Can Stalin be everywhere? Can he oversee everything? No, no. Don't you understand? Tito *knows* him. He has actually talked to him! They have discussed the world revolution together. If we cannot trust Tito, then whom can we trust? You must stop thinking about things so much, Stevan. Or, if you must think, you must ask yourself whether your thoughts are in accordance with Marxist doctrine. Also, I think you are being too idealistic.' Through the dusk of the evening Stevan could feel the brown eyes staring at him and could imagine their earnest expression. 'Did you know that Lenin said idealism was reactionary?'

Stevan remained silent. In all his life he had never had more respect for anyone than he had for the big man standing in front of him. Except, perhaps, for David Ristić. But David had been a close friend, almost a brother. That was different. One thing he did know: If Alex Miletić could swallow whatever had to be done to bring the communists to power, surely to God he, Stevan Matić, could also do it?

Slowly they turned back in the direction of the camp. He had, Stevan realized with an empty feeling in his heart, never felt lonelier in his life.

* * *

In December 1941, after Draža Mihailović had been promoted to the rank of major-general by the young King Peter and his government in exile, he was appointed minister for war for Yugoslavia. In March 1942 David Ristić found himself summoned to the general's presence. Not sure whether the long-anticipated posting to his own unit was at last in the offing, or whether he was being designated to liberate yet another village, he stood to attention before the general and saluted smartly. Mihailović, who had set up a rather rickety temporary office in an abandoned hut, waved him almost absent-mindedly towards a chair, finished scribbling some notes, and then looked up with a smile.

'So,' he said. 'Lieutenant Ristić.'

'Yes sir.'

'Tell me, lieutenant,' he leaned forward on the small school desk, eyes twinkling, 'can you ride a motorcycle?'

A motorcycle? Well, he thought he knew how to start one. Had ridden back-saddle once behind Stevan on a borrowed bike that had nearly finished up being wrapped around a tree.

'Yes sir.'

'You can? Fine, fine.' He removed his glasses in an absent-minded fashion, stared at them for a moment, then replaced them. 'You have heard that our government in London has appointed me minister of war?'

'If it's not too late to congratulate you, sir, all of us are very proud.'

Mihailović nodded and gave a slight smile. 'Thank you. I have to confess, though, that it is not an honour I have accepted too eagerly.' He hesitated, then went on. 'It has projected me onto the political scene, you understand? And the truth of the matter is, I am a military man, not a politician.'

David nodded, not too sure what this had to do with him. Or with motorcycles.

'When I entered this conflict it was with one thought only. To rid our country of its enemies, no matter how formidable they may be, and to demonstrate to the world that honest Yugoslavs were unequivocally on the side of the Allies.' He frowned at some inner thought, before continuing. 'Today, however, it seems that the enemy is not only an external one.' The blue eyes behind the glasses searched David's face. 'You have heard, of course, of the terror our own communists are bringing upon the population in Montenegro?' Without waiting for a reply he rose abruptly, walked to the doorway of the hut and stood staring out at the cluster of firs surrounding the area. He stood there for so long that David, who had leapt to his feet the moment the general stood up, began to suspect he had been forgotten. Just then, however, Mihailović turned around, retraced his steps and again lowered himself behind the desk with an audible sigh.

'Let me tell you something, lieutenant. Since observing the way in which our opponents wage their political war, I am extremely grateful not to be mixed up in such a dirty business. I am more grateful than ever that I *am* a military man. In fact, except for being opposed to fascism with all my heart and my strength, I have never been interested in politics, thank God. Never have been, most certainly never will be. However,' he continued with another heartfelt sigh, 'this new appointment means that I will probably find myself involved whether I wish to be or not. So I need someone who is here on the scene with me. Someone who can give me sound advice. You understand my situation?'

'Yes sir.'

'Good.' He was suddenly brisk. 'I have been in touch with Belgrade. They have arranged to send . . .' he hesitated and gave his shy, rather charming smile. 'They have arranged to send someone they think will be able to give me sound political advice.'

'Yes sir?'

'If you will come here for a moment?' He had opened a map on his desk and his forefinger was tracing a route. 'The gentleman will be travelling by train for part of the journey. But he will need someone to pick him up.'

At last David knew why he had been summoned to the general's office. It seemed that he had been chosen to pick the political functionary up and bring him back to headquarters. He was to make his way to a certain village by foot and by horse. When he arrived he would find a motorcycle waiting there. His instructions were simple. He was to wait at the village until the gentleman arrived, then bring him to headquarters immediately.

He left on his mission the next morning and arrived at the village in the afternoon. The functionary, he was told, was expected to arrive some time the following morning.

The moment he saw that tall, towering figure stride into the village square and glare fiercely around, he realized he should have known. Bless Mihailović! God bless the man.

'Uncle Mikhail!' he shouted at the top of his voice. 'Uncle Mikhail! It is me, David!'

And then he was being embraced in that warm bear hug as the old man nearly lifted him off his feet.

'David! But they didn't tell me. They didn't say it would be you.' His booming voice echoed through the village.

'Nor me. Not a word!' He was laughing exultantly, near tears at the sight of the fierce, wise old man he loved so dearly.

There was no time to be wasted. David's instructions were to leave the village immediately his passenger arrived. The motorcycle was wheeled out, a miracle of shining black and silver chrome, complete with a sidecar. Nothing but the best for this new adviser to the minister for war!

'I didn't know you could ride one of these contraptions, my boy.' His uncle had settled his huge body into the sidecar in which he seemed to only just fit. He turned to make some comment about the comfort or lack of comfort, but his words, whatever they had been, were lost, carried away with the wind and the noise of the engine.

David had started the machine, and now pushed his foot down hard on the foot pedal. With a roar the bike lunged, lurched, and shot out of the village like a cannon-ball, leaving in its wake flying chickens, squealing pigs, a donkey frozen in its tracks, open-mouthed villagers and a screaming infant.

Up, up, up the hill it howled, leaping over boulders, taunting trees with its near misses, plunging down gulleys, veering precariously off whatever beaten track it managed to find. At first frozen in his seat with shock, Mikhail Ristić began to yell as his body began to react with bruised indignation to each new unpredictable twist and turn of the infernal machine. His words, however, were again borne aloft past his nephew's ears, to be swept up and away, lost in the wind. By the time they reached headquarters some time later he was hunched down in his seat, eyes closed against the wind, lips moving whether in profanity or prayer no one but himself and the wind would ever know.

David roared up to Mihailović's makeshift office with a flourish, proud of the fact that it had taken him no more than half an hour or so to master the splendid big machine. He leapt off the bike and held out his hand to his uncle to help him out of the sidecar in which he was hunkered down as though in some unsatisfactory dugout that offered the minimum of protection.

Ignoring his outstretched hand, Mikhail heaved himself stiffly up and out of the seat, paused to give him a glare from the pale brown eyes that rooted him to the spot, opened his mouth to say something, found it too dry to utter a word, then limped slowly towards the delegation that had appeared to greet him.

David, the recipient of that outraged, furious and terrible stare, could not move from shock. *My God! No wonder we won at Salonika.*

Later, much later that evening, his uncle, apparently recovered from both his rage and from what he was ever after to refer to as 'that maniacal ride through hell', strolled with him on the outskirts of the village. It was a beautiful, if freezing evening with a full moon that hung so low it seemed to skim the upreaching firs and pines and lit up the path they followed as though it was a giant, softly glowing lamp.

'For God's sake, boy. Why did you tell the general you could ride that infernal machine? We could have come on foot, you know. Or with horses.'

'But that would have taken us twice as long. I know. That's the way I reached the village. As for the motorcycle,' he gave his uncle a sideways grin, 'aren't you the one, Uncle Mikhail, who has told me hundreds of times through the years that one should never say one can't do something until one has tried?'

For a brief moment he thought he was going to receive another terrible glare, but then his uncle relented and burst into a great roar of laughter. 'By God, you are right! So I did. So it is true, after all? One's words *do* come back to haunt one. Eh?' Again he gave a short burst of laughter and placed an arm around his nephew's shoulders. 'Serves me right, eh, my boy? Yes, yes. It is true. Serves me right.'

David joined in with his laughter, then eagerly began to question him about the family. Was Aunt Draga coping all right? How was Andjela's marriage going? Did her husband treat her well? Was the occupation interfering with Zora's studies? And Aunt Kaja; he hoped she was well.

Yes, yes. Of course Draga was coping wonderfully well. It would take more than Hitler's riff-raff army to unsettle that one! Zora's studies were coming along nicely, so far as he knew. As for his Aunt Kaja, well, there had been a slight problem when she learned that her husband had agreed to join Mihailović here in the mountains, but, of course, one simply had to treat women with firmness, so it had not taken long to resolve that. As for Andjela . . .

Here he stopped walking and turned to David with a

smile. 'Such news for you, my boy. By summer you will be an uncle.' The smile broadened until it reached the proportions of a delighted chuckle. 'If it's a boy, Andjela said she intends to call it David Mikhail! What do you think of that?' He stood there beaming proudly.

His nephew patently thought it was wonderful news and did not hesitate to say so.

'I'm sorry, you know, David. I'm sorry I couldn't tell them that I was joining Mihailović. The fact is, I didn't even know *you* were here with him at headquarters. It was a matter of their own safety. The less people know the safer they will be. Otherwise, of course, I would have direct messages for you.' He sighed. 'I sent your Aunt Kaja to stay with relatives outside Belgrade. So I hope there will be no problem there. The family, by the way, think I am with her.'

David nodded agreement. There was one more member of the family he wanted to ask about. He did not quite know how to approach the subject. As usual, his uncle seemed to guess what was in his mind.

'If you wish to ask me about my ex-son,' he said gruffly, 'please don't.'

Saddened, David remained silent. He was fond of his wild, charming cousin. Had always felt his uncle was far too harsh with him. Perhaps if Nikola's father had tried to talk to him, if only he, David, could have found the time to see him again, to reason with him . . .

He glanced at his uncle's stern profile and realized it was a subject best left alone. In any event, there was something he had been waiting to ask since he'd first glimpsed Mikhail Ristić's big frame stride into the village square that morning.

'I've been wondering, Uncle.' He hesitated, feeling almost shy, then pressed on. 'Do you remember Irina Mirskaia? I took her to meet you and Aunt Kaja one afternoon last summer. Do you remember?'

They had resumed their stroll, but now his uncle again stopped and turned to look at him. 'The little Russian girl? Yes, yes. Of course. Odd you should ask that. As a matter of fact she called on your Aunt and me only three weeks or so ago. Was asking after you.'

'She was?' David stared back at him eagerly.

'The damnedest thing! Said she wanted to join you. She said she had heard the communists accepted women into the ranks and she asked if I knew whether the Chetniks were doing the same.'

David gave a delighted laugh. 'The devil she did? Did she say that? My God, Uncle, I hope you told her we aren't so desperate that we have to hide behind women.'

'Even if we were, my boy,' Mikhail boomed, 'I don't think that little slip of a thing would last long. Mind you,' he said, turning back in the direction of headquarters, 'she is such a beautiful little girl. Absolutely beautiful. I must congratulate you on your taste. Although she seemed so . . .' He hesitated, searched for the right word.

'Yes, Uncle?'

'She seemed a little lost. Yes, yes. That's the word. That little girl is well and truly lost I would say.' He stared at his nephew in surprise as David pulled up short.

'What do you mean, she is lost?' he shouted. 'Irina is *not* lost! She will stay in Belgrade until I return, do you understand? And believe me, Uncle, I *intend* to return. I intend to return and marry her. I shall survive this damned war! I shall survive this war and I will return to take care of Irina. She will not be lost! I assure you of that.' He stood there trembling with rage, glaring at his uncle in much the same manner the old man had glared at him earlier.

After his first start of surprise, Mikhail shook his head. 'There is no need to shout at me, my boy.' His voice was surprisingly gentle. He placed an arm around his shoulders. 'Of course you will survive! I have been told,' he said proudly, 'that you fight like a tiger. And your little Russian girl will be all right, too. Yes, yes. I was mistaken. I am sure I was mistaken. Everything will be fine for both of you.' He shook his large head ruefully. 'But it is hard on the women, David. War is always so damned hard on the women.'

Changing the subject, he began to talk about Mihailović,

the problems he faced. 'You would think it enough that he has to rid the country of these barbaric Germans, without worrying about the communists who, by the way, seem to be as mad as the fascists, madder! What kind of men are they when they see in this terrible suffering of our people only a way in which they might grasp power? You know, son, the very thought of them hurts me much more than the thought of the Germans. These men come from our own people. If you knew the reports the general has received about their behaviour in Montenegro. Madmen! These are madmen, I tell you.'

David had something else on his mind. 'Listen, Uncle. Do you know I've been trying to get transferred to a unit in the field ever since I've been here? Do you think you could, you know, now you are here, do you think you could give someone a push? A reminder anyway?'

'Give someone a push?' Mikhail removed his pince-nez, polished each glass carefully and frowned. He replaced it on his nose then and glared down at his nephew sternly. 'Are you asking me to use my influence to get you something you want?'

'Yes,' David said without the slightest hesitation.

'Damned if you are!' His uncle roared with laughter and slapped him on the shoulder so hard he nearly stumbled. 'Well, if you are so brazen, son, let me see what I can do. Yes, yes. I will see what I can do.'

What he could do became quickly evident. Almost immediately, David received notification that he was to be posted to the elite Avala Corps, which was operating in Posavina, an area in West Serbia embracing Loznica, Valjevo, Mladenova, Kosmaj and Rudnik. Prior to his departure from supreme headquarters at the end of April 1942, however, an order signed by the German puppet General Nedić's Minister for Internal Affairs appeared in the Belgrade paper *Novo Vreme, The New Times*. It called upon Draža Mihailović and his collaborators to surrender within five days to the Belgrade police authorities. Failure to do so would result in families of all Chetnik leaders being taken as hostages.

No Chetnik surrendered.

David left for Posavina with a heavy heart, shortly after word was received that the wives of several Chetnik leaders had been arrested and placed in the infamous German concentration camp in the Belgrade suburb of Banjica.

8

News of the difficulties the partisans were encountering in Montenegro continued to bother and irritate Tito. In a letter dated the 3rd of March 1942, Milovan Djilas and Mitar Bakić, both delegates to the Central Committee of the Communist Party of Yugoslavia, wrote that they 'considered the success of the Chetniks in the area was due to false political attitudes about all basic questions by certain partisan elements', an apparent allusion to comrades who continued to eliminate local authorities.

'Well, perhaps Djilas has learned something,' he grumbled, handing the letter to Stevan one brisk March morning. 'After the mess he himself made in Montenegro last year!'

By the end of April, however, the chaos among the communists in Montenegro could no longer be brushed aside. Word came through that the partisans had got out of control in their determination to force their various versions of the dictatorship of the proletariat down the throats of a resisting population. Although the Italians continued to hold the towns, the countryside was in the hands of warring factions of Chetniks and partisans, and from all accounts the latter were getting the worst of it. It was also learned that under pressure from a frightened and furious population, Mihailović himself was rumoured to be considering moving his headquarters to Montenegro to take charge of operations and to rid the countryside entirely of partisan bands.

Tito decided that enough was enough.

Despite the cease-fire arrangement with the *Ustaši*, in Eastern Bosnia the communists were still doing badly in clashes with German units and the Croatian home guard. With the support of the population the Chetniks, on the other hand, were managing to hang grimly on and, as had been the case during the communist terror in Hercegovina, there was still a steady stream of defections from the partisans into their ranks.

Temporarily giving up what appeared to be a losing battle in eastern Bosnia, therefore, and under heavy attack from all sides, Tito made the decision to withdraw from Foča and move southwards in an effort to save the rapidly deteriorating situation in Montenegro. Grim-faced and determined, he left with the First and Second Proletarian Brigades early in May, only to face an even worse situation in the inhospitable and barren Montenegrin mountains with their sullen and hardheaded population that patently wanted no part of the proletarian revolution. Once again he found that the Chetniks were clearly receiving the support of the people and although as poorly armed as the partisans, again and again they emerged as victors in battles and skirmishes. With what seemed to Stevan to be an almost childlike faith, the secretary-general again appealed to Moscow for help, and again received nothing.

As always during the stress of battle, Tito seemed nervous and irritable, although every effort was made for his comfort and protection. There was never any question about his courage. As he himself had let it be known he had, in fact, been awarded a medal by the Austrians during the First World War for conspicuous gallantry against the Allies. It was simply the general consensus, with which he agreed, that if anything should happen to him, the Communist Party in Yugoslavia would be lost.

Still, there was no doubt about it. The continual shortage of food, the worry about lack of arms and ammunition and the perpetual skirmishes were taking their toll. He was short-tempered and on edge. Forever after Stevan was forced to remind himself of these circumstances whenever he recalled the brutal slap in the face he was given one bright morning in May after being summoned to the secretary-general's presence for some trivial task.

Tito was ensconced in a warm, dry cave with some rugs and a makeshift table and chair. He had rather irritably asked Stevan to try to get a message through to one of the partisan commanders in the field. Then, just as Stevan was leaving with his notes, he called him back.

'One good piece of news. We have begun at last to get some excellent intelligence from Belgrade. Direct from the office of General Bader, the German commander for Serbia, you know?' He picked up a piece of paper, waved it. 'According to German reports, Mihailović now has at least a hundred thousand men in his so-called army. No wonder our revolutionary struggle is suffering so many set-backs. But, here is some more good news. The British supplies to him have so far been negligible, so he is as short of arms as we.'

'Good.' Stevan nodded and again made to leave. But Tito had not finished.

'You are not curious? As to our source, I mean.'

'Curious?' Stevan stared at him, a little surprised, not sure what he was getting at.

Tito smiled, although the pale eyes remained cold. 'It's from a friend of yours. That young woman, Olga. The sister of Comrade Miletić. It seems she has managed to find a friend in very high places.' His good temper seemingly having been restored, he lowered himself down onto an old fur rug, leaned back against the cave wall, and began to read a report in an obvious gesture of dismissal, leaving Stevan to stumble out of the cave in a fury of humiliation and bitterness.

* * *

By June 1942 Chetnik action combined with the hostility of the civilian population had made the partisan position in Montenegro completely untenable. The decision had been made to move back into Bosnia, although they had not anticipated the six long weeks it would take them to withdraw. Single file as always and with the perpetual shortage of food, miserable weather and Chetniks never ceasing to snap at their heels wearing away at their morale, it was with a sense of relief that they finally came to halt if only temporarily in Central Bosnia.

Although they had occasional brief and fierce encounters with German or *Ustaši* forces necessitating several hasty withdrawals and some bitter losses, the Axis forces in the main left them alone. By the time they had rested up and regained some strength, Tito had made the decision to move onward to Bihać, a small town on the border of Croatia. The decision to move so close to the now independent fascist state necessitated, of course, that some more definite undertaking be agreed upon with both the Germans and the *Ustaši* that would enable the Axis forces to concentrate on Chetnik fighters while Tito proceeded with his all-important political agenda.

Drawing upon pre-war contacts the communists had with the *Ustaši* when both groups had been outlawed by the Yugoslav government in fact proved even easier than the secretary-general had envisaged and it was quickly agreed that the main force under his command would be left in peace although, as his *Ustaši* contacts foretold, small bands of partisans operating throughout Bosnia did find themselves occasionally under military attack and even on occasion themselves launched short attacks against Axis forces. Little could be done to prevent these brief sorties. Neither the partisans nor the *Ustaši* were anxious to broadcast their 'mutually beneficial' cooperation. The least said or known about it the better, particularly amongst their own sometimes unsophisticated forces.

Relaxed and seemingly content for the first time in months, Tito temporarily shed the mantle of 'military commander' with which he was clearly ill at ease, and returned to his natural forte of administration and propaganda.

The forces under his command, perhaps twenty thousand men, were overnight transformed into an 'army' of one hundred and fifty thousand for the benefit of the outside world. No doubt, Stevan thought with a pang, a number prompted by the report they had received from Olga that according to the German General Gelen was the number of forces Mihailović now commanded. With another sleight of hand, the twenty thousand were then divided into 'corps', 'brigades' and 'divisions', and given the lofty title of the National Army of Liberation and Partisan Detachments of Yugoslavia. At least they were now comparatively well fed and not badly armed.

Triumphantly, like a small child eager for praise from his teacher, Tito eagerly radioed to Moscow details of his 'army's' new status. *We shall now set up something like a government, which we shall call the National Liberation Committee of Yugoslavia.*

Moscow seemed to have its doubts. The stream of messages Tito received stressed the importance of the new committee being presented as of a national, not a communist nature. The partisans were under no circumstances to consider the committee to be any kind of opposition to the legal Yugoslav government in London. No mention was to be made about the abolition of the monarchy in favour of a federal republic. Tito read Moscow's instructions, gave a slight shrug, and began to make preparations for the first meeting of the anti-fascist National Liberation Committee of Yugoslavia, which he had decided to hold at the end of November and which was to be attended by delegates from all over the country.

The meeting proved to be both uplifting and encouraging, despite some grumbling among the delegates at the rough likenesses of the decadent imperialists Winston Churchill and Franklin Roosevelt that flanked that of their beloved Stalin in Tito's new spirit of unity. For once he really was trying hard to follow instructions from Moscow. It was not the Party's intention, he said in his address to the delegates, to form a government, but rather to put together the political machinery that would enable them to help *all* national forces fight against the fascists.

His comments received a favourable reception, although there were muted rebellious mutterings when the leadership of the Party endorsed his comments about 'incorrect' methods used by certain elements within the partisan groups to try to force the population to gather together beneath the banner of the red flag.

But the leadership, under Tito's guidance, stood firm. From now on it must be made clear to the masses that the communists, far from being bloodthirsty Bolsheviks were, in fact, democratic patriots who took a broad, liberal view of things. To reinforce this new and rather revolutionary approach, a resolution was passed for the delegates to take back with them to spread amongst their members. It guaranteed not only the inviolability of private property, but also the freedom of individuals to pursue their own initiative in trade, industry and agriculture and particularly stressed that the partisans would bring no radical changes to the social life and activities of the people. It finished with a grand flourish by promising 'free democratic elections'.

And having thus pronounced the Party's intention to turn over a brand-new leaf the partisans sat back, well pleased with themselves, to await the response of a population that had so far proven to be so unjustly suspicious of the intentions of its would-be communist liberators.

* * *

David Ristić was never to forget the scene that presented itself to him when he arrived late one afternoon at the end of April 1942 to take up his new posting with the Avala Corps. Gathered together in a small valley near Umka were some three thousand men. Most of them bearded, and some, whose hair reached the middle of their backs, David recognized as peasants who had announced that they would not cut their hair until 'the little king is back on the throne'. They were dressed in a variety of clothes from bits and pieces of army uniform to the Serbian peasant's national costume of jodhpurs and *gunjaks*, a short top coat made from heavy woollen homespun. They were carrying a variety of arms from short machine-guns of English, Italian or German origin, which they wore slung around their necks, to long 'rifle machine-guns' as they called the Czechoslovakian *Zbrojovkas*. Most of them, however, carried rifles from the former Yugoslav army that had been made in Belgium or Yugoslavia. Slung across their chests were a variety of bombs, daggers and munition bags. Many wore cartridge belts across both their chests and their backs. The insignia on their sleeves bore the proud Serbian motto *Liberty or Death*, a reminder of their vow to live up to their proud heritage. In the grey afternoon mist they looked unreal; an army of fierce, ragtag ghosts risen up from Serbian soil to once again respond to the need to banish an invader from their beloved land.

'They look impressive, don't they?' Lieutenant Branko Jelić, his good friend from Belgrade with whom David had served in Negotin, smiled. 'The trouble, of course, is that the ammunition they carry is about all we have. Once that is gone . . .' He shrugged.

Their commanding officer, Kosta Marinković, a former bomber pilot in the Yugoslav air force, who had joined the Chetniks after the capitulation of the army on the 17th of April the previous year, had handed David over to Jelić shortly after his arrival and had watched with a wide grin as the two young men had given whoops of joy and embraced each other Serbian-style with kisses on both cheeks. Neither had known the other was with the Chetniks. Jelić, like David, had joined the movement in Belgrade, and also like David, had been transferred to the mountains when it was felt by the Belgrade command that the Gestapo was snapping too close at his heels.

'What a bit of luck that you were posted here, David. And you know you will be serving in my brigade? The Posavska Brigade. It's the best one in the corps.'

Later he was to assure him he would enjoy serving under

Marinković, who was an impressive-looking man with a thick beard and piercing green eyes who had already made an excellent impression. Jelić's tales of his courage in battle, his tremendous energy, his voice 'that can shake mountains when he wishes' did not come as a surprise. 'The men have boundless faith in him, and you know how important that is,' Branko said.

Marinković had already explained the general set-up of the Avala Corps which, it seemed, was fairly representative of Chetnik units in operation all over the country. The Posavska Brigade consisted of three battalions and a staff company. In theory it was intended that several separate areas of action could take place by each battalion under separate commands. Therefore, each battalion had three officers, each of whom could assume command if the others were killed or wounded. However, in practice the situation in the field quite often required that the whole brigade take part in a unified operation. At other times the battalions might split into companies or even smaller units, depending on the action required. The situation was so unpredictable that quite often individual action had to be taken.

'Flexibility,' Marinković had boomed. 'That is the answer to guerrilla warfare. Flexibility and patience. We attack when we can, but we must be prepared to simply take defensive action when we lack ammunition and arms and are faced with an enemy of vastly superior strength.' He had spoken rather wistfully of how easy it would all be if they were only facing the Germans. 'But at the same time to have the *Ustaši* dogs aiming for our throats, those blasted *Domobrans*, the Croatian home guard *and* the Bulgars – the Hungarians. And now they have brought in Muslims from Bosnia and treacherous Albania has of course supplied them with Arnauts from Kosovo and Metochia. We have also learned that they have recruited white Russians from Belgrade, some seven thousand of them I believe.'

Marinković had shaken his head with exasperation. 'Not

to mention the *Ljotićevci*, those treacherous Serbs without souls – fascists every one – worse than Nedić's puppet army if you ask me.'

David had shaken his head gloomily. 'And yet I think General Mihailović is more worried about the communists. He said the pattern is beginning to fall into place. What they are trying to do is further create, and take advantage of, internal disorder. I suppose they know they have no hope of grabbing power under normal conditions.'

Marinković nodded. 'Yet our orders from Čiča...'

David was to learn that the whole corps used the affectionate derivative when referring to Mihailović. '... Čiča has given clear instructions. We are to concentrate on driving the Germans out.' He had smiled, revealing white, slightly uneven teeth. 'We can take care of the rest after the war.'

That evening David was to eat better than he had done for months. Sitting with Jelić and several other officers outside a makeshift tent he attacked a tin plate piled high with smoked meat, cheese, bacon, boiled eggs and *pogatcha*, the domestically-made wheat bread he loved, all washed down with a large tin mug of coffee. 'My God,' he said, 'at headquarters they would give their best captured Italian *Berettas* for a meal like this.' They all laughed.

'Enjoy it while you can, lieutenant. We do not eat like this every day.'

They went on to explain that the previous day 'Zeka' had ambushed a German convoy. Taken by surprise, the Germans had been disarmed and left by the roadside, alive in order not to provoke reprisals against nearby villagers, but 'naked as the day they were born', chuckled Jelić, 'Anyway, we'd hoped the trucks would be full of ammunition, but as it turned out they only contained food. Not,' he added, munching happily away at a large piece of corn bread, 'that we are really complaining.'

'Who, or what, is Zeka?' David held his mug out for another cup of the bitter coffee.

Kosta Marinković, who had joined them half way through their meal, gave a great roar of laughter. 'When you find out,' he said, 'you will be doubly grateful you are sharing the post of second in command of the Posavska Brigade with Branko. A few more Zeka's and we would win the war with both hands tied behind our backs, eh, Jelić?' He moved off with his own mug full of coffee.

'A few more Zeka's and a few more Marinković's,' a dark-eyed officer said softly.

It was a cold evening, but the air was crisp, fresh and invigorating. Unable to get over their good fortune at meeting again, and of actually sharing a brigade, David and Branko talked far into the night. David repeated the conversation he had had with their commanding officer earlier that evening about the various forces ranged against them, and discovered that Jelić harboured his fiercest hatred for the partisans. 'And so would you, David, if you had seen them in action as I have. Wait until you have been with us for a while and you'll see what I mean.' He went on to describe how during an attack he had led on a German patrol some partisans had sneaked up from behind and opened fire on his unit. 'We had intended to disarm the Germans and take them as prisoners to make sure there would be no reprisals against our people. But what happened? We had to return the partisan fire, and in the confusion three Germans were killed. The rest escaped and the partisans disappeared into the woods. And the result? Neither arms nor ammunition taken and three hundred – *three hundred* – Serbian civilians died for those three Germans. God only knows, I hate the bloody and barbaric Germans and the unspeakable *Ustaši*, but at least I know they are not Serbs. But the communists...' he spat and echoed Mikhail Ristić's words of several weeks previously. 'There are many Serbs amongst them. Our own people! And they yearn for power the way a hungry wolf yearns for red meat. They have no compunction about wading through the blood of their own people to get it!'

First thing next morning David was wakened by a dark, softly-spoken Gypsy, who introduced himself as Jovan, handed him a mug of tea and told him that he had been assigned to be his orderly. From that moment on until he left the Avala Corps he was never far from David's side.

Jelić appeared bright and early, explaining that he especially wanted him to get to know their third battalion. He introduced him to Zeka, the battalion commander. The short, grey-haired man in his early forties, whose quick movements contrasted oddly with his rather stout build, wore no beard. He was, however, unshaven, and rubbed his hand several times over his bristly grey stubble. He did not wear his hair long. A sign of independence, wondered David? He remembered what Jelić had said about Zeka's outstanding qualities as a fighter. Certainly there was no indication of that in his appearance, except perhaps for a rather chilling half smile that never seemed to leave his lips. As Jelić said later, 'that smile is on his face when he eats, when he drinks, when he sleeps and when he kills. Damned if I'm not sure it isn't still there when he makes love. A real chiller, is Zeka. But wait until you see him in action. My God, then you will be glad he is on our side!'

Of the men in the battalion, about a hundred and fifty were known throughout the Posavska Brigade as 'Zeka's fighters', and many of them were now clustered around him. They were to stay in David's mind as a collection of cold, dangerous faces, except for a young lad called Yaruga.

'*Yaruga*?' David smiled. 'Ditch? But what kind of nickname is that?' The gentle-faced boy just smiled and shrugged. Later Branko told him that Yaruga dogged Zeka's footsteps the way Jovan had already begun to dog David's.

'He's too young to be here, but refuses to return to his village,' he said.

Within a month David had settled into his position within the Corps, and was familiar with the individual strengths and foibles of the men under his command by the time the signal for *pokret* – movement – arrived. Quietly and with a minimum of fuss some three thousand men prepared themselves and their horses for the move. Battalions joined their brigades, with special patrols at their head and at the rear. David and Branko were both up front with the Posavska

Brigade when Kosta Marinković caught up with them and explained that the corps would be moving southward towards Valjevo, where it would spread out in the hills and mountains. Word had been received from headquarters that strong German units had been despatched to 'clean out all Chetniks from Mačva and the western Morava area'. It was obvious that if they stayed in the valley they would all be 'sitting ducks'.

For David's benefit, Kosta went on to explain that as a result of the lessons learned at Šabac and Loznica, when so many Chetniks had been wiped out by German forces with their vastly superior numbers of troops and firepower, the strategy was to withdraw, avoid direct confrontation on a large scale and concentrate on smaller operations, particularly sabotage. This strategy had, in fact, proved of great value to the Allies in the autumn of 1941 when the German divisions the Chetniks had tied down in Serbia might have contributed to a vastly different outcome in the battle for Moscow, had they been free to be sent to the Eastern Front.

'Even with all these restrictions, we must be hurting them badly,' Marinković added, 'because they keep launching these all-out attacks in an effort to wipe us out. And, of course, their search for Čiča has intensified. God protect him from them and for us.' He leaned forward in his saddle, urged his horse into a canter, and in a few moments was riding at the head of the brigade.

'It all sounds a bit vague,' David said. 'Do you think we might have a special task in the near future, Branko?'

His friend shrugged. 'I don't know. It seems to me that we have to play it by ear. And meanwhile—'

'Meanwhile,' a voice came from behind, 'meanwhile the enemy are allowed to kill us, but we must try not to kill them!'

David half turned in his saddle and grinned at Zeka, who sat stolidly on the ugliest grey mare he had ever seen. 'Never mind, Zeka. You will no doubt get your reward in heaven.'

Zeka hunched down into the saddle and managed to

scowl and at the same time retain that chilling half-smile. They rode on in silence.

My dear David,
The general has told me a courier is going to your corps commander so I have prevailed upon him to include this letter for you, to let you know this 'old man', your uncle, is in good health and hoping you too are keeping well.

You will know by now that Čiča has been appointed general and deputy commander-in-chief of the 'Yugoslav army' in the fatherland (which he would prefer we call ourselves, but the Chetnik label, identified so strongly by our people with their country's bravest liberators will, of course, stick). This latest honour from London seems to have caused something of a panic in the German command here. Believe it or not, General Dankelmann, the military governor of Serbia, has been seeking to arrange an armistice with us, but as he refused to accept Čiča's terms, which were, of course, that the enemy evacuate our country, it all came to nothing. Until that day comes, however, as Čiča informed them, we shall continue to fight, to the last man if necessary.

Brave words, which I heartily endorse! But it has not been easy here. The German response has been to organize special task forces designed to hunt our general down. Along with the usual puppet curs, they have formed special German divisions. The Brandenburg Division which our people in Belgrade tell us consists of three first mountain units and four siege divisions, and the Seventh SS Division Prince Eugen which we believe consists partly of *Volksdeutschers*, with some of their own specially trained people. All in addition, of course, to the usual German SS motorized police units. Together with the Italians, they have been buzzing around like packs of virulent Macedonian mosquitoes in an effort to capture our Čiča. Fat hope they have with the people guarding and hiding him as though he were their last ticket to heaven. I'm afraid, however, we *have* been forced to retreat. Not only our supreme command here, but all other corps or local brigades in Mačva and West Serbia as far as the Homolje Mountains where, as you know, Major Piletić has been extremely active in fighting both the Germans and the soulless *Ljotićevci*.

You will also know by now that we have succeeded in pushing the partisans out of Montenegro, right back into eastern Bosnia where I have no doubt our people there will take care of them. Rumour has it that they were led by that Tito fellow and all I can say is he certainly should take some lessons in guerrilla warfare. I cannot pretend to understand the mentality of those who would try to take advantage of their country's agony to grab at perfidious power and my only regret is that we had to waste our ammunition chasing them out! The peasants, as always, kiss Čiča's hands and press food upon us. They have so little, however, after the German and Italian bandits steal from them, that we take the minimum. Thank God London keeps us supplied with money, so at least we can pay them for what we do take!

I must close in haste! The 'mosquitoes' are closing in again! Take care, my boy.

Your loving Uncle Mikhail

Over the next few months they were constantly on the move. David was never again to eat as well as he had that first evening with the Avala Corps during the remaining period he spent with them. There were compensations, however. His friendship with Jelić was one of them. The two young officers, both blond and blue-eyed, both voluble in their desire to rid their country of every last fascist, both at a loss to understand the actions of the communists who were trying so hard to sabotage their efforts in that direction, would talk long into the night, visualizing the direction

Yugoslavia would take once the war was over and their enemies had been disposed of. They would get rid of treacherous Croatia, strengthen bonds between all other provinces, establish a democracy that would embrace all Serbs and Slovenes, and utilize the rich minerals and natural resources of the country to modernize it without destroying the land's rich agricultural heritage.

While they talked David's orderly, Jovan, would hover nearby, bringing tea from time to time, listening intently whenever possible.

'And this new democracy of yours,' he shyly asked David once. 'Will it still have room for Gypsies?'

'But of course. Hasn't Yugoslavia always had room for your people?'

'Yes. But we have been very poor.'

David was nonplussed. 'Perhaps our country has not always managed well. But we had such little time to put it all together, you understand? After the war it will be different. You will see.'

'And the young king? He will be back?'

'The people will decide. I should think so, but it is for the people to decide.'

Their days were given over to fighting off attacks, mainly by the Bulgars and the *Ljotićevci*, or to initiating acts of sabotage that included the blowing up of a munitions train and the destruction of bridges and railway lines. One evening David left the camp with Zeka and some twenty men to liberate a village that had been occupied by the Germans who, as usual, were apparently confiscating everything they could lay their hands on.

'They have taken our corn, are forcing us to round up our cattle, horses, pigs and cows. They are going to leave us nothing,' the old peasant who had been despatched to the Chetniks to enlist help had cried.

They were met on the outskirts of the village by a group of excited villagers. The Germans, they whispered, had taken over the home of the mayor. For once they were being rather careless, mainly because they had three large, fierce

German shepherd dogs loose in the yard. 'I don't know how you can kill those dogs without making a noise,' one old man said. 'If you could do that, the rest would be easy.'

'Any ideas, Zeka?' David had learned long ago that what Jelić had told him about Zeka's fighting abilities was true. He was a swift, fearless and deadly killer. More important, however, he had an instinctive grasp of military situations and an innovative mind that quickly suggested solutions. In the present circumstances David did not hesitate to turn to him, expecting to find the stocky figure standing at his shoulder.

But Zeka was already on the move. He was gliding into the village at a quick, silent pace, gesturing for the rest of them to stay a distance behind. David seethed with inner exasperation. He had no idea what the grey-haired guerrilla's intentions were, but had no other recourse than to follow. Damn the man. He'd give him hell when they got out of this!

As the house occupied by the Germans loomed up – damned if they weren't singing that song he'd hoped never to hear again as long as he lived, *Lili Marlene!* – they hesitated and watched as Zeka ran lightly across the dirt road, scaled the high fence and disappeared.

'Mother of God, those dogs will eat him alive,' a young peasant whispered. But there was nothing but silence, and the sound of guttural voices singing that cursed song.

They waited.

Within a few moments the high gates leading into the yard were opened and Zeka beckoned impatiently. The rest, as the old peasant had said, was easy.

David led the men into the yard, expecting to see, although he could not understand how, three dead German shepherds. Instead, he saw the three huge dogs hunched up in a row, very much alive, softly whimpering, each one of them with its eyes fastened upon Zeka, who paused briefly to give them a quick glance before bursting into the house with a bloodthirsty yell.

Jelić threw his head back and roared with laughter when

David described the scene to him the following morning. 'Yes, yes, I know,' he said. 'He has that effect on all animals. I asked him how he does it, but you know Zeka. He just looked at me with that smile.'

At the beginning of August the Avala Corps undertook a series of sabotage actions aimed against the important railway lines the Germans used to move troops, arms, ammunition and other war supplies. They began by blowing up the railway lines between Valjevo and Čačak and returned to camp to face a German attack, but not before learning that the Allies were not only benefiting from action taken by the Chetniks, but were deeply appreciative. Headquarters had sent the text of a telegram Mihailović had received, jointly signed by Admiral Sir Henry Harwood, commander of the Mediterranean fleet, General Sir Claude Auckinlech, supreme commander of the British forces in the Middle East, and Marshal Tedder, commander of the air force in the Middle East. *With admiration we are following your directed operations which are of inestimable value to our Allied cause.*

They also learned that several offensives had been launched by the Chetniks against the *Ustaši* and the Croatian home guard near Zvornik on the mountains of Vučjak and Lipljak. Successes were also reported from the townships of Gorazda and Foca, where well over two thousand Chetniks had liberated the people from the crazed *Ustašti*.

Just before the corps moved further south-east towards Sandžak and East Bosnia in the hope that conditions might at last allow them to take offensive action, Branko received word that a Chetnik unit near Sarajevo under the leadership of his friend Sava Derikonja, had taken the valley of Ljubinje in eastern Bosnia. Almost before they could begin rejoicing, however, further news came that the Germans had launched a fierce counter-attack with a battalion of the 738 Regiment of the *Wehrmacht* and retaken the area at heavy cost to the Chetniks.

The unmitigated gloom this news brought was quickly followed by ominous reports that the Germans had brought in Bulgars to help them force out Chetniks who were still fighting fiercely on the Mali Yastrebatz ridge. This pattern of good news, so swiftly followed by bad, seemed never ending.

On the 8th of September 1942, David returned to camp with three wounded men. He had been sent by Kosta to reconnoitre a district that had recently been occupied by a large German patrol. In the late afternoon they passed through a small, poverty-stricken village whose inhabitants told them the Germans had passed through only two days previously. A short time later they found themselves under heavy attack from a thickly wooded ridge, but managed to pull back with less severe losses than might have been expected.

David discussed what had happened later that evening with Branko. He had just returned from the brigade first-aid unit where he had checked up on his men with the 'doctor', a second-year student of medicine nicknamed 'Ziss' for no reason he nor anyone else seemed to be aware of, and whose eternal complaint was that 'the war has come too early. It could at least have waited until I got my degree.'

David accepted the mug of coffee Branko offered him, mentioned how relieved he was that none of the men was seriously wounded, and went on to say that things could have been much worse. 'The truth is, they started firing too early from the ridge. It gave us those few extra minutes to pull back that made all the difference between wiping us out or inflicting the light casualties they did. The odd thing is, Branko, that this kind of thing is so unlike the Germans. If nothing else, they are usually so damned efficient. But it was the same thing that night we entered the village with Zeka. They simply seem to me to be getting careless. And it is not like them. Have you noticed the same thing?'

'Maybe we are really getting to them,' Branko agreed. 'It must be frustrating for them. They've thrown everything they have into trying to capture *Čiča*, but with nothing to show for it. Besides which, the news from the Eastern Front must be unnerving for them.'

Jovan appeared with a skimpy meal of corn bread and

cheese, but at least for once they had a good supply of coffee. They sat around the fire drinking it, discussing the war situation, and then turned to the latest gossip from Belgrade they had heard at a nearby village. General Nedić, according to the villagers, was reported to be furious now that 'Čiča had been appointed Minister for War, a post he himself had held in pre-war years. They were both chuckling over small details of the story when Kosta joined them. He was bursting with excitement.

'I think it's going to happen at last!' he exclaimed. 'The British must be going to land a force along the Adriatic coast.' Hurriedly, his words stumbling over themselves in their anxiety to leave his mouth, he told them the news received from supreme headquarters by the corps commandant, Lieutenant-Colonel Trifković. The British had requested Mihailović to order civil disobedience throughout the country. '*Čiča* will be issuing the order tomorrow, the ninth of September,' Kosta said. 'So we must expect the British to invade shortly after that.'

The call to the civilian population went out from Mihailović, as Kosta had predicted. The response from the peasants and townspeople alike was fearless, unstinting. Until the end of the year, groups of civilians or stalwart individuals were responsible for the destruction of German military cars, trucks and supply depots on an unprecedented scale. Under Chetnik direction bridges and railway lines between Kraljevo and Krushevatz, Kraljevo and Rashka and Kraljevo and Stalaćh were damaged or destroyed. A German train containing arms and munitions was blown up near the village of Mrshatz and over a hundred locomotives were immobilized along the Belgrade-Salonika line.

The German response was instantaneous and brutal. There were mass arrests of citizens in Belgrade and throughout Western and Eastern Serbia. Thousands were shot, others were sent to labour or concentration camps in Greece and Germany. The Gestapo was let loose on a mad rampage.

Villages were razed to the ground. Women and children

were bundled into churches which were then set alight, or were murdered in bestial fashion in front of relatives. When they found the village of Kriva Reka was sheltering the well-known Chetnik officer, Major Keserović, the village was burned down and over six hundred inhabitants executed by the Germans and Bulgarians.

The culmination came on the 25th and 26th of December 1942, when close to three thousand suspected Mihailović sympathizers were executed at the village of Jajince, close to Belgrade. The dazed population withdrew into itself in horror. The massive rebellion petered out, and the British never did make their landing on the Adriatic coast.

PART THREE
1943–1945

A small group of rebels led by the former colonel, Draža Mihailović, is engaged in mutiny against the legal Serbian government of General Nedić. These rebels consider themselves as the regular Yugoslav army and, motivated by a criminal desire for notoriety, are attempting to continue the state of war between the German and Serbian people which was concluded on April 17, 1941.

Proclamation by General Bader,
German military commander,
Belgrade, January 19 1943

I recognize, Duce, *a special danger in the long-term plans of the Mihailović movement. The followers of Mihailović are preparing for the destruction and disarming of your units in Hercegovina and Montenegro. With regard to the danger which the movement of Mihailović conceals within itself, I have issued an order for the destruction of all his followers in the areas occupied by my troops... no easy task considering the forces he has at his disposal.*

Letter from Adolf Hitler to Mussolini, 16 February 1943

[Tito] has fooled and humiliated the British and Americans in the most amusing way. He is, of course, a Moscow man.

Speech delivered by Heinrich Himmler,
21 September 1944

1

By the beginning of 1943, the euphoria of the Bihać meeting had faded. The Croatian home guard were slowly beginning to take back various small towns and villages throughout Western Bosnia that the *Ustaši* had almost casually let fall into the hands of the partisans. The population's bitter experience at the hands of communist bands who had displayed all of the characteristics of 'bloodthirsty Bolsheviks' made them extremely wary about the partisan's professed 'new democratic line'. Accordingly, their cooperation was both minimal and reluctant. To rub salt into the wound, Moscow radio broadcast from Tiflis details of a message sent to Mihailović by the supreme commander of the Allied forces in North Africa, General Dwight Eisenhower, to start the new year. *The American armed forces in Europe and Africa greet their brothers-in-arms in eminent and gallant military units under your resolute command. These brave men who joined your ranks in their birthplaces in order to expel the enemy from your homeland, are fighting with complete devotion and sacrifice for the mutual cause of the United Nations.*

Clearly, something drastic needed to be done to restore rapidly deteriorating partisan fortunes. Shortly after Moscow's report about Eisenhower's message to the Chetnik general, Stevan found himself summoned to an informal meeting of the communist leadership in an area outside Bihać. As usual he went to the meeting with a feeling of reluctance.

Something had seemed to die within him all those

months ago in Montenegro when Tito had rather spitefully let him know that Olga had begun a liaison with a German officer in Belgrade. In addition, the thing about these meetings that he disliked most was that he quite often not only felt inadequate, but sometimes something of a fool. It was always made quite clear that he was not there to offer his views or suggestions about any matter dealing with Party policy. He was there, quite obviously, simply for Tito's convenience, for the odd occasion when the secretary-general would glance in his direction and give a slight nod, which simply meant 'Make a note of that'. Supposedly, Zdenka was his secretary for God's sake. Why in the devil didn't he use her, then?

The bitter thoughts remained unspoken. When summoned he always appeared and sat impassively through the sometimes interminable and boring meetings, until required to jot down a few notes. This time they were discussing the apathy shown to the partisans by the illiterate masses who had, after all, been well informed about the Party's new democratic policy. It was no secret, however, that despite their resolution to behave in a democratic manner, certain partisan units were still adhering to the theory that Tito often expostulated himself when discussing the German policy of severe reprisals against the population when dealing with guerrilla action.

'Yes,' he would agree, 'it is too bad if hostages are shot, women and children bereaved and molested and driven from their homes. We all regret that. But isn't it a fact that they are at war, too? Why should we be the only ones to risk our lives? And in any event, after any severe German reprisals, you know as well as I do, our own ranks are immediately swelled by angry relatives. This is war, after all. One must be realistic.'

This point of view, and the opposite one, that such an attitude was continuing to push people into the Chetnik camp, were being argued vigorously. Stevan had heard it many times before. His mind began to wander, he was not sure for how long, and knew only that suddenly he had caught a few words that made him sit up straight in his chair and pay attention.

During the brief period when his mind had wandered, the leadership had moved on to a discussion about the feasibility of approaching the Allies with the accusation that Mihailović was collaborating with the Germans. Incredible! Stevan was stunned. Yet there it was.

Tito was now musing about the efficacy of 'repetitive propaganda' and the miraculous way that something repeated often enough could overnight become truth, no matter how incredible, not only in the minds of the masses, which might be expected, but even amongst the so-called intelligentsia. God only knew, he had seen this happen often enough while he was in Moscow. It was a fascinating process to watch.

Hard to think, someone said, that the Allies would swallow this, yet there was, after all, that strange business of the British flying in those Canadian Croat communists to act, so they said, as British intelligence officers. Tito had spoken to some of them personally and there was no doubt they were aware of the opportunities inside Yugoslavia to further the aims of the world revolution. Was there any significance in their arrival and the fact that shortly afterwards the Moscow-run radio station from Tiflis had begun to broadcast accusations that Mihailović, far from being a national resistance leader, was actually collaborating with the Germans? Just coincidence? Of course, no one had taken the accusations seriously at the time and even now, asking the world to believe that Mihailović was collaborating was a rather tall order, particularly at this time when he had just received a resounding endorsement from the supreme commander of the Allied forces. On the other hand, perhaps something could be done in concert with the Tiflis 'Radio Yugoslavia'. Certainly, given the Chetnik leader's almost invincible reputation, this would not be easy, and yet...

Afterwards, Stevan really never could recall who it was who had found the solution. Tito? Ivan Ribar? Djilas?

Although it could also have been the ruthless Ranković. Or the wily Moša Pijade from Belgrade. In any event, the question had eventually been asked: could not a start be made by simply accusing some of the Chetnik commanders in the field of collaboration?

The meeting came alive.

It was immediately grasped that the opportunity for creating confusion certainly existed. There was, after all, already a group in Belgrade led by that blackguard Kosta Pećanac, which had already occasionally been mistaken for Chetniks because they too not only grew beards, but also wore the Chetnik Šubare. Pećanac quite openly collaborated with the Germans. Then, too, there were those small roving bands of criminals, often bearded, who rampaged through the countryside taking advantage of the disruption caused by the occupation to rob and murder. Surely it would be possible to convince the Allies that many of these groups were, in fact, Chetniks. No wonder Mihailović kept trying in vain to insist that his was the Royal Yugoslav Army in the fatherland, and should be known as such. The Chetnik label had stuck, however, because of the brave and patriotic connotations it held for the Serbian people.

The idea had instantly caught everyone's imagination. For the rest of the afternoon they discussed eagerly the pros and cons, the viability of such an approach, the expected reaction from the Allies, and what their own response should be to such a reaction. And, finally, which Chetnik commanders should be placed under suspicion? A decision was finally made and agreed to by all concerned.

It was then that Tito had glanced towards Stevan and nodded for him to take note of their secret resolution. An official note was to be drawn up and sent to the British accusing Chetnik commanders who were in control of three provinces. The men named were Uroš Drenović in Bosnian Krajina, both Djujić and Jevdjević in Dalmatia, and Stanisić and Djurisić in Montenegro. After a final short discussion it was agreed that the note should be signed by Tito as secretary-general of the Party and co-signed by Ivan Lola

Ribar as secretary of the Young Communists of Yugoslavia. It went without saying, of course, that this would all be done in concert with Radio Yugoslavia. Moscow could be relied upon to cooperate in what would initially need to be a very delicate exercise in propaganda.

The decision made, everyone relaxed and began to idly discuss internal Party matters of less importance. Tito glanced in Stevan's direction and gave a slight nod of dismissal. Slowly, methodically, he gathered up his loose sheaf of notes, his pencils, the now empty mug of coffee he had brought with him to the meeting, and walked out into the bitterly cold night. He shoved the sheaf of papers into his breast pocket, dropped the mug outside the billet he shared with two other partisans, and walked into the woods. Finally he stopped, grasped the trunk of a tall pine with both hands to steady himself and vomited out what seemed to him to be the rest of his heart and the whole of his stomach.

A long time later Alex Miletić found him. He was sitting with his eyes closed, his back against a birch that stood silvery and shining and clean in the pale white glow of the moon.

'My God, Stevan, what's the matter?' Anxiously the big man dropped down on one knee and peered at him. 'I've been searching for you everywhere. What are you trying to do? Commit suicide? You will freeze to death out here!'

Stevan opened his eyes, looked at Alex, and closed them again.

'Are you sick?' Alex reached out, took hold of his shoulder. 'Come on, I'll help you. You had better get back to camp.'

Calmly Stevan reached up and removed the large hand from his shoulder. 'No. No, I'm not going back, I'm never going back.' He pulled his knees up against his chest, wrapped his arms around them, and then tersely told Miletić what had taken place at the meeting.

'Do you understand, Alex? These men they are planning to dishonour. I *know* most of them. All anti-fascists. All patriots. All brave men. If I was asked to fight them face to face I would do it. But *this. This* I cannot stomach. Do you understand me? Not, of course,' he added tiredly, 'that the British will swallow it. They are not that stupid. It's just that it's so … why it's almost as though they were to accuse *you* of such baseness.'

After what seemed to be a long time the other man began to speak in a hoarse whisper. Stevan had to lean forward to hear.

'But if it was for the good of our cause, I would *want* them to accuse me. I would want *you* to accuse me.'

'Yes, I know. I know, Alex.' His voice was infinitely weary, infinitely sad. 'I have, after all, read something of the manifesto. *Communism rejects all absolute concepts of morality.* Plain as *Mein Kampf*, isn't it? The trouble is, at heart *I* am just a common bourgeois, I suppose. Anyway, I'm getting out. I want to get out.'

'What do you intend to do, then?'

'Do? Nothing. Just not go back. I am not going back.'

'But you must. This whole area is held by the partisans. You wouldn't get further than five kilometres. Don't you understand? You know too much. You would give them no alternative. You would *have* to be liquidated. Don't you understand?'

In the white light shining down from the moon Stevan peered at the shadowy face of the other man. There had been grave concern in his hoarse whisper. Grave concern, and something else. He felt an icy chill permeate his whole body. A chill above and beyond the numbing coldness he had been feeling for some time. There was something in the big man's voice. *Was it a warning? Or was it a threat?*

* * *

My dear David,

Thank you for your answer to my letter of last summer. No need to apologize for the delay, my boy. We, too, have been continually on the move. Čiča has had so many narrow escapes from those German brigands that we are almost finding it a bore. There are times when I actually miss such excitements as going on a motorcycle ride with my nephew! (That maniacal ride through hell you might remember!)

In a more serious vein, I was saddened when I read how you felt about your first encounter with the partisans. You said you were in front of your unit when they attacked from a hidden gorge and that you downed their leader with your *Zbrojovka*, only to discover when you searched him that he was a Serb from Valjevo. I have read your words over and over, at least a dozen times. 'For the first time since the war began,' you wrote, 'I felt I might go to pieces.' You added that you pulled yourself together only by a tremendous act of will, told yourself 'I am sorry, my brother, but it was either you or me,' and carried on, feeling perhaps stronger than before. It might help you to know that in my opinion, these men have given up their right to be called Serbs. They are communists, son. Outlaws! Or, as the Montenegrin peasants rather charitably call them, bloodthirsty madmen!

You heard, of course, of Nedić's latest demand published in *The New Times* in January, that Mihailović surrender? Ludicrous! I hear he is seething with resentment at Čiča's popularity with the people. Well, he chose his own path. Now he must learn to live with it.

For the rest, our forces continue to be active in the field. As a suitable reply to Nedić we initiated a bitter battle against the Germans at Zajchar, and just for good measure our people blew up the railway track at Ugrinivtzi-Kriva Reka and cut the telephone lines. At the moment our brave men are engaged in heavy fighting against the Bulgars at Osnich. The enemy has retaliated by arresting all priests and other leaders in the district of Bolyevatz. The Bulgars, of course, are experts at terrorizing defenceless civilians. A very primitive band of criminals, I must say. You have perhaps heard that the German field commandant at Vrnjačka Banja, a Major-General Fischer, has published the names of two dozen or so followers of Čiča who were shot at Kraguyevatz? We were much saddened by this terrible act of barbarism. God knows, we try to protect our civilians as much as possible, but these terrible reprisals cannot be completely avoided.

Our Belgrade people have informed us that the Germans have launched an attack against the partisans who fled into western Bosnia, after which, it seems, we are again on the list. You remember Major Perić? He has information about an 'operation Schwartz' to be launched against our army, apparently after they have destroyed the Bolsheviks. They will certainly be doing us a favour should they succeed. It is my belief that without these shameless communists shooting us in the back each time *we* launch an attack, the fascists would long since have been driven from our beloved country.

The Italians in Montenegro have indicated that they have had enough, that they will respect a 'truce' if we will. We have hit them hard since Čiča took over operations in Montenegro and, as you know, they are hardly the bravest fighters in the world. It is giving us a chance to regroup, to prepare to face whatever it is the Germans are preparing for us with their Schwartz operation.

David was reading the letter while sitting on a rock in a sun that only just took the chill off an icy wind. He had finished his skimpy lunch of boiled eggs and hard cheese and now frowned as he tried to decipher several more lines written in his uncle's hand with an obviously blunt pencil. Finally, he realized that it was a note saying that he would continue the letter in a few days, by which time he hoped to have either a better pencil, or maybe even some ink. He was not sure when a courier would be leaving for the Avala Corps, so he would keep adding a few lines until he could send his letter. The following page, which gave no indication of when it had been added to the previous text, was written in weak black ink.

> I am not sure whether you know that we recently welcomed a new military mission from Britain. They brought with them an encouraging letter from Anthony Eden and a pair of field glasses for Čiča as a kind personal gift from General Alexander. Although he would, as you can imagine, have much preferred more concrete aid in the form of war *matériel*. Throwing a pair of field glasses at the *Wehrmacht* is not something that will be of much help to the Allied cause! I digress, and am unkind, furthermore. It was indeed a kind thought!
>
> We were rather astounded, however, by the attitude of the mission. Despite all of the kind words, they actually asked whether our forces could not embark upon more energetic action against the Germans! Considering that single-handedly and against all odds the general has taken and is controlling almost the entire countryside, together with provincial towns from East Serbia to Sandžak, Eastern Bosnia, Montenegro and Hercegovina, leaving only the well-fortified cities in the control of the Germans, I considered this remark to be both impertinent and singularly stupid. Incredibly, they also asked whether *we* could stop fighting the partisans, and concentrate on the fascists. Since Čiča has been appealing to London for months in an effort to have them influence Moscow to bring pressure upon the partisans to, if not cooperate with us, at least direct their attacks away from us and towards the occupying forces, this also seemed to me to be a singularly stupid remark.
>
> I was present during this exchange, and thought Čiča handled the situation very well, although he was obviously extremely angry. When they began to press him to 'kill more Germans', he pointed out that in fact what

he was trying to do was cause as much damage to them as possible *without* doing this, because of the severe reprisals against the population. When they persisted in this line of thinking, he asked them rather drily whether, in his situation, they would consider one hundred *English* lives a fair price for one German life. They seemed offended at the suggestion!

All of which indicates I suppose that one cannot expect the same kind of brilliant leadership the British have at the top to filter through to the lower ranks. At least we have been assured often enough that our contribution has been of inestimable help to the Allied cause by their top command, who are in a position to more fully understand the situation. You will have heard, in this connection, that the French General de Gaulle has bestowed the Croix de Guerre with the red palm spray upon the general, calling him a 'legendary hero, a symbol of the finest patriotism and of the highest Yugoslav qualities'. So much for minor British military missions!

Before I forget. You might be interested and pleased to learn that an old friend of yours, Bogdan Bošković, is apparently being of some help to our intelligence people in Belgrade. He runs a restaurant there, as perhaps you know, that is much frequented by German officers, and he has been able to give us some quite useful bits of information.

I know this will encourage you should you hear of old friends who may have joined those bloodthirsty fellows, the Bolsheviks. I'm afraid some of these young fellows, who must be completely mindless, have broken the hearts of their fathers.

Forgive me if I close abruptly, but I have just learned a courier is about to depart for the Avala Corps. No news of the family. Let us pray they are all well.

Love from your Uncle Mikhail

David read the last part through several times. His uncle,

he suddenly realized, must have learned about Stevan. Resolutely he shook off the feeling of sadness that enveloped him. Best to think about Bogdan. At last he had found the courage to act; in the interests of his country and for his own honour, considering what the Nazis had done to his wife and her people. Yet despite his determination not to think about Stevan, thoughts of him crept back into his mind. What was it his uncle had written? He again consulted the letter. *These men have given up the right to be called Serbs. They are communists, son.* Was it possible that Stevan had given up his heritage so easily? Had he really thrown in his lot with the Bolsheviks? How he wished he could talk to him for an hour or so. Where are you, Stevan? And what in the name of God are you doing?

* * *

They had been moving at an agonisingly slow pace through the Neretva Valley in the direction of Mount Prenj. Streams of refugees, many of them barefoot, clad in rags, cold, hungry, typhus-ridden, together with the depleted partisan forces, themselves badly demoralized, limped past Stevan and Alex who were sitting with their backs against a large rock, tiredly watching Jelena make one last round of the sick and dying who were lying on makeshift stretchers a couple of hundred yards away beneath some trees that were leafless enough to let the weak sun filter through.

Alex had been a little irritated with her. 'You will drop from exhaustion,' he had snapped, almost himself at the end of his endurance. 'And then you will be of no help to anyone.'

She had reached out and lovingly caressed his cheek. 'Just a quick last look,' she said softly, 'then I will join you both. I really will have a rest then. I promise.'

Stevan yawned, squinted up at the cold blue sky, now brushed across with several high white clouds, and then closed his eyes. When he opened them something made him again glance up at that blue sky that had been raining death down upon them so often during the past couple of months. He frowned. *It's almost the same as that day Tito . . .*

His voice exploded into the crystalline air with the force of rock-shattered glass. 'Jelena!' He screamed the name in unison with Alex's anguished 'No! Noooo . . .'

Like a deadly silver bullet the Stuka dived down with its high-powered, whining shriek, scattered a spray of bullets haphazardly amongst the stretchers, and zoomed up and away, disappearing amongst the clouds. Following his own wrenching scream and Alex's tormented denial before the fact came moans and sobs and then an even more terrible silence from the little bower of the sick.

They had both leapt to their feet, and now raced towards the slowly spinning figure of Alex's wife. The partisan cap with the red star she had been so proud to wear had fallen off, releasing the rich chestnut hair in a halo around her face. Alex reached her first. 'No,' he was still repeating, but now in a whisper, an entreaty. 'No, no no.'

With his large hands he brushed the hair from her forehead, while Stevan stared with horror at the gaping wound in her chest from which the blood was gushing in a red, ever-strengthening stream. Her face was contracted with pain, but then, as though someone had reached down to draw across it a gentle veil, it cleared and relaxed into a look of great beauty. She was staring up at Alex, her lips were moving in what was obviously a tremendous effort to say something. As he leant down the words came out clearly, proudly. 'Long live Stalin!' She smiled and with a last great effort lifted her hand, began the sign of the cross, but was dead before she could finish. Gently, Alex lifted her hand, completed the sign, then buried his head in her lap and began to sob.

A long time later, Stevan bent down and touched him on the shoulder. 'Alex, we have to move on. I'll try to find a priest among the refugees. We must bury her. We–' He gave a gasp of pain as the big man swung his arm up and hit him a tremendous blow across the chest that sent him reeling against a giant fir tree. Seconds later a phenomenon he had been experiencing with increasing frequency over the past few months occurred. He seemed to be standing outside of himself, outside his own body, observing the whole scene, including his own role in it, from a great distance. This time, however, instead of the one scene showing Alex's huge frame covering that of his dead wife as he grieved in mortal anguish, with himself sprawled dazed against the tree and the other hazy figures hovering around, what he observed was a series of 'film clips'; selective scenes from the past few months that had burned themselves into his consciousness and that were to reappear in his mind's eye for the rest of his life.

From a great distance he relived within the framework of seconds his reluctant return from the woods with Alex that day he had vowed to leave the partisans; the subsequent estrangement from Tito, who with his uncanny antennae had sensed some change in him and had coldly withdrawn his sponsorship, leaving him feeling alone, isolated. Now he was observing himself, frozen with fear and panic as the bombs rained down on headquarters at Bihać at the beginning of the German offensive – the operation Weiss intelligence had warned them about, but which they kept hoping would be put off until the enemy carried out operation Schwarz which they knew had been planned against the Chetniks.

Flick, flick, flick. The desperate partisan messages crying for help, despite the accommodations made with the Italians, despite the undoubted courage shown by the rank and file and some outstanding guerrilla leaders, nothing but desperate news from all sides where the Germans were attacking.

Flick, flick, flick. Tito's panicky appeal to Moscow, the belated reply: *Insurmountable technical difficulties prevent us from offering you assistance ... you are all doing great things ... fraternal greetings and best wishes to our comrades-in-arms...*

Suddenly, with great clarity, he saw himself standing beneath a clear blue sky identical to the one under which he now sprawled. He was aware that he was standing in a valley at Drvar and that Tito had come down from headquarters to talk to the partisans, to encourage the sick and the wounded. Once again there was that flash of silver in the cold blue sky, a swift, unexpected glimpse of a solitary reconnaissance plane swooping down...

From a long way off he watched himself move with a speed he had never known he possessed, watched with complete detachment as he threw his body against the communist leader as a shield, heard the hail of bullets, felt the stinging pain in his shoulder, and listened to screams similar to the ones he had heard just a few moments ago...

Flick, flick, flick. Tito. Wonderfully, warmly friendly again and concerned about his shoulder which was, after all, nothing. A flesh wound, he was telling the communist leader. Nothing! And Tito confiding in him again. Telling of his anger towards Moscow who, after offering no help other than lofty words, was now complaining because he had been in friendly contact with the Germans and had exchanged a few prisoners.

Tito's complaining voice faded. He was looking down now at a dazed, lost-looking woman who had been included in the prisoner exchange with the Germans. Whispers swam around his head. It was Tito's second 'wife'. The mother of his second son. What would happen now that his real wife had returned? Would the unpopular Zdenka be banished? It was understood that the pathetic-looking Herta Hass had suffered indescribable horrors at the hands of the *Ustaši*. There was no way she could be abandoned. But she was. 'I have a new comrade now,' Tito was informing her in that reserved way he had.

Her lost face refused to go away. Stevan again watched her as she wandered around the camp, the object of Zdenka's furious looks. 'What happened?' she asked Stevan. 'What happened?' she asked anyone and everyone. 'What has happened to him?'

But the crumpled face of Herta Hass began to blur and faded away. Now he was watching a long, endless line of refugees. Thousands upon thousands of them stretched into the distance. Old men, women, children. Hungry, frightened, silent, here and there perhaps an old woman asking plaintively, *What have you done to us, brothers? Why did you need to come here? What did we do to deserve this?*

The scene changed.

He was with Tito in the little grey stone cottage he used as headquarters in the Rama Valley. There was another man sitting with them over the remains of the best meal Stevan had eaten in months. Fresh fish, fruit and cheese, coffee served with brandy the high-ranking German intelligence officer had in his despatch bag when captured.

From his great distance Stevan again listened as the two men, close in age, laughed and joked together.

'You know, we should really be on the same side,' *Stari* was saying. 'I was with you in the last war, you know. But if we don't take care the Allies are going to win again.' The German was answering that he could not agree more. 'Is it not possible we could come to some arrangement?' Tito again, fastidiously removing the butt of a cigarette from his holder, replacing it with the new one offered by the German. 'After all, we partisans have no real quarrel with you. We could be of great help should the Allies land along the Dalmatian coast. Particularly now that your hands are full on the Eastern Front. You understand? We could be of great help to you.' He was shrugging in that frank way of his. 'Of course it would be understood, should you lose, should you be forced to withdraw, the country would be left in *our* hands.'

The German was nodding agreement. 'When I get back to Zagreb you can be sure I will place your suggestion before General von Horstenau.' Now he was expressing his admiration for Tito's 'great survivability'. 'We have also been surprised at the amount of arms you have. Where do you get your guns, your ammunition?'

Tito settled back, slapped his knee, laughed heartily. 'Wo sonst? Von unseren gemeinsamen Italianischen "Freunden".' He beamed happily, proud of his smattering of German. 'Where else?' he repeated in his own language. 'From our mutual Italian friends.'

The German again, amazed: 'Lieber Gott, schütze uns von unseren alliierten!' God preserve us from our allies! The German officer's voice faded.

Flick, flick, flick. Alex. His open face tight with concern. 'But he has asked us to blow up all of the bridges. All of the bridges over the Neretva.' From his distance Stevan watched himself nodding, a little hesitant. 'But this will cut off all means of escape. Where shall we go with the wounded? The typhus is spreading, you know. And the Germans have us surrounded.' He watched himself scowl.

'I understand he intends to confuse the enemy as to our intentions, Alex.'

'Yes, but...'

'For Christ's sake, Alex! You have your orders. You are the engineer! Stop asking questions. Just demolish the bloody bridges.'

Flick, flick, flick. Alex. Dumbfounded. 'He wants us now to *rebuild* the bridges? Impossible! With what? We have no materials, no time, nothing...' His voice was fading away, bewildered, despairing.

A voice kept repeating his name. 'Comrade Matić? Are you all right, comrade? Comrade Matić?' He opened his eyes slowly, closed them again against the brilliant sunlight, opened them once more. He was back in the present. A burly partisan was peering down at him anxiously. 'Is all well with you, comrade?'

Slowly he nodded, passed his hand over his forehead, and sat up. 'It's Comrade Alex. He won't leave his wife. We can't get near him. He keeps lashing out. And we must move on. That plane might be back, it might bring others with it.'

A short distance away Alex still knelt, his head in the lap of his dead wife. Cautiously Stevan rose, trying to ignore the stinging in his left shoulder – where the wound he had received when he threw himself over Tito seemed to have reopened – and the throbbing pain in his chest where the big man had hit him. This time he stayed at a safe distance.

'Alex,' he said softly, urgently. 'We have to leave. We have to move on.' There was no reply, simply a muffled sound that could have been a sob. 'You are practising self-indulgence, comrade!' The voice, authoritative, cold, callous even, rang loudly in his ears. With a sense of surprise he recognized it as his own. 'Your wife died with the name of Stalin on her lips. At least allow us to bury her with dignity. You should be prepared to mourn her loss by renewed dedication to our cause. Now, *get up!*'

A quiver ran through Alex's body. Slowly he rose, turned. Stevan braced himself for another blow. Instead the big man stared at him confusedly for a moment, then reached up to wipe the tears and dirt from his face. 'I'm sorry, Stevan,' he muttered meekly. 'I'm sorry.'

Stevan found an old Orthodox priest in the stream of refugees still shuffling by. They buried her in a shallow grave next to the rock they had both been leaning against such a short time ago.

Then began the slow, tortuous crossing of the mighty Prenj Mountain, with its narrow, slippery, snow-covered tracks. An endless ragged stream of refugees and partisans. The food supply soon ran out. Typhus went on a rampage. Of those who escaped its deadly talons many were to drop dead along the wayside from cold, hunger, and sheer despair.

The Germans, however, having reached their goal of driving them out of Western and Central Bosnia mercifully left them more or less alone. Eventually the survivors reached the safety of Glavatičevo. There they stopped to regroup, lick their wounds and review their chaotic situation.

2

At the beginning of April 1943, a Montenegrin officer who had been stationed with the Chetnik forces in the Neretva Valley arrived at Avala Corps headquarters on his way to the supreme command where, he ruefully told a group of fellow officers, including David Ristić and Branko Yelić, he fully expected to be 'given hell' after having been forced to withdraw his forces from a partisan attack. The truth of the matter, he said, was that when the partisans had so idiotically blown up the bridges that would have allowed them to retreat from an expected German attack across the wide, turbulent Neretva River, the Chetniks, who had been holding the area in the valley for some time in a successful bid to halt communist attempts to push their way into South Serbia, had relaxed and become careless. They had expected, after all, that the Germans would be busily engaged in a rout of the mad partisans and when the latter had effectively destroyed the bridges that were their only exit from the expected battle, the Neretva Chetnik commanders had felt they and their men could relax.

Who could guess that not only would the Germans fail, inexplicably, to press their advantage, but that the partisans would have engineers who seemed to know a damned lot more about bridges than their leaders did about military matters? You had to give those engineers credit! Using the wreckage of two bridges as bases, they had constructed planks out of ripped up telegraph poles and wires and other materials they had dug up from only God knew where, and put up makeshift structures that had allowed them to cross the river into the valley.

'They took us completely by surprise,' he admitted shamefacedly. 'In addition, they had a great many weapons, and were not short of ammunition as we were. Apparently they have made some arrangement with the Italians, who have given them a good supply of food and clothing. We managed to capture an Italian officer who was with them. He admitted they are teaching those mad communists how to use their modern weapons. They even have Italians driving their light tanks against us.' He shrugged. 'None of this, of course, is really any excuse. As I am sure,' he added drily, 'the supreme command will take good care to point out.'

David grimaced at Branko. 'There, but for the grace of God, I suppose...' he muttered softly. They continued talking long into the night about the irresponsible behaviour of the partisans who may have taken the Neretva Chetniks by surprise but who were now, thank God, reported to have been more or less wiped out by the Germans who had, it appeared, rallied after all to drive them out of Bosnia.

'Perhaps they will let us fight the bloody fascists in peace, now,' Kosta Marinković said.

Still, the partisan defeat had been achieved at a terrible price. Not only thousands of communists dead, but streams of refugees who had been bombed, killed or driven out of their villages and townships. Thousands of civilians had become victims of the erratic, sometimes irrational decisions by communist leaders who seemed more intent on causing internal chaos than in fighting the enemy, and who were completely insensible to the suffering of the people.

'There is really no end to their dirtiness,' the officer from Neretva Valley said. 'Do you ever listen to Radio Yugoslavia? Do you know they have actually been accusing some of our officers of collaborating with the vile fascists? What they think they will achieve by such patent lies I'm damned if I know. They must be getting desperate, is all I can think.'

'Well,' Branko said slowly, 'we know they have been making overtures to the British. It's in their interests to try to discredit us.'

David laughed. 'They are going the wrong route, then. The British will never swallow *that.*'

'You think not?' Branko seemed doubtful. 'Yet from what we hear, the British have been supplying them with war *matériel.*'

'Well, if it's the same amount they are giving us, that's not going to cause much harm.'

'No. But, I mean, do the British really know what is going on here?'

'Surely. They have their own officers here. If they have any doubts, if they don't want to believe the evidence of their own eyes, all they have to do is talk to our peasants. Enough of them know our language.'

'Well, perhaps...'

'Look, Branko.' David rummaged around in the breast pocket of his leather jacket, took out his wallet and removed an old, yellowed newspaper clipping. 'You know the last letter my uncle wrote to me? He enclosed this. Said he had been carrying it around for years, and thought I might be interested in reading it.'

They were sitting around a flickering fire, and he leaned forward to get better light. 'Listen. *Bolshevism means in every country a civil war of the most merciless kind between the discontented criminal and mutinous classes on one hand, and the contented or law-abiding on the other. It means war of the most ruthless kind, the slaughter of men, women and children, the burning of homes and the inviting in of tyranny, pestilence and famine.*' He glanced around the group of tough, determined faces. 'Do you know who wrote that?'

'Someone who knows what he is talking about,' Kosta answered.

David nodded. 'Yes. He does. The man who wrote that was the British Prime Minister, Winston Churchill! More than twenty years ago. But, my God, how he read them through and through. Well! You think *he* is going to be fooled by a few outrageous lies by people he himself has classed as criminals?'

There was a murmur of assent around the by now dying fire that was broken by a grizzled veteran who had listened to David carefully, 'And yet,' he said now, 'isn't that the same Churchill who just a few years ago was in love with that accursed fascist, Mussolini? What was it he called him during that visit he paid to Italy? "A great Roman". That's what he said. Mussolini was a great Roman.' He chewed for a moment on the stem of his empty pipe, then spat. 'A great Roman!' he repeated.

For a moment David was nonplussed. He recalled now, vaguely, his uncle talking about that visit that had elicited the highest praise from Churchill for the Italian dictator. When had it been? A few years back. Eight? Ten? He ran his fingers through his hair, then shrugged. 'Anyway,' he said, 'we have to trust someone.'

'Why do we?' The fierce response in a shrill young voice came from the outer circle around the fire. 'Why do we have to trust anyone?' For a moment there was silence, as everyone peered into the dimness trying to identify the speaker, who turned out to be Yaruga, Zeka's youthful shadow. Identification was followed by a roar of laughter and a chorus of agreement.

'You are right, Yaruga, let's not trust any of the bastards!'

'You have taught him well, Zeka.'

'Well, we certainly have to think about that, Yaruga.' Kosta, who had joined in with the general laughter, yawned. 'Time we turned in, eh? We'll be up at dawn.' Just before the group broke up, however, he drew David aside and asked that he report to him the following morning. 'There is something afoot that I think might be of interest to you.'

David did not give this too much thought, and the next morning he duly reported to Kosta, now a good friend albeit the commander of the Posavska Brigade, and was a little taken aback to find that the commander of the Avala Corps, Lieutenant-Colonel Trifković, and Major Kobas, commander of the corps' staff company, were also present.

'We need someone to undertake a rather sticky operation for us,' Kosta began, after the officers had returned David's smart salute. 'The person required needs to know Belgrade like the back of his hand, speak German and have his wits about him! As I have just finished telling Colonel Trifković and Major Kobas, I think you fit the bill.'

Trifković and Kobas, both solidly-built men well over six feet tall, studied him thoughtfully for a moment. Trifković finally nodded his head.

Kobas said, 'Yes, yes,' in apparent agreement. 'Although,' he added, 'that beard will have to go!'

In his slow, methodical way, Trifković began to explain that all their intelligence sources were reporting that now that their operation Weiss had been successfully concluded against the partisans, the Germans were preparing to launch another all-out attack against the Chetniks. A message from the German south-east command to the German supreme command in Yugoslavia had been intercepted on the 14th of March 1943, making reference to their plans for 'a concentrated attack against Mihailović'. The full objective of what had previously been identified as operation Schwartz was 'the destruction of all insurgents in Montenegro and East Hercegovina, especially the command of Mihailović with all his assistants and liaison officers which must be discovered and destroyed'.

Major Kobas took up the story as Trifković hesitated. 'According to the reports we've received, Mihailović's supreme command is also to be the main objective of the *Luftwaffe*, which is apparently to play a role in this operation Schwartz.'

'I hope someone is going to make sure we have plenty of arms and ammunition to defend ourselves with, sir.'

Trifković gave a short, harsh laugh. 'Don't rely on it, lieutenant. As usual it's rather a case of fending for ourselves. That's why...'

David listened carefully as he went on to explain that an

approach had been made by several of General Nedić's police corps to the Avala Corps, claiming that they wished to get out of Belgrade, desert Nedić, and throw in their lot with the Chetniks.

'I think they are genuine,' Trifković continued, 'not to mention wise. With the way the war is going in Africa and on the Eastern Front you don't have to be too bright to see the writing on the wall. I think these men realize it is now simply a matter of time before the Allies invade, whether it is along the Dalmatian coast or in Southern Europe does not make too much difference now. We think these fellows simply want to make sure they get on the winning side before it's too late.'

'On the other hand,' again Kobas took up the tale, while Kosta stood quietly to one side with a map in his hand, watching David. 'One can't be too careful with these fellows. Anyway, to cut a long story short, we have asked them to supply us with some arms and so forth as a gesture of their sincerity. They have agreed. We think in view of the expected heavy attack by the Germans it is a risk worth taking. The point is, we need someone to go to Belgrade, make contact with them, and bring them back here, together with the promised arms. You understand?'

'Yes, sir.' David beamed, tried to control the swell of excitement that raced through him.

'But you will have to get rid of that beard! Some of the bloody *Ljotićevci* wear them, but Nedić's men do not. And by the way, avoid the *Ljotićevci* like the plague. They are worse than the Germans. May each and every one of their souls sizzle in hell!'

'I will be disguised as one of Nedić's men?'

Trifković nodded. 'A Captain Pačić. We have been told he is not in Belgrade at the moment. Just hope you don't have any kind of run-in with someone who knows him. We can supply you with an identity card which should get you through German checkpoints. As we see it, the main dangers in order of degree are firstly that you might be walking into a trap, secondly the bloody *Ljotićevci*, who seem to smell Chetniks coming a mile away, thirdly an encounter with any of Nedić's men who know Pačič, and last but not least, the Germans themselves.'

'What kind of arms have they promised us, sir?'

'Not too many, but beggars can't be choosers. Mainly heavy machine-guns and ammunition. But they have also promised money, food, medical supplies, clothes, not to mention...' He suddenly laughed, 'several boxes of cigarettes, without which I doubt whether I for one can continue in this bloody war much longer.'

The rest of the meeting was taken up with instructions about David's movements once he reached Belgrade. His mission had obviously been carefully planned.

Shortly after receiving his instructions he left for Belgrade on the back seat of a motorcycle driven by a young soldier called Dragan, feeling slightly vulnerable without the beard that he had proudly worn as a badge of kinship with those Chetniks of the past who had fought so fiercely against the Turks.

After showing his identification papers and being waved through several German checkpoints without incident he decided that as things were going so smoothly he could surely pay a quick visit to his family, to Irina. Against orders, but still...

They had first driven to the police headquarters of General Nedić in Misharska Street, arriving in the early evening. After being welcomed by an extremely nervous, red-faced man who introduced himself as Lieutenant Janković and explained that this was where they would spend the night, David had announced his intention of going out again to 'have an early dinner'. Janković had protested volubly.

'No, no. Something can be brought here to the station for you. You must not leave the station. It is too risky, too...'

David nodded absent-mindedly, patted him on the shoulder, and then simply walked out of the station, a nervous Dragan following. He gave him Irina's address. 'Do you know where it is?'

'Yes, lieutenant, but...'

'No "buts", Dragan.'

It was a pleasant, if cool evening and for the first time since leaving camp David allowed himself to think about his darling Irina. How excited she would be when he walked in! He hoped to God she had been coping all right with this bloody German occupation. She was so sensitive, so fragile. Despite his furious denial when his uncle had told him she seemed 'lost', he had been unable to think about her since without a nagging worry at the back of his mind. Perhaps he should, after all, have remained in Belgrade to look after her. Yet how could he? The whole history of his people had propelled him automatically into rebellion against the latest upstart invaders. How could one be expected to resist history?

They drove at a slow and hopefully inconspicuous speed through the by now almost deserted streets of Belgrade. Deserted except for a few bands of the unspeakable local fascist thugs, the *Ljotićevci*, a few members of Nedić's puppet army or police, and German soldiers, some with giggling blonde Fräuleins on their arms, no doubt brought from their own country to keep them happy. No decent Serbian woman would, of course, be seen dead with any of them. There were a few motorcycles on the road similar to their own, an occasional supply truck and a few German staff cars. But the curfew was doing its job. The once lively streets of Belgrade were slowly emptying.

They reached Miloša Velikog street and drove slowly along until David asked Dragan to pull over to the kerb on the opposite side of the Mirskaia apartment building. The first thing he had noticed was the German staff car outside. No doubt it belonged to the German officers Madame Mirskaia had been so taken with, he thought with a flash of irritation. Bastards! In any event, even if he encountered one of them, he felt quite secure with Pačić's identity card, and with his own ability to talk himself out of most situations.

He swung off the bike and was about to tell Dragan to

accompany him as it was too dangerous to leave him sitting there by himself, when the front door of the apartment house opened. Framed in the doorway stood Irina, flanked on either side by two German officers. A heavy-set, middle-aged captain and a younger, good-looking man of the same rank. She was wearing the red dress he disliked so much, with a short fur jacket thrown over her shoulders.

Laughing and chattering in that breathless way she had, she tripped gaily down the steps, with her escorts. The driver opened the door of the car and saluted smartly. Just before getting in, something made her lift her head and glance across the street to where David stood, frozen, beneath the soft yellow glow of a street lamp. For a moment their eyes met and he watched her soft lips silently form his name. Then she was being helped inside. The car drove off. He stared after it, catching a glimpse of her white face framed in the back window just before it reached the corner, turned, and disappeared.

'But you look so grim, son. What has been happening to you?' At least, he thought bitterly, his aunt had not changed. Dependable, solid as a rock, she sat opposite him with Zora. Both of them had been rapturous at seeing him again, safe and in one piece. At one end of the table sat the shy Dragan, sipping coffee, trying to make himself unobtrusive during this family reunion.

Quickly David learned that he was now an uncle. Andjela had produced a seven-pound two-ounce baby girl some two months previously. Her name was Ivana, and Andjela and her husband had taken her to visit his parents. They were not expected back for a week or so.

His Aunt Kaja and Uncle Mikhail, they told him, had also left Belgrade to stay with some relatives. A very wise decision, considering Uncle Mikhail's temperament. He would most assuredly have been in trouble by now had he remained in Belgrade.

Zora's studies were going well, considering, and yes, of course, Aunt Draga was healthy as ever. Money? Yes, yes. They were managing well, although the price of food had sky-rocketed. But he should remember that story about his father. Before leaving for the front in the First World War, David Ristić senior had left his wife and sister-in-law a bag full of gold coins. When he returned from the war, Aunt Draga related proudly, for what David thought must be the millionth time, every coin was still in the bag. Yes, yes. She knew how to manage. And both Andjela and Zora were sensible girls who knew how to stretch a dinar to its utmost.

One last piece of news, before they forgot. He would be so happy! Quickly they explained that just two weeks ago, late one afternoon, Aunt Draga had been shopping at the market. Zora had not yet returned from medical school, but Andjela had been home with the baby. Well, there had been a knock on the door and when she opened it David would never guess, it was Jack Cohen! Andjela had hardly recognized him, he was so thin. He had grown a beard and was dressed like a peasant. And if David remembered how *fastidious* he had always been with his clothes he would *realize* . . .

'Jack? Thank God!' For the first time since he arrived David's face relaxed into a look of genuine pleasure. 'But what was he doing, still in Belgrade? Surely to heaven he would be better off in the country. You know there are some villages that are so remote the Germans haven't even touched them. If he could find his way to one of them . . .'

'Well, it seems that is what he was going to try to do. But he had a bag full of gold and jewellery. He first of all asked Andjela where you were, and when she said you were no longer in Belgrade, he explained he had intended to ask you to keep the bag for him. If all went well he would return for it after the occupation. If not, you were to keep everything. He said you were to consider it all to be yours.'

'But why shouldn't he return? Of course he will return! If he has survived for *this* long. You have the bag in a safe place for him, then?'

His aunt and sister exchanged a look.

'What is it? What's the matter?'

'Well, nothing, really.' It was Zora who answered slowly. 'It was just that Andjela was scared. She was too scared to take it.'

'Scared? What do you mean? Too scared to help a friend? Since when have either of my sisters been too scared to help a friend in trouble?'

'You don't understand, son.' His aunt was looking at him anxiously. 'Andjela has a child now. Her first duty is to protect that child.'

'Besides,' Zora added in a low voice. 'Andjela has changed. Since she married.' In a voice that was suddenly harsh, she added, 'Thank God I will have a profession. *I* will be able to look after myself. You can be sure of that! I shall *never* put myself in a position where I must rely on a man.'

'Zora!' His aunt was patently distressed at the tone of her niece's voice.

David stood up. 'I have to be going.' There were things going on inside his family, he realized, undercurrents that he was certainly in no position to cope with now. Afterwards, he thought. Afterwards, when this bloody war is over.

At the doorway to the apartment he paused before joining Dragan, who had tactfully moved outside as his aunt and sister embraced him. 'Take care of yourself, son,' his aunt said, holding back the tears with a struggle. She hesitated, surreptitiously wiping her eyes with her apron. 'Son? I hope you won't try to see Irina. She ... we'll let her know you are all right. But there are a lot of German officers billeted near her apartment house. I hope you won't try to—'

'No,' he interrupted shortly, trying hard to keep the bitterness from his voice. 'I won't.'

He kissed them both, and studied Zora thoughtfully for a moment. 'We'll have a long talk,' he said. 'After the war. We'll have a long talk.'

Once outside he directed Dragan to a small restaurant in the Čubura district. 'God knows when we'll have a chance to eat a decent meal again!' They parked the motorcycle outside and walked into the small, clean dining room with its spotless linen and tapestry-lined walls. Just as they entered they encountered a group of four swaggering *Ljotićevci* on their way out. Their leader was a huge, black-bearded thug, clad in a black leather jacket and riding boots. For a brief moment the eyes of the two men met. David felt his blood begin to boil. Something of the intensity of his feelings seemed to reach the *Ljotićevci*, who paused and glared back at him. 'Do you have your identification?' he asked in a loud, bullying voice.

David didn't miss a beat. 'Yes I do!' he snapped in his best upper-class military manner. 'Do *you*?'

For a moment they stood eye to eye. David sensed the sudden tension in Dragan, who was standing rigidly at his side. Then the *Ljotićevci* relaxed, shrugged, muttered something to the man behind him, and they all walked out, the last man turning to give them both a baleful glare.

'Whew!' Dragan sat down at the nearest table, removed his cap, took out a handkerchief and mopped at his forehead. 'My God, sir, you were cool. How do you do it?'

David shrugged. 'Never let fascist scum think you are afraid of them, soldier,' he said shortly, then suddenly smiled. 'Besides,' he added, patting his breast pocket which contained his identification papers, 'I was quite sure Captain Pačić outranked him.'

Dragan laughed with him, then withdrew into his usual shyness. He was trying to work out what had happened to the young lieutenant since they had arrived in Belgrade. There had been the brief call to the police headquarters, then the quick surveillance of Miloša Velikog Street. Only the good God knew for what purpose *that* had been. Then the visit to his family, where Dragan had sat quietly drinking coffee and taking occasional surreptitious glances at the lieutenant's good-looking sister. She had seemed to be one of those self-assured, strong young women Dragan fervently admired, but would never in his wildest dreams have the courage to approach.

But the lieutenant...

Some time after they had entered the city an invisible, tight, hard armour seemed to have closed around him. But the precise moment it had happened was something Dragan could not pinpoint. One instant he had been taking orders from a relaxed, laughing young man who was clearly delighted to be back in Belgrade, the next he found himself accompanied by a cold, rigid officer whom he, Dragan, for one, would not wish to encounter in battle. The way he had glared at the *Ljotićevci*! Dragan was still not sure whether it had been that terrible glare or the *Ljotićevci* themselves who had scared the devil out of *him*.

A waiter was approaching with a large menu and Lieutenant Ristić seemed to relax slightly. 'Order what you want, soldier,' he said with a slight smile. 'Courtesy of the Avala Corps. And bear in mind you are not likely to have another meal like it for a long, long time.'

An hour later they were back at the police station where a relieved Janković showed them into his own quarters at the back of the building, and supplied them with coffee, pastries and a few newspapers and magazines for the night.

The following morning they were taken to a truck bearing a special pass ticket identifying it as a supply vehicle for the Serbian State Guard. A burly young man with narrow brown eyes drove them to a supply depot where the truck was quickly loaded with boxes of food, clothes, medical supplies and boots. Surprisingly enough, it seemed the arms and ammunition were still packed away in a room at the Misharska Street station. When they returned, two heavy machine-guns, boxes of ammunition and a few large boxes they were told contained cigarettes and money were quickly loaded onto the truck by two of Nedić's police, watched by an alert, wary David and an uneasy soldier Dragan. When the truck had been loaded full to the top, Lieutenant Janković asked David to accompany him to the courtyard. There he found about forty policemen lined up in two rows. Janković stood in front of them, his hands clasped loosely behind his back, swaying slightly back and forth. He nodded towards David.

'This, as some of you may have gathered, is an officer with the Avala Corps of General Mihailović. Many of you have expressed the intention of leaving Belgrade to join the Chetnik guerrillas. There is an opportunity right now for perhaps half a dozen of you to leave with this officer. Any who wish to do so, step forward. You will wear your own uniforms and take your arms.'

Five men stepped forward and were given leave to collect their personal things from the station locker room. David took Janković uneasily to one side.

'Look,' he said, 'wasn't that rather risky? If there is just *one* traitor amongst them. They *did* join Nedić, you know.' He hesitated, not sure how to continue. After all, so had Janković himself joined Nedić!

'You don't understand,' Janković said. He nodded towards the remaining men. 'They would all join you except for their families. They have all – *we* have all – had it up to here,' he abruptly drew a hand across his throat, 'with the bloody Germans.'

David nodded. 'But you? You are not coming with us?'

'I too worry about my family.' He sighed. 'Still, it is plain to see who is going to win this war, you know. I think it is a good time for the wise man to get out of Belgrade. Tell your commandant that we will try to gather some more ammunition and repeat this operation as soon as possible. Next time I think I will be accompanying you.'

The truck left shortly afterwards. Dragan followed on the motorcycle with a policeman riding pillion. David sat in the front of the truck with the driver and a huge police sergeant, the remaining men positioning themselves on each side of the running board with their rifles, looking every inch an authentic convoy of the Serbian State Guard. They passed through the German checkpoint at Banjica without the slightest problem, headed towards Mladenovac and then roared triumphantly on in the direction of Čačak.

A few days later David was discussing his mission with a delighted Kosta Marinković. 'The colonel couldn't be happier,' he said. 'He had not expected things to go so smoothly. He had expected a trap, to be quite honest. I don't think he would have been at all surprised if you'd been grabbed and tossed into one of Nedić's prisons! But he is extremely pleased with the way you carried everything off.'

David nodded. 'Yes, I know. He told me.'

Kosta hesitated, giving him a penetrating look. 'There is nothing wrong, then?'

'Why should anything be wrong?'

'No reason at all,' his friend said in a puzzled voice. 'There is no reason at all.'

* * *

Tito's good spirits were slowly returning. The endless smoking, the gallons of coffee he had drunk and the bouts of nervousness and temper that had left those around him apprehensive and reluctant to be the bearer of all the bad news in Bosnia, were slowly being replaced by more moderate behaviour now that he was enjoying the comparative peace and safety of Glavatičevo. He had, however, during the past desperate weeks, lost his fresh looks of rude good health. His eyes were bloodshot, his skin puffy and pale, his hair almost entirely grey. Yet despite the vastly depleted partisan forces and despite the indeterminate news brought back from Zagreb by his peace delegation, he remained optimistic.

Under the leadership of Kŏca Popović, his representatives, including both Milovan Djilas and Vladimir Velebit had left for Sarajevo shortly after Tito had released the German intelligence officer he had entertained at Rama Valley. They carried with them Tito's offer to the Germans of partisan aid in fighting the British should the latter make their expected landing along the Dalmatian coast. The personal message from Tito was that the partisans did not consider the Germans to be their enemies. He himself, after all, was a Croat, and had fought alongside the Austrians during the Great War. He had no desire that the allies should again prevail and emerge as victors. Nor did he have any quarrel with the Croatian fascist state headed by Ante

Pavelić. In fact, this might be an excellent opportunity to remind him of the secret agreement that had been signed in Sremska Mitrovica in 1939 by Stipe Javor on behalf of the *Ustaši* and by Moša Pijade representing the Communist Party of Yugoslavia, binding both parties to coordinate action aimed at the destruction of Yugoslavia.

Would it not, therefore, benefit all concerned if a truce were to be declared between the partisans and all Axis forces, thus freeing the former to concentrate all of their strength against the common enemy inside Yugoslavia, the Chetniks? There was surely no need to elaborate upon the benefits to the Germans of a partisan agreement to join forces with them against the expected landing of Allied forces along the Adriatic coast!

As the first step towards what Tito hoped would be a fruitful partnership for both sides, he suggested an immediate exchange of prisoners. From the German side, he also asked, initially, that they cease all hostilities against the partisans, and that they allocate to his beleaguered guerrillas an area in Sandžak where they could reorganize and continue their struggle against Draža Mihailović.

The reply brought back by his delegation was undoubtedly a disappointment. Although the German commandant in Sarajevo had been interested enough to send them to Zagreb under German protection and although both Hitler's personal envoy, Siegfried Kasche, and General von Horstenau had seen the advantages of having the partisans join with them in a common front against the Chetniks, not to mention the Allies, and were themselves quite enthusiastic about the suggestion, the fact was that permission would be required from Berlin before Tito's extremely interesting proposition could be put into effect.

However, all the signs were extremely hopeful. The Germans had, after all, designated Hans Otto, a trusted member of their security service, the *Sicherheitsdienst*, to act as liaison between their own and Tito's headquarters. This fact, together with the news that divisions of the First Bosnian Corps and the First Croatian Corps had moved back into the areas now vacated by the Germans, and expected to be able to move slowly back into Bihać, which the Germans were also expected to vacate, had put Tito into an optimistic frame of mind.

'They thought they had driven us out,' he said to Stevan. 'But to what purpose? They must have known they couldn't stay there for ever, that we could move back in again the moment they left.' He despatched a message of congratulation to the First Bosnian Corps and, in anticipation that Hitler would give his stamp of approval to his plan, added: *You must take this new situation into account and concentrate all your struggle against the Chetniks in Central Bosnia and Krajina.*

For Stevan, the period spent in Glavatičevo had seen a slow reconciliation of his inward struggle to accept the harsh doctrine and decisions of the Marxists. It was not just the loneliness, the bereft feeling he had experienced during his brief period of alienation, not only with Tito, but with Alex Miletić after that night he had been so sick in the woods near Bihać. Although both he and Alex had tried to hide their feelings of mutual distrust from Jelena, they had been patently uneasy in each other's company until Stevan had redeemed himself by protecting Tito's body with his own, thus apparently proving to Alex that he was absolutely loyal to the cause, despite the doubts he had obviously experienced from time to time.

No. It was not just the devastating feeling of loss he had felt then. It was not even the wave of death and destruction from the skies he had witnessed during the bombing of Bihać, or the subsequent frantic evacuation across the Neretva where at least they had had the chance of surprising some of the cursed Chetniks who had been so sure the partisans were trapped on the other side of that river. No. What was burned into his memory, what he was never to forget, was that terrible trek of starvation, typhus, freezing cold and barbarous acts of inhumanity he had witnessed during the withdrawal over the harsh, rocky, unforgiving terrain of the snow-covered Mount Prenj. He was never to forget that for each act of compassion he had witnessed during that journey into hell there had been a dozen more of instant and murderous retribution directed against anyone, innocent refugee or bewildered peasant, who had questioned any part of the Marxist doctrine as interpreted by men and women whose own inner conflicts seemed to demand that they give rational human reasons for irrational inhuman acts. He had learned two unforgettable lessons from it all. One was that the communists were obviously correct in their declaration that there was no God, which suggested that they were also correct in many of their other assumptions. The second was that in one thing big Alex was certainly right.

It was best not to think.

For the first time he found himself entirely at ease with whatever direction Tito deemed it necessary to take in order to ensure victory for the people's revolution. And Tito himself could not have been more charming. He had reverted, in fact, to that easy, pleasant relationship they had developed when they first met in Belgrade. The condescension had disappeared. He now consulted Stevan on the same level as the other communist delegates.

So far as Alex was concerned, since Jelena's death a subtle change had come into their relationship. It was no longer Stevan who deferred in most things to the big man, but rather the reverse. Alex followed Stevan around, eager for a few words, any words, that would convince him he had followed the right path.

'I should have left her in Belgrade with that God of hers,' he would say tearfully. 'I should never have allowed her to join us.'

'It was her own decision,' Stevan would reply in the stern voice that seemed best to calm Alex. 'She died with Stalin's name on her lips, remember. She would not have had it any other way.'

Then, to Stevan's great pleasure, the one leading communist with whom he had always felt at ease, Nikola Djerdja, joined them just before they left Glavatičevo and moved north to Kalinovik. Although Djerdja was fiercely loyal to Tito, he did not hesitate to say out loud what others were whispering. 'We should never allow him to make military decisions. All that vacillation. It has cost us thousands of lives. And yet, if anyone can lead us to political victory, Tito can. He is the man who can do it.'

It was while they were still at Kalinovik, just before moving on to establish their headquarters at the Piva Plateau, that they learned that the German offensive against the Chetniks was now to be put in operation. According to their intelligence sources, the German command had assembled a huge number of troops for the operation: the 118th Division, the 7th SS Division with some twenty thousand soldiers, including parts of the Brandenburg Division, four brigades of the Croatian army and several battalions of the Bulgarian army. 'The time has arrived to destroy the Chetniks before they, in alliance with the English, inflict heavy damage to our forces' was the message they intercepted from General Lütters to the German command in Belgrade.

As an introduction to the offensive, word was received from their German connection in Zagreb that posters offering a large reward for the capture of General Mihailović would soon be flooding the country. Unfortunately, at the same time these posters had been printed similar ones offering a price for Tito's head had also been produced, and until word was received from Berlin giving approval to the plan for collaboration between the partisans and the Germans, the plan for distribution of these would have to go ahead. Tito was, however, to understand that they would be null and void the moment word was received from Berlin.

The partisans rather gleefully sat back and waited for the assault upon the Chetniks. They did not have to wait long. On the 14th of May 1943, the First Mountain Division of the Schwartz operation swooped down and surrounded the famous Chetnik commander, Pavle Djurisić at Kolasin in Montenegro, killing or taking prisoner some two thousand of his Chetniks. Together with Italian units from the

Perudja, Venecia and Taurinese Divisions, similar operations were successfully carried out against the poorly-armed Chetniks in other areas of Montenegro, Hercegovina and Sandžak. Three to four thousand more were killed or taken prisoner and quickly despatched to forced-labour camps in Germany and Greece.

Fierce fighting was also reported from the area between the Neretva River and the upper course of the River Drina, where the Chetniks had attacked the townships of Goražda, Čajnice, Foča and Dobro Polje in retaliation, only to be driven back by the heavily-armed forces of Italian, German and Croatian troops, although not before the latter had been forced to urgently request help from the Seventh SS Division, which brought in its tanks and the *Luftwaffe*. Excitedly, Tito sent off a message to his Second Proletarian Division, ordering them to help 'liquidate the danger of Chetniks around Foča and Čajnice'.

'The Germans are wiping them out,' he exclaimed to Stevan, after reading an intelligence report from Belgrade one afternoon. He glanced up from the report and beamed happily. Gratefully, Stevan had noticed that these days he referred to 'our intelligence people in Belgrade'. No mention was made about 'your friend Olga'. Today, particularly pleased, he also mentioned that 'Belgrade intelligence' was getting some very useful information from a new source. Some fellow who managed a restaurant that was frequented by high-ranking German officers. Name of ... he peered again at the paper he was holding. 'Bogdan Bošković.'

'Bogdan?' Stevan gave an exclamation of laughter. 'But he's a friend of mine.'

'Is that true?' Tito stared at him over the rim of his glasses. 'What kind of fellow is he?'

Stevan chuckled. 'Well, let me put it this way. He must have heard we are having less trouble with the Germans than the Chetniks are. He tends to sway with the wind.'

Tito nodded thoughtfully. 'A realist! Good, good. The kind of man I like. You know then what you are dealing with.'

The euphoria of those first few days of operation Schwartz when it seemed the Germans at last were well on the way to wiping out their Chetnik rivals, however, was to end in a rude shock. Tentatively at first, and then in an ever-increasing stream, reports began to come in that the Germans were also attacking neutral partisan units. At first, frankly disbelieving, the secretary-general froze in his head-quarters which were now situated on the Piva Plateau, unable to accept or comprehend the outright treachery of the Germans.

Until the morning they awoke to find themselves under heavy and formidable air attack and almost completely surrounded on all sides by Axis forces. The nightmare of Bihać had begun again.

3

Apple on the tree
Apple on the tree, my Milan
When you go to the army
Wave to me with your handkerchief
Apple on the tree, my Milan

The column moved slowly alongside a gently bubbling stream, encased on the left by cliffs washed white by centuries of rain and snow, and on the right by majestic firs whose deep green reflection in the water below took precedence over the blue sky with its rapidly withdrawing sun. The deep voices echoing through the canyon as they sang the old Serbian folk-song rang with satisfaction and pleasure despite the loss of three of their comrades-in-arms and the two wounded men they carried on rough stretchers.

At dawn that morning they had successfully achieved their objective of the destruction of the railway line near the Italian garrison of Priboy, after which an unexpected encounter with Bulgarian troops had netted them a substantial booty of food and ammunition.

Just as night fell they came across a small hut in a clearing in front of the heavily wooded area to the right of the stream. There was no sign of life, although smoke was sending out small puffs of grey-white that lingered and swirled before turning into mist. David Ristić, riding at the head of the column on a large black gelding, held up his hand. The small column of men slowed down and came to a stop.

'Wait here,' he said to his companion, 'I'll be back in a moment.' He rode ahead until he reached the small hut, dismounted, and knocked on the door. As there was no response, he cautiously pushed it open and peered in.

'Doesn't seem to be anyone around.' The voice coming suddenly from behind made him gasp and spin around, one hand on his luger.

'My God, man, don't come up behind me like that. You could get hurt.'

'Sorry.' Alan Woods gave his hesitant, apologetic smile and stepped into the cottage. 'The fire's going. The owner can't be far away. Do you think he'd allow us to have some hot water? I could at least wash some of the wounds those two chaps have.'

David nodded. 'Should be no problem.' He stepped outside again and was about to beckon his sergeant to join them, when from the woods a voice suddenly cried out. 'Ko je tamo?' Who is there?

David instantly withdrew into the shadows. 'Ko je tamo!' he shouted back. Who is *there*?

'Kaži ti prvi.' You say first.'

'Ne,' he called back. 'Kaži ti prvi.'

A few more long moments and then from the woods emerged a small, shadowy figure, both hands raised above his head. David let his breath out sharply with the release of tension.

'It's all right,' he said to the still invisible Woods. 'It's the shepherd.'

Later, as they sat by the fire, drinking warm goat's milk pressed upon them by their voluble host, an amiable old man dressed in baggy trousers and a scrupulously clean, richly-embroidered if rather shabby *gunjak*, David explained to the British pilot that in a recent evening encounter two units of Chetniks had fought each other, each thinking the others were partisans. 'Luckily no one was hurt,' he said, 'but they wasted a great deal of ammunition.'

'Ah, yes. Ammunition! Serbian gold these days.'

David laughed. 'That's about it.'

For the first time since he had led his men out of

headquarters the previous day he found himself feeling comfortable with the fact that Woods had accompanied them. It was all very well for the supreme command to issue orders that any Allied airmen who bailed out over Yugoslavia were to be rescued at any cost, treated as 'brothers' and protected as 'sons', but when such 'brothers' insisted, as Woods had, that they take part in operations against the enemy, the strain of keeping an eye on them as well as directing and taking part in the operation was an added burden that he, for one, could do without. On the other hand, the Englishman did know something about first aid, and had been able to cleanse the wounds of the two Chetniks and make them much more comfortable, which David appreciated as deeply as the two men themselves.

The old shepherd began again to talk to him rapidly as Woods watched with a look of bemusement. 'He certainly can talk. What is he saying now?'

'Nothing much,' David laughed. 'He is a bit of a chattering machine, I'm afraid. He doesn't get a chance to talk to people often. He was saying that some Germans passed through here a week or so ago. Probably looking for us! He stayed hidden until they moved on. He said he was lucky, they came during the daytime so he was able to see who they were. With us, all he could make out was that we were a military group with horses and mules. We could have been anyone.' He shook his head. 'I think he wasn't sure whether to stay on the mountain with the bears and the wolves, or to risk showing himself.'

They left the two wounded men in the hut with the shepherd fussing over them and walked outside to find themselves a sleeping place on the ground near one of the fires the men had lit. David watched Woods with a slight smile. The Englishman, since being rescued from a German patrol by Zeka and his guerrillas, had been having some difficulty getting used to the egalitarian nature of the Chetnik army. As David had explained to him, while the peasants and townspeople responded well to military instruction, neither were very taken with the idea of military discipline. In fact this had proved to be beneficial because it allowed men who were on the whole extremely self-sufficient and enterprising to initiate what often proved to be bold and effective action against the enemy. 'You will find, of course, many men who were in the army previously. These are the ones who look for, respond to, and promptly obey orders.'

Woods had seemed rather dubious.

When Zeka had first presented him to the Avala Corps with rather a flourish, as a kind of gift, he had been delighted and obviously relieved to discover that David spoke English, and then overjoyed to learn that the corps was also taking care of another allied airman, an American called Abe Powis. Powis was a tall, slim, wise-cracking Yankee who, despite his upper-class New England background, seemed to fit in with Chetniks of all ranks. The stiff, aloof manner of Woods that had alienated David until he discovered that it hid a pleasant, rather shy nature, seemed to irritate the American. After a rather stilted exchange of the experiences that had led them both to bail out over West Serbia, Powis tended to ignore him, preferring to spend his time with Zeka trying to learn the secret of his uncanny hold over animals, or with Bosa, the pretty young nurse from Belgrade they had acquired through her Chetnik brother.

Powis had been picked up by the Chetniks almost the moment he landed. He claimed they had 'frightened shit' out of him when they materialized from the thick forest to surround him; huge, fierce-looking men with thick beards, holding an assortment of weapons. In fact they had had some trouble convincing him that he was, in fact, their 'brother', and that they sought merely to defend him from any lurking Germans. His description of the encounter could still send David into gales of laughter.

Woods, on the other hand, had almost been taken by a German patrol which had, however, temporarily retreated under Chetnik fire. Still, he claimed, he would have welcomed the Chetniks had they each and every one resembled old Nick himself. To his eyes they had all looked 'Absolutely capital, each and every one, beards and all'.

That evening he sat with David and Sergeant Veljko, talking drowsily and seemingly at ease at last with the rank and file. Veljko showed him his wineskin full of the brandy he had been saving for months now so that he would have something to 'celebrate my Slava', his family name's day due in November.

'You're a bit of a terror, you know, Veljko,' Woods said, only half-jokingly, wagging his finger at the burly Chetnik. 'Those fellows in there,' he nodded towards the hut, 'could have used some of that.' David translated for him. Veljko looked guilty and quickly hid his wineskin within the confines of his jacket much to the amusement of both officers.

Next morning they took their leave of the shepherd, who continued chattering until they were well out of sight, and made their way back to headquarters at a good pace, arriving just before noon. David made his report to Kosta, who arranged to have details sent to supreme headquarters through the radio section, then sought out Woods, Powis and Branko Jelić for what he felt was a well-deserved lunch.

That evening the young men gathered together with Kosta around the radio he kept in his tent and prepared to listen to the evening report from the BBC, always so anxiously awaited by Woods. As David had explained to both airmen, since those inexplicable reports had started emanating from the Soviet Tiflis radio that the Chetniks, far from fighting the Germans, were, in fact, collaborating, supreme headquarters had taken care to radio details of all action taken by its various units to British headquarters in the Middle East.

'Maybe,' he said, 'they will mention our operation yesterday. After all, we caused a good deal of damage to that railway line and successfully engaged the Bulgars. Not a bad day's work!'

In fact, the BBC announcer did, in his round, fruity voice, describe in good detail the action taken by David's Chetnik unit. The thing that was to leave Woods deathly pale, the three Serbs silent with shock, and produce a startled 'Shit!' from Powis, was that he attributed the action taken to the partisan rebels of the communist leader Tito.

*   *   *

Much later that evening Powis found David leaning with his back against a tree, looking up at the brilliant stars, and smoking a cigarette, a habit he had begun since his trip to Belgrade.

'Christ! I still can't get over that broadcast. How can you take it so calmly?'

'I'm not taking it calmly. I cursed the British for an hour. We all did! Not in front of Woods, of course. It's not his fault.'

'The news is all over the camp. You people must be disgusted with us.'

'What makes you say that? I just said, it's not Woods' fault. And it is certainly not yours.'

'I know. But still. You know Woods. Christ, I feel badly enough, but Woods! He's still in a state of shock, I think.'

David nodded, made no reply.

'The thing I don't understand about you people, the thing I'll never understand...' He broke off and remained silent until prompted by David.

'Well?'

'You know that sergeant of yours, Veljko?'

'What about him?'

'You know that wineskin he's been guarding with his life for the past few months?'

For the first time that evening David laughed. 'All it contains is some very bad brandy.'

'I know. He's been saving it for his birthday or something.'

'Something like that.'

'Well believe it or not I saw him offering it to Woods. I think he must have decided to celebrate his birthday early. They were both well on their way to drowning their sorrows.

Old Veljko had his arm around Woods' shoulders as though he were his father. What in the hell *gives* with you people?'

'What gives?'

'I mean, what makes you act like that?'

David thought the question over gravely. 'I think,' he said, 'Veljko simply understands how Woods feels. We Serbs have a very long history, you know. We understand that when a government, or its bureaucrats if you like, does something stupid or dishonourable, it shames its people. Veljko is a simple man, a peasant, you understand? But he understands that. Our history has taught him that. He must be feeling very sorry for Woods, that's all.'

'Sorry for him? Shit!' growled Powis. 'If it was me I'm damned if I'd be filling him with brandy. I'd be kicking his ass all over the side of the mountain. That's what *I'd* be doing.'

For some reason the American's furious indignation released the tension David had been feeling. He gave a short laugh and slapped him on the back. 'Come on,' he said, 'I don't have any brandy, but I do have half a bottle of wine. Let's go and finish it.'

Two days later David was on his way to supreme headquarters, again on the back of a motorcycle driven by the soldier Dragon. With him he carried a letter from Colonel Trifković asking, so the colonel had explained, 'Just what the hell is going on with the British? Try to see General Mihailović,' he had added, 'but if you can't, perhaps your uncle will know what's going on.'

In fact, when he arrived, it was to discover that the general was absent at a village some fifty kilometres away where he had been invited to act as godfather to the grandchild of the local mayor. His Uncle Mikhail, however, was very much present, older, carrying much less weight, yet looking extremely well.

'I'm beginning to think going without all that good cooking of your aunt's is healthy for me.' He was still brimful of the old fire. He had enfolded David in his huge embrace, then stood back and studied him for a moment. 'You've lost weight, too,' he pronounced. 'But you look well, son. You look very well. I think you have matured, too. You have really matured.'

'I wish there were easier ways of doing that, Uncle.'

They both burst out laughing.

Later they sat under a rough canvas canopy that Mikhail used as his temporary office, and he read the letter from Colonel Trifković.

'We can't understand what's going on, Uncle. Would it be possible for you to get in touch with the British command in Cairo? Luckily, you know, just by accident I happened to have a British airman with me during the two operations. We do have a witness, an independent witness, you see. If they want some kind of proof.'

'Proof? Proof? The place is riddled with British officers! They can see what is going on with their own eyes. They must report these things back to their headquarters.' His uncle's huge frame was atop an overturned wine barrel. He closed his eyes, placed his elbows on his knees and rested his head in his hands for a moment, giving a deep sigh before looking up. 'David, the thing that happened to you, taking part in sabotage and fighting against the enemy, only to listen later to your exploits being credited to the partisans, has happened to several other units. Even to *Čiča* himself!' He went on to describe an attack Mihailović had led on the town of Vishegrad, occupied by close to a thousand German troops. His objective had been to take the garrison and then blow up the rail bridge linking Serbia and Bosnia over the River Drina. The mission had been successfully completed, the Germans driven out of and beyond the town of Rogatitza. The Chetniks had then withdrawn to their headquarters in the woods, only to listen to the evening broadcast from the BBC credit Tito's partisans with the taking of the town of Rogatitza 'after a glorious battle'. Mikhail shook his massive head, and again gave a deep sigh. 'As for witnesses, both American and British officers were present. They participated in the action with the general and later listened with him to the British broadcast. I have no doubt they were as embarrassed as you say your airman was!'

'But what the devil is going on then, Uncle? You know, if it was Moscow radio, I'd understand, but–'

'What is going on?' His uncle rose and began to pace up and down the confined space covered by canvas. 'That's what we are trying to find out. We have sent a detailed report to our government in London and until they take the matter up with the British government there, I don't think we'll know what is going on. It's not the only kind of thing we've been discussing, you know.' He sat down again, heavily. 'Some very strange things have been happening with British military headquarters in the Middle East. For instance, they complained that we were not doing enough against the Axis. They asked us to commit certain acts of sabotage that required materials we simply do not have. When we asked them to send the necessary dynamite and so forth, they agreed. But they did not send it. Yet a week or so later they asked, in a damned impertinent manner, I might add, why we had not carried out their instructions! Ten days later they again demanded action. This time telling us to do something that in fact would have meant completely cutting off our own supply lines.' He stared at David in genuine puzzlement. 'They have even asked us, you know, to take some action that, so far as we can see, has no useful military objective, will achieve nothing other than the death of a handful of Germans or their murderous friends, for which hundreds of our civilians will die. When we mention this to the British mission for instance, or ask questions about the objectives of action they ask us to take, all we get in response are glazed or angry looks and no reply.' His voice was loud with anger.

'What do you mean, no reply?' David was suddenly shouting in an explosion of frustration, anger. 'Damn it! Do they think Serbian blood is of such little value? I thought it was Hitler who was supposed to think Slavs were an inferior race!'

His uncle peered at him over his pince-nez. 'Don't shout,

son,' he said, his own voice suddenly mildly reasonable. 'There is no need to shout at me.'

'Sorry.' David could not help, angry though he was, giving an inner smile. His uncle, as he well knew, could out-shout him or anyone else for that matter.

Mikhail sat there thoughtfully. 'I tell you, David. Do you know what I think it's all about?'

David shook his head.

'During the last war, as you know, I fought alongside the British at Salonika. They were marvellous! Fought like tigers, helped us immeasurably with supplies. Well, after that war, when some of the inept and irresponsible actions of their military and political leaders were revealed to have cost thousands of lives quite unnecessarily, someone made the comment that the British soldiers were "lions led by donkeys". Well, today, with the political leadership they have, I begin to think it is a case of donkeys being led by lions! If Churchill knew what was going on here, things would be tidied up very smartly, of that I am sure. I am positive that once our government in London explains matters to him, we will have no further problems.'

He was still holding Trifković's letter in his hand and he now waved it in the air. 'Anyway, tell your colonel when you return that the moment we receive a report from London we will be in touch with him. Meanwhile, we must have faith that these misunderstandings will be sorted out. The British are our traditional and faithful allies. We must keep our faith in them.'

They turned to other things and began to discuss the terrible losses the Chetniks had suffered at the hands of the Germans during the bitter summer campaign when the latter had made another all-out effort to capture Mihailović and destroy his army. David described the fierce fighting that had taken place between the Avala Corps and the German First Alpine Division, which had resulted in the Avala Corps suffering grievous losses. As always, the problem had been lack of arms and ammunition. When were all these materials the British kept promising going to materialize anyway? He told of his visit to Belgrade, and Colonel Trifković's hope that they might find a source of arms through the police lieutenant, Janković. The latter had, however, been picked up by the Germans and shot only a few days after David had left the city. There were traitors everywhere!

'Tell me, Uncle,' he asked, 'you must have heard the radio broadcasts from Belgrade. Is it true what General Lütters is boasting? That some six thousand of our men were killed or taken prisoner during the summer campaign?'

His uncle nodded mournfully. 'It's been a terrible time, son. But, you see, we have survived, you and I, to fight on.'

Later they had dinner together under the stars. David was able to tell his uncle that the family was well, that they believed he had left Belgrade with his wife. Yes, they *had* heard from Aunt Kaja who apparently was keeping up the myth that Mikhail was with her. She had said she was very glad to be out of Belgrade.

His uncle did not mention Irina. He was grateful that the old man seemed too preoccupied with other things to think about her. He did say that the burden of being the general's sole political adviser would soon be lifted. At the instigation of the government in London a National Political Committee would soon be joining them. He had been asked to be its chairman, but he preferred his status of special adviser.

The following morning David left supreme headquarters to return to his corps. He carried with him as a souvenir from his uncle a copy of the proclamation signed by the supreme commander of the *Wehrmacht* in Serbia that had appeared in Belgrade's daily newspaper *Novo Vreme* on the 21st of July 1943. He certainly did not need it. It was plastered throughout the country on trees, in railway stations, post offices and city halls. Perhaps though, he thought, Alan Woods or Abe Powis might like it as a souvenir.

A REWARD OF 100,000 REICHSMARK
IN GOLD
will be paid to the person who brings the bandit Draža

Mihailović, alive or dead, to the legal authorities. This criminal has plunged the country into its greatest tragedy. As an English agent he has contributed to the destruction of all national values sacred to the people from time immemorial. He has disrupted the peace of both peasants and townspeople and plunged the country into an indescribable misery. For this reason a price of one hundred thousand Reichsmark in gold has been placed on the head of this dangerous bandit. The person who proves that he has disarmed this criminal, or who surrenders him to the nearest German authority, will not only receive the amount of one hundred thousand Reichsmark in gold, but will also receive recognition of having accomplished a national task, because he will liberate his people and fatherland from the scourge of terror.

When he arrived back at camp, however, it was to find that both Powis and Woods had left. A major operation against the Germans was about to be launched near Boka Kotorska and it had been decided to move them to a safer place. They had been spirited away on a peasant's cart, buried beneath some old blankets and rags, just one hour before his return.

* * *

As Tito was so often to say, they should not have been too surprised by the German betrayal. After all, was it not true that Hitler had been the first to break his pact with Stalin? No, they should not have been surprised. Their biggest mistake had been to accept the German explanation that it was lack of communication between their headquarters in Zagreb and their Belgrade command that had caused the latter to include partisan rebels in operation Schwartz which had originally been designed only to wipe out the Chetnik danger.

By the time word had reached them that their proposal

for collaboration had been turned down by Hitler himself, who saw Mihailović as the main danger to his forces in Yugoslavia, they had found themselves completely surrounded on all sides by the German army.

It had been a terrible time. Their efforts to break through the German encirclement had been repulsed time and time again. Finally, however, their First Proletarian Brigade managed to break through to the Kalinovik-Foca main road, enabling their remaining forces to dissolve into the forest. It had meant sacrificing the sick and the wounded and they lost almost ninety-nine per cent of their Third Division. But they had survived!

But only just. Crushed, many of them full of despair, they withdrew into East Bosnia to once again lick their wounds. Tito himself seemed to grow older each day in front of Stevan's eyes.

Yet he had not lost his instinct for survival, his determination to out-wait what he was convinced would be an eventual German withdrawal from the country, at which time he would use every means at his disposal to wrest power for the Party.

Even the triumphant bray of General Lütters to all German units that *Soldiers, the operations against Chetniks and communists are ended. The main body of the enemy troops are annihilated,* produced only a shrug.

'That's what *he* thinks,' he was often heard to say. 'But at least they've wiped out many of the Chetniks for us. And it's not over yet. Our breakthrough will come. You will see. Something will turn up.'

In fact in the late summer of 1943, something did indeed turn up. A few months previously a young British officer named William Deakin had dropped into their midst by parachute while they were at Mount Durmitor. An Oxford don and intimate of Churchill, he had at first been greeted with the mixture of dislike and distrust Tito was always to entertain towards the perfidious British. To general astonishment, however, Deakin had seemed almost immediately to identify himself with Tito and his cause.

Although the only partisan action against the Germans he was to witness was their withdrawal under attack, he accepted without question the tall tales they spun about action they had supposedly taken against Axis forces. He had eventually departed, vowing to carry back to the British his knowledge of partisan heroism and effectiveness against the fascist enemy.

And now, several months later, they were surprised to receive word that due to Deakin's report about their activities the British were sending a military mission to join them. It was to be led by another friend of Churchill's, a British officer called Fitzroy Maclean. When the mission arrived, Tito could not have been more pleased.

'Maclean tells me he received his instructions direct from Churchill. The old man told him to "See which side is killing more Germans. The Chetniks or the partisans". And there is something else,' he added. 'This is a man I can get along with. He served with the British foreign office before the war. The diplomatic service. He actually served with the British embassy in Moscow.' He positively beamed. 'Yes, yes. This is definitely a man I can get along with.'

To the partisan leadership's astonishment Maclean did indeed prove to be a man the secretary-general could get along with. They had all listened somewhat nervously as Tito plied the British brigadier with the same astonishing lies about partisan activity that he had fed to a credulous Deakin. 'He even swallowed the story that we had an army of two hundred and twenty thousand,' chuckled a bemused Djerdja who, nevertheless, was never to forget that Churchill's instructions to Maclean to 'see who is killing more Germans' had shown a total lack of concern for the hundred Serbian civilians who would die for each one of those dead Germans. Their dislike and contempt for the British reached the level of hatred when they later received information that the British prime minister's advice to the French underground had been *not* to kill Germans if it would harm the civilian population. 'Our people's lives are so cheap, then?' they had fumed.

Yet there was no doubt at all that Maclean's visit had saved them from certain disaster. Before he left Maclean made it clear he would not be carrying through his instructions to also check with Mihailović and his Allied mission. With no knowledge of the language and with his movements closely monitored by partisans who ensured he had no contact with those who might tell him otherwise, he was to send a report to London in late November in which he unhesitatingly confirmed the wildly exaggerated claims of the communists concerning how many Germans they had killed, dismissed as unfounded any concern the Allies might have about Tito's commitment to communism, painting the partisans pink rather than red, and linking the Chetnik name to the unspeakable deeds committed by the *Ustaši*.

Ludicrous and riddled with inaccuracies as the report was, it proved to be a turning point in the fortunes of the partisans and effectively sealed the doom of both the Chetniks and the Yugoslav people.

4

The furious attacks launched by the Germans against Chetnik units in July of 1943 had taken their toll.

Supported by Bulgarian troops, *Ljotićevci* and members of General Nedić's State Guard they had attacked Chetniks under the command of Captain Nikola Kalabić of the Gorski Royal Guard, in an abortive effort to capture the renowned and courageous officer. Although they failed in their main purpose, the elusive Kalabić once again slipping through their fingers, they did inflict heavy losses against his guerrilla fighters.

Simultaneously the *Zicherheitsdienst*, the German security police, struck at Chetnik forces in the districts of Obrenovac, Veliko Gradište and Užice, inflicting heavy losses. The treacherous *Ljotićevci* earned fulsome praise for their 'valuable' contribution to the ultimate destruction of the 'bandit' Chetnik forces from General Bader in his monthly broadcast throughout the land.

In retaliation against the detested *Ljotićevci*, the Rasina Corps struck back with deadly effectiveness against the fascists in the district of Kruševac, only once again to find themselves pitted against German reinforcements who immediately inflicted terrible reprisals against the population.

When the elusive Captain Kalabić again struck back against a German garrison in the town of Stragari, he took these brutal reprisals by the fascists into consideration and executed all German prisoners. His moment of triumphant retribution proved all too fleeting, however. While the

Germans often proved ineffective against the wild attacks of the bearded guerrillas, even when patently superior in arms and numbers, no one could surpass them in brutal reprisals. They brought in reinforcements, murdered every civilian in sight, and burned the small town of Stragari down to its very last home.

The fighting, the killing, seemed never ending.

It continued into August when in a large operation undertaken near Arilje lasting some two weeks the Pozega Corps captured an entire company of Bulgarians and wiped out a unit of *Ljotičevci*, killing the latter's commandant. Punitive action was immediately launched by the fascists, who burned to the ground several small villages including Pranjane and Kamenica and executed several hundred peasants. They then undertook further action against several districts controlled by the Chetniks within Western Serbia, burning down more villages and launching a bombing attack against the area of Kosjeric.

The allied landing in Sicily and southern Italy came just in time to revive the reeling Chetniks. In central Serbia the Avala Corps, along with every Chetnik corps in the country renewed and intensified action against the Germans, the Bulgarians and the discouraged Italians. David Ristić took part in several vigorous attacks against German units, German garrisons, German convoys, German munitions depots. The Posavska Brigade began to accumulate an impressive number of successful sabotage operations, cutting enemy supply lines, blowing-up still more bridges, liberating villages and destroying lines of communication leading to Bulgaria and Greece. Eventually, though, short of food and arms, they retreated to the hills outside Belgrade to regroup, to try to find ways of again building up supplies.

On the 6th of September 1943, David was sent alone to a rendezvous at a house situated just outside the city in order to make contact with a civilian Kosta had described as 'A friend of Mihailović, but a nervous friend'. It was hoped but by no means certain that he would agree to act as liaison between the Avala Corps and a group inside Belgrade which had promised to do its best to gather a cache of much needed food and anything else it could gather or steal for the corps.

Dressed in innocuous civilian garb and riding a bicycle David lifted his face up to the sun and pedalled easily along the rough, winding mountain path at a leisurely pace, enjoying the beautiful autumn. He was seven kilometres outside Belgrade when he became aware of a deep roar emanating from north-east of the city. Another bombing raid by the Americans returning from Rumania to a base in Italy, he realized. His bike skidded to a halt. The sun had disappeared behind a wafting group of clouds that also hid the Allied planes, although the deafening explosions as bombs hit the earth reached him loud and clear.

Squinting his eyes upwards and then towards the city he tried to assess the area where the bombs were being dropped. If his assessment was correct, and the billowing dark smoke assured him it was, they had hit not the German military command or administration, but the middle-class suburb of Pasino Brdo. An incredible mistake. Or were they just off-loading bombs? With a sick feeling in the pit of his stomach he remembered the girls' school that was situated in the suburb. Many of his friends' youngsters attended the school. He began to furiously peddle towards the suburb.

He reached the site where the school had been just as the last of the small bodies was being placed on top of open garbage trucks by a group of men who were working silently, tears streaming down their cheeks. 'We have no other transport,' one of them said in response to his question. 'These trucks are all we have.'

'Four hundred of them, brother,' another worker broke in, his voice cracking with fury and grief. 'And all of the school staff. No survivors.'

The bombs, he was told, had been 'air-pressurized' and the strangest thing was that none of the children appeared to be injured except for a small trickle of blood that ran from their mouths and nostrils. Otherwise it could almost appear that the lifeless objects being loaded so gently onto the trucks were nothing more than straw-filled dolls, their jointless limbs sprawled this way and that.

For the first time since the beginning of the war David found his eyes filling with tears. This had been done, in the name of God, not by the barbaric Germans, who apparently knew no better, but by the Allies. Did any of them know what they were doing? *Any* of them?

He was overwhelmed by a great and bitter and terrible anger. *Only pay them back, God! Please pay them back. Pay them back, God!* The refrain turned over and over in his mind as he slowly got back on his bike and cycled away, his limbs feeling heavy, awkward, as though great weights had been attached to his ankles, as though his very arms and legs too were weighted down with bitter grief and anger.

He returned to camp several hours later. At least his contact had proved to have more courage than had been expected and there was hope that through him they would receive provisions from inside Belgrade, including some arms and ammunition stolen from the Germans for which several civilians had paid with their lives. The terrible anger he had felt at Pasino Brdo of necessity was buried deep within him as were so many other outrages and betrayals that would continue to haunt him for the rest of his days.

The bitter war went on.

From Bor, the centre of the rich copper mines in Eastern Serbia, came news that the Zagubica Brigade had successfully attacked the German force that was guarding the large Bor mine, proving so successful that the latter had to call for reinforcements and resort yet again to murdering civilians and burning down villages.

From the frontier between Serbia and Bosnia the Zlatibor Corps swooped down upon the enemy and took the town of Bajina Bašta after a bloody battle with German units, while the Javor Corps routed the Albanians.

In Croatia, Chetnik action was equally successful, until sabotaged by the perfidious partisans. In Hercegovina the local Chetnik commandant had attacked and taken the

Italian Tourinese Division, liberated all of the towns and launched an attack against Mostar when his men were struck from the rear by communist units, throwing them into disarray and causing them to fall back, unable to sustain fighting against the Germans, the *Ustaši* and the partisans.

When news of the Italian capitulation reached supreme headquarters, at that time situated on the frontier of Serbia and Sandžak, General Mihailović at once ordered all action against the enemy to be intensified. Towns began to fall like flies into Chetnik hands. Nova Varoš, Prijepolje, Bijelo Polje, Berane, Andrijevica and Kolašin. The Sandžak commandant, Major Vojislav Lukačević, who played a large part in the planning of this action, captured some two thousand Germans and easily took the whole Italian Venezia Division.

The successful campaign by Chetnik forces reached into Eastern Bosnia, where the Drina, Romanija and Cer Corps launched fierce attacks against the enemy, capturing Rudo, Goražda, Prača, Rogatica and Ustiprača.

News of these successes were greeted everywhere by Chetnik forces with whoops of joy, with the singing of patriotic songs, the resurgence of a hope that alleviated hunger and mitigated the chilling cold of the mountains that penetrated their threadbare clothing. Their pleasure was enhanced by the knowledge that much of the action their forces had taken against the enemy had been witnessed by British and American officers, thus putting a lie to the vicious, dirty and stupid rumours the communist bandits were trying to spread that Chetniks were collaborating with the enemy. Some collaboration, they laughed. Some collaboration!

Early in October, frustrated and furious after their abortive attempt to destroy the village of Visoko, where they believed Mihailović to be stationed with several of his top commandants, the German command launched a fierce new initiative against the guerrillas. General Felber, who had replaced General Bader, ordered operation 'Maiskolben', launching fifteen battalions of German, Bulgarian and

Ljotićevci, with the help of the *Luftwaffe*, against the main body of Chetnik troops on the 3rd of October 1943. The operation went on for five days. The general's report to Belgrade announced glumly that despite the best efforts of his forces most of the Chetniks had 'escaped to the west, although five hundred persons have been retained as hostages'.

Three smaller operations – 'Krum', 'Herbstnebel' and 'Hamelbrot' – were not much more successful. The German general did point out with some satisfaction, however, that winter was fast approaching. With their severe lack of even basic winter clothing and their obvious shortage of ammunition, the situation for the elusive Chetniks was now extremely serious.

In December, in fact, the Chetniks paused to take stock, to look back upon a year during which they and their people had suffered terrible losses. Yet they could take heart from the knowledge that severe as those losses had been, those they had inflicted upon all enemy forces had been equally or more devastating. It was during this lull, during this short pause for breath, that they were to receive the most bitter, unbelievable and terrible blow of all.

All over Serbia and in areas of Bosnia, Hercegovina and Montenegro where they had fought so long and hard against the fascist foe, they stood around in groups, stunned, disbelieving, listening to the radio news that told them that at a meeting in Teheran a decision had been made by Prime Minister Churchill, President Roosevelt and the secretary-general of the Soviet Communist Party, Joseph Stalin, that: *Yugoslavia would be liberated by its own people and the only movement which, from now on, would be supported by the Allies would be the partisans, under the leadership of Secretary-General Josip Broz.*

* * *

It fell to David Ristić to address the men of the Posavska Brigade, to try to explain the inexplicable.

The commander of the brigade, Kosta Marinković, was incapacitated by a leg wound he had received during a recent attack by heavily armed German and *Ustaši* forces. Branko Jelić, too, was incapacitated not only by a stomach wound that had left him in constant pain, but by the deep bitterness and depression that overcame him after hearing of the Teheran decision.

In fact it had become a custom with David to sit around the fire with the men after battle, discuss the action they had just taken, and try to answer their increasingly curious questions about the communists. Why were they expending their precious ammunition against their own countrymen, the Chetniks? How was it that they preferred to sabotage Chetnik action against the real foe, the fascists, instead of helping to rid Yugoslavia of these murderous intruders? When were the British and the Americans going to send the Chetniks supplies? From one side of their mouths they proclaimed that what *Čiča* and they themselves were doing was invaluable to their cause, while from the other they said he was hand in hand with the fascists. Were they mad? Were the Chetniks themselves mad to ally themselves with such treacherous and slippery allies?

This bitter evening the questions were the same, but more intensified.

'Yes, brothers, my fellow Chetniks. It is, of course, a grave blow. But will it really make that much difference to us? We must always bear in mind our original purpose in joining *Čiča* here in the mountains. It was to rid the country of external enemies who attacked us and invaded our land without even the civilizing gesture of a declaration of war. Certainly, we have received many promises of assistance from the Allies since we began our resistance, but all of you know how little assistance we did receive in real terms. So, why should we despair? We shall carry on with our purpose. To rid our beloved country of the fascists. The only difference I see is once we have achieved that, we will then have to direct our efforts against this internal threat – against the traitorous communists.

'You are saying we must carry on the fight as though nothing has happened?' Zeka's cold eyes rested on him with an expression of hostility.

'What else? What *has* happened? As I said before, not that much has changed. At least we can take pride in knowing that when the whole of Europe bowed down to Hitler, we were the first in the field to have the courage to take him on. History will record that fact, Zeka.' He laughed, reached out and gently shook the other man by the shoulder. 'I would wager you never expected to make the history books, brother.'

'What you say about nothing having really changed is true enough.' A huge, dangerous looking Montenegrin spoke up. 'But *something* is going on. How is it possible that these communist underworld bandits get away so easily with their murderous lies? Are the Allies stupid? Or are they truly mad?'

David leaned forward and held out his hands to the warmth of the fire.

'Not mad, Tomo. As I see it, in this war we are faced with a conflict that has developed beyond a military struggle into a *political* war. To put it bluntly, I think our own leadership was simply not prepared for this kind of war. It has taken them too long to grasp what it is all about. And it seems to me that the Allies are equally slow in this regard. So far as the purpose of the communists within our country is concerned, why all the lies and propaganda at a time when our dear Yugoslavia is fighting for its life? It seems to me their purpose is clear. They wish to create chaos and confusion so that they will have a better chance to grab power for themselves the moment an opportunity presents itself.'

'You mean they wish to *steal* our country? Like common thieves? They wish to steal our country without fighting for it in an honest way?' Yaruga's squeaky voice, coming from his permanent place near Zeka's side, was so indignant that the men began to chuckle.

David joined in with their laughter. 'I think you are right

there, Yaruga. But we should be warned, you know, by how effective their methods have proved so far. No need to tell any of you that we Chetniks have always bettered them on the battlefield, or that our people all over the country have repudiated them again and again, but the way I see it we have certainly lost, if only temporarily, on the international field. Yet if our Allies have not yet understood that an unseen political war is being waged, if our Allies are as blinded by the military war as we have been, then we cannot be blamed too much for taking so long to understand what has been going on in our country.'

'It is enough to make a man's head burst,' Tomo muttered. 'Here in our own country the communists are our enemies. Yet how can we not admire the military success of the brave Red Army? How can we not be proud that our fellow Slavs in Russia have routed these fascist bastards?'

David nodded. 'You know, Tomo, I also wonder if perhaps that is why the Allies have abandoned us so readily. *To appease the Soviet Union*! Especially as they seem unable to gather their courage and open up a second front. Perhaps we are being offered up as a concession,' he said, for the first time allowing a note of bitterness to creep into his voice. 'Perhaps they have forgotten why they entered this war in the first place – to save Europe from totalitarian fascist aggression What an irony if they now meekly hand it over to the communist totalitarians.'

'What *I* want to know is this: these Allied airmen who get themselves shot down over our territory. Are we still expected to risk our lives saving them from the bloody Germans?' It was Zeka again, in an obviously truculent mood despite the perpetual half-smile on his thin lips.

'Why should we?' Tomo again. 'If you ask me, we should hand the ones we *do* have over to the dirty fascists. If the Allies want to brand us as bandits, well, let us teach them a lesson. Let us *behave* like bandits.'

'Ah yes, Tomo,' David interrupted quickly. 'And how those bloody partisans would like us to do *just* that. "You see", they would say to the Allies, "we *told* you they are hand in hand with the Fascists".'

'What *I* would like to know is how many Allied airmen have the communists risked *their* lives to save? Can someone tell me that?'

'None that I know of,' David said, 'although they did capture an English journalist when they first entered the field, and promptly murdered him. Which one would think would be enough to show where their sympathies lay.'

'You know what I think?' Zeka lit a cigarette, placed it between his thin lips, and continued speaking out of the side of his mouth. 'I think we should never have become involved in this bloody war in the first place. Tell me,' he stared at David unblinkingly, 'is it true that the British got us into it? Is it true that they were the ones who pushed those bloody stupid officers into that putsch?'

David returned the cold look unsmilingly. 'I don't know. Certainly they handed Prince Paul over to the British in Greece. I don't think they were too surprised to receive him. But what part they played in the scheme . . .' he shrugged, 'I simply don't know.'

'You don't know. Yet you are telling us we should stay here in the mountains, half-starved and half-frozen to death and keep on fighting the enemies of the British. You are telling us we should lay our lives on the line and keep on rescuing any of their men who are shot down over our territory. Is that what you are telling us?'

A hush fell over the by now quite large group of Chetniks who had gathered around to listen. David was a favourite of theirs. They admired the courage and leadership he showed in battle. He seemed to unthinkingly emulate the deeds of his renowned uncle from the First World War – his unflagging optimism, his energy, the way he laughingly insisted that their sojourn in the mountains, from Shar-planina in the south to Kopaonik, Jahorina, Zlatibor and Tara to the Slovenian Kranjska Gora and Planica in the north-west, was little more than a 'hunting and skiing trip', that the exhilarating air of the mountains would add years to their lives, or at the very least gave them an opportunity to 'live with nature and away from this confused and cruel world'. They liked him. They believed him. Yet it was Zeka, the ultra-realist, who would give them their direction.

David had still not offered any reply to the cold-eyed guerrilla leader. After a moment, however, he had a question of his own.

'Tell me, Zeka,' he asked quietly, 'what made *you* join the Chetniks in the first place?'

Zeka scowled. 'Who wouldn't have?' he grunted. 'You know I come from Umka. You should have seen those bloody fascists strutting around my village as though they owned it. You should have just seen the bastards!'

David nodded. 'And has anything changed since then?' he asked. 'Has anything really changed?'

Zeka stared back at him. Almost imperceptibly, the cold half-smile widened into something like an admiring grin. 'No,' he admitted. 'By Christ you are right! Nothing has really changed.'

* * *

From the 25th to the 28th of January 1944, a meeting of Mihailović's National Congress was held at Ba village, nestled next to a small river near Suvobor Mountain, close to the Kadina Luka railway station in Western Serbia.

By the time David, who had been sent by the Posavska Brigade as its delegate to the meeting, had arrived after an exhausting journey over bitterly cold, snow-capped mountains, the congress had been in progress for two days, and had already chosen its new president, Dr Živko Topalović, and agreed on a federal vision for Yugoslavia that would include Serbia, Slovenia and a Croatia returned to its pre-war borders.

The congress had been called in order to refute the vicious lies and propaganda that emanated each day through BBC broadcasts from London, the Middle East and from the Soviet Radio in Tiflis. The general theme was not only that the Chetniks were collaborating with the enemy, but that General Mihailović himself entertained political ambitions, that he was 'A reactionary Serbian nationalist-chauvinist', whose main political objective was the return of the Serbian monarchy, and the total domination of Yugoslavia by a 'reactionary clique of corrupt Serbian politicians' to be led, presumably, by the Chetnik leader himself. This 'corrupt' group, the broadcasts implied, was intent on preventing the Yugoslav Communist Party from forming its 'people's democracy', which would bring with it the protection of human rights, freedom of political speech, free democratic elections and social justice not only just for the working class, but for the whole population.

After making inquiries about the whereabouts of his Uncle Mikhail and discovering that the old man was closeted in a meeting with the heads of the various democratic parties, David had rather wearily made his way to the quarters allotted to him in the home of one of the villagers.

He was about to knock on the door of the house when a sudden, ear-splitting roar rang through the air.

'David! David Ristić! By God! It's David.'

Turning, he found himself almost swept off his feet by warm embraces from what looked to be two large grizzly bears.

It was only when he extricated himself from their bone-crushing hugs that he realized who they were. 'Janko! Vladimir! I don't believe this!' He hugged them back, kissed them on both cheeks, shook his head, kept repeating, 'I don't believe this. I don't believe it.'

It was true enough. The Petrović twins had, it seemed, learned of Mihailović's stand against the fascists at approximately the same time as David. They, too, had immediately joined the guerrilla force. As, too, they told him, momentarily quietened and saddened, had their friend, Lieutenant Ljubić. 'Taken by the partisans in late 1942. Those Godless bastards sent a message to his unit, suggesting they discuss mutual action against a nearby German garrison. When Ljubić turned up with most of his unit, they found it was a trap. Most of them were slaughtered, although one or two escaped to tell the tale. Our friend, well, the bastards drove a stake through his mouth. What barbarians! I would not,' Janko said grimly, 'wish to be in their shoes when the day comes for them to face God.'

David nodded. 'We will remember these things after the war,' he said grimly. 'We cannot afford to dwell on them now.'

'You are right. We would all go mad! But look, where are you billeted? Come and stay with us. There is much to talk about. And God knows when we will meet again.'

In the end David relinquished his own room to share that of the Petrović brothers in the home of the local miller. Warmly and hospitably supplied with a huge platter of pork, *kajmak*, black bread to be washed down with *rakija*, followed by cheeses, pastry and coffee supplied by the plump, cheerful woman of the house, they sprawled out on a large sheepskin, nibbling away and softly talking.

It did not take long to exchange details of each others' movements since they had all joined Mihailović. Both David and the twins were careful to exchange anecdotes concerning the lighter side of life as hardy guerrilla fighters. David told them a few tales of adventures he had enjoyed with Zeka and described that cold-eyed Chetnik's uncanny hold over animals. The twins acted out a hilarious tale of their first night with Mihailović's army. Following their practice when they were in the army reserve, they had changed out of their woollen trousers and *gunjaks* into silk pyjamas, only to be awakened at dawn by an attack by a German patrol. While Janko mimed the indecent haste with which they had dragged on their clothes, Vladimir slapped David on the back and roared with laughter. 'My God, David. It's the last time we've even *seen* our pyjamas.'

Later, they joined some of the other delegates, who numbered well over two hundred and fifty, to exchange greetings and news with old friends, compare experiences, discuss the inexplicable decision taken by the Allies at Teheran and the extraordinary behaviour of the British.

Most of them had a rueful story or two to tell about action taken by their units against Axis forces that had been witnessed by American or British officers, only to return to base and have to listen to their exploits being credited by the BBC to Tito's partisans. Despite assurances by the often excrutiatingly embarrassed Allies that these lies would be reported back to Allied headquarters, nothing seemed to change. The lies continued. Anger flared, as they each recalled individual experiences, until someone ruefully told how the Serbian peasants had now coined a new phrase. *Ti lažeš kao London*, they would occasionally tell each other. 'You lie like London!' They all dissolved into laughter. God bless the Serbian peasant. A wonderfully humane, generous and compassionate fellow who would give you the clothes from his back and his last morsel of food and who wanted nothing from life except to be allowed to enjoy his own rich culture, his church, his little king, his family and his land and village.

But why, in God's name, did the British want to hand him over to the communists? Well, no doubt about it, it was the sacred duty of them all to save him from the clutches of those Godless bastards, whatever the motives of the Allies.

Perhaps, David mused out loud, those motives had something to do with the speech Mihailović had made the previous year while attending a baptism in a small Serbian village. In an uncharacteristic burst of anger he had apparently said, in the presence of a British officer, that the English wanted to fight the Germans 'to the last Serb in Yugoslavia'. He understood from his uncle that the remark had somehow got back to Churchill, who had been furious although, God only knew, when you considered that the Serbs were the only resistance forces in Europe being asked to kill more and more Germans despite the horrendous reprisals against their own civilians and that the British had continually failed to honour their own promises to supply arms and other *matériel* to the general, Mihailović would be less than human if he didn't occasionally explode with frustration.

'And what about that business with the Italian Venezia Division?' someone asked.

There was much shaking of heads at this reference to another totally inexplicable action by the British. After a fierce fight the Chetniks, under the leadership of Major Vojislav Lukačević, had accepted the surrender of the Italian division and had looked forward to disarming the Italians, at last obtaining much needed supplies. Instead, the British officer with them – what was his name? Lees? Armstrong?

'No, no. Not Lees,' roared a bearded giant. 'He was with us. A hero. Like the English who fought with our fathers at Salonika, not one of this new slippery breed.'

'It wasn't Armstrong, either,' David interjected. 'I believe his name was Bailey. A Colonel Bailey.'

'You are right. Bailey! That's the name.'

'Well, before Lukačević could disarm them, this Bailey made an arrangement with the Italian commander that he could keep his arms provided he agreed to join with the Allies and fight the Germans. Of course the bastard agreed. Who wouldn't?'

'So Lukačević returned to headquarters no doubt feeling bitter as stale *rakija*. And then what happened!'

'What happened? This slippery British colonel allowed the partisans to come in, "accept" the Italian surrender and take all their arms, supplies, clothes, food – as though they were not already getting enough from our infamous allies.' The speaker spat into the fire with disgust. 'What in God's name ... why are the British acting like agents of Stalin? Do they no longer love *their* king? Would they deprive us of *our* little king? How can they do these things to us Serbs, all of whom would risk lives and families to rescue just one of their sons? How can they do these things?'

'I'll tell you what it is all about!' the bearded Serb from Bosnia who had spoken up about Lees roared. He placed a large finger on the side of his nose, then wagged it at them. 'I can explain. I can explain *everything*.'

They all laughed.

'Explain, then, Misha,' David said. 'Go ahead and explain.'

'You see, we captured this group of German bandits. They were mocking us about our slippery Allies who were selling us out to Stalin. They seemed to know all about it. So, before slitting their throats, you understand, I asked one of them . . . I speak some German, you know . . . I asked him, well, you know all about it, tell us why they are doing these things. And he said, true as I sit here before you, he laughed and he said, "Maybe," he said, "Stalin has initiated a plan of germ warfare against the British. Maybe his agents have put something in their water to make them all mad." So, you see, that's what it is. I know for a fact – don't ask me how – but I know for a fact that what he said is true.' He sat back with an air of great satisfaction. 'I told you. I told you I could explain *everything!*'

As they again all burst out laughing, Vladimir slapped him on the shoulder. 'Misha,' he said, '*Ti lažeš kao London. Ti lažeš kao London.*'

On that note the group broke up and moved off in twos and threes to await the speech about to be given by General Mihailović.

It had been well over a year since David had last seen the general. During that time he had undoubtedly suffered grave setbacks and disappointments, all added to the hunted life he was forced to lead: never sure where he would lay his head that night; never sure that for all of the visible goodwill and love shown to him by his people wherever he went that he would not this day or the next be betrayed, handed over to the Germans who never ceased their yapping at his heels.

He had, however, changed surprisingly little. The black beard was now heavily streaked with grey, but the mild eyes remained steady behind the wire-rimmed glasses, the wiry figure upright, the head held high. His address to the congress was delivered quietly but forcefully. It dealt briefly with the Allies, referred to their insulting silence when presented again and again with evidence by their own officers in the field that virtually all action taken by his army was inevitably broadcast over the BBC and Tiflis as having been initiated by the partisans. He spoke of British insistence, unique in the whole theatre of the war, that his guerrillas should kill more and more Germans, regardless of the murderous toll that took of civilians who suffered swift and terrible retaliation from the enemy. Does that mean, he asked bitterly, that Serbian blood is cheaper than that of other Allies? It was not that he would not, where there was a clear and important military objective, sacrifice if need be, the lives of his people. They would not have it otherwise. But when demands were made for seemingly senseless action to be taken?

The British had also, almost from the beginning of the Chetnik struggle, demanded ever more destruction of military objectives and the sabotage of railway communications than the guerrillas were already carrying out. He had always been perfectly willing to order such action, indeed, when the necessary *matériel* was available, had often initiated it, but often they did not have the *matériel*. When he had requested explosives from the Allies, and all the other necessary equipment needed to carry out their requests, promises were made to give him such supplies, but these promises were never kept.

With an expression of distaste he referred to the accusations that his men were threatening revengeful reprisals against Croatia, against Muslims and political dissidents, once the war was over. It had never been and never would be the policy of the Yugoslav army in the fatherland to institute mass reprisals against anyone. At the end of the war the regular courts in a free and democratic country would examine each case against war criminals and hand down just sentences in accordance with the law of the country. To do otherwise could only be the act of barbarians such as the fascists and communists, against whom all of his people were fighting. Democracy was based on political dissent and not on totalitarianism. Therefore political dissidents had nothing to fear provided they had not committed unlawful crimes against the population.

He mentioned the partisans. Their recent action in making it known that they would welcome any *Ustaši* who wished to throw in their lot with them now it was clear that the Axis forces were going to lose the war was totally reprehensible, but typical of this lawless rabble. It showed the actual paucity of their scattered groups of bandits that the Allied and Soviet press referred to as an 'army'. Some 'army' he said drily. Almost drowned by supplies from the British and Americans, yet they could not make a dent inside Serbia, where the people hated them perhaps even more than they hated the Germans. In any event, any Croat with a clear conscience, including members of the Croatian home guard who had been forced to join the Germans, was welcome to join his own army. As for the *Ustaši* criminals who at this date were responsible for the bestial murder of well over seven-hundred thousand Serbs, they would be dealt with eventually by the law courts, although even that was more than they deserved.

In conclusion, he wished to make one thing clear. The only political ambition *he* had was *to liberate the country from all occupying forces*; to bring peace, freedom and true democracy to all peoples of Yugoslavia, without any distinction with regard to ethnic, linguistic, religious, spiritual, cultural or political heritage. That was the tradition of the past and that was his genuine aspiration and dream for today and for a better order for tomorrow.

After short speeches by leaders of the assembled democratic parties, the delegates broke up into meetings where they discussed what effective measures might be taken against all fascist forces in the country, and how to counter the actions of partisan groups, now heavily armed and continuing to receive an ever-increasing supply of materials from the British and the Americans. It was by now clear to everyone that the hitherto inexplicable actions by the communists were simply ploys to discredit the Chetniks with their Allies, create internal chaos, and place themselves in a position to grasp power once the Axis forces were driven out. Satisfaction was expressed that, despite the new injection of supplies the communists were receiving from the Allies, they still fared badly in any encounters with Chetniks, scoring only when they utilized their cowardly tactic of attacking from behind once the Chetniks were engaged with one or another of the Axis forces. In addition, everyone was encouraged by the knowledge that the Serbian population remained firmly behind their national movement.

In the afternoon there was a march past by several hundred soldiers of the guerrilla army. They assembled at the village school, took the salute from the general, then marched proudly through the main street behind torn and tattered regimental colours, preserved from the Balkan wars, their fierce spirit plain to see despite their ragged uniforms. Watching them, David felt a prickling of the skin, a surge of warmth and affection for these proud patriots. It was an oddly moving and sad scene. Despite their threadbare uniforms these men represented all that was best in the Serbian people. All that their fathers had so proudly fought for in the Balkan wars, in the Great War. Glancing over at the official party, he could see that the group of well-known Belgrade politicians now standing close together were also deeply moved, one of them visibly brushing tears from his cheeks. His uncle, as always, towered over everyone on the platform. He stood there, straight as an arrow, rigidly at attention, his right hand resting over his heart.

Oddly enough, although they were still in the heart of winter, the evening proved to be clear and mild. At the suggestion of General Mihailović, tables were brought out from the local school and set up around the river-bank where the delegates were served a variety of chicken dishes, bread, cheeses and wine by the villagers. The feeling of solemnity that had been so evident during the march past remained, and the meal was completed in a hushed, almost reverential atmosphere. The men gathered together that evening instinctively felt that their meeting here at the small village of Ba in the soft Serbian hills was something very special. A beginning? David wondered. Or, he thought with a feeling of chill, an ending?

It was while he was still in a sombre mood that he finally managed to locate his Uncle Mikhail and stroll with him briefly by the side of the river. Mikhail Ristić too, seemed subdued, thoughtful, absent-minded even. However, he assured David that the meetings he had been attending with the leaders of the national democratic parties had gone extremely well. There was a new feeling of reconciliation in the air, an awareness that at this critical stage of their country's history their traditional bickering and rivalry must of necessity be brought under control in the interest of post-war unity. One thing the communists had done for them was make them aware of just what a fragile thing their hard-won democracy was, how easily it could be brought crashing down around their heads by a few unscrupulous scoundrels who were determined to grab and hold power whatever the cost.

They had all been extremely pleased and relieved by General Mihailović's obvious sincerity when he had assured them he personally had no political ambitions. Nor was it his intention to throw his support behind the government in exile in London when the time came for post-war elections to be held. While he appreciated the financial and psychological support the government had given him, as far as he was concerned his fight was against the enemy forces in his country. Once the Axis forces were driven out of Yugoslavia, he simply wished to pursue his military career and allow the people to decide through their cherished democratic process which political party they wished to guide them through the necessary rebuilding and rehabilitation of the country.

'Yes, yes,' Mikhail said, 'it has gone very well. Better even than could have been expected.'

They discussed briefly the decision that had been made by the Allies at Teheran. Here, too, David found his uncle's view to be optimistic. 'Let me tell you about some British officers we had here in the field, son.' He went on to say that, of course, the British actions were inexplicable, even to many of their own officers who had accompanied Chetniks on many of their attacks against Axis forces. These officers openly expressed their bewilderment and embarrassment at the orders they were receiving from Cairo, although there were others, he regretted to say, who adopted a defensive, even arrogant stance, delivering their instructions in a quite obnoxious tone, staring past *Čiča* at something they could apparently see on the wall behind him when he raised the question of heavy civilian reprisals for their often incredible demands, remaining obstinately silent when *matériel* they themselves had promised failed to materialize. 'A few of them even had the gall to suggest that if they did supply us with arms we would merely use them against the partisans. When we supplied overwhelming evidence that in fact it was the partisans who were using Allied weapons against *us*, again that obstinate and insulting silence.'

However, it was the former officers Ristić wished to talk about. During one discussion at the general's headquarters, he explained, one quite high-ranking British officer had expressed the suspicion that an English officer named Jack Klugman, a known dedicated communist, was tampering with the information coming out of Yugoslavia by crediting all action taken by the Chetniks to Tito's partisans. This highly inaccurate information was then, according to this officer, sent on to London. Mihailović had not at the time given much credence to this. After all, he had reasoned, surely there was more than one British officer at Cairo headquarters? Then, however, two other officers who had been assigned to the Chetniks had paid him a brief visit after they, too, had been to Cairo. Both of these officers not only mentioned Klugman, but said that, in fact, most of the Cairo staff at British headquarters were either communist or leftist. In addition to this, the Cairo staff had a huge map on which they had pinned markers that they claimed showed the partisans held most of Yugoslavia under their control which was, of course, patently absurd. Sheer nonsense! But when these two officers, who had come directly from the field, bluntly questioned the accuracy of the map, they were treated with outright hostility and were from that moment on denied access to any material concerning events that were supposedly taking place inside Yugoslavia.

These officers had assured Mihailović that they themselves would be attending the meeting of the big three in Teheran and that they would 'set things very right indeed'. However, it seems that they never reached Teheran – contingencies of war no doubt – but it was certain that once they reached the right ears with their story there would be a complete reversal of the Teheran decision.

David, who had listened to his uncle carefully, could only shake his head. 'Well, I hope so, Uncle. You know what they have done, don't you? They have said: "The Yugoslav people will save themselves", and then, by announcing that they would arm only one side, the communists, in what they well know is a full-scale civil war, they have tried to make sure that our people have no say at all in their own fate.'

'I know. I know, son. But we must be patient. *Čiča* himself has faith that the Allies will soon come to their senses.'

'Another thing. I noticed, during the march past, there were a few British soldiers with *Čiča*'s party. And an American officer?'

'Ah yes. Captain Musulin. He is here to try to arrange with us the evacuation of their American airmen. Altogether there must be over five hundred airmen being protected by our forces. A few Canadians, even one or two Russians, I believe, together, of course with the British. We are trying to arrange for their safe evacuation.'

'Are we mad, Uncle? With one breath they accuse *us* of collaboration, claim that our country is in the hands of the partisans, and with the next they confidently ask *us* to undertake the safe evacuation of their own people! Tell me, what have you heard from our own people in London? What are they saying? Do they have an explanation?'

'Don't talk to me about our people in London, son! All we get from *them* is some garbled nonsense about their trying to fight something they call "invisible forces". What invisible forces! What do they mean? We get no sense from our people in London. As for the British, what can I say? They must somehow believe they are acting in their own interests, although what those interests can be I do not know. They are certainly, *most* certainly, acting against their own principles. And let me tell you something, son. At some time in history most countries act against their own interests, but it is when they begin to act against their own *principles*, against what their country stands for, that they are in deep trouble. I begin to wonder whether this, for the British, is not the beginning of the end.'

'And the Americans?'

'Ah, yes. The Americans I think I can understand, if not approve. I have not a doubt in the world that they realize what is going on here. Their officers on the scene here with us have shown no hesitation in not only believing what they see with their own eyes, but in quite vocally advising their government of what they see. We have also heard from Ambassador Fotić in Washington that he has had several interviews with President Roosevelt during which, incidentally, he was promised that several plane-loads of supplies would be sent to us. These, of course, never did arrive! However, from our people in Washington, if not in London, we do get a clear picture of the situation. Firstly, picture if you can, a president who is not well. Our ambassador wonders whether he will survive the length of the war. An obviously sick man, he tells us. And this man, under severe strain from events not only in Europe, but in the South Pacific, is given an opportunity on a platter to, at the same time, please Winston Churchill on the one hand and Joseph Stalin on the other! An opportunity, one suspects, that does not occur too often. In addition to this, we are reliably informed, he does have on his staff a number of leftist sympathizers who are happy to promote the socialist cause. I cannot condone the American position but at least thank God, I understand it, which is more than I can say for the British.'

'So what is going to happen, then, to *our* country? Are we really nothing more than a bargaining chip for these big powers? Is that what we are fighting for? Is it really possible that they can seal our fate by treating us as figures they can move willy-nilly on a chess board?' David could hardly control his anger, although his voice remained low and level.

'Perhaps we had better go back now, son. I admit to feeling a little weary. It's been a long day.' As they slowly retraced their steps he reached out and rested his hand on his nephew's shoulder. 'No, no, David. Do not worry. It is *our* people who will be deciding our fate. The key words to remember from the Teheran decision are *Yugoslavia will be liberated by its own people*. I admit that now our financial support has dried up from London things are becoming difficult. Yet the countryside remains firmly in our hands. The partisan outlaws are sprinkled only sparsely through Serbia, despite all of the supplies the Allies are lavishing upon them. When the fascists have been driven out, it will be a matter to be settled between us and the partisans. There is no doubt as to the outcome. There is no doubt as to whose side the people are on. No, no, son. If there is one good thing that came out of that treacherous decision at Teheran it is that. Our fate will be decided by the Yugoslav people. So we need have no fear, you see.'

They parted, as usual, with his uncle giving him a warm bear-hug, counselling him to look after himself. It was unlikely that they would see each other again before David returned to the Avala Corps early next morning. Mikhail, however, still seemed oddly distracted. His mind, obviously, was on the events of the day. Watching the tall figure as he strode resolutely away towards his quarters at the other end of the village, David suddenly experienced a piercing feeling of such sharp loss that he almost cried out. It was a terrible feeling of desolation, a premonition of such painful implication that he could not bear to face it. 'Uncle!' he called urgently. 'Uncle!'

The old man stopped, turned, gazed at him in surprise. Quickly David caught up with him, reached out, touched his arm.

'Look, Uncle, you will take care of yourself? You will take

care?' Mikhail continued to stare at him, not quite able to grasp what the problem was. After a moment he chuckled, nodded.

'Don't worry about me, my boy. How often have I told you? It will take more than a gang of fascist thugs to finish off your old uncle, my boy, I can assure you of that.' Affectionately he reached out and ruffled his nephew's hair in a gesture he had used when David was a child. 'You had better get some sleep, David. You're off early in the morning, I know.' With another fond chuckle he turned and continued on his way, leaving his nephew gazing after him, trying to cope with the most devastatingly helpless feeling of loss he had experienced in his whole life.

5

Despite Tito's optimism about the British mission headed by Brigadier Maclean, Stevan himself was nervous, apprehensive about the outcome of the mission's mandate to 'find out who is killing the most Germans'. Clearly, for the past few months the Chetniks had been killing not only large numbers of Germans, but also whole units of *Ljotićevci*, Albanians, Croatian home guard, Bulgarians, Italians and *Ustaši*. News of the intensified attacks the Germans had launched against Mihailović's guerrillas reverberated throughout the land, spread by radio exhortations from Belgrade against the Chetnik 'bandits' by Generals Bader and Nedić, by word of mouth, by the posters spread throughout the country offering large rewards for the capture of the elusive leader of the Chetniks, by long lists of names of civilians who had paid with their lives for supporting him. Details of Chetnik deeds, together with a grim warning about the retribution that had followed, were printed almost daily in *The New Times*.

In addition to these embarrassing facts was the knowledge that although Tito's messages to Moscow still referred to the partisan forces as being 'well over a hundred thousand strong', by Stevan's estimation it was doubtful whether they were even ten thousand strong. He knew that when they had first entered the field in order to assist the 'First Socialist Land – The Soviet Union', the figure had been in the vicinity of twelve or thirteen thousand. This had increased a little due to the initial policy of forced recruitment which, however, had proved to be so counter-productive that Tito had been forced to put a stop to the practice. When the *Ustaši* terror had been at its height in Bosnia, they had also attracted several thousand Serbs in the area, and a number of Croats, who had expressed horror and disgust with the barbarism of Pavelić's puppet government. However, they had soon lost many of these recruits to the Chetniks when the communists seemed incapable of stopping their policy of murdering local authorities in order to set up National Liberation Committees. At no time, in his estimation, could the number of partisans throughout the country have exceeded twenty thousand, and that was probably an over-estimation. Then, of course, there had been the devastating losses during the botched up Neretva operation – at a conservative estimate they must have lost at least eight thousand men. While he had no quarrel with Tito's using, as he seemed to be doing, estimations of Mihailović's strength as his own when he appealed to Moscow, as always, for help, how on earth did he think he could fool a British mission whose officers were on the spot?

He need not, however, have worried for a moment. Tito, as usual, proved to be a wonderful manipulator of men. At one and the same time he despatched messages to partisan units, instructing them to sabotage all Chetnik efforts against Axis forces, while assuring the British officers that the Chetniks, far from fighting enemy forces, were actually collaborating. The British, indeed, seemed to be almost indecently anxious to believe every word he said.

The Second Proletarian Brigade was sternly warned not to undertake battles with the Germans, but to concentrate their efforts on preventing Chetniks from 'mobilizing the local population of Muslims'. The Second Corps was advised its task was to 'wipe out the Chetniks'. Upon learning that Chetnik forces had cleared the area of German forces, Tito ordered his Fifth Partisan Division to 'move immediately in the direction of Goražda and Rogatica and take Visegrad', reproving them sternly for having taking action against the Albanians. 'You should have directed your forces against

Serbia. This is the most important strategic political task for the present, to disable Draža Mihailović. You must urgently pursue your action in that direction for reasons of foreign policy.' Similar orders were despatched to his Third Partisan Corps, stressing that Chetnik groups 'must be destroyed'. He had been grimly satisfied to learn of successful action taken by partisans at Sokolac where they had launched an attack against Chetnik forces that had been engaged in fighting the Germans and the *Ustaši*.

The communist leadership was also happily aware of the problems the Chetniks were having with British missions which, apparently following instructions from their headquarters in Cairo, were forever pressing them to do 'more' while at the same time ignoring the visible and considerable action taken by the Chetniks against Axis forces.

The communists also benefited greatly by the Italian surrender. They moved quickly to seize a large number of areas, arms, food and clothing abandoned by the Italians, many of whom, upon learning that the partisans were not at all fussy about accepting Axis forces into their ranks, quickly joined the thousands of Hungarians, Bulgarians, Croatian home guard and whole units of *Ustaši* who almost overnight flocked to join the comrades after having seen the Italian surrender as the writing on the wall. Partisan ranks swelled rapidly to unheard-of proportions. They not only now possessed a large supply of *matériel* from the Italians, but could look forward with confidence to even more largesse from the Americans and the British.

A confident, indeed jubilant, Tito immediately set about calling a meeting of his anti-fascist council where he informed his delegates that from now on their council would be considered a proper constitutional body that would form a national committee of liberation with full powers of a provisional government. Their government would, of course, supersede the monarchy and the government in exile in London. The response was gratifying. The delegates moved that their leader be given the title of Marshal of Yugoslavia;

that he should assume the posts of both prime minister and minister of defence.

When the decision made by the 'big three' at Teheran was received, the communist triumph was complete although, as usual, Moscow seemed ever ready to dampen their enthusiasm, and let it be known that their assumption of the authority of a government over the legal government in exile was not only too early, but a little unseemly. In fact although the Moscow radio reported that the meeting of the council had taken place, no reference was made to their formation of a provisional government, or that such a government superseded that of the young king in London.

It was the BBC that came to the rescue, reporting in full the developments that had taken place at their meeting in Jajce. Soon afterwards a patently puzzled Moscow followed suit.

December brought with it severe problems in addition to all of the good news. The Germans, seemingly disheartened by their abortive attempts to destroy the Chetniks and capture their leader, turned their efforts against the partisans, who were forced to fall back from Jajce and Banjaluka. Tito withdrew to Potoci where his good friend Maclean again made a brief appearance to hearten him with a personal letter and signed photograph from Winston Churchill.

By the end of February the communist leader had again been forced to withdraw and set up his headquarters near the town of Drvar where he was to receive, a month or so later, a visit from a Soviet military mission led by General Korneyev. Every effort was made to welcome and impress the Soviet visitors, who seemed, however, not so inclined as the British mission had been to extend uncritical and unquestioning admiration and aid. If Tito was disappointed, he hid it well, and contented himself with the fact that at least this was an acknowledgement from Moscow of his new importance, now that he was receiving both help and recognition from the Allies.

So far as Stevan was concerned he could not have been more grateful that the inaccessibility of their hide-out gave an opportunity to relax, to escape for a while the incessant movement, the withdrawals, the uncertainties. He had come to realize and to accept the motive behind all of Tito's actions. This was not a military war between the Yugoslav communists and the fascists; this was a deadly, internal, civil war. In Mihailović, adored as he was by the Serbian people, lay the greatest obstacle to a communist takeover once the Allies won the war. He had to be destroyed. Tito had recognized that right from the start. He must have been considering how he could go about it as far back as that first meeting with the Chetnik leader, when he had agreed to everything, then coolly abrogated every agreement.

The thing that puzzled Stevan was the attitude and actions of the British. If, as Tito's intelligence people told him, the British military missions had, almost from the moment the partisans entered the field, seemed to treat Mihailović more as an enemy than the invaluable ally all their own military leaders claimed, what was their motive? From whom did they receive their instructions? The British foreign office? Their headquarters in Cairo? What was it they called the latter? SOE: Special Operations Executive, that was it. If their instructions came from either source, what was the motive? The whole thing truly puzzled him. The more so because of Moscow's blunt and realistic assessment of the situation, and the pressure they had brought to bear on Tito to cooperate and coordinate his activities with Mihailović. From Moscow's point of view, of course, they were aware that the effective action taken by the Chetniks had tied up enemy divisions that might otherwise have been sent to the Eastern Front. It was obviously in the Soviet interest that the Chetniks be given every assistance possible; that the 'people's revolution' inside Yugoslavia be set firmly on the back burner until the war had been won.

It was impossible to discuss these thoughts with anyone. Certainly not with Alex. He did exchange a few comments with the pragmatic Djerdja, who was not much help. 'Just let us be grateful Tito has them in the palm of his hand. No sense in asking questions.'

He decided to take Djerdja's advice. Until Tito, who did indeed seem to hold the Allies in the palm of his hand, asked them to bomb Belgrade. Obligingly, the Americans, either ignorant of or not concerned about the fact that the day chosen was the Orthodox Easter Sunday when the streets would be full of people on their way to church, once again rained destruction down on the battered city. The news struck Stevan like a blow. *Why Belgrade! Why not Zagreb if you are so bloody well intent on destroying civilians? Because Zagreb was Tito's city? But, Christ, at least you would be destroying the enemy.*

Aware that such thoughts would and could only bring destruction, he closed his mind against them. It was never again, really, to be opened.

* * *

A week or so earlier, David's detachment had been marching along a country road in a wooded, mountainous area that gave them excellent cover. Kosta Marinković, at the head of the brigade, suddenly held up his hand, setting off a reaction that at first slowed down and then completely stopped the entire chain of men.

Stiffly, he dismounted from the large black gelding David Ristić had insisted on giving him since his own mount had been shot beneath him a few days previously by a marauding partisan band. Already David was down on one knee, examining an empty canister of aluminum, several more of which were lying in a clearing about a hundred yards off the road.

At first no one spoke. It was a sad and depressing scene they were being forced to witness more and more often. Everywhere they turned it seemed there was further evidence of the lavish amount of supplies British and American planes were dropping to the partisans. Remembering the grudging and skimpy material their 'allies' had given them even during the days when they were praising their contribution so fulsomely, the reaction could not help but be one of deep bitterness.

'Why are they betraying us?' Lieutenant Siriski, an energetic and courageous fighter from the northern part of Serbia suddenly shouted. 'They are supporting not only our enemy, but their own. Don't they understand that? This is treason! It is beyond me to understand what they are doing, it is simply beyond me!'

Kosta was shaking his head in a bewildered fashion. 'Still, the war is not over. We must wait and see. Let us wait and see.'

David, noticing that the men behind them were beginning to mutter rebelliously, grasped Siriski's arm. 'For God's sake, Pera,' he muttered, 'aren't our men demoralized enough? Must you shout that we are betrayed by our Allies? Already our men have had enough of this bloody game of war.'

'You are saying we should not let them know the truth?'

'What truth? They are supporting the partisans in what they believe to be their military struggle against the fascists. But they will not support them in the political struggle for our country. I am sure of that. Can't you understand that?'

'No, I can't understand that! Nor can I understand that statement that came out of Teheran. *The Yugoslav people will liberate themselves, but we will only help the communists!* Don't *you* understand to whom they have tossed their political card?'

His voice, however, had quietened. He shot David an angry look, remounted his horse, and anticipated Kosta by giving the signal to move.

Trudging silently alongside a morose Kosta, David wondered just how long they could expect the men to stay with them in this bloody and treacherous struggle. The realization, however late in coming, that they were not only involved in a military operation to rid their country of the fascists, but in a political struggle against the equally unscrupulous and murderous communists, had made survival his one aim. To survive! At least until he saw the day when the former were pushed out of his beloved country and the latter resoundingly defeated. He was aware, however, that since Teheran a number of Chetniks had defected, simply shaved off their beards and returned to their villages or towns. Could he blame them? Why fight for such treacherous and stupid allies? A sullen and rebellious Montenegrin had asked this a few nights previously before deserting. Let *them* die if they want to kick the fascists out of Europe, he had said.

At least Zeka was sticking! Although a few days previously David had expected him, too, to vanish overnight. They had been marching along another country road for several hours, and had finally reached the top of a hill that gave a commanding view of the lush valley below. It had been a glorious spring day and their position gave them a clear and splendid view for miles around. He had been standing quietly talking to Kosta when their attention had been drawn to a cluster of tiny white clouds some thirty kilometres away. They instantly realized that the 'clouds' now drifting towards the ground were parachutes. The three planes that had been dropping them were now some ten kilometres away, heading north-west, when there was suddenly the sound of heavy machine-gun fire filling the air. They both swung around to find Zeka shrieking at the top of his lungs, firing furiously if futilely in the direction of the rapidly disappearing planes.

'Are you mad? What is wrong with you? They are British planes!' It was Kosta, shouting with that mighty voice that reverberated through the air, almost a match for the heavy gunfire.

'Don't you see what they're doing? *Do* you see what they're doing? They supply our enemies with guns to turn against us! *They* are our Allies? To hell with them! I'll kill them. I'll kill them all!'

It was David who wrested the heavy gun away from him, while Kosta stood by, shaking his head. 'Zeka, Zeka. We don't have enemies enough? You want to add the Allies to our long list of enemies, Zeka?'

Zeka spat. 'They have added *themselves* to the list.'

After that he was silent, however. After a short break the column had moved on.

Now, thank God, at least they were having some rest, in the lovely Serbian hills some fifty kilometres south of Belgrade. They could not possibly, David thought, have found themselves in a better place for Easter. God willing, perhaps next year, perhaps for Easter 1945 he might actually celebrate the holiday with his family in Belgrade.

It was a beautiful spring day which had begun for them with a short Easter service given by an Orthodox priest from a nearby village that had also supplied them with much needed food. Much to David's amusement Jovan had earlier that morning produced a coloured egg for his breakfast and had beamed shyly when David slapped him on the back and complimented him on his undoubted ingenuity in so often producing the right thing at the right time.

After his usual early morning consultation with Kosta and Dragan concerning their next *pokret*, David accepted a mug of tea from Jovan and wandered away by himself to find a tree to lean against, drink the scalding liquid, and gaze towards Belgrade. Regardless of the occupation, he was certain that his aunt and his sisters would by now have joined the throng of Belgraders who would be packing the churches, dressed in their best Easter clothes, doubtless intent on praying to God for an early end to this interminable war.

He glanced at his watch and discovered it was close to 11 a.m. He was about to return to the makeshift tent where Kosta and Dragan were still talking quietly together when the familiar sound of bombers drew his startled attention. They were filling the sky from the direction of Rumania and were over the city almost before he could grasp what was happening. Even then he could not really believe what he was seeing. Allied bombers, *American* bombers, dropping their deadly cargo over the centre of his city on the bright, beautiful Easter Sunday morning of the 22nd of April 1944.

From the periphery of the city the German anti-aircraft guns began spitting fire. First one and then another of the bombers began to spin downwards, rapidly putting a distance between the tiny parachuted figures that began to dot the thundering sky.

David still stood rooted to the spot, simply unable to comprehend what he was seeing. *Allied aircraft bombing Belgrade? Germans* defending Belgrade? He became aware of nearby movement of voices. Still in a daze he walked slowly towards Kosta, who had gathered some officers and men around him.

'We will need someone to go and try to pick them up.' The big commander was pointing towards the spiralling parachutists. 'Could I have some volunteers?' Almost automatically his eyes turned in the direction of David, always the first to volunteer for any of the more dangerous assignments. This time, however, all he received was a terrible glare from the young officer. His face was contorted with such rage that Marinković quickly looked away.

Still in something of a daze, almost in a state of total incomprehension, David turned and walked back to the tree. This time he sat down, leaned his back against the trunk, and gazed towards the thick haze of black smoke that hovered above the city.

Half an hour later a second wave of deadly Allied bombs hit the city, this time aiming at the southern part that contained many of the most beautiful homes and historic public buildings in Belgrade. The Royal Palace, situated in Crown Street, was in that area. Dully, he wondered whether it had been hit.

A long time later he was aware of Jovan hovering anxiously at his side, handing him a cup of something that he accepted but put down beside him, untouched.

In the late afternoon he was brought out of his deep, wounding introspection by the harsh sound of Zeka's voice. The guerrilla leader squatted down next to him and handed him a plate of food.

'Eat up. Eat up. God knows when we'll have as much food again.'

David rested the plate on his knee and stared dully ahead

at the still smoking city. 'God only knows,' he said, 'why I was so surprised. At the extent of the bombing, I mean. They've bombed Belgrade "at the request of Marshall Tito" any number of times. Not to mention Nish, Smederevo, Leskovac, Podgorica. Wherever there have been Serbian civilians to kill. Thousands of them. And how much harm has it done the Germans? Did they hit even one tank? Not that we know of! I've known all this. It's *seeing* it, Zeka. *Seeing* Allied airmen hitting Belgrade, *seeing* the bloody Germans defending our city and–'

'And knowing that Croatia declared war on our great Ally the United States even before Germany, and Zagreb has not been hit once. Because, no doubt, they don't want to upset that great Croat guerrilla, Josip Broz Tito! Does that bandit not have one Serb with him with guts enough to put a bullet through his brain? Are the Serbian comrades totally devoid of guts? I understand you, brother. I understand you.' Zeka nodded grimly. 'But, anyway, we picked one of their airmen up. I don't suppose they can help having a half-witted government any more than we can. No casualties, except that one of our men got an arm wound. Nothing serious. The bloody Germans were everywhere, using all kinds of transport trying to pick them up before we got there.'

'You mean *you* volunteered? *You* risked your neck to rescue one of our marvellous bloody Allies?' His voice was nearly breaking with bitterness, bile.

There was no reply. He looked up, then, and found Zeka watching him with that blasted half-smile of his. 'You know, David,' he said, 'I've been thinking these past few days. You know what the bastards want? *All* of them. They *want* us to behave in as bloody dirty a way as they have. I don't know why. I don't even care. I'll tell you something, Zeka for one would find it no trouble, no trouble at all, to cut any of their throats from ear to ear. I would do it with pleasure. The bloody fascists, the filthy communists, the treacherous, dirty Allies.

'But I've worked something out, you see. That's what they *want*. And as long as that's what they want, why, I'm going to be the most faithful bloody ally they have ever had in their lives.' He gave a short, harsh gust of the chilling sound that passed for his laugh. 'Now eat up brother! None of them is worth a cracker! None of them is worth losing a man's appetite over. You understand?'

David stared at him dully for a moment, then slowly nodded his head, lifted the plate still resting on his knee, and began to eat.

Later that evening they all gathered around the radio for the BBC newscast from London. 'Today,' the rich, plummy voice announced, 'at the request of Marshal Tito, the Allied forces have bombed Belgrade.'

The Allied forces were to bomb Belgrade again the following day, the 23rd of April 1944. This time, however, David simply watched, cold-eyed but accepting, along with the rest of the grim, silent band of Chetniks.

6

Although their intelligence sources had given some indication that the Germans had decided to rid the territory of 'all rebel forces', they had felt reasonably secure in their headquarters overlooking the small Bosnian town of Drvar. Tito and Zdenka had settled down with their usual aptitude for comfort and Stevan, on excellent terms now with the partisan leader, hoped that things would somehow resolve themselves without further skirmishes. Deep in his heart he yearned for peace.

It was in this frame of mind that he lay down to sleep one evening towards the end of May, only to be rudely awakened at dawn by the familiar sound of bombs falling and exploding. Leaping to his feet he discovered that Drvar was under bombardment. For a moment he stood there uncertainly, his hand shading his eyes as he gazed upwards at the awesome sight of hundreds of German parachute troops blocking out the sky, almost unaware of figures rushing around him, orders being shouted, until suddenly Alex was at his side, pulling him along, yelling something about Tito, about withdrawal into the hills.

In fact it was only by the skin of his teeth that he found himself with Tito, Zdenka, their little dog, Alex and other members of the inner circle being spirited away from the raging battle, away from the noise and chaos. He learned that Tito, with his usual calm instinct for self-preservation, had instructed the British mission to arrange for their evacuation. In no time they were all being miraculously delivered safe and sound to an Allied airfield in Italy. Events had overtaken them so rapidly, the general confusion had been so great, that it was to be several days before either he or Alex were to feel pangs of concern and remorse, for their desertion of their comrades. Alex in particular, to Stevan's exasperation, seemed unable to overcome a deep feeling of shame over that desertion.

More important matters loomed. It soon became apparent that the main problem presented by their hasty withdrawal was that of image. It would not do, all agreed, for the world to learn that the man Churchill called that 'hardy guerrilla fighter' had chosen not to lead his heavily-armed fighters in the defence of their headquarters, or that he now showed no inclination at all to rejoin his partisans in Yugoslavia. Hasty consultations ensued. A compromise solution was quickly found. Tito would set up headquarters on the Adriatic island of Vis, far enough from the hazards of the Yugoslav mainland to be sure, but at least he would not be operating from foreign soil. An added plus was that he would be under strong British protection, although once comfortably settled on the island, Tito made sure that his personal quarters were surrounded by his own bodyguards. One could never really trust the imperialists.

Other small irritants arose, but were soon dismissed. The most pressing of these was the questions from the outside world when German radio claimed that Tito's headquarters had been overrun and captured. Someone somewhere proved adept at a quick sleight of hand. Soon the BBC was rather primly denying the German claim. In the United States Yugoslav ambassador, Constantin Fotić, came under attack and was roundly accused of being a liar when he spoke of Tito's ignominious retreat from Drvar.

On the other hand, there was no doubt that the Allies fully expected Tito to eventually return to the mainland and liberate the country with the 'army' they had armed so lavishly. Stevan knew there was no way he could do that. The Germans held the cities in their iron grip. The Chetniks held the Serbian countryside and East Bosnia and enjoyed the help and support of the people. Tito had no strikeforce and his partisans were spread very thinly through the rest of the country. It would take a miracle to both conquer Mihailović's army *and* force the Germans out.

Yet all of this seemed to be the least of the marshal's worries. During June he received a visit from Dr Ivan Šubašic, who represented King Peter, in order to discuss means by which the Teheran decision might be implemented. It was yet again agreed that democratic elections would be held in order to allow the Yugoslav people themselves to choose what form of government they wished to have after the war.

Stevan first began to realize what was really in Tito's mind when on the 5th of July 1944, he dictated a letter to Stalin, begging him for help and asking that the Red Army move into Yugoslavia once it had crossed the Carpathians and Rumania. While still awaiting a reply from the Soviet dictator he flew in early August to Casserta where he held talks with the supreme Allied commander in the Mediterranean. A few days later he met with Churchill in a villa overlooking the Bay of Naples, proudly wearing a white marshal's uniform, all aglitter with gold braid, specially ordered from Moscow for the occasion. Whether Churchill was impressed by the display of elegance was not recorded. What was clear was the fact that Tito smoothly, albeit with a touch of exasperation, dismissed the British prime minister's concern that Stalin might have intentions of infiltrating Yugoslavia. He also assured the old warrior that he himself had no intention of imposing communism upon the people of his country.

Yes, he agreed somewhat wearily, he was willing to issue a statement to that effect, and also to the effect that he would not use armed force to influence the 'free expression of the will of the people' concerning the future regime of their country. The meeting had gone extremely well, despite a burst of anger from the marshal when Churchill was so ill-advised as to mention worrying reports he had received from certain British liaison officers with Mihailović that not only was the whole of Serbia firmly held in Chetnik hands, but that the partisans themselves were 'divorced from the Serbian people'.

Tito returned to Vis bursting with confidence, seemingly unimpressed by his historic meeting with the British prime minister. In response to Stevan's eager questions concerning Churchill, he had simply shrugged. 'What's he like? He was quite cordial.' He paused and added: 'He is no match for Stalin. No match at all.'

Shortly afterwards he graciously received a representative from the United States government and somewhat ruefully dismissed the American's concern that the Soviet Union might have intentions of entering Yugoslavia through Serbia. No, no. He himself would be the one to liberate Serbia, of that they could be sure.

Recalling the letter the marshal had written to Stalin, Stevan could only shake his head and smile to himself. What a magician Tito was! What an actor! What, it must be said in all honesty, a practiced and persuasive liar.

In fact the only weakness Tito showed so far as he, Stevan, was concerned, was his seemingly indestructible faith in Stalin. After all, had not that pragmatic dictator shown again and again that the fate of Yugoslavia was down very low indeed on his list of priorities? What if, in fact, Tito was somehow forced into free and democratic elections? The preference of the Yugoslav people for almost any other than what they considered to be the bloody Bolsheviks was a lesson the partisans had long ago bitterly learned. Nor could they hope to defeat the Chetniks in an armed battle even with the superior weaponry so lavishly supplied by the Allies.

No doubt it was with similar thoughts in his mind that Tito quietly arranged to be spirited off the island of Vis in a Soviet aircraft which took him first of all to Rumania for a brief discussion with Marshal Tolbukhin, the Soviet supreme commander, and then on to Moscow for an audience with Joseph Stalin, from whom he sought aid in ensuring that, in fact, the Yugoslav people would *not* be allowed to decide who should govern them after the war.

When he returned to Vis it was with the sweet knowledge that not only had he at last succeeded in winning Stalin over to his side, but that as the Allied military command had officially recognized his partisan movement as the legal authority inside Yugoslavia, they would now require his permission to enter the country. It was imperative, of course, that they be kept out of Yugoslavia in full force. If they were to find out what was really going on, all hell would break loose. They might even once again throw their support behind Mihailović, in which case, undoubtedly, the whole glorious revolution would be lost.

For now it remained only for the marshal to despatch the hapless but ever-faithful Brigadier Fitzroy Maclean to try to explain away to the furious British his stealthy visit to Stalin, and to instruct all his commanders in the field to continue to concentrate all efforts on the liquidation of their true enemy, the Chetnik forces.

To Stevan, the incredible thing was that during the time Tito had been engaged in so brilliantly fooling the Allies, the Americans had had no qualms about seeking the help of Mihailović in arranging for the evacuation of several hundred allied airmen who had bailed out over Yugoslavia and been rescued by the Chetniks. The Chetnik leader, he knew, had for some time been trying to contact the Americans about the evacuation of their airmen, through the British headquarters at Cairo, but his messages had not been forwarded. The British were no doubt somewhat embarrassed and hesitant to admit that the Chetniks were holding the airmen in areas that they themselves had insisted were in the hands of the partisans. Mihailović had eventually bypassed the British and sent a message directly to the Yugoslav embassy in Washington.

Stevan was thinking about the implications of all this during an afternoon's swimming and sunbathing on the beach. It was while he was lying on his stomach, head resting on his arms, that he overheard two British officers, who were also taking the opportunity to soak up some sun, discussing the operation Mihailović had undertaken, speculating about the risks the Chetniks had taken not only in preparing an airstrip for the main evacuation, but in guarding it from German attack. It did not seem to occur to either of them that there was anything strange about the fact that the Chetnik 'collaborators' were thus engaged while the leader of the partisans was enjoying what amounted to a summer vacation on an Adriatic island under British protection.

Stevan felt a sudden gust of anger towards Mihailović. All of the Chetniks! What innocent idiotic fools they were. No one had any right to be that innocent! No wonder Tito had been able to outmanoeuvre them although, no doubt about it, the fact that men like Deakin and Maclean had turned up and proved to be putty in his hands had certainly helped. But what cynics the British are, he thought, listening to the two officers. He remembered all that talk he used to hear when he was in London about 'fair play', all that emphasis on 'doing the right thing'. What bloody cynics they really were. Thank God he had found himself on the side of the partisans. Ruthless? Unscrupulous? No doubt about it, the communists were both of these things. But at least they made no bones about it. There was none of that bourgeois nonsense about decency and morality. In their own way they were more honest about their intentions, their motives.

He rolled over lazily onto his back and closed his eyes, shielding them with one hand. God, how he wished he'd known what he knew now the last time he had seen David Ristić. If only he'd known, he was sure he could have explained everything to him, prevented him from throwing in his lot with the doomed Chetniks.

It would not have been easy.

Ristić had always been so much under the influence of old Mikhail, his uncle, who had always believed so implicitly in the country's traditional ties with Britain, who had always believed so completely in the concept of democracy. No! It would not have been easy. Yet if he, Stevan, had believed then as he did now in the communist cause, he could have done it. He was sure of that. This, he now realized, was what had first attracted him to Nikola Djerdja It had been the man's total, unswerving, uncompromising faith in the rightness of the cause he served. When a man was so totally committed it was almost impossible not to be affected by him one way or another. Yes, he thought drowsily, I could have done it. If only I'd *known*.

Just before he dropped off to sleep he had another flash of insight. It was about those promised democratic elections in Yugoslavia. Democratic elections? Over Tito's dead body! The revelation came with such force, such clarity, that he sat up and gave a sharp hoot of laughter, causing the nearby British officers to glance in his direction and stare at him for a moment. Just another one of those unruly Balkan communists, their mildly amused glances clearly said. With a wide grin Stevan gave them both an ironic little salute, lay down again, and was almost instantly asleep.

* * *

All Chetnik units close to the site of the evacuation had been asked to supply men to help build the airstrip and help guard the Allied airmen. Kosta had sent what men he could spare under the command of Branko Jelić. David was in charge of a group on the periphery of the operation, holding them in readiness in case of a German attack.

The initial evacuation had, however, a weary Branko told him later, gone quite smoothly. The airmen had been a mixed group, mostly Americans, a few Canadians and British. It was the Americans he felt sorry for. 'They seem to be very generous men,' he said. 'They clearly expected the plane that arrived to take them out would be loaded with supplies for us. Of course there was nothing.' He went on to explain how many of the Americans had silently removed their own jackets, boots and coats, and handed them to their Chetnik escorts, whose own clothes were in tatters. Many had seemed close to tears. 'Who could blame *them*?

Branko asked. 'They are men like us. They do their best, try to trust their government.'

Since that devastating Easter when they had watched from a distance as Belgrade once again burned, the Posavska Brigade had been continually on the move. Ironically, they at least had a small supply of British and American weapons taken from partisans they had encountered and successfully routed. The *matériel* had come in extremely useful for sorties against the Germans and the *Ljotićevci*. Nor, they learned from time to time, were other Chetnik units idle. In May the Timok Corps had inflicted heavy damage to the Germans on the Deli Jovan Range and had successfully engaged the Bulgarians at the village of Mali Izvor. Such good news was always mitigated by the brutal reprisals that followed. The Germans had executed all Chetnik prisoners taken and destroyed Glogovica village. The Bulgars had slaughtered as many civilians they could get their hands on once the Chetniks left the district.

In Eastern Serbia the Mlava Corps had taken forceful action against the Germans and at Zajecar hostages were brutally murdered because of attacks against Axis forces by the Knazevac Corps which later joined up with the Deligrad Corps in taking the town of Svrljig. During the very month when the Avala Corps was concentrating on assisting in the airlift of Allied airmen, the Krajina Corps had successfully attacked the German garrison at Majdan Pek.

The Chetnik fight against the fascists was proceeding almost as relentlessly as the betrayals against themselves.

At the beginning of September General Mihailović issued a proclamation for general mobilization that quickly resulted in the taking of several German garrisons, the blowing up of a German armoured train and the destruction of the line from Belgrade to Uzhitzé, in addition to a multitude of smaller skirmishes throughout the country. A few days later a grave Kosta Marinković was to gather his officers together and warn them to brace themselves against the latest blow they were about to receive. It was the intention of the young King Peter II, he said, to broadcast to his people a request that they transfer their support from Mihailović to Tito. The government in exile in London had notified the general that the decision had been made because of intense pressure put on the young King by the British government. The great Winston Churchill himself, it seemed, had advised the young King that 'should we be so unlucky as to not receive the assent of His Majesty to make this broadcast, things will proceed in any event as though we *had* received his assent.'

The broadcast was made. Most of the Chetnik officers shrugged, went on fighting, continued to endure, to absorb this blow as they had so many others. For many of the rank and file, however, this final apparent act of betrayal proved to be the last straw. They began to desert in increasingly larger numbers.

* * *

By the end of August the Red Army had entered Rumania and was well on its way to liberate Hungary. They crossed the border into Yugoslavia in the middle of October 1944, and two days later David Ristić was summoned to the presence of Lieutenant-Colonel Kosta Trifković, commander of the Avala Corps, where he was quietly told that receiving the message that the Red Army had entered Yugoslav territory, his beloved uncle, Mikhail Ristić, had given a great cry, lurched in the direction of General Mihailović, and dropped dead after taking two steps.

'It is a great loss,' the colonel said. 'We are all aware of what a great patriot your uncle was, of his tremendous contributions to instituting and preserving our democratic country. Let us be grateful to a merciful God for at least granting him a quick and painless death.'

David experienced a violent surge of anger and bitterness. *Could not that 'merciful' God have granted him such a death before he learned that the Red Army had crossed into his beloved country?* To the colonel, however, he merely nodded. 'Yes sir.' Deep in his heart he had known the last time he saw his uncle at the January congress in the village of Ba that he would never see him again. Before Colonel Trifković could dismiss him, however, he quickly asked what policy the Yugoslav Army would be following towards the Red Army.

His commander hesitated, then said briskly that the policy would, of course, be one of cooperation. 'We are both fighting the fascists, after all,' he went on. 'I see no reason why we should not cooperate. This is an *army* we will be dealing with, not groups of undisciplined partisan terrorists.'

It was in that spirit that Lieutenant-Colonel Dragutin Keserović, after liberating the town of Krusevac in the Greater Morava Valley from German occupation, advanced to meet the Russian troops and escort their commandant into the cheering, celebrating little town. While his Chetniks were engaged in the town's riotous celebrations, partisan units approached the outskirts of the town and launched an attack against Keserović's guerrillas. The Soviet commandant ordered his troops to surround the town and asked the Chetniks to surrender their arms.

'They took two thousand of our men,' an angry Branko Jelić, who had just received the news from the staff company commander, Major Kobas, related to David. 'They even arrested an American officer who was with Keserović when he liberated the town. Luckily, Keserović himself managed to escape with the help of the townspeople. So much,' he went on bitterly, 'for our cooperation with the Red Army.'

After learning of a similar incident when, after several days of heavy fighting against strongly-armed German troops who were installed in Čačak, Chetniks under the command of Captain Predrag Raković had welcomed a Soviet unit and invited them to take part in the liberation of the town, only to find themselves surrounded, disarmed by a Red Army division, and handed over to some nearby partisans who had been hovering on the edge of the fighting. It was agreed that no further attempt should be made to cooperate with the Soviets.

Still battling the Germans, who more and more were

having to deal with the advancing Red Army, the Chetniks, after controlling the whole of central and Eastern Serbia for so long, now found themselves forced to withdraw to the west, to Sandžak and into Eastern Bosnia. To add to their discomfort, a typhus epidemic broke out, eating viciously and heavily into their ranks.

Towards the end of January 1945 the Avala Corps, on the move since October, having survived severe losses through encounters with the still heavily-armed Germans and small groups of well armed and, to add to their bitterness, warmly clothed and well-fed partisans, had withdrawn into Eastern Bosnia, had come to rest close to the border of central Bosnia and dispersed in a triangle spread between Zvornik, Gračanica, Doboj and Gradačac, overlooking the wide valley of Gradačac. Here they hoped to rest for a while and take stock of their situation, out of the way of their numerous enemies. Instead they found themselves again under heavy attack, this time, surprisingly from partisans who appeared to be on their own. Instead of the longed-for rest, the corps found itself engaged in a fierce and deadly battle against a foe smaller in number but heavily, indeed extravagantly, armed with American and British weapons and ammunition.

The battle had been raging non-stop for two days and nights when Kosta Marinković called on an exhausted David and asked him to take a small, nearby village that was believed to be under partisan control and where it was suspected much of their food, arms and ammunition was stored.

'I don't know what the hell these partisans are doing here in the first place,' a weary Kosta grumbled. 'They have been running behind the Red Army in Serbia like scavengers trailing a tiger. But, anyway, take what men you need. See what you can do. But be careful. You know how well armed they are these days.'

It proved to be a routine operation, except in one respect. After leading his troops down a steep hill with his usual blood-curdling yell, and breaking through the first barrier of partisan lines, David found himself on the periphery of the village where stiff resistance brought his unit almost to a halt and the first fight developing into a hand-to-hand battle that was both intensive and bloody. Slowly, however the Chetniks gained ground, moving from house to house with heavy losses to both sides. After spraying a hail of bullets from the machine-gun he was carrying at the entrance to a large barn, watching as two bodies fell out and slowly crumpled, David levelled it at three attackers who appeared from his right, then ran on rapidly until he reached the wall of a farmer's house. His attention was caught by a group of partisans who seemed, like children, to be playing a game of hide-and-seek behind a large vegetable cart on the opposite side of the street. It took a split second for him to realize that, in fact, at least one of them *was* a child. He could surely not have been more than sixteen, if that. David hesitated, automatically lowering his machine-gun, caught up for a fatal instant in a feeling of incredulity. Had it come to this? In this barbarous, stupid war, were they now having to fight children? Without turning to look at the Chetniks he knew were close on his heels he raised an arm, and pointed towards the youngster. *Uhvati Ga Zivog. Take that one alive!* The next moment he found himself falling, knocked to the ground by a crushing blow to the left side of his head. Dazed, he struggled to get up but could not make it. He was aware of blood pouring out of his head, onto his face, over his old leather jacket. From a great distance he heard another burst of gunfire and a loud voice crying out. 'We got the bastards! We got them.' Then rough hands were grabbing him under his arms. He was being dragged away.

When he came-to it was to find himself with a rough bandage around his head and being half-carried, half-pulled through deep snow by two Chetniks. With a tremendous effort of will he tried to stand, tried to stumble along under his own motivation. Just before they reached the village of Gornja Krecana, where the main body of the Avala Corps was camped, he again collapsed.

Afterwards he was to retain a hazy memory of a feverish,

nightmarish night spent at the village. Oddly, he did not feel any pain and was never sure whether he had received a visit from Branko Jelić and Kosta Marinković, or whether he had dreamed it all. Next morning, after learning that, ironically enough, the entire partisan force had withdrawn the previous evening, he was despatched to the nearest field hospital, taken there by an old farmer in a sleigh with, he was to remember clearly for years after, two large brown horses. The doctors who examined him were short and to the point.

'You have had the maximum of luck. A fraction of an inch more and you would have lost your eye entirely. As it is, if it is to be saved you will need to see an eye specialist. And quickly.'

After that things had moved with incredible speed. The brisk colonel in charge of the hospital had despatched him to supreme headquarters, now situated near Doboj. There he was to meet with General Mihailović for the last time. There he was to be told that he now held the rank of captain, and almost immediately after he was to receive an honourable discharge from the Yugoslav army in the fatherland.

PART FOUR
1945–1951

In spite of inadequate supplies and having to fight under exceptional difficulties, General Mihailović and his forces substantially contributed to the Allied cause and were participants in the struggle for the final Allied victory.

President Harry S. Truman
On the occasion of the posthumous award to General Draža Mihailović of the Legion of Merit, 29 March 1948

The Communist Party of Yugoslavia should make less noise about its achievements... which are not so very much. After German paratroopers broke up Yugoslav partisan headquarters, when the people's liberation movement in Yugoslavia was in severe crisis, the Soviet army came to the rescue of the Yugoslav people, evicted the occupying forces, liberated Belgrade and allowed the Yugoslav Communist Party to assume power.

Letter from Joseph Stalin and V. M. Molotov to the Yugoslav Central Committee, May 1948

1

By the beginning of October 1944, the Red Army, led by Marshal Tolbukhin, had broken through the fierce and bloody German defence and fought its way to the outskirts of Belgrade. There they paused and waited for the arrival of the Yugoslav partisans in order that they might visibly take part in the liberation of the city.

The truth was, however, that Tito's partisans were nowhere in sight, caught up as they were in a bloody battle with the Chetniks who were, as always, fiercely supported by Serbian peasants horrified at the thought that their beloved country might well be handed over to the Bolsheviks. It was all very embarrassing, to say the least, for the Yugoslavs, although the problem was eventually solved after an almost two-week delay by smuggling Tito and a few of his top aides into Belgrade in order that they could appear on the all-important balcony and thus project an image to the world of being the 'patriotic deliverers' of the country.

The whole thing had left a bitter taste in the mouth, particularly as Stalin had initially insisted that, as the Red Army was being called upon to liberate Yugoslavia, it followed that the Yugoslav partisans should come under the command of Marshal Tolbukhin. It had taken all of Tito's persuasive powers before the Soviet dictator had grudgingly agreed that he could retain command of his own partisans. The very minimum the Soviets expected, however, as they let him know in their usual tactless way, was that he would help liberate the capital city.

All of this unpleasantness was forgotten as Tito held a triumphant review of his troops a few days after the liberation of Belgrade, although, standing well back on the platform, Stevan could not quite rid himself of a feeling of unease that persisted in lingering despite the exhilaration and pride of the moment. One of the drawbacks to his closeness to the partisan leader was that in addition to taking part in the moments of great triumph, he also had the dubious honour of being aware of all the problems.

The most pressing of these was the ever-present fear that now that the Soviets were installed in Yugoslavia, the Allies would demand an equal presence in the country. Through the ever-increasing number of liaison officers sent to join partisan units, there was the continual danger that they would discover the embarrassing truth that the Yugoslav people were waiting for the Americans and British in order to save them, not only from the hated Germans, but also from the Bolsheviks. Having given the partisans such unstinting and generous support, it was obvious that both Churchill and Roosevelt expected as great a share of influence in the country as did Stalin.

It was not to be.

Foreseeing the danger, Tito instructed General Arso Jovanović to issue orders to all partisan detachments that Allied liaison officers were to be refused permission to leave the units to which they were attached unless under the most rigid partisan supervision. This, predictably, led to problems. One or two of the more enterprising British and American officers had managed to slip away on their own, talk to villagers, learn only God knew what. There were others who had chafed and protested to the extent that they had had to be physically restrained, sometimes to the point where the partisans had no option other than to imprison them. The irritating thing was that the situation was too delicate to resort to that most effective of partisan tactics – speedy liquidation of anyone who questioned their revolutionary behaviour. Before long Tito had found himself faced by an indignant General Lloyd-Owen, his own British liaison officer, asking for explanations. The marshal, of course, had brushed the complaints aside with his usual aplomb. As usual, the partisan leader was able to keep his eyes and mind on the main problems. There were certainly enough of them to distract his attention from the bleatings of a pompous British officer.

And one by one the solutions were being found. The Red Army, successful where the partisans had so dismally failed, had driven the Chetniks out of Serbia and into Bosnia. The essential task of preventing the Allies from learning the extent of the murderous massacres that were taking place throughout the whole country, or of learning that the huge army they thought they had been supplying with military *matériel* was non-existent, was the most difficult, but not insoluble, although the partisan forces were stretched so thin that Tito had to refuse General Maitland Wilson, British commander-in-chief in the Mediterranean when the latter offered to join up with his guerillas in attacking German troops who were withdrawing through the range of mountains from Albania and Macedonia.

How to admit to the British general just how few partisans there were to join up with? His refusal resulted, as General Wilson had predicted, in allowing the Germans to establish an almost impregnable defence along the Srem front. Tito's consistent refusal to accept offers from the Allies to assist partisans who were often in dire straits, always heavily outnumbered and whose inadequacies again and again allowed the German forces to prevail, led to British puzzlement, outrage and finally a suspicious concern that had an increasingly embarrassed Brigadier Fitzroy Maclean scurrying back and forth bearing messages and excuses for Tito's behaviour that satisfied no one and eventually led to a plaintive rebuke from Churchill: *You seem to view with suspicion and dislike every military operation on your coast that we are making against the Germans!*

One by one the marshal dealt with these problems, handling the British coolly and contemptuously, bemusing the suspicious but naïve and ill-informed Americans, solving the difficulties on the Srem front by mobilizing the youth of Belgrade. When that folly resulted in the mowing down by the still coldly efficient German machine of some twenty-five thousand untrained young Serbs whose bodies and blood were all too soon strewn over the fertile plains of the Vojvodina, he threw open Party ranks to anyone who wished to join, knowing that the idealists would be followed by an army of opportunists, criminal elements, *Ustaši* and Italians and Bulgarians who had failed to escape the country and who were well aware that their only hope for survival in the turmoil of the revolution would be to join with the communist forces.

Although these tactics brought fierce criticism from members of the Central Committee who were not at all happy about accepting just anyone into their ranks and who were uneasy about the slaughter of the youngsters at Srem, Tito's will, as always, prevailed.

'One has to be realistic,' he said. 'Any criminals or ex-enemies of ours who survive will be the easiest to control once we have established our government. It is those who have guilty pasts who will be most obedient to our future directives. As for the youth of Belgrade who died at Srem – why weren't they in our ranks in the first place? If they were not for us then they were undoubtedly against us and would only have caused trouble in the future.'

Certainly in one way he was right, Stevan had to admit to himself. For the first time since German troops had entered the country, partisan ranks swelled to hitherto undreamed-of proportions. And anyway, they all soon found themselves so caught up in the onrush of hectic events and the accelerating pace of history that such minor details concerning correct behaviour were swept away with the wind.

There was the bitter discovery that their Soviet brothers had made an agreement with the British that Yugoslavia would fall evenly between their 'spheres of interest', and the resulting trauma that followed. Was it not a basic tenet of Marxist doctrine that socialist states must under no circumstances indulge in the criminal behaviour of the imperialists who so ruthlessly ground small states beneath their heels and subordinated the masses to the interests of their empires? The very concept of 'spheres of interest' was as much of an anathema to the more serious intellectuals within the Party as was the private ownership of property – the subordination of the Party to private interests. It was a bitter pill for them to swallow.

But swallow it they must, although Tito made it clear, if only through the occasional veiled remark, that he would see to it that the British sphere of interest would not last for long. As for the Soviets, well, were they not all brothers, after all?

So with muted grumblings they accepted the resumption of negotiations with Dr Šubašic, representative of the Yugoslav government in London. Under the agreement they approved it was agreed that a combined government would be formed from members of their own National Committee and members of the royal government. At least they were able to ensure that their anti-fascist council remained the supreme legislative body. The original agreement made with the Allies that democratic elections would be held at the end of the war was reaffirmed and it was further decided that until these elections were held the young King Peter II would be represented in the country by a regency. The agreement was approved by both the British and Soviet governments. After all, as Tito explained to his Central Committee, who were patently unhappy about the swearing in of Dr Šubašic as foreign secretary, even though Tito himself was now Prime Minister, this 'comedy' did ensure Allied recognition of their government, which was crucial at this uncertain stage. As if to stress his point, British and American ambassadors arrived almost immediately on the scene to join their Soviet counterpart.

For Stevan, events were moving so rapidly that all thoughts of his private life had been pushed well into the background. He was constantly by Tito's side, overseeing administrative implementation of the marshal's directives, accompanying him as he made a tour of palaces and villas that were to be appropriated for the use of the new prime minister. Afterwards he was to reflect gratefully upon the fact that he was kept so busy it was a matter of falling into bed every eighteen hours or so to snatch a few hours of sleep and regain enough strength to continue with his ever-increasing round of duties.

He was thus largely, if not entirely, able to ignore or at least subordinate the knowledge that in Belgrade a bloody purge was taking place not only by the true partisans, but by the latecomers who were taking the opportunity to rid themselves of old rivals and settle old scores. One had only to be wearing a partisan uniform to be in a position to round up a rival, label him 'collaborator' and have him arbitrarily shot. Neither law nor order prevailed. Even the pragmatic Djerdja was heard to mutter that it was one thing to follow Stalin's practice of eliminating all enemies but another thing to eliminate the whole population! 'It's time Tito put an end to it,' he told Stevan. 'He has let it go too far.'

Stevan had shrugged. Best not to think about these things, as Alex had always told him. In any event, even if the marshal showed no inclination to discourage the murderous behaviour of his partisans, at least he himself showed no sign of personal bloodlust, except for the oft-expressed intention to liquidate the traitor Mihailović once the secret police managed to find him. They had already learned that the general had refused offers by the Americans to get him out of the country.

Meanwhile the population, having suffered so much already during the German occupation, cringed, living from day to day in fear, not knowing which member of their family might next be picked up by one of the bloodthirsty Bolsheviks and murdered in cold blood. It was later estimated that at least fifty to sixty thousand 'enemies of the people' had been marched out of Belgrade, never to be seen again.

At least Stevan had been able to make sure his own parents were safe. He had seen to their evacuation to a small cottage they owned in the country. His mother had been hysterically grateful, his father coldly contemptuous.

He tried to keep his thoughts determinedly away from Olga Miletić, as he had done since learning about her wilful betrayal of their love. The police, he assumed, were protecting those who had gathered intelligence for the Party. Yet sometimes, during the rare moments when he had time to think, he would visualize his eventual encounter with her. He would be cool, brisk, would congratulate her in an icy tone on her contribution to the Party, would brush aside her apology good-humouredly, would turn away to more important matters. She would, of course, be contrite. Or would she? Perhaps not. The old, wilful, Olga might still be much in evidence. In any event, he promised himself, he would be cold, noncommittal, non-judging even. He would, however, *never* forgive her. Never! Not if she got down on her bended knees. Which, he was forced to admit to himself with a bitter smile, was highly unlikely.

In fact, he was totally unprepared for his own reaction the day he did finally see her.

He had been busy at the White Palace, overseeing the massive redecorations the prime minister had ordered – Tito made no secret of his disappointment at the relatively modest furnishings of the royal palaces – when big Alex Miletić had burst in.

'I'm sorry, Stevan. I'm sorry to disturb you. I know how busy you are. But it's Olga. Could you possibly come? She's asking for you.' Quickly he explained that some women had burst into the Miletić home, vowing vengeance upon the *Švapska prostitutka*, the German prostitute! They had beaten her, tried to hack off her hair. 'God knows what would have happened if Stana Radović hadn't arrived back from the market,' Alex exclaimed. 'She flew at them, routed them, badly wounded one of them with some kitchen scissors. I know how busy you are, Stevan, but ... He broke off and hurried to catch up with the other man who had dropped the list of furnishings he had been checking off and was running, running...

She was not as badly beaten as he had thought from Alex's hurried description. The beautiful shining hair had been roughly and unevenly chopped but, as she assured him between tears and hysterical laughter, 'I'd been meaning to have it cut anyway! Oh, Stevan,' she cried, 'Stevan I've missed you so. I know you've been busy, but...'

Over her left eye there was an ugly black bruise and she had a cut on her chin. Otherwise, she assured him, 'Just a few bruises, more to my dignity than to my body. Do you know what they were calling me? They called me a German prostitute!' She began to cry. He was holding her gently, cradling her in his arms, frightened to death of hurting her even more, bursting with love, trying to hush her as she made the dreamed-of apology. Not for wilfully betraying their love, but for what she called her 'bourgeois attitude' when he had on that long ago morning handed her Tito's letter suggesting that she might be able to contribute invaluable aid to the Party by perhaps forming an alliance with one of the German occupiers.

'It wasn't until you left that I realized what an honour the Party had done me,' she confessed. 'But by then it was too late. You were gone. How *could* I have acted so like a stupid little bourgeois? How *could* I?'

To which he found he had no answer. No answer at all. Except to repeat over and over how much he loved her. The past was all to be forgotten. Now that they were together again he would never let her go. Never!

They were in her bedroom on the second floor of the Miletić home. When Stevan had followed Alex up the stairs and burst into the room, she had been sitting up in bed reading. She was wearing a high-necked gown of some kind of soft, flimsy material. It had taken just one welcoming look from those wonderful dark eyes and he had known instantly that nothing had changed. He was as much her slave as he had ever been. Nothing had changed, nothing.

Now, as he glanced around the room, he became aware of

the anxiously hovering figure of Stana Radović and of Alex, shifting uneasily from foot to foot, obviously embarrassed at being witness to such an intensely private and emotional scene.

'Your mother?' he asked, turning back to Olga. 'Is she . . .'

'She's asleep. We gave her a sleeping draught.'

He nodded. 'Look, Olga, I can't stay. I have a luncheon appointment with Tito. But I'll come back as soon as possible. Have you been in touch with the police? Those women could be back.'

'The police!' It was Stana, nearly spitting her contempt. 'Those bandits? Who has the courage to call the police? All *they* do is plunder and murder. I tell you it was better with the Germans. At least there was order. At least one could walk the streets.'

'Hush, Stana. Hush. You must give the government time.' Olga frowned lovingly in the direction of her old nurse. 'You must give them time.'

'Alex, you'll have to stay here with her. As soon as I've finished lunch I'm going to call Ranković.' He turned back to Olga. 'You know Comrade Ranković? He's been put in charge of organizing the police. I'll make sure you get some protection. It wouldn't hurt for you to get hold of an army uniform, either. People will hesitate before they touch someone wearing the uniform of a partisan officer, I can tell you that,' he said proudly. He leaned over and kissed her. 'I'll be back as soon as I can.'

On his way out he suggested to Alex that as soon as the police arrived he should arrange to move back into his old home with his sister and his mother, glad of an opportunity to get the big man out of the old apartment he had moved back into, with its memories of Jelena. It's not healthy for him to be living alone like that, he thought. It's not healthy. And at least if Alex moved back home he would know that Olga was safe. God only knew how long it would take before he himself would have time to take care of her.

He arrived for his appointment with Tito just as Comrade Milovan Djilas was walking out. They nodded warily at each other. Oddly enough, it transpired that Djilas had been to see the marshal concerning the problem of lawlessness in the streets. His complaint, however, had not been levelled against the partisans, but had concerned the scandalous and riotous behaviour of the Red Army.

Djilas, who like so many members of the central committee, was strangely impervious to murder committed in the name of the Party, was himself engaged in plundering the valuables belonging to the state. He had appropriated a beautiful villa for himself, was oddly puritanical about sexual behaviour. The fact was that the Red Army was not only murdering and pillaging in as frenzied a manner as the partisans themselves, who were, after all, entitled to the spoils of war in their own country, but in addition they were raping every woman they could get their hands on.

'Even Party members,' said a mildly scandalized Tito. 'Imagine! They are even raping the wives of Party members. I must say, it's hard to understand such behaviour. But there you are.' He went on to tell Stevan that the previous day he himself had been forced to deal with an indignant commissar whose wife and daughter had both been raped by members of the Red Army, regardless of the fact that the daughter had screamed at them that she was a card-carrying member of the Party. Naturally the commissar had been very upset. It was only natural. 'Still,' he added thoughtfully, 'one must be tolerant, after all. The Red Army is made up of a lot of Asiatics, you know.'

What he really wanted to talk to Stevan about was the scandalous state of the royal train. 'I can't be expected to ride in *that*,' he fumed. 'Absolutely shabby. The furnishings are very shabby. Could you take a look at it? Do something?'

He listened sympathetically to Stevan's tale about what had happened to Olga Miletić. 'Yes. Yes, you are right. You must speak to Ranković, and we must get her into an army uniform. I'll give her a medal,' he added generously.

The bulk of the Red Army, having thundered through Belgrade and cleared it of the Germans, was to move on in its quest to liberate Hungary, leaving only a couple of thousand troops behind, which at least alleviated some of the 'lawlessness' problem. By the beginning of April the partisans themselves were at long last in a position to launch their own offensive, to push the remnants of the German army out of Croatia and Slovenia. By the 8th of May the remaining Axis forces under the leadership of General von Löhr, although still formidable, had been forced to comply with orders from Berlin to submit to unconditional surrender.

The first phase of the people's revolution was at an end. Yet endless difficulties lay ahead.

Even before the country had rid itself of the Germans the problem of Trieste confronted them. Tito had always made it clear that the moment he took power he intended to reclaim the valuable port city from the Italians, bring it back into its rightful orbit within Yugoslavia. The Western Allies, however, had different ideas. This, they claimed, was a question that must be discussed with *them*.

The British dug in to the extent that they made it clear that Tito's partisans would find themselves facing British troops should they go ahead with their plan to grab Trieste. At first the marshal brushed this threat aside. Friendly Allied sources had quietly informed him that the British were bluffing, were aware that their own troops, mainly drawn from the working class, would refuse to fight against the heroic partisans they had heard so much about through the BBC and the Allied press.

When he learned that the tactic of General Alexander was to allow his troops to observe partisan behaviour – the indiscriminate brutality, arrogance, killing and thieving, before asking them to confront Tito's men, he flew into one of his rages that was not at all alleviated by reports that the British general's tactics were working. Within only a couple of weeks of observing partisan behaviour, British troops were expressing outrage. Eventually he had no alternative when faced with a strong display of British resolve other than to withdraw. He was to brood for a very long time over

General Alexander's statement that the future of Trieste would be decided at the peace conference and that Marshal Tito's apparent intention was to 'establish his claim by force of arms and military occupation', going on to compare such action with that of Hitler and Mussolini. 'It is to prevent such actions that we have been fighting the war,' the general had concluded.

To add salt to his wounds, Tito's appeal to Stalin for support was refused. Unable to prevent himself, this time, from speaking out angrily about his disappointment with the Soviet attitude, he received a sharp rap on the knuckles from Moscow for his temerity. For a time he withdrew into himself.

The humiliation of Trieste, however, did not prevent him from re-emerging from his brief period of resentful silence to enter into quiet negotiations with certain British officials over the Austrian province of Carinthia which, he stoutly insisted, should belong to Yugoslavia by virtue of the fact that its inhabitants included a number of Slovenes. These negotiations resulted in thousands of refugees who had poured into Austria to escape the vengeful partisans being coolly cajoled by the British into returning to certain and brutal death in Yugoslavia by a variety of questionable methods, including one instance which eerily echoed the German procedure used to persuade their Jewish victims to travel quietly and without resistance to their doom. Some twenty thousand refugees were placed on trains, their fears assuaged by British assurances that they were being sent to safety in Italy, without knowing that each guard's van was full of partisans, some of whom appeared to rob and murder their victims even before the trains reached Yugoslavia.

As word filtered back to Belgrade of the bloody massacre of these refugees – a mixed bag of white Russians, Croatian and Slovene peasants with their wives and children together with some *Ustaši* and a few Chetniks – a wave of consternation spread through the ranks of certain partisans such as Nikola Djerdja, whose pragmatism had almost reached breaking point.

'Thousands of them,' he hissed to a pale Stevan, 'shot, knived, bludgeoned to death. So many bodies they had to dynamite them to try to destroy the evidence. But not before removing all valuables, including gold teeth for god's sake, from the bodies. It's a replay of the Jewish holocaust! Has *Tito* gone mad? What if the international community finds out about this?'

'International community? Well, what about the British role?' Stevan found himself automatically leaping to Tito's defence despite the queasy feeling in his stomach. 'They broke international law, you know, returning refugees like that. *They* won't be saying too much about it to the international community, I can tell you.'

Mercifully, the crisis was swept aside in the rush of historical events precipitated by Tito at last clearly revealing his hand to the West by taking steps to establish a purely communist regime within Yugoslavia. Dr Šubašic and the rest of the representatives of the royal government were rudely ousted and placed under house arrest. 'Free democratic elections' were held as promised, despite Western propaganda which questioned the fact that of the five-hundred and ten candidates nominated, four-hundred and seventy were communists and the remaining candidates all communist-sponsored. The resulting victory was rightly hailed in the communist press as a resounding endorsement of the Yugoslav Communist Party, which now felt entitled to abolish the monarchy in favour of a federal republic based on the Soviet system.

The unfavourable reaction from the West was brushed aside. It was Stevan himself who informed the marshal that the great Winston Churchill himself had exclaimed: *Tito tricked me!*, causing Tito to give a roar of laughter and slap his hand heavily down on his knee. 'I wish he was here,' he shouted, between gusts of laughter, 'I'd love to tell him how easy it was!'

The only discordant note at that triumphant moment was the knowledge that General Mihailović was still moving freely around the countryside, warmly welcomed by the people, who still revered him as the first man in Europe to actively stand up to 'that maniac Hitler'. In addition to the irritating fact that he was being protected by the ungrateful masses, there was the worrisome knowledge that he had some fifty thousand men still at his disposal, although it was generally felt that without military supplies there was little he could do to upset the 'legitimate' government of Yugoslavia.

There was no doubt, however, that the 'Chetnik factor' was an extremely delicate matter. While the propaganda machine turned out endless stories about the 'collaboration' of these dastardly traitors, the embarrassing truth remained that throughout the country there was hardly one family that had not witnessed one or more of its members being arrested or executed by the Axis forces for their part in supporting 'Chetnik enemies of the German occupation'. Lists of names of those executed by the fascists for the crime of supporting the Chetniks could still be found in post offices and municipal buildings throughout the country, together with posters offering a substantial reward for Mihailović's capture, despite a concerted effort by Party members to find all such posters and destroy them.

The situation obviously called for drastic measures. These were drawn up and quickly implemented. A law was introduced by the constituent assembly banning all 'political' discussion about the war or events that might have taken place during the German occupation. The ban applied not only in public places, but within the homes of the population. Another purge was undertaken to 'cleanse' the country of those suspected of having belonged to or sympathized with the Chetniks; thousands more citizens were gathered together, summarily executed or thrown in jail. The country was blanketed with fake photographs purporting to show Chetniks drinking and carousing with German officers and soldiers. A massive indoctrination programme was launched in the schools where children were encouraged to report to their teachers any 'illegal' political discussion overheard in their homes. Ranković's secret police were everywhere, ready to pounce upon anyone so unwise as to even ask in a puzzled voice why, if the Chetniks had been collaborators, had so many of them been arrested and executed by the Germans?

Tito himself made several trips into the countryside, explaining to silent villagers, who were slower to grasp the situation than the townspeople, that Mihailović had been a German spy 'even before the war'. He stopped going, however, when it was drawn to his attention that on each such trip he was of necessity accompanied by a large assortment of bodyguards, while it was well known that Mihailović was still in a position to wander alone or with only one or two aides into most villages. 'People are ungrateful,' the marshal was heard to mutter. 'Let them learn the hard way, then.'

And learn the hard way many of them did. Stevan did his best to remain detached from the purges, the killings, and tried to hide his anger when confronted with the shamelessness of some partisans who showed themselves capable of branding innocent, apolitical citizens 'collaborator' for the simple reason that they coveted their homes, their furnishings, cars or other possessions. When such by no means infrequent cases came to his attention he simply turned his head away and buried himself in his work.

His relationship with Olga had entered upon a period of pure bliss. They met as frequently as possible, although the heavy demands made upon his time by Tito and the fact that Olga herself had been allotted a heavy workload at the university where a complete reorientation of all subjects to fit in with the Marxist–Leninist dialectic had been undertaken, precluded their being together for more than a few hours at a time. A period of three to four weeks often elapsed before they could snatch an hour or so together, usually at Stevan's apartment where at least they had some privacy. Occasionally they managed to meet briefly for a coffee or lunch at the old Three Violins restaurant, now rebuilt state-owned and flourishing under its proud new name 'The Red Banner'. It was still, however, managed by their good friend Comrade Bogdan Bošković, who occasionally joined them to entertain them with some hair-raising incident he had experienced because of his dangerous work gathering intelligence for the partisans during the war.

Olga quite obviously adored Stevan, was in awe of the close relationship he enjoyed with the marshal, and was tenderly aware of the ascendancy he had attained in his relationship with her brother Alex, who unquestioningly looked to Stevan for most of the answers to any of his problems. Sometimes, Stevan thought, he got more pure satisfaction out of this new respect Olga had for him, than from the love she gave him so unstintingly.

For himself, thinking back to the time during the war when he had brooded about her so bitterly, he could only renew the vow he had made that he would spend the rest of his life making her happy, trying to repay her for the hell she must have gone through in having to enter into a liaison with some brutal Nazi bastard for the sake of the Party. It had obviously never occurred to her that he, Stevan, had not expected her to make such a sacrifice. And it was, indeed, a terrible sacrifice for her to have had to make. She had sacrificed everything. He must never forget that for a moment. He must never forget that while she was suffering only God knew what humiliation, he had been concerned not about *her* feelings, or the obvious danger she had exposed herself to, but about his own petty little bourgeois emotions of jealousy and rage.

There had been no discussion of marriage. Neither of them had time to think about their personal future, they were both so caught up in the implementation of the people's victory. When the subject *did* come up, surprisingly enough, it was the marshal himself, who showed no signs of legalizing his own relationship with Zdenka, who was to mention it.

It was a week or so after the great victory ball presided over by Tito and a thin, tired-looking Zdenka. The ball, looked forward to eagerly by so many as a consolidation, a celebration of the great gains the Party had made under the leadership of the marshal, had, in fact, hardly been what one could call an unqualified success.

Stevan had looked forward to it and had been greatly amused at finding Olga, always so contemptuous of such bourgeois activities in the past, in something of a dither. What should she wear? What *did* one wear to a 'people's' ball? The occasion, obviously, was not going to be one of those shallow social events where dim-witted females vied with each other over who was escorting whom, whose gown was the more beautiful, who was wearing the most expensive jewellery, the best fur. This, she was convinced, was to be an occasion of great dignity and joy, where modestly-dressed comrades would gather together to celebrate the great victory and triumph of the people over the greedy capitalists. 'Should I just wear my uniform, perhaps?' she asked Stevan, who had laughed, and shaken his head.

'Wear what you like, my darling. You will outshine every woman there anyway.'

In the end she chose a simple white gown that was beautifully cut to enhance her spectacular figure. She wore no jewellery, and slipped into a plain white woollen coat when Stevan arrived to pick her up. Her short hair had been transformed into a shining cap that accentuated her high cheekbones and drew attention to the brilliant dark eyes. She looked absolutely stunning.

Which, he was to think later, was probably what had drawn the ire of the Party matrons who, when Stevan and Olga arrived, accompanied by Alex and a sloe-eyed little Slovenian girl, Olga had insisted her brother invite, were lined up in as formidable an array of pomp and glitter as any flock of bourgeois ladies of the royal court had ever managed to display in the decadent past.

They were certainly, he was to discover ruefully, already angry and eager to draw blood.

Stevan's little party had apparently arrived too late to witness an unpleasant scene caused by the celebrated partisan fighter, Cana Babić, who had arrived wearing the army uniform she considered appropriate for a heroine of the revolution under the most glittering of social circumstances. Cana had long been celebrated in poem and song as one of the bravest heroines of the revolution, having fought fiercely alongside her male comrades, displaying the kind of courage any man would be proud to possess. It seemed, however, as Stevan learned from a hurried aside from Nikola Djerdja, who was present with his plump, pretty wife, that Cana had taken one look at all the ladies present, all dressed to the hilt, and begun screaming 'Is *this* what we fought for? Is *this* what the revolution was all about?' The hefty, red-faced peasant woman could not be quietened. When she had wrenched a diamond necklace from around the neck of the wife of one of the more prominent Party members and began to shout obscenities, she had been forcibly evicted. She fought back so violently that there had then been no alternative. She had been placed under arrest.

It was into this unsettled climate, then, that Olga had walked with her beautiful, stunning simplicity. They had not been there for more than ten minutes when from a table behind their small party a loud feminine voice was to comment upon the scandalous fact that not only those partisans and their wives who had actually fought bravely for the revolution were allowed to attend the ball, but apparently any *Švapska prostitutka* who could use her wiles on high-ranking partisan members could also attend.

An instant hush fell over the immediate area. Stevan swung around in his chair in a blind fury, encountered a group of bland, smiling faces and turned helplessly back to Olga, who was sitting up very straight, her chin held high.

Into that tense situation had entered, of all people, Marshal Tito, resplendent and handsome in a white and gold uniform. He had approached their table, greeted them all warmly and then, no doubt to the intense fury of the Party matrons surrounding them, swept Olga off to dance.

The Marshal did not appear to be aware that he had inadvertently prevented Comrade Matić from causing a scene which, Stevan realized, he had most certainly been about to do, but had returned a flushed Olga to him several minutes later and complimented her on her dancing ability, before turning away to chat with some Central Committee members and their wives at a nearby table.

It was not until he met with him a week or so later that Stevan fully realized how little escaped the attention of the president of the new Yugoslav republic. After discussing plans for the annexation of a state hunting lodge for his own use, Tito had suddenly glanced up and stared at him shrewdly. 'I hear,' he said drily, 'that some of our women have seen fit to comment about Comrade Olga's contribution to our cause during the war.'

Stevan gave him a startled look. My God, he thought, does *anything* escape his attention? 'You know women,' he said after a moment. 'But I think Olga is too intelligent to let a little thing like that worry her.'

'Such little minds they have. Such petty little minds.' Tito shook his head sorrowfully. He returned for a moment to studying the plans spread out on his desk in great disarray, before glancing up again. 'There's only one thing to do,' he announced. 'You must marry her. Yes, yes,' he insisted, meeting Stevan's startled look with something like a twinkle in his eye, 'that's what you must do. You must marry her. And *I*,' he beamed proudly, 'will give the bride away. *I* shall be the one to give the bride away.'

They were married a month later. The civil ceremony was brief, the bride beautiful, the marshal impressive and the groom, so he kept repeating to anyone who had the patience to listen, was the happiest man in the world.

2

Despite the best intentions of the supreme headquarters of the Yugoslav army in the fatherland, David Ristić was not to reach the safe haven of Switzerland until the end of April 1945.

Armed with an honourable discharge and instructions to cross the half-frozen River Bosnia and proceed from there to the village of Rudanka, where he was to receive further instructions and new papers, he had no sooner completed the river crossing than he collapsed, was picked up, and taken prisoner of war shortly afterwards by a roving German column. The diagnosis: typhus.

When he regained consciousness he was in a hospital in Zagreb, with a mixed bag of Germans, Croats, partisans and Chetniks all sick or wounded. All, as he was told by a pretty young Dalmatian nurse, were kept carefully apart! She was also to tell him that he had been given countless injections before his typhus was controlled.

'To have survived what you have survived,' a German doctor later informed him, 'means that you have an iron constitution. You are indeed lucky.' David stared back at him with mixed feelings of detestation and grudging appreciation of the excellent care he knew he had received.

As soon as he was considered to be strong enough he was transferred to the Rebro hospital, where a German eye surgeon operated on his eye, removing the cornea and some small splinters. 'If you ever find yourself in Switzerland,' he was told, 'go and see a specialist. Another operation and you should be able to retain most of your sight.'

He was to spend two months in the Rebro hospital before being sent to a convalescent hospital in the Austrian Alps with another small group of POWs. The train taking him to Badgastein was packed, not only with prisoners, but with refugees. News that the Red Army stood poised to take Vienna had spread rapidly through the train. David listened with grim amusement to the stories about the atrocities that could be expected from the Russian 'beasts', and almost muttered *It takes one to know one* to a fellow POW, but was too tired to make the effort. Later he was to remember looking out of the train window when it pulled into a small station, his attention drawn by loud and cheerful singing which, he found, came from a large detachment of what at first appeared to be German soldiers. A closer look revealed them to be young boys of thirteen, fourteen, certainly not more than fifteen years old. *Good God*, he thought drowsily, *why doesn't someone stop this? Why don't they take those guns away from them, send them back to school?*

He was indescribably weary. It was as though the years of bitter fighting, of disappointments and betrayal that he had kept pushing to the back of his mind for the sake of survival, had suddenly descended upon his shoulders, a weight so heavy it blocked out all feeling and left only this terrible tiredness. He could, he thought, sleep forever.

When he did awaken fully it was to find that the train had arrived at Badgastein. With the other POWs he was transferred to a truck and driven to the hospital on the outskirts of the small town. As the truck lumbered slowly through the town he could just make out the defiant slogan covering most of the walls. *Unsere Wände brechen aber nicht unsere Hercen.* Our walls break down but not our hearts!

A month later he was sent to another camp in Innsbruck and from there to yet another POW camp in the village of Landeck, some forty miles from the Swiss border. On the evening of the 29th of April 1945 he was tersely told by a sergeant in charge of the Austrian guard to *Nehmen Sie Ihre Sachen mit!* Get your things together! Without further explanation he was ushered outside with two hundred or so French, Russians, Italians and Yugoslavs – both Chetnik and partisan – and taken on a long overnight march. He was not to discover until the next morning that they were moving in the direction of the Swiss border. Some time after three in the afternoon of the 30th of April they were called to a halt at a spot about one kilometre from the Swiss frontier and released by the Austrian guards. *Vorwärts! Vorwärts!* And go forward they happily did, across a small stone bridge, into the safe haven of Switzerland.

It was also, David was to discover later, at some time after three in the same afternoon that Adolf Hitler sat down next to his bride in a bunker in Berlin, held a pistol to his head and pulled the trigger.

Although the method of his arrival in Switzerland was hardly, David thought with wry good humour, what supreme headquarters had in mind for him, at least he *had* arrived in the beautiful, neutral little country.

The Swiss proved to be efficient, if reluctant, hosts.

He was sent first to Bern, where he stayed in a refugee centre set up in a school until he was 'processed'. By the time the war had ended on the 8th of May he had passed through the small town of Nussbaum, and had his eye examined by a Swiss doctor who recommended that he be sent to the eye clinic in Zürich. The subsequent operation in that sparkling, clean city was to keep him in hospital for another few months.

Later he was to marvel that at a time when he seemed incapable of making decisions in connection with his own fate; so many shadowy figures had emerged to tell him what he must do. He was to go here or go there, do this or do that. He complied quietly. The last thing he wanted to do was to think, to have to make decisions.

From Zürich he was sent to another refugee camp, this time in the beautiful Lake Lucerne area where he spent his days with several other displaced persons dismantling bunkers for the Swiss, for which he received marvellously clean accommodation, excellent food and a few Swiss francs. He lived from day to day, grateful for the air that reminded him of his beloved Serbian mountains, grateful that he was engaged in a physical effort that ensured him of a deep, drug-like sleep each night.

Gradually his mind, that had slowed down like a rusty machine, began to respond to the lubricants of hard work, nourishment and rest. The pure Swiss air cleansed his lungs, roused his brain. The process of thought returned. The questions began.

How had it happened? How could it be that his beautiful little country that had had the courage to stand up to Hitler and his gang of thugs, that had stood up so bravely to that bloody and terrible occupation, could have been so coolly, so treacherously, handed over to another murderous totalitarian regime? Could something have been done to prevent it? Could *he* have done anything to prevent it? Yet what? What could you do if you wakened one morning to discover a horde of barbarians in your back yard except take up arms, try to evict them? Yet the communists had not done this. They had waited until a country that was *not* theirs had been overrun before being stirred into action. And then that action had been directed not at the enemy but at their own brothers. They had launched a dirty political game that had allowed them to steal something that was not theirs by right. Thieves! That was the word. Common thieves. Who had said that? Yaruga! A simple country lad, yet he had certainly hit that nail on the head. And where was Yaruga now? What had happened to him? To Zeka? Branko Jelić? Kosta? He was overwhelmed then by such a sense of loss, of pain for whatever unknown anguish his brave comrades must be going through ... or were they all dead? Would he ever know? He had to stop thinking! Best not to think!

And his beloved Uncle Mikhail. Was *this* what he had fought for so bravely during the Balkan wars, during the Great War? Was all that great courage spent in vain? So that he might put his trust in unworthy allies who had so chillingly shrugged off their own professed moral ideals? Already, so the newspapers told him, they were finding out that yesterday's ally remained what it had always been, their own mortal enemy. What had caused them to so easily betray not only *his* little country's interests, but their own? Was it guilt? The guilty knowledge that dictator he might be, yet Stalin alone had held back the tide of fascism with his people's blood? Had little Yugoslavia, then, been tossed to the new double-fanged beast as temporary appeasement, as they were now in the process of tossing Poland? Yet Britain had gone to war for Poland, for God's sake! It did not make sense. None of it made sense.

And what of his aunt, his sisters? What of Irina? He'd thought once that he would never forgive her that terrible betrayal. Yet was *that* his fault, too? Should he have stayed with her? God only knew, he had been aware enough of her fragility, her inability to cope with a life that showed signs of becoming too brutal, too terrible. Was *that* where his real duty had lain? With his family, with his love?

Once they began, the questions refused to stop. The deep, drug-like sleep he had enjoyed for so long began to fail him. No matter how hard he worked now, the nights suddenly became long, nightmarish hours of tossing and turning. Thinking, thinking . . . the questions never stopped.

Until one morning he was called to the camp office and given some good news. Shortly after his arrival in Switzerland, one of the endless forms he had completed had been an application to the Serbian National Defence in the United States for a scholarship that would allow him to remain in Switzerland and pursue his studies in languages. He had been granted the scholarship.

He made an instant resolution. What he needed now above all else was not deeper knowledge of the several languages he already spoke but to try to understand the political expediencies that had led to the betrayal of things he had been brought up to believe in all his life. At the beginning of December 1945 he began his studies with the Graduate Institute of International Studies at the University of Geneva. He was to emerge two years later with a masters' degree in political science.

Without, however, having learned any answers to any of his questions.

3

Problems arose almost the moment they returned from their honeymoon on the Adriatic coast. Stevan had kept Tito's main wedding gift as a surprise, leaving Olga's mother in charge of putting the final touches to the luxurious villa on Rumanian Street, not far from the one Tito had appropriated for himself in addition to both palaces, although he was still grumbling about the deficiencies of the Royal Palace, the old home of King Alexander. That problem was eventually resolved by turning it into a residence for official guests.

They had arrived back in Belgrade by train and were taken by car to Rumanian Street. Olga, a little drowsy from the journey, had rested her head on his shoulder. 'We are going to see Alex and mother first, then?'

'Yes. We'll be seeing them,' he replied, and refused to say a word when the taxi entered the perfectly groomed grounds of the spacious white residence the marshal had chosen for them. As planned, Olga's mother was waiting with outstretched arms and a small group of Party comrades assembled for the house-warming.

At first Stevan had thought Olga's silence merely indicated that she was stunned, overwhelmed by the thoughtfulness shown by the marshal. She does not know him as well as I, he thought proudly. This will make her realize what a generous man he is. He could not have been more stunned when she turned to him when the last of their guests had departed and quietly announced that they could not possibly live in this house.

'What are you saying? What do you mean?'

'You can ask *me* that, Stevan?' She returned his stare with equal incredulity. 'But you know whose villa this is. It belongs to...' She named a well-known Belgrade family with whom they were both well acquainted.

He felt the blood flooding to his head. His face must have been crimson. 'What are you talking about? There is no private ownership of property, you know that. This house belongs to the state. And you and I are officials of the state. High officials. Do I have to tell *you* that?'

'But don't you understand? *This* is not what Marx meant. That we substitute one privileged class for another! It is even worse when it applies to *us*, to you and me. We have *always* been privileged! Besides,' she moved over to one of the wall paintings, stood staring at it with a slight frown, 'this painting alone, it is priceless, Stevan. It belongs in the museum. All these furnishings, they belong to the state, perhaps in one of the official residences, but for *us*? No, no. We cannot live here. We must return to the apartment. God knows, even that is much more luxurious than the homes most of our people are forced to live in.'

Her attitude had, of course, provoked a bitter row. In the end she did come to realize that there was no way in the world they could leave the residence without deeply offending the president of the new republic. The pleasure they might have enjoyed from their beautiful new home, however, had effectively been destroyed.

Not, Stevan had to admit to himself, that Olga was the only one who was disturbed by the manner in which so many Party officials were displaying endless greed for the bourgeois life they had railed against for so many years. The jealousies and intrigues that flourished as the Party leaders and the bureaucracy competed to grab the most desirable homes, furnishings, paintings and *objets d'art* might have been amusing had not some of the more sober thinkers amongst them not seen fit to mutter darkly that this was hardly what the communist promise of equality was all about.

The fact was, however, that the latter were definitely in the minority. Besides that, such mutterings could be and often were, interpreted as being dangerously close to treason. After all, there was not a man or a woman amongst them who could deny that the power they held had been grasped for them by Marshal Tito. And the marshal himself was displaying an aptitude for acquisition, for luxury, pomp and splendour that far outreached anything displayed by members of the royal court during previous regimes. Yet he was not selfish about this. His own love of the good life enabled him to show great tolerance and understanding to those of his officials who made no effort to hide their predilection for the bourgeois life style. In fact it was the more modest officials who aroused his ire, his suspicions. 'A strange attitude he is taking,' he would mutter. 'Don't think I haven't noticed!'

Yet these things were only trifling problems compared with the major difficulties that confronted the new government.

Astonishingly enough, the most pressing of these proved to be the Soviet brothers who had been rushed in from Moscow to guide the fledgling Yugoslav government in the right Marxist-Leninist direction. If the Yugoslav communists had expected some degree of tactfulness from their Soviet counterparts concerning the role the latter had played in leading them to victory within their own country, they were to be rudely disillusioned. Their Russian comrades made it abundantly clear that without the Red Army, the Yugoslav partisans had stood no chance of attaining the power they now enjoyed. Nor did the Soviets prove to be at all shy about appropriating acquisitions their Yugoslav hosts had requisitioned from state storage for themselves. Their needs, too, proved to be alarmingly bourgeois in character.

There was no doubt in the world that they were welcome in Yugoslavia. For years both the Party leadership and the rank and file had idealized not only their iron leader, Joseph Stalin, but also their status as the first socialist society that was destined to lead the world into a new and just order. They were also quite humbly grateful to the Red Army for its liberation of their country not only from the fascists, but from the decadent old order against which they had themselves fought so ineffectively for so long.

It was not only the Soviet's rude – even, in the opinion of some, indecent – grabbing of the best material possessions that caused concern, but also their failure to grasp that they were visiting a foreign country whose cultural, agricultural and industrial background differed in a great many ways from their own. In the agricultural sector, for instance, many of the Yugoslav comrades felt the Soviet experiment should be used more as a guide for what should *not* be done than as the 'successful' operation the Soviets boasted about. Although this sector could certainly do with some modernization, the very fact that the peasants of Yugoslavia supplied the country so well with food, leaving a great deal over for export, had indicated to much of the Party leadership that, in agriculture at least, the new government should proceed with caution. There was certainly no need for any five-year plan. Collectivization was a dream that should be handled with great caution. It should be examined very carefully before being forced upon the intractable and often intransigent farmers of Yugoslavia.

Their efforts to explain this to the Soviets inevitably, however, resulted in frustration. 'What do *you* know about such matters?' was the hardly tactful response to just about any idea the Yugoslavs put forward. And the truth was, they simply did not like to argue too forcefully with their Soviet guests to whom they owed so much.

The thing that hurt most, however, was the ambivalent chuckle from the Soviets when the Yugoslav partisans mentioned their own role in the liberation of their country. There would be coarse winks and rough laughter and ambiguous remarks about the Chetnik contribution that had been so much appreciated by the Soviet fatherland when that gangster Adolf Hitler had launched his attack against their country. That attitude of theirs towards the name of Mihailović or any mention of the traitorous Chetniks not only caused genuine pain to members of the Party leadership, who were reminded of the Soviet ambiguity towards Mihailović during the war, but genuine outrage to many of the rank and file, who had been fed as much propaganda about the Chetnik role during the war as had the Western Allies. Such misunderstandings were sure to, and did, provoke all kinds of incidents that had to be dealt with and hushed up by the Party propaganda machine.

The only person who took it all in his stride, who seemed able to rise above any small storm, was Marshal Tito. Stevan's admiration for the marshal grew month by month. He would return home to Olga full of enthusiastic comments about the new leader of Yugoslavia. More often than not, however, he would be confronted by an inexplicable silence on the subject of Tito that he found more infuriating than if she had offered criticism. As time went on, Olga made it abundantly clear that she was gravely disappointed with the end result of the people's revolution.

'What is going on with the secret police?' she would ask bluntly. 'In many ways they are as bad as the Nazis. And they are infinitely worse than the police from the previous regime. Is this what we fought for?'

Stevan tried hard not to be provoked by such remarks, and would patiently point out that what Yugoslavia was experiencing was an interim period. No one had ever promised instant paradise. He had never heard any leading communist promise that. 'Not even you and Alex,' he would joke gently, 'promised that.'

'Well, no one is asking for instant paradise, as you call it. But don't you think a little instant justice is long overdue?' No one could be quite as provocative as Olga when she wished!

He learned to contain his enthusiasm for Tito in her presence. Usually she would listen to his comments about the communist leader in silence. On the rare instances that she did respond, however, the resulting fracas could leave them both white-faced and furious with each other.

'Why can't he act with more restraint?' she would ask. 'He is the leader of an egalitarian socialist state. He is not a king! Why does he try to act as though he were? Not even king! He is acting as though he was an emperor! It is ridiculous!'

The truth of many of her complaints did not, of course, make them any more palatable. The idea of special stores available only to top officials in the party left Stevan himself feeling uneasy, especially at a time when the people themselves were suffering obvious deprivation as a result not only of the wartime occupation but, unfortunately, of the subsequent plundering by the communists.

In his heart, also, he wished that the marshal had at least let a little more time pass before personally acquiring the vast estates and hunting grounds in Karadjordjevo and Belje. Even under the royal regime these areas had been considered the property of the state. When he and Olga were invited to join one of the president's hunting parties and she refused to attend, Stevan had had to invent a plausible excuse. He was furious with his wife. She remained unrepentant.

There was also the problem of rumblings amongst the Serbs about the comparatively gentle treatment extended to Zagreb, the capital of Croatia, compared to the bloody activities that had taken place in Belgrade immediately after the liberation. The truth was, Croatia had shown as much enthusiasm for its new masters as it had for the fascists. The enthusiasm was in part, of course, for the new leader of the country who had, after all, been born in Zagorje, the heart of nationalism in Croatia. Although Stevan did not believe Tito to be anything other than an international communist, again in his heart he could not help thinking of the crowds he had seen in Zagreb welcoming the Germans while Belgrade was still burning. He kept silent, but at home, Olga did not. Nor did Alex, so busy at the time with the rebuilding of Belgrade. But during his rare visits to their home (Stevan suspected that the big man also disapproved of their lifestyle) Alex could not help grumbling about the Serbian 'bloodbath'. 'Does it pay, then, to be a traitor?' he would ask enigmatically.

Yet despite the problems, the embarrassments, the ambiguities, those first few months of the liberation undoubtedly were amongst the happiest of Stevan's life. For all their misunderstandings and frequent quarrels, he loved his wife with all his heart. Always had, he would tell himself ruefully. Always would. It was a great joy to return home and find her waiting for him at the end of a long hard day. A joy to go to sleep holding her tightly in his arms. And he was enjoying his new work which now mainly centred around the Department of Agitation and Propaganda. He also enjoyed, he had to admit to himself, his new status as a close associate and friend of the marshal. He was not fully sure as yet that 'power corrupts' but was certainly ready to admit to himself that it was indeed heady. The truth was, things could have been so different. Had fate not kept him so close to Tito's side he could, he well realized, today be a man without a country, like David Ristić who, the secret police had informed him, was now residing in Switzerland. Stevan was glad his old friend had survived. But the thought that he too might have been fool enough to follow the Allied cause at the beginning of the war brought with it a feeling of chill. What a young fool he had been in those days. What an idiotic young fool. Had he followed his own inclinations God only knew where he would be today. Well, fate had dictated otherwise. It had led him into the iron arms of the Communist Party, for which he must always be grateful. God willing, he thought without irony, he would repay that wonderful stroke of luck by unwavering dedication to the Party and to Tito, the man who led it within Yugoslavia. And should Olga or Alex or anyone else complain about actions taken by the Party or about the direction it might or might not be taking, he, Stevan, need only remind himself of the manner in which the decadent capitalist imperialist states of Britain and the United States had treated their adherents within the Chetnik movement. And that, he would think to himself with a chuckle, should be enough to ensure his fidelity to the Party that had given him so much.

It was unfortunate that Tito should be on a visit to Poland when news was received that after some eighteen months of intensive search Ranković's secret police had at last captured General Mihailović in the mountains near Vishegrad.

'I would give anything to have seen Tito's face when he received the news,' Stevan exclaimed excitedly to Olga late one evening in May 1946. No need to tell her that the extensive protection that had been given the general by most of the population had been a constant thorn in Tito's side ever since they had attained victory.

They had just retired to their large bedroom. Stevan was sprawled out on the comfortable little settee, watching his wife as she sat in front of the dressing table, idly brushing her hair. They had come to a tacit agreement over the past few months not to discuss anything over the dinner table other than trivia. Ranković's ubiquitous spies were everywhere and God only knew how many of their servants were on his payroll, even though Olga, to Stevan's secret chagrin, had brought Stana Radović over from her mother's house to manage their household. 'She knows who can be trusted,' she had said enigmatically to her husband's mild suggestion that Stana might be more useful to Alex and Mrs Miletić. He did not press the point, knowing how grateful he should be to the stern old mountain woman for her fierce protection of Olga immediately after the war. It was simply that he could not forget the contemptuous way she used to look at him in the old days when he was courting Olga; nor did he really feel comfortable even today when those hooded, guarded eyes rested upon him from time to time.

Olga stopped brushing her hair and frowned into the mirror. 'So they've finally found him,' she said. 'Well, I hope they have enough sense to let him go. They cannot allow him to remain in the country, of course. Banishment is the answer, to the United States perhaps. I understand the Americans tried to persuade him to leave the country months ago, offered him asylum.'

Stevan sat up straight and stared at her. 'Are you mad?' he asked. 'Let him go? You expect *Tito* to let that traitor go?'

The dark eyes met his in the mirror. She slowly resumed brushing her silky hair. 'Stevan,' she said with infinite patience, 'must you pretend with *me*? I know the story too well, my dear. If I heard it once I heard it a hundred times, right through the war.' She put the brush down, ran her hands through the short, straight locks and swung around to look at him directly. 'It was a mania with Kurt. "We *must* capture Mihailović" he kept saying. "He is our biggest danger in this country. The communists are a mere nuisance".'

There was a brief silence.

'Kurt,' Stevan said finally. Added slowly. 'So his name was Kurt.'

She shrugged. 'I never told you?'

'Being with him ... it must have been terrible for you. I know how terrible it must have been. God only knows, they were such brutes, the Nazis. Brutes!'

'Kurt? A Nazi? No, no. I could never have coped with a Nazi. Not even for the Party. He was a regular army officer. I think he detested the Nazis as much as anyone. He most certainly loathed the SS. Feared them, too, I suspect.'

His heart began to beat rapidly, painfully; there was a roaring, a rushing in his ears as he sat as though frozen on that ridiculous little settee, staring at her. 'You...' He swallowed, his throat was quite dry. 'You did not hate him, then?'

'Kurt? Hate him? Of course not.' She stood up and tightened the belt around the cream-coloured, satin dressing gown. 'Hadn't you better undress? It will be another busy day tomorrow.' She moved over to the huge double bed, sat down and smiled at him.

'Stupid of me,' he said slowly. 'I always thought you must have loathed him.'

'Loathed whom?' Her expression was one of frank puzzlement. After a moment she nodded. 'Oh. Kurt! No, no. Why should I have loathed him? Most of the Germans were brutes. I grant you that, Stevan. But many of them were decent human beings, just like the rest of us. That's why I chose him. He seemed to be decent. Quite kind, really. He was very kind to mother. No, no. He was quite a decent man. Attractive. He had connections in the right places. Otherwise I could never have done it.' She laughed. 'Not even for the Party. Not even for . . . Stevan?'

He had leaped to his feet and was striding towards the door, aware that if he stayed in that room one instant longer he would strike out at her. Hit her, hit her, hit her . . .

'What is it, Stevan? Where are you going?' she asked sharply.

He paused in the doorway for one brief moment and gave her a look of pure hatred. 'Where am I going?' he almost snarled. 'I'm going to get drunk, my dear Olga. I am going to get very, very drunk.' He stalked out, slamming the door viciously behind him.

* * *

Comrade Bogdan Bošković gave a deep sigh and refilled his brandy glass from the half-empty bottle in front of him. He was alone. All alone in The Red Banner restaurant. The rest of the staff had departed hours ago. But he could not go home. Every night it was the same. After all these years, he still hated returning to that silent apartment. Would it always be haunted by Rachel's presence? He tried to put off returning to it until the small hours of the morning when he would fall onto the bed in a drunken stupor.

The time was coming, he realized, when he would have to take action of one kind or another. Yes, yes, the time was undoubtedly coming when he would have to make an irrevocable decision. Should he stay in Yugoslavia and further ingratiate himself with the Party? Rid himself of this obsession with finding Rachel who, he had been assured a thousand times, was undoubtedly dead, a victim of one of those terrible camps that had flourished under the Nazi flag? Should he remain in Belgrade? Make an effort to find some comely little comrade with whom, he thought sentimentally, he could settle down. Someone who would welcome him of an evening, give him children, take care of him.

Or should he get out of the country, via a route he had planned for himself 'just in case', even before the communists took power? Although he had tried to allow for every contingency, the ascendancy of the communists within Yugoslavia had come as something of a shock. The truth was, as he well knew, that although the Germans had undoubtedly considered Tito and his partisans to be something of a nuisance and were always pleased to destroy any group of Bolsheviks they could get their hands on, their main target, the one who had caused them endless trouble, was Mihailović. They had, in fact, terrorized the whole population of Belgrade, let alone the country, in an effort to force the people to withdraw their support from the Chetniks. It had simply never occurred to Bogdan that the Allies would not reward the general accordingly at the end of the war. Thank God that the instinct for survival that was always with him had made him at one point during the war ask himself why, if he was endangering himself by handing over snippets of gossip he heard from his German friends or overheard in the restaurant to the Chetniks, he should not cover himself twice, as it were, by handing the same information over to the communists?

How ironic life was. Right up until the very last moment he had sat almost in the same spot, staring at a snapshot of himself taken a few years before the war on a cycling trip. On one side of him stood Stevan Matić, on the other David Ristić. It had not been until the communists actually entered the outskirts of the city that he had made the decision, risen, gone into the kitchen, returned with some scissors, cut off the figure of David Ristić and carefully torn it into small pieces. Yet his memory had been unable to rid itself of the candid face of his old friend as it had a moment previously stared at him from the faded photograph. After a moment he had again returned to the kitchen, this time bringing back with him a small pot of glue. He had carefully patched the pieces of David's likeness together again and stuffed it into the back of his wallet.

Perhaps the instinctive gesture had been providential? Perhaps, after all he was meant to join his old friend, David, in the Western world which, he suspected, would be much more to his liking anyway. No man wished to leave his country, but the truth was that life under the communists was turning out to be not exactly a bowl of roses. It was, in fact, not only uncertain and dangerous, but even worse. It was spartan in the extreme. It was all very well if you were someone like Stevan, who had had the good luck to really land on his feet, grab himself a slice of the good life he had always been used to. But when you were merely a poor worker under suspicion for close association with the Germans, even though he had shown them the snapshot of himself with the well-known Comrade Matić, even though he had proved he was supplying them with intelligence during the war and had, in fact, been one of the first to join the partisans the moment they entered Belgrade, there was still that air of belligerence they effected every time they entered the restaurant to check on this or check on that. He simply did not feel entirely safe with them, to be honestly truthful.

His drunken musings were suddenly interrupted by a loud banging on the front door. For a moment he sat quite still, frozen with fear, remembering a similar loud banging on his apartment door that had culminated in the disappearance of Rachel. It was only when he heard Stevan's voice that he was able to rouse himself.

'Bogdan! Are you there, Bogdan? It's me, Stevan! Open up! It's me, Stevan!'

'Stevan! There is something wrong? What is it?' His friend stood in the entrance to the restaurant, his face pale, distraught almost, beneath the dim light that shone in from the street.

'Something wrong? No, no. Not a thing. It's just, I was just passing by, you see. Remembered you saying you often worked late. Thought I would drop in. Say hello.'

'I could not be more pleased, Stevan. Come in, come in. I was just about to stop work and have a little nightcap, you understand. Thought I would just have a little nightcap to relax me, you know, before going home. Perhaps you would join me?'

'Nothing I'd enjoy more, Bošković.'

Daylight was beginning to penetrate the restaurant by the time Stevan left. Or at least, by the time he was carried out. Bogdan had been forced to call his home and suggest they send his car, his chauffeur, to pick him up, before returning to his own apartment, where he threw himself on the bed, gazed up at the ceiling and tried to cope with the distinctly unpleasant sensation of fear which he could not seem to dismiss.

He was now quite sober. Very sober indeed.

What, he kept asking himself, would Stevan remember of their conversation? Would he remember anything at all? Probably not. They had both drunk so much. Yet Bogdan knew how often he could remember with sharp and perfect clarity the events of a whole evening when he had drunk himself into a stupor. Other times he could not recall a thing – more often than not he could not recall a thing! Surely Stevan would not remember anything? Yet if he did? Well, was it *really* so bad?

There had been the sentimental remembrance of days long past. School days, days of their early manhood. Nothing there. That had been all right. But then they had begun to talk of the great partisan victory, of the subsequent takeover by the communist government in Yugoslavia.

'Tell me, Bošković, I mean tell me honestly,' Stevan had

insisted, 'how do you think we are doing? How do you think we've done, so far?' He had started to chuckle as Bogdan launched into a veritable landslide of praise for the new order and held up his hand. 'Come on, Bogdan, fellow. It is me, Stevan, you are talking to. We have made mistakes, let me be the first to admit it. For heaven's sake, you don't have to be careful with me. If you and I cannot be honest with each other, then who can?'

Which had led to his cautious comment that the handling of the economy might, well, might not be all that could be desired. 'The shortage of food, you understand, Stevan. We are not used to that in Yugoslavia. Why, even under the Germans, expensive, to be sure, but...'

All of which had been extremely well received. Stevan had nodded, sighed, agreed. He felt that the agricultural industry should have either been left alone, or handled with extreme caution. It was the Soviets, really, with their damned insistence that Yugoslavia follow in *their* footsteps, whether those footsteps had been successful or, as the whole world knew, spectacularly unsuccessful, so far as agriculture was concerned.

'Now,' he had added, 'our prisons are overflowing with peasants ... damn it, we can't arrest *all* of them. We are trying, though, to control the bureaucracy. But it's like a giant octopus. You cut off a tentacle, turn your attention to another one, and the first one grows back.'

Which had led to even more cautious criticism of their Soviet friends. All extremely well received. Which had led to Bogdan's big mistake.

'Yes, yes,' Stevan had said. 'We still have many problems, no doubt about it. But, tell me, Bošković, this is a popular restaurant. You must hear a few things. You must overhear what people really think. What are they saying?' He sat back with a tolerant smile.

How he's changed, Bogdan thought, from the days before the war. No longer slender, Stevan had put on weight, acquired a slight paunch since leaving the arduous life of a guerrilla fighter for the comforts of Belgrade. His face, too, had undergone an undefined transformation, had coarsened with age, with experience. The mouth had hardened, the eyes tended not to look directly at you. As a matter of fact...

'Come on, come on.' Stevan had interrupted his flow of thought. 'What are our people really saying, Bogdan?'

'Well, they say, they whisper,' he added virtuously, 'they know they are not allowed to speak about wartime events. They know it is illegal, you see, yet, they whisper.'

'Yes, yes, go on.'

'The *Ustaši* thing. The holocaust. They wanted Pavelić's head you know.'

'Can we help that? The British had him, handed him over to the Vatican. Can we help that? Of course he had friends in very high places indeed inside the Vatican. And Stepinac! At least we gave them Archbishop Stepinac's head on a platter. What more do they want?'

'But they say he was not the one who ... I mean ... the sin of omission, yes. He could have done something to stop those criminals, you know. How many did they prove he saved at the trial? Eight was it? Ten? Out of a million Serbs and Jews!'

Stevan chuckled. 'That's what happens in a war. You see what you want to see!'

'And what they say. Not that *I* agree, mind you. No, no. They say that many of the partisans who liberated us, they say many of them were *Ustaši* criminals who overnight put on the partisan uniform and claimed to be heroes. Over a million Serbs were murdered by these ghouls and yet–'

'Nonsense.' Stevan frowned. 'No more than seven-hundred and fifty thousand. I know that for a fact. I've seen the German records myself. Where do they get all this nonsense?'

Bogdan was still carried away.

'And they ask. They ask "Why are the Croats still allowed to keep the borders given them by the Germans?" There is a lot of concern about that, Stevan. A lot of concern.'

Stevan nodded sympathetically and sighed. 'Our people

are so simple-minded. Don't they understand? Under communism, as the marshal points out time and time again, Yugoslavia will remain one country united forever. Borders are no longer relevant. In the name of brotherhood and unity, we–'

'Another thing. They want those crimes. All those *Ustaši* crimes, you know? They want them all exposed. They want ... well, you see how the German people are made to pay for *their* government's crimes. Our people feel the Croats should also be made to at least *look at*, at least *acknowledge*, what was done in *their* name. Let them understand and apologize and then maybe ...'

'A great contribution to unity *that* would be. A great contribution to brotherhood!' Stevan shook his head with resigned good humour.

'Well, that's what they say.'

'Simple-minded. So simple-minded.'

'And they ask, why always the Serbs? So many murdered by the Germans and their gangster allies. So many killed while the Croats and Slovenes collaborated and worse. They murdered and tortured and mutilated our people, our Serbian women, our children. Terrible things. You know the terrible things they did. And where is the world? our people ask. The world is crying out about the terrible things done to the Jewish people and so it should, but what about the Serbs? Why does the world turn its head away from the plight of the Serbs, the terrible things done to the Serbs?'

Stevan reached for the brandy bottle, filled both glasses and drained his own. 'Yes, yes. I understand, Bogdan. I understand what you are saying. Our people went through a terrible time. No doubt about that.'

Bogdan took a deep gulp from his own glass and gazed into it moodily. About to continue, he hesitated. A brief warning stab of self-preservation made him hesitate. Why was he babbling away like this? He looked up to meet Stevan's tolerant gaze and found himself rushing on. 'There is this *rage*, Stevan. This simmering rage. Why have the

Allies done this to us, they ask? We were the first ones to fight Hitler, and where has it brought us? And how many of our people died protecting Allied airmen? Does that mean nothing? It's what they ask again and again. Why have the Allies deserted us? Was Nedić right, after all? Is it that Churchill cares for nothing except his empire? And, of course, they listen to the Russians. You know what the Russians say? It was Mihailović, they say, *who* did all the fighting before *we* came. But we were the ones who liberated you. Without us your partisans would have been nowhere. And they add,' he went on with a puzzled look, 'we and Stalin's Englishmen. Without Stalin's Englishmen and us your partisans would have been nowhere. Whatever that means.' He frowned, momentarily lost in thought. 'But it's the people, you see. The same refrain, again and again. Why us? First the criminal Croat Pavelić and his gang of murderers set free, and now this Croat gangster Tito and his gang of criminals who–' He stopped abruptly, realized too late.

Do you understand what we've done, Stevan? We've brought a gang of criminals to power. Don't you understand what we've done? Olga's constant lament rang shrilly in Stevan's ears. He reached up to cover them, found himself peering into the scared yellow eyes of Bogdan.

'What was that you just said?' The lazy, half-smile was gone, the faded dark eyes had narrowed into such a malevolent glare that the coward sitting opposite him shrunk back.

'No, no. Not me, Stevan. *I* didn't say it. It's the people. I didn't . . . not me . . . not me . . .'

But Matić had already reached into his pocket, pulled out a small pistol and was pointing it directly at Bogdan's panic-stricken heart. 'Explain yourself, fellow! You'd better explain that, fellow, or . . .' Mercifully he had suddenly slumped forward, knocking over Bogdan's half-empty glass of brandy and an empty bottle which fell to the floor and rolled under a nearby table.

Comrade Stevan Matić had passed out cold. But what

would he remember when he came-to? Just how much was he going to remember?

*   *   *

The months David had spent at the Graduate Institute of International Studies in Geneva had been tumultuous. Despite the intransigence of both the Soviets and the Yugoslav communists during those first few months after the war, when it became apparent that they considered, as one of his friends put it, 'all agreements made by the Allies to have been written in stone, while their own commitments are infinitely fluid', the sympathies of many students seemed to lie with the communists. Even the American students, he noted with disgust. Even after Tito had ordered American planes over Yugoslav territory shot down with the resultant loss of American lives. What kind of people are they, he asked himself?

'There is definite proof available that the Chetniks collaborated,' one young American announced one day apropos of nothing during a class on international law. David had leapt to his feet.

'With Allies such as *you*,' he shouted, 'I wish to God we *had* collaborated. I wish to God we had!' At least he had enjoyed the resultant uproar, had watched with satisfaction as his plump professor wrung his hands. 'Gentlemen! Gentlemen! This is an academic institution, not a house of parliament.'

On the whole he enjoyed his studies, enjoyed the endless political discussions and arguments, the vital life that existed within the university, despite the restlessness he could not seem to control. Whether it was a result of the endless movement during the war when he had rarely laid his head down on the same spot for more than a few nights at a time, or of the restless, violent dreams or the bad headaches caused by pieces of shrapnel that still remained embedded in the side of his head, he was not sure, but he found he simply could not settle down at any one of the small rooming houses in Geneva. He changed his place of residence almost monthly.

And, of course, there was the bitterness, the deep sense of betrayal that all of the Chetniks he came in contact with during his stay in Switzerland experienced. He wondered whether it would ever be possible for him to fully trust anyone in this world ever again.

He worried about his family, although he had managed to learn through the connections the Yugoslav émigrés established with sympathizers who had remained in his country that his aunt and his two sisters had at least survived. Of Irina he learned only that the communists had 'thrown out' all white Russians and German residents it considered had collaborated during the war. He also learned with some bitterness that the term 'collaborator' was applied very loosely by the new rulers of his country.

David had not agreed with General Mihailović's decision to remain inside Yugoslavia. He believed he should have escaped, perhaps into Greece, where he could have kept up a military fight against the new totalitarians, or at least accepted the American offer of asylum, so that he could do his best to ensure that the free world knew the truth about what had taken place in his country during the war. The general, however, had taken the attitude that nothing had really changed. To him the communists were no different in character from the fascists. They were all international outlaws who must be driven from his country; nothing could convince him to do anything other than remain with his people and direct all of his efforts towards their eventual liberation.

David was prepared for the news he received one morning in May 1946, that the communists had finally captured that brave, decent warrior. What was to come as a pleasant surprise, what he had not expected, was the worldwide response from men and women of conscience to the announcement from the communists that they intended to 'give Mihailović a fair trial and then shoot him!'

Suddenly the questions began. Suddenly, those American

and British officers who had been with the Chetniks and observed with their own eyes what had gone on, found they could no longer remain silent whether or not they incurred their government's wrath. Almost simultaneously they burst free of the constraints they claimed their governments had placed upon them during the war and began to tell the truth as they themselves had witnessed it, to relate their personal experiences.

'If Mihailović is a traitor then so am I,' cried one British officer with uncharacteristic emotion. Others rushed into print to express the bewilderment and shame they had felt when forced to present Mihailović with streams of contradictory instructions from their headquarters in London and the Middle East, of their embarrassment when so many promises of aid to the general were left unfulfilled.

Sitting in his small room with his Chetnik friends, David searched through the international press in order to gauge world reaction to the capture of Mihailović, to the announcement that he would be executed as a traitor.

From the London *Time and Tide* came Rebecca West's lengthy article in which she referred to Churchill's policy in Yugoslavia as 'a great man's moment of imbecility' and concluded that: *This is a senseless story. Or is it, on the contrary, a story disconcerting in the glimpses of a sense as cold as steel?'*

There was total agreement among the Serbs with the American journalist David Martin's thoughtful analysis and comment that: *In the case of the British foreign office, there was a marked bias against Mihailović from the beginning.* Yes indeed! *But why?* The questions kept coming. A great outcry from the liberal conscience of the world. If Mihailović and his Chetniks had been collaborators, only fighting the communists, why were they not well supplied with war *matériel* by the Germans? Why was this an army in rags from beginning to end, fighting almost with bare hands, freezing and hungry in the mountains when, according to their accusers, they could have been well fed, well armed by the fascists? Why, when it could not be denied that Mihailović was the first man in Europe to defy Hitler, would he throw in his lot with the fascists towards the end of the war, when it was obvious the latter were losing?

The most heartening news came from the United States where five hundred or so American airmen, joined by Canadians, marched on Washington and demanded that pressure be brought to bear upon the communist government in Yugoslavia to give the general a truly fair trial. Their demand was simple enough: that they be allowed to go to Belgrade as witnesses for the defence.

'What a hope,' David said. 'But thank God there are still such honest men here in the West.'

Despite, or perhaps because of, the ominous silence from Belgrade to the request from the American government that the Allied officers who had served with or been rescued by the Chetniks be allowed to give evidence at his trial, a committee for a fair trial for Draža Mihailović was formed in New York, made up of prominent American citizens who accepted depositions from American and British officers who had been attached to General Mihailović's headquarters; former members of the American military mission attached to Marshal Tito's headquarters; and former members of the army air forces grounded and saved by Chetniks in occupied Yugoslavia.

The committee duly reported its findings that there was no contradiction nor conflict in the depositions received from the missions with Mihailović and the mission with Tito. The evidence, which included facts, names and figures, completely supported the conclusion that General Mihailović not only did not collaborate with the Germans, but had desperately fought them to the last day of their occupation of the Balkans.

The real crime of which General Mihailović is accused is that, in the minds of eighty per cent of the Yugoslav population, he became and remains the symbol of the simple, sturdy Yugoslav peasant resistance to tyranny, foreign or domestic, concluded Colonel Robert McDowell, leader of the last American military mission to Mihailović.

All of which, of course, made no whit of difference to

what went on in Belgrade, where an obviously bewildered and exhausted Mihailović was duly dragged before his accusers.

It is known on good authority, reported the *New York Times*, *'that he was subjected to torture. More was at stake in Belgrade than the life of the one-time Serbian hero, who was the first man in Yugoslavia to lead a well-organized resistance to the Nazis. Tito's government was also on trial. By the verdict it too has been found guilty.'*

The General was shot on the 17th of July, 1946.

And so the murder of Draža Mihailović becomes, like the murder of Jeanne d'Arc, a case for the English conscience, wrote Robert Speaight.

From French writer Georges Bernanos came a cry from the heart: *I am not going to pray for this world any longer, as it sits crouched on the atomic bomb, yellow with hatred, with its tongue babbling of social justice and its heart devoid of love.*

Incongruously a letter that appeared in a Hamburg newspaper from a German soldier who had served in Belgrade during the war: *If the Chetniks were collaborating with us* he asked with genuine puzzlement, *why were we killing so many of them?*

The last word, however, was to come from David Courtney who wrote in the *Palestine Post*: *Bit by bit a crazed world seems bent on finishing Adolf Hitler's job for him.*

4

Some time later Stevan was to look back and try to pinpoint the beginning. At what point had the pure happiness he had experienced during the first months of his marriage begun to sour? There must have been a beginning. When was it?

There had been the reconciliation after she had told him about her German lover, Kurt. 'But of course I never loved him,' she had cried. 'Never! Yet how could I hate him? He agonized over the killing his people were responsible for. He was so kind when mother became ill. And all the time I was using him, pretending to care for him when all I cared about was the information I could get from him for the Party. Hate him? No, no. I did not love him, but if I hated anyone it was myself.'

Stevan had not been able to swallow all of the bitterness, all of the violent jealousy that had racked him that night he had rushed out and drunk himself into a stupor with that traitor Bošković, who must have been planning to defect to the West even as he drank with him, while pretending warm friendship for him and loyalty to the Party. He only wished he could remember more of what they had talked about that night. If only he could remember. But most of it was simply a haze.

Was it the show-trial Tito had insisted on holding with Mihailović as the star attraction? The trial had caused worldwide revulsion, but Tito had insisted that would soon pass. 'People forget things,' he insisted. 'What they *will* remember,' he had added with grim satisfaction, 'is that Mihailović was found guilty and shot because he was a fascist traitor. *That* is what will go into the history books. *That* is what they will remember.'

Olga had been tearful. 'He is copying Stalin,' she had said. 'That's the way Stalin destroyed his enemies.'

'But of course,' Stevan had exclaimed angrily. 'He is Stalin's best student. Isn't that what you and Alex wanted?'

She had burst into loud sobs and rushed out of the room, leaving him frustrated, bewildered.

Then there had been the day Mihailović had been shot. He had rushed home after the urgent call from Stana Radović to find his wife sitting in front of the fire, wrapped in an old bath robe, shivering, on a warm July day.

'What have we done?' she kept asking. 'Did we have to *murder* him, Oh, Stevan, I so longed for us to be *better*. Don't you understand?'

No. As a matter of fact he did not understand. They had *won*, for God's sake. They had fought an admittedly dirty war, no one had suffered more than he, because of the dirtiness of that war, because of that stupid bourgeois morality that Olga and her brother had ridiculed so, that it had taken him so long to get rid of. And now, when he had *finally* come to realize what the world was really all about, when he had *finally* managed to rid himself of those ridiculous bourgeois attitudes well, they were not happy with *that*, either! Neither of them. He knew quite well that Alex and Olga discussed him behind his back. They did not agree with his disillusionment with the Soviets, for one thing. But then they did not have his access to the top echelons of the Party, were not aware of the grave concern the Central Committee was expressing about the Soviet tendency to assume that Yugoslavia was no more than an extension of the Soviet Union, that its considerable resources existed solely for the purpose of advancing the interests of the first socialist state.

They even had an excuse for the arrogant behaviour of the Soviets towards the population in general. 'This is just a stage they are going through,' big Alex had explained. 'They have never had anything before, you see. Perhaps it will even take another generation before we see the true result of Stalin's great purpose.'

Exasperating!

And when had Olga begun the secret drinking? Why had it taken him so long to find out? Stana Radović, no doubt! That fierce old mountain hag had no doubt had a part in deceiving him about what was going on when he wasn't around.

Mira! Had Olga found out about Mira? Who could blame him? To face a tearful and accusing wife, forever complaining about the betrayal of the revolution when, for God's sake, they had *won*, hadn't they? Having to face that after a truly difficult day spent trying to walk a fine line between the traps Party members were forever setting each other ... my God ... what a suspicious lot they were! And they had always envied his close relationship with Tito. They were dying to catch him out in something, anything...

So who could blame him, really? Brisk, cheerful, yet soft, pliable and rounded Comrade Mira, always ready to start his day off at the office with a joke and a laugh. Always so devoted, always ready with a word to soothe, to flatter, to build a comrade up for God's sake, not make him feel it was his entire responsibility for letting the whole world down.

Mira, of course, had proven not to be so pliable as she seemed on the surface. God! How was it possible for a woman to be so soft on the outside, yet hard as steel on the inside? It had taken every ounce of prestige and power he possessed to wriggle out of that one. Had she really expected him to divorce Olga for her? As though he would *ever* divorce Olga. It had taken enough pain and effort for him to win her in the first place.

These days when he reached his office it was just not with the same enthusiasm he had started out with, when was it? Almost three years ago! He could not believe time could have passed so quickly. Unbelievable!

Unbelievable! And so was the panic and confusion that greeted him that morning when he arrived at his large, airy office. For one thing, there was a message that the president of the republic wished to see him. Now! Immediately!

He rushed over to Tito's home on Rumanian Street, where he liked to conduct his day-to-day business and was hurriedly ushered up the staircase by an aide, into his spacious study. The marshal had been waiting for his arrival, so he was told.

Tito was sitting behind his desk in a corner of the study, his face half-hidden by the hand covering his forehead. Stevan walked up to the desk and stood there, a little disconcerted as the marshal lifted his head and looked straight at him, yet at the same time seemed to look straight through him.

'You sent for me?' he asked softly, trying to hide the shock he felt at the marshal's appearance, which reminded him of the time following the German fourth offensive, when they had only just survived that murderous trip over Mount Prenj, when Tito had seemed to age overnight. This morning, too, his skin was pale, puffy. There were dark smudges beneath his eyes. Grey was beginning once more to show through the hair he had taken to dyeing. He looked overweight, unhealthy.

To Stevan's consternation, although the blue eyes seemed to remain focused on him, the marshal made no acknowledgment at all of his presence. Instead he began to whisper, seemingly to himself, a soft, hissing stream of words that Stevan could make neither head nor tale of, except for the word 'Meshetov' that kept emerging hoarsely and clearly.

Just as he was about to consider calling for help, Tito sat up straight and said loudly: 'He's sent Meshetov, you see.' He stood up abruptly, came around from behind his desk, and began to pace up and down the room. Stevan watched him, trying to conceal his bewilderment, concentrating instead on the startling array of medals that covered the beautifully tailored jacket of one of the remarkable assortment of uniforms the marshal maintained. How *he* loved and cherished those medals! How jealously he collected and guarded them...

He was talking about the incorrect attitude of the Soviets. Right from the start. Right from the very start they had done little other than try to grab the whole of Yugoslavia's natural resources for themselves, had done their level best to prevent the country from developing and expanding its own industries. *You have heard them, Stevan, you have heard them yourself! Why does Yugoslavia need heavy industry? You know, comrade, that everything you could possibly need we have in the Urals!* He had stopped the restless pacing and stood in front of Stevan, imitating the slurred, ill-educated voice of one of the Soviets they both knew well.

'They want to leave us nothing! We are not even to make decisions concerning our own iron and steel, our own shipping industry! By God! Do you know their latest proposition is that they set up a joint Soviet-Yugoslav bank? By God! They want to take over our sovereignty in finance and foreign exchange even. Did you know that, Stevan? Do you know that?

'And their *spies*. Their spies have infiltrated every department, every administrative section, the police, the military, all *infected* with Soviet spies. Spying on *us*. Spying on their comrades! And now, because of my protests, because of my resistance to this complete Soviet takeover of our country, Meshetov! *He* sent him! I know it. *He* has sent him!'

Once again Stevan stared at him blankly, relieved at least that the marshal seemed to be returning to his normal self, seemed to have a grasp on what was going on around him.

'Meshetov?' he asked after a moment. 'I don't seem to...'

'In Moscow. In the thirties. During the time of the purges, you understand? One day there would be a comrade, a friend, in good standing, you understand? In good standing with the Party. Impeccable background. Impeccable Party credentials. And then suddenly Meshetov...' He spoke the name with a mixture of such loathing and fear that again, Stevan could only stare at him.

His voice once more had dropped to a hoarse whisper. 'Meshetov! That grinning, leering face. That smile, that terrible smile, and another comrade gone. *Gone*. Just like that. And now *he* has sent him *here*. To *me*. Comrade Stalin would be *so* pleased if I would attend the next Cominform meeting in the Ukraine! They think *I* don't know what they are up to? Oh, they are cunning! *He* is cunning! An unfortunate accident, is what they would call it. Marshal Tito fell out of a window! Or fell from his horse in a hunting accident! By God! They think I don't know what they are up to?'

He stared hard at a Stevan, who had gone suddenly pale.

'My God! Is it true? Would they be so brazen?' A sudden fear took hold of him, left his throat dry. 'But then they could attempt something *here*, here in our own country. My God! There are enough of them here.'

Tito's pale eyes glazed over and he passed a visibly trembling hand over his well-groomed hair. 'Well,' he said, 'I would rather it happened here. If I must be killed, at least let it be in my own country. Go to the Ukraine? After seeing Meshetov? Never!'

Stevan shook his head, unable to find appropriate words to help the marshal. In fact he had not realized before that the problems with the Soviets had moved from the area of profound but manageable differences into the murky realm of crises.

Tito dismissed him shortly afterwards, with a friendly pat on the shoulder, although the blue eyes had hardened as he asked after Stevan's wife. He had not seen her at *any* of the little social events he arranged from time to time with his closest comrades from wartime.

Stevan, relieved that Tito seemed merely to have needed him as a sounding board, had recovered, at least outwardly, his equilibrium, felt himself nevertheless redden. Despite his entreaties, threats and shouts, Olga had steadfastly refused to accompany him to any of what she called 'the bourgeois activities of the new court'.

He muttered something about her not having been very well lately and became aware that the marshal's eyes had softened and were now expressing something like amusement. 'You mean she has heard something about a young lady called Mira?' he asked with a smile. He laughed out loud as Stevan began to stutter, to deny. 'She'll get over it,' he assured him. 'Women get over these things.'

Returning to his office he found his staff still in something of an uproar because of an earlier visit by the Soviet 'expert' in the field of agitation and propaganda. Comrade Aleksei Bukovsky, Stevan thought with a sigh as he tried to soothe the several ruffled feathers, might or might not be an expert on propaganda. He most certainly, however, must be the world's foremost expert on agitation! He made these fleeting appearances from time to time at Stevan's office, made sarcastic if not very useful comments about the quality of the staff's work, then strode out, leaving in his wake a great deal of agitation. It often took a week or so for Stevan to get his resentful staff back on track.

What preoccupied him throughout the day, however, was not the unscheduled appearance of Comrade Bukovsky so much as the impression he retained of Tito. Although the marshal had seemed to be in revived spirits when Stevan left him, he still looked both tired and ill. Stevan could not help worrying. He made a quick decision to drop by and see Nikola Djerdja that evening. Sound him out, if nothing else, on what he thought about the marshal's state of mind, his health.

Djerdja, sitting in the living room of the same modest apartment he had lived in with his wife before the war, did not seem too concerned about the state of the marshal's health.

'He is lonely,' he said, referring to Zdenka's untimely death the previous year. He smiled. 'I understand steps have been taken to bring a new young woman into his life. I think it will make the world of difference.'

'Lonely? But he has two sons. Surely...'

'Well, you know, the first one is from his first wife,

Pelagia. Not a very happy marriage. The boy was neglected by both parents. Not that one can blame Tito. His life has been the Party. There was no time to be a father. Then, of course, Herta's son ... well, you know Herta, she is still bitter over the way she feels he treated her. So, you see, there is bitterness on the part of both sons. Hardly conducive to alleviating loneliness. No, no. I think once he has got used to this new young woman, he will be his old self again. Have you met her? A good, modest Serbian girl. Name of Jovanka.'

Stevan nodded, stirred uneasily. Somehow Olga had heard of the efforts of certain Party officials to find someone as a suitable companion for the marshal.

'And where did Marx write that Party officials should act as procurers for their leader?' she had asked bitterly, precipitating yet another row. It did not help that Stevan *had* met Jovanka. A quiet, extremely attractive girl, she had been enticed into the marshal's household 'to manage things', like a lamb led to the slaughter. Personally, he *did* feel slightly uneasy about the arrangement.

Best not to think about these things.

'Have you met a man called Meshetov?' he asked Nikola, who had lit a pipe and now settled in his comfortable chair with a contented sigh.

'Meshetov? Yes, yes. He arrived recently from Moscow. Quite an affable kind of man. I had a chat with him. It seems Stalin would like to see the marshal attend the next Cominform meeting. It's being held in the Ukraine, you know. I think it might be a good idea.' Djerdja frowned, his comfortable line of thought disturbed. 'Something needs to be done to straighten out our problems. There have been too many misunderstandings. As you know.'

Stevan nodded. 'Do you think the Soviets are right? *Is* it our fault?'

'Our fault? Of course not. For my own part I'd certainly like to have some explanation about that agreement Stalin reached at Yalta with the imperialists. You know as well as I do that communist nations do not indulge in that dirty 'sphere of influence' game. Yet there it is. It is clear enough. An agreement that Britain and the Soviet Union should retain a fifty-fifty sphere of interest in Yugoslavia. Of course, it is my opinion that Stalin meant to break that dirty little contract as soon as he decently could. Agreements made with the imperialists are hardly things one needs to honour. But still, the whole matter is disturbing. I think the marshal should have a word with him about it. Clear things up. Then, you will see, Stevan, things will improve between us and the Soviets. Yes, yes, once the air has been cleared, things will improve.'

The marshal, however, it transpired, held a different view of the matter. He did not attend the Cominform meeting in the Ukraine. Things did not improve with the Soviets.

They did, indeed, seem to grow progressively worse.

* * *

Shortly before completing his master's degree in political science, David returned home one afternoon to find he had a visitor.

'Bogdan!' He embraced his grinning friend with great warmth and delight. He could hardly believe his eyes. 'But what are you doing here, fellow? I understood you were still in Belgrade. God! If you knew how worried I've been about you.' He took his arm, held onto it, greatly moved. 'I know about it, you know. I know about the work you did for Mihailović. I can't tell you how good it made me feel to know that you *were* with us, after all, Bogdan.'

'Well, after all,' his friend replied modestly, 'it was not so very much, you know. One becomes used to risking one's life daily. One just accepts things after a while.' His eyes misted over with quite genuine emotion.

David nodded. 'Yes,' he agreed. 'I know. But listen, Bogdan, what are we doing standing here?' David glanced around his modest room. 'This calls for a celebration. I tell you what! I don't have too much money, but I know a little place I *can* afford from time to time. I'm going to take you out to dinner. You can tell me all the news. Have you seen the family? How did you manage to get out of the country? I want to know *everything*.'

As it happened, it was Bogdan who took *him* out to dinner. 'I foresaw the day, you see, when I would need to slip out of the country. Made some plans, as it were. I'm certainly not rich, but I *do* have a little nest egg. Right here in Switzerland as it happens. Enough to get me through a year or two. I'm going to try to get into the United States, you see.'

They had a wonderful reunion. Yes, Bogdan had visited David's family just a couple of weeks before he had had to slip out of the country. *They* were hot on his trail, he explained. Yes, yes. The communists, suspicious of him always, had been hot on his trail. He had realized he had to get out. As for David's family, they were all well. A miracle really, considering what Belgrade had gone through. It was a miracle *anyone* who lived in Belgrade had survived. First the dirty fascists. Bogdan had realized shortly after he last met David that he would have to fight them. It had been his intention to join the guerrillas in the mountains, as a matter of fact, but a persuasive case had been made that he would be more useful if he stayed on and worked in the underground in Belgrade. Of course it was ten times more dangerous. Still, what could one do? Then there had been that terrible bombing by the Americans over Easter. Luckily, Bogdan had been spending the holidays with some relatives at a village outside the city. Thank God! When he had returned he could not believe the ruins! Yes, yes. It was much safer altogether to be a guerrilla in the mountains, in his truthful opinion. Then, of course, there had been their 'liberation' – he gave a hollow laugh – by the Red Army. What a nightmare that had been! No woman – from ten to a hundred and ten – had been able to put her nose out of the door for fear of being grabbed. Bogdan himself had actually been stopped by a couple of their primitive troops the first day *he* had ventured forth and had been relieved of his wallet and his cuff-links. They had been waving their guns around pretty freely. It was quite some time, he assured David, before he had again ventured forth!

Then, of course, the Yugoslav partisans had trickled in on the heels of the Russians. As bad as the Red Army! Worse! Not with the women, but there were no such trifles as cufflinks with *them*. They went for the big stuff! Anyone who owned a home, a car, *anything* of value, was automatically labelled 'collaborator' and his possessions promptly removed. Not for the use of the state, of course, but for the use of whichever partisan happened to get there first! Thank God *I*, Bogdan began, hesitated, changed his mind about whatever it was he'd been about to say. Well, he said, thank God I didn't own anything of value they wanted.

As for the family, well, Aunt Draga had not changed a bit. A few white hairs, perhaps. Zora was working at the hospital in Belgrade and was fast earning a name for herself as one of the most competent doctors. Andjela seemed to be happy. She was expecting another child in a few months. Yes, yes, she appeared to be cheerful although, of course, everyone was suffering from the shortages of just about everything, including food.

David nodded. 'I've heard they have managed to create a mess with the peasants. It is true, then?'

'It is indeed.' He gave David a sly look. 'You know, of course, that Stevan, Stevan Matić, is a very important person with the Party these days?'

David nodded. 'Every time I see a group photograph of them, he's always there in the background.' He hesitated. 'I owe you an apology, Bogdan. You tried to tell me, yet I still find it almost impossible to believe. How long had it been going on? How could he have deceived us for so long? Not only you and me, but his family.' He shook his head. 'I'll never understand it.'

'And Irina? Have you heard from Irina, David?'

'Irina? No. I have not heard.'

'I visited their apartment, you know. But they were all gone. There were all kinds of rumours about what happened to them. The white Russians, you know, who lived in

Belgrade before the war. All kinds of rumours. About the ones...' he stared unblinkingly at David, '...who were supposed to have fraternized with the Germans. But I could not find out what happened to Irina.'

'And Rachel? Did you ever find out...' he stopped talking as Bošković scowled and shook his head.

'I've been to the Red Cross, everywhere. But there is no record. I'll find her, though, David. I *know* she's still alive. If she's not on anyone's list, surely that means *something*. I *know* she's still alive, I tell you.'

'I hope so, Bogdan. I hope so.'

They parted in the small hours of the morning and agreed that they would lunch together before Bogdan completed his business in Geneva and went to West Germany. He was convinced he would be able to gain entry into the United States from there, although he became evasive when David pressed him for details. 'Come with me, David,' he said. 'I'm sure I could get you into the United States too.'

David shook his head. 'Perhaps one day, Bogdan. But I don't feel ready to leave Europe yet. I think I'll stay here a while longer. Work on my doctorate. I don't feel ready to leave yet.'

'Not ready to leave Europe?' Bogdan shook his head. 'Don't you realize, David? Europe is finished. Just as well, too. What an old whore she is, after all.'

A week or so later he left Geneva. David went to the station to see him off. As they shook hands and embraced, he hesitated.

'Bogdan?'

'What is it?'

'Nothing. I mean, if you should hear anything. About Irina, I mean. You will let me know?'

'Yes, of course.' Bogdan swung aboard the now slowly-moving train. 'I'll let you know,' he called.

Several months later David received a postcard from him. It was from Los Angeles. 'Doing nicely,' it said. 'Will write.'

He never did, though.

David kept working on his doctorate in a desultory fashion. The truth was he could no longer seem to focus on his future and lived from day to day, aware that funds from the Serbian National Defence were running low. It would not be so bad if the headaches had not returned. They pounded in the back of his head, making his eyes blur, a mist rise before him and the paper he was trying to read or write. He was also afflicted by sudden, irrational flare-ups of temper. He would explode over some trifling incident on a bus, in a restaurant, in the middle of a conversation with friends who would stare at him with surprise. Often he did not recall what he had said, what had happened, and would wonder why someone he was on good terms with would suddenly avoid him, or begin treating him with apprehensive caution.

He had great difficulty sleeping. A loud voice, the slamming of a door, distant music, could all awaken him in an instant, leaving him wide-eyed and awake for the rest of the night, unable to focus on his studies the next day.

At least his last move had proved to be a wise one. He had taken a large, spotlessly clean room in the home of a cheerful and warm-hearted widow, Madame Robert. Sparsely furnished, which he much preferred to some of the overstuffed quarters he had had previously, the room had a lovely view of the lake and its walls were lined with shelves containing books left there by Madame Robert's late husband and by transient students who, like David, had rented the room from time to time.

One day he realized with a start that it was almost two years since he had said goodbye to Bogdan Bošković. He was thinking about Bogdan that afternoon as he ran lightly up Madame Robert's front steps after having had a late lunch at a nearby café. He was aware that he, too, should begin thinking about his future. He had already inquired at the US embassy and learned that there was a long waiting list for migrants in his category. Heaven only knew how Bogdan had managed things. Perhaps, David thought, he should check with the Canadian embassy? Or simply brace himself for the bureaucratic battle that would follow any decision to remain in Switzerland. Then there was the United Nations. Perhaps if he could find work with the United Nations his future might automatically resolve itself.

He was surprised by an excited Madame Robert opening the door for him before he had even begun fishing in his pocket for his key. He had a visitor! A lady. Madame was quite excited. It was, in fact, unusual for her young boarder to receive a visitor these days. He had become rather solitary. David stood there for a moment looking at her with a puzzled expression. A lady?

'Oui, oui!' Madame was all aquiver. 'Une dame bien distinguée, peut-être votre tante?'

'Ma tante?' David was sprinting up the wooden stairs leading to his room before completing the sentence. He flung open the door, expecting against all reason to see his plump, regal, beloved Aunt Draga sitting in the one comfortable chair in the corner of his room and pulled up short at the sight of a slightly built, dark-eyed woman with grey-tinged black hair caught in a neat if severe bun at the nape of her neck.

He stood stock still, stared at her for a fraction of a second. 'Good God,' he said. 'It's Marya. Marya Mirskaia.'

She smiled and came over to kiss him on the cheek. 'I'm so glad, David. I'm so glad to see you.'

'Please...' he led her back to the chair, picked up the wooden chair in front of his small desk and sat down in front of her. 'What a surprise'. I never expected ... you look very well. You are looking very well.'

'And you, too, David, except ... older, perhaps. You look older, and...' She reached out gently, touched the side of his left eye. 'They hurt you, then? Those monsters! They hurt you?'

'Oh, nothing. It's nothing.' His tone was brusque. He preferred not to talk about the wound that reminded him of things he did not wish to remember.

'And these lines.' The probing fingers ran down his face

to touch the lines etched deeply into the side of his mouth. 'They have made you bitter then, David? Don't let them do that to you. Bitterness eats internally. Don't let them win *that* battle, David.'

He shrugged. 'I know. I try to think rationally, you understand. I try not to dwell on the past.' He hesitated. 'And Madame Mirskaia ... Irina?' He spoke the name with some difficulty. 'They are here with you in Switzerland?'

Her eyes filled with tears. 'No,' she said quite harshly. 'They are dead. They are both dead.'

Madame Robert chose that moment to knock on the door and enter with a tea tray. David automatically rose to his feet, thanked her, said the necessary things, introduced her to Marya Mirskaia and sat down again heavily as his landlady exited in an aura of benevolence and goodwill.

'Dead? *Irina*? Dead?' Of all the possibilities he had considered, of all the ... that 'little golden butterfly' as Aunt Draga called her ... his beautiful little love ... *dead*? The sheer finality of the word made it impossible for him to grasp. *That* word? In connection with *Irina?*

Marya Mirskaia, however, had recovered her usual calm. Simply, with no outward signs of emotion, she told him the story.

Shortly after the communists had taken over the country they had rounded up the German population, many of the *Volksdeutschers* and many white Russians, put them on a train and sent them to Austria. 'It was Irina's nightmare,' she said simply, 'exactly as she used to tell us. The train reached the Austrian border and then was returned to Belgrade, where they sent it back again to Austria, then back to Belgrade ... we discovered later, you see, that the Red Army had closed the Austrian border. But at the time all that we knew was that we were living Irina's nightmare. Back and forth ... we had no idea where we were supposed to be going or what was to happen to us. Irina's mother became a little hysterical, you understand, although Irina seemed to remain calm. She insisted, the third time they sent us back to the Austrian border, that her mother and I swallow some sleeping pills she had managed to take with her. Anna had been having problems with her heart. Since the occupation, you understand. Well, Irina gave us both these pills, told us to try to get some sleep. When we awakened it was as though we were not awake, but caught up in some kind of terrible nightmare; Irina's nightmare, perhaps. It was around dawn. I remember the first thing that struck me when I opened my eyes was this ghostly mist that seemed to swirl into the carriage from the open windows. People were shouting, crying. Gradually we comprehended what it was they were saying. A woman! A young woman had thrown herself from the train. No one had realized her intentions. She had simply pushed past everyone to reach the carriage door, opened it, stepped out and...'

Marya took a deep breath, staring past him, reaching back into that terrible dawn. She closed her eyes, then began to speak again in a level voice.

'It seemed to take ages for us to understand that it was Irina who...' Again she stopped talking and stared down at the handkerchief she was twisting between her hands. 'As a matter of fact,' she added, 'I don't know what would have happened, how we would have coped, but ... Do you remember the man who used to be in charge of your apartment building, David? Otto Schmidt. Do you remember him?'

'Otto?' David nodded, 'Of course.' He heard his own voice, observed himself sitting there very still, quite detached, as he listened to Marya's story. Yet had someone asked him to move at that moment he would have been unable to do so. He felt almost paralysed.

'How strange life is,' she went on. 'We met him only once at your apartment. Your aunt introduced us when he came in to look at a light fixture she was having problems with. Only that once. Anna and I met him just that once. But he was also on the train, you see. He was looking for his wife. They had become separated at the station and he could not find her on the train. He was almost frantic with worry. The Red Army was still in Belgrade when we left. Some of the soldiers were at the station. We heard they were just grabbing women...' Her voice faded, then seemed to regain strength.

'I think in a way Otto was relieved to find something he could do. He took care of everything. When we were finally allowed into Austria he spirited Anna and myself out of the station and took us to a small town outside the capital where he had relatives. When Anna had a heart attack, when she died, they were so kind to me. So kind.'

She looked at him directly, smiled her sad smile.

'You see, even Germans ... some of the Germans could be very kind, David.' With a brisk movement she leaned forward to the tea tray Madame Robert had placed on a small table between them. 'Your landlady also seems to be very kind.' She picked up the pretty china teapot and poured him a cup. 'Here,' she attempted another smile. 'I'm sure you can do with this.'

They drank the tea between them, leaving the small plate of biscuits untouched.

'And now?' David asked after a long silence. 'You are living in Switzerland?'

She shook her head. 'Just visiting.' She held up her left hand, showing off the thin golden band around her third finger. 'I recently married. An old friend I met in Vienna. He had lost his family in a boating accident. We offer each other consolation. We assuage each other's loneliness. It is more than I could have expected really. He is very kind.'

She sighed. After a moment went on to explain it was their intention to leave 'the sad continent' that contained so many unhappy memories for them both. They wished to live quietly somewhere. Perhaps in England. As they both had many friends in Geneva this was in the nature of a farewell visit. Someone had mentioned one day that there were quite a few Chetniks still in the country, many of them students. It had occurred to her to inquire, to see if it was at all possible that a David Ristić could be enrolled at the university and, 'Well, you see,' she said, 'here I am.'

He kissed her warmly on the cheek when she left. They

promised to keep in touch, though both knew they would not.

That night he lay in his bed, wide awake, staring up at the darkened ceiling. Slowly a great keening began within him.

Irina began to dance before his eyes. She was dressed in something filmy, something yellow. Of course! It was the dress she had been wearing when he had first laid eyes on her. His little butterfly. His beautiful little golden butterfly, whose fragile wings had been so brutally broken.

And with his keening for Irina came at last a great and terrible mourning for his people. For his Uncle Mikhail. His family, doomed now to live within a dictatorship that would be as hard to dislodge as the Turks had been. For his fallen comrades. Through a letter received from Sergeant Veljko, now in Italy, he had heard that they were all gone. He was the only officer from his brigade who had survived. The others were all dead. The mighty voice of the courageous Kosta Marinković silenced forever. The scholarly and brave Branko Jelić and all of the others. All dead. Zeka, too, his chill smile now turned to dust. And the innocent young Yaruga. Dead! As was Draža. Draža Mihailović who had started it all. Whose crime, it was now perfectly clear, had been his innate decency, his total inability to comprehend the unscrupulous lengths to which his adversaries were willing to go in order to grasp power.

Long into the night and through the early morning hours he mourned. For all of them. His lost love. His people. His lively, warm-hearted, hospitable, innately loving but terribly innocent people. What was it Mihailović had once asked? Will we ever be free of the Turks? he had said. Hadn't his people suffered enough through five centuries of barbaric occupation? Shouldn't they at least have been granted a little more time to solidify the democratic institutions they had yearned for right through their long and bloody history?

He thought about the British. Perhaps he was still as innocent as Draža, as innocent as his people. He simply could not grasp the extent of the arrogance that led them to believe they were capable of making decisions that would affect other countries and other peoples in such a profound and devastating way. He thought about William Deakin and Maclean, Fitzroy Maclean, who it seemed had been the main actor in the drama that had led Churchill to abandon a man like Mihailović for the unscrupulous liar and dictator Josip Broz had again and again proved himself to be. What motivated such a man? Was it gold? Women? Rumour amongst the Serbs had it that Tito had lavished him with gifts. Hard to believe, but on the other hand, what kind of a man was it who could take it upon himself to deliver a small country that had made so many sacrifices in search of democracy into the hands of a ruthless communist dictator?

He thought about Alan Wood. A decent British officer of the same mould his uncle had talked about so often when speaking of the Salonika front. Were there many others like that amongst the British? With a flash of insight he realized that probably in any country there was only a handful of men who truly lived up to their country's professed ideals. Others, the majority, perhaps, could only try. And, always, there was a small group of malcontents who through self-hatred or God only knew what kind of twisted inner turmoil, seemed to live only for the destruction of whatever attempts at decency they saw around them.

He thought about war. How long ago it seemed that in his innocence he had thought it an act of heroism to take up arms against whatever barbarians you found in your back yard. Now he knew that war was simply a state of madness during which the cream of youth died on bloody battlefields while cynical politicians chewed cigars in safe back rooms and hatched plots that betrayed and made a mockery of every ideal and value the young thought they were dying for, while still others thought only of how they could profit from all of the carnage.

He finally drifted into a restless sleep of nightmarish dreams about dead comrades and mangled butterflies. When he awoke he knew with cold clarity that it was time for him to get out of Europe.

5

Stevan stared at his wife, trying to fight the familiar feeling of helplessness that swamped him whenever they began one of their seemingly endless arguments.

'Olga,' he said patiently, 'I haven't asked you to attend *anything*, *any* social event to do with the Party, not since...' he hesitated. Even saying the name caused pain. Pain to them both. To *him* too. Couldn't she understand that?

'Not since Goli Otok!' After all these bitter years she was still unable to compromise.

'All right,' he said bitterly, furiously. 'Not since Goli Otok. What I can't understand,' he went on, desperately trying to insert a note of reason into the discussion that could, as he well knew, suddenly blow up in their faces, develop into shouts of mutual recrimination that would leave them both weak, ill, and which would resolve nothing. 'What I can't understand,' he repeated, 'is why all this moral outrage *now*? When *I* was asking the questions. When *I* was questioning the methods and morality of the Party, I was a petit bourgeois! Remember?'

'Must we go through all that again, Stevan? *Must* we? We – Alex and I – we *believed*, don't you understand? Won't you *ever* understand? Whatever they did, it was *for* something. It was for a *new world*. Can't you understand?'

'What I *can* understand is that if it had not been for the marshal we would not be in the position we are in today.'

'Exactly,' she said quietly, bitterly.

'Don't you understand at all the strain he was under?' No,

he thought angrily as she stared at him coldly, then picked up her drink, not even bothering to reply. No, you can't comprehend. You don't *want* to comprehend.

When the Soviets had demanded that Yugoslavia unite with Bulgaria, cast itself, as it were, in the same obsequious 'puppet' mould as the Bulgars, Tito had consulted with the Central Committee. The decision to at last make a stand against the stifling embrace of their Soviet brothers was almost unanimous. Tito had subsequently made an impassioned speech at the opening of congress in July 1948, repudiating the accusations of the Soviets, who had been spreading lies about his efforts to collaborate with the Axis powers during the war and about the real role played by the partisans in the liberation of Yugoslavia. Yet he still left the door open, indicated his great desire to restore the previous warm relations his country had enjoyed with the first socialist state.

Throughout the anxious months that followed – the Soviet economic blockade, the barely concealed threat of invasion emanating from the Kremlin – the Yugoslav leader had outwardly maintained his composure. He was, he intimated to Stevan, sure of two things. One was that, in fact, Stalin would not risk an international war that could be precipitated by invasion of Yugoslavia. Once again Tito was counting on the Western Allies. There was no way, he was convinced, that the Americans would allow Stalin into the Adriatic. He was also convinced that the not-so-subtle attempts by the Soviets to incite the Yugoslav people to overthrow him would fail. Memories of the behaviour of the Red Army and the subsequent stream of arrogant Soviet advisers that had followed were too fresh in the mind of the population. In fact, in one way, the differences they were having with the Soviets were beneficial. This new danger to their country made the people push to the back of their minds wartime memories that were still of great embarrassment to the Yugoslav communists, spoken or unspoken; made them unite at last behind their communist government.

He had been proved right on both counts. Both the American and British governments brushed aside their feelings about the outright contempt and various small humiliations the Yugoslav leader had inflicted upon them almost from the moment the Red Army had entered Yugoslavia, and deemed it in their interest to offer him substantial arms and economic aid. Thus the crisis passed due, ironically enough, to the despised imperialists. Yes, the crisis passed. But it had taken its toll.

No one seemed to understand the depth of Tito's despair when Stalin had orchestrated his expulsion from the Cominform. No one seemed to understand what it had cost him to have to liquidate his old comrades – Žujović, Hebrang, Arso Jovanović – all of whom, like Alex and thousands of others, had been unable to overnight shake off their faith in and love for the Soviet Union and its iron leader.

Yes, the break with Stalin, the humiliation of having to deal once again with the decadent and gloating imperialists had certainly affected the marshal deeply. Yet it was, perhaps, an entirely unrelated incident that Stevan believed had taken him over the edge. It was an attempted rebellion by Muslim peasants that proved to be the straw that broke the camel's back. What had given them the idea that King Peter II had dropped into Bosnia by parachute? Not that the uprising had been allowed to gain momentum. Very rough steps indeed had been immediately taken to quell the outbreak. But the lack of loyalty, the implication that they were not appreciative of the great things Tito had done for them, had affected the marshal deeply.

Yes, yes. Tito had been under terrible strain. Still, as a matter of fact, in his heart, Stevan himself had been appalled by his actions in connection with Goli Otok. To himself make the decision to send some fifty thousand comrades who simply found it impossible, after years of being encouraged to worship Stalin, to overnight turn around and condemn him, to that island hell-hole to be beaten, tortured and humiliated, without consultation with either the Central Committee or the Politburo, no, whatever the strain, that should not have been done.

Yet Stevan felt he could understand the marshal's behaviour, even though he could hardly approve it. At least, he *could* have understood it, if he had not had to visit the place himself to retrieve big Alex, who could understand nothing of what was going on inside Tito. All he understood was that if he had been wrong about Stalin, then he must have been wrong about everything else to do with communism. He would have to accept responsibility for the death of Jelena, for all of the things he had seen and heard and pretended not to have seen and heard in the years since he had joined the Party. No, no, Alex could not understand, could not accept. For Alex, even Goli Otok was easier to accept.

For Stevan, however, even today the name of that hell-hole evoked nightmares that he doubted would ever leave him.

It had begun with the strange disappearance of Alex. Then the futile inquiries, until his brief discussion with a worried Nikola Djerdja who, just prior to Alex's disappearance, had attended a meeting with Tito and a group of engineers to discuss the building of a bridge in Croatia that was to be named after the marshal. Tito himself had presided over the meeting and perhaps Alex might well have swallowed the glittering splendour of his uniform, top heavy as always with a colourful array of medals, had he not suddenly burst into a tirade against 'that tyrant' Stalin. Alex, Djerdja told Stevan, had not said a word.

Shortly after the meeting broke up, however, just before leaving the room, the big man had glanced towards the marshal and said quite loudly: *Stalin wears a simple tunic of the people.*

'Might as well have held a red flag to a bull,' Djerdja had said, shaking his head. 'I tell you, Stevan, he was *asking* for trouble.'

It had all led to Stevan having to visit that stinking hell-hole off the Dalmatian coast, Goli Otok. The smells, the sights, he knew would be with him until the day he died.

And the sight of Alex. Big Alex, broken, sitting in those unspeakable rags in a corner of a cell, rags soiled with his own filth, wearing that fiendish sign around his neck. *Traitor!* Alex. A traitor? The big man had been beaten, tortured. Yet it was that terrible sign they had hung around his neck that had almost broken Stevan.

He brought himself back to the present with an effort.

'You know quite well,' he said, 'that the marshal was under a terrible strain at the time of Goli Otok. You know what he's *really* like. Why, these days he refuses, even, to sign anyone's death warrant. It is years since he has signed a death warrant.'

'And even longer,' she said remorselessly, 'since he has signed a reprieve.' They were in the bedroom, that beautiful, large, airy room which had been so often turned into a battleground. He wondered, dully, why they even bothered to retire there before beginning their endless arguments that so often developed into bitter screaming at each other. God knows, he thought, any spies in the place must be able to hear us for miles around.

Olga had risen to her feet and was refilling her glass from the bottle she no longer tried to hide. She took a mouthful of the liquid, settled down again on the settee and stared at him resentfully.

'Do you know the difference between us, Stevan? The difference is *you never believed.* You never *did* believe, did you? So you had nothing to lose. Nothing at all.'

He was overcome by a deep feeling of fatigue. How long could they go on like this? How long could *he* go on? Trying to cope with the endless intrigue, the tension caused by the knowledge that the Party members with whom he worked were watching him like hawks waiting to pounce the moment they saw a chink in the armour he had managed to build around himself over the years. They knew, of course, that his relationship with the marshal was not what it used to be. Ever since he had walked into Goli Otok of his own volition and plucked Alex out over the protests of the rat-faced comrade who ran the whole evil, stinking operation,

Tito's attitude towards him had changed. Not that he had ever said anything. Stevan had waited, God only knew, with trepidation, for the summons that would banish him from Tito's side forever, might even deliver him into the hell of Goli Otok. At least, he had thought bitterly, if they place the sign of 'traitor' around *my* neck it would be more ironic than just. How could you be a traitor to something you did not, deep in your heart, truly believe in? Olga was right about that!

The marshal, however, had not sent for him. Nor had Ranković's ubiquitous and ruthless police appeared on his doorstep. He had simply been shown, through a certain coldness in Tito's manner when they met, that he was no longer in favour. A very slight chink in his armour indeed. But the Party hawks had seen it immediately. They were all on tiptoe. Ready to pounce. Which was why it was so important that he go to this blasted ball which was being held for the sole purpose of honouring Tito. He *had* to go. And so did Olga. But did she recognize this? He gazed at her bitterly as she sat there brooding, sipping her drink. That was another thing! Not only did he have to cope with the constant fear of a stab in the back at the office all day long, but with endless quarrels and recriminations when he returned home and found her drinking, drinking. When, for God's sake, what he really needed, and surely deserved, was a little peace. A little love. Was that really too much to ask?

'Stevan?' The dark eyes were gazing at him intently over the rim of her glass. 'Why don't we just separate? Or divorce? We can't go on like this. It's not fair to either of us.'

They'd covered this ground before, too.

'Because,' he said coldly, 'you are my wife and I will never let you go.'

'But why?' She drained the glass, put it down, got up and began to wander around the room, not quite steady on her feet. Then with a quick change of mood she ran to his side, fell on her knees and buried her face in his lap before looking up at him. 'I know, Stevan. I *know* it's our fault. Alex and I, we were the ones who drew you into all this. I know that. It is our fault. Mine if you like. I take all of the blame. I was wrong! That is all. But *please* don't make me live in this house any longer. It hangs around my neck like a stolen necklace. Let me go. Maybe if I could go to one of the villages, help the people somehow. Maybe I could save myself.'

'What are you talking about? Save yourself!' *Was his patience supposed to be inexhaustible?*

'Don't think I'm not grateful. Don't think that.' She lifted her head, gazed up into his face. 'What you did for Alex, when they took him to that ... that place ... don't think I don't know what courage that took, Stevan. Why, I don't think I've ever loved you so much as I did then. If only we could have packed, just packed a few things and gone away with Alex. Even now, it's not too late. You and me. We could ask them to send us to a small village. We could...'

He smiled gently and caressed her face. 'What are you talking about? You want me to give up everything I've worked for?' He gave a short, bitter laugh. 'Oh, yes,' he said. 'They are waiting to pounce. There are plenty of them waiting to pounce! But Tito has not *entirely* discarded me, you know. They are all aware of that.' He put her gently to one side, got up, began to undress. 'Come on. I'm tired. Tomorrow evening we will go to the ball. I want you to be especially gracious to the marshal. That's all I'm asking. Especially gracious. I think this might be the turning point. I think he might wish to put Goli Otok behind him, even in his own mind.' He bent down and kissed her lightly on the lips, trying to hide a frown as he encountered the sour smell of liquor. '"We could ask them to send us to a small village,"' he parroted lovingly. 'You would be bored stiff within a week, my darling. And so would I.'

He could not quite believe his eyes the following evening. He had been held up at the office and rushed home to find her curled up in bed, reading, a half-filled glass, as always, by her side. 'You have not started to get dressed yet?'

She shrugged, turned a page of the out-of-date magazine. 'I told you. I'm not going.' Reaching out, she picked up the glass, sipped it, replaced it before looking at him. 'I can't,' she explained. 'I have nothing to wear.'

'Nothing to . . .' With a short exclamation he stormed over to the wardrobe and threw it open. It contained a few simple day dresses. She had long ago given up wearing the partisan uniform. About to turn back to her, his face contorted with anger, he caught a glimpse of something that had been pushed right to the back, the bright colour catching his eye from its place behind a long dressing-gown. It was the red dress she had worn all those years ago, before the war. To that club dance. David Ristić had been there. That evening when he had first asked Olga to marry him.

He pulled it out, walked over to the bed, threw it down and grasped her by the arm, jerking her off the bed, ignoring the sharp gasp of pain. 'You can wear this! I'm going to bathe and change,' he added between gritted teeth. 'You had better be ready by the time *I* am or, by God, you are going to regret it. You will live to regret it, Olga.'

Two hours later they stood together in their place in the official line gathered in the reception hall of the old Royal Court, waiting to pay their respects to the marshal.

He was standing a little inside the entrance to the ballroom, immaculate as ever in his most glittering gold and red uniform, the heavy, pure gold belt he wore around his waist resting against the slight paunch he had acquired over the years. Stevan waited a little apprehensively, hoping desperately that Tito would choose this moment to publicly effect some kind of reconciliation. Hoping against hope that instead of looking past him to a place behind his shoulders, as he had tended to do since the Goli Otok incident, he would again look directly at him with those pale blue eyes, smile, perhaps even place one of the blunt, capable hands on his shoulder. It was not just the regaining of his prestige, Stevan realized. What he yearned for most of all was that warm feeling that came to those who basked in the sun of the marshal's approval. How he had missed that. He had not fully understood until this moment how much he had missed that.

All of the Party hierarchy were present, he noted as he glanced around, smiling where appropriate, or stiffly inclining his head. The Party matrons were also overwhelming in their presence, awash in a sea of silk, jewels and furs, their cold and restless eyes coming from time to time to a disapproving halt when they reached Olga who, with neither furs nor jewels, still managed to outshine them all. Stevan felt a stab of pride at this. The drinking, thank God, had not yet harmed her magnificent figure. There was just that slight puffiness around her eyes. He suddenly made up his mind to take a few days off from his duties and take her on a holiday, talk things out with her. She was right about one thing. They could not go on indefinitely like this.

With a start he realized they had almost reached the marshal. Just one couple ahead of them. A moment later they were themselves standing in front of him. Stevan pushed Olga forward, straightened his shoulders and tried to calm the beating of his heart, aware that his future was about to be decided either by a friendly if not affectionate greeting from Tito that would in an instant restore him to that prestigious place he had grown so used to, or by a cold look that would forever relegate him to at best a minor bureaucratic role, at worst an entry on Ranković's police list.

The gasp, the harsh whispers, that came from the assembled dignitaries as his wife, now directly in front of the marshal, ignored his outstretched hand but instead, with a movement of infinite irony and grace, swept low in a royal curtsy, reached Stevan only after his own heart momentarily stopped, his own blood froze within his veins, his own desolate future loomed, receded before his eyes . . .

He reached out angrily, blindly, and was about to pull her roughly to her feet and walk out in humiliation, when the mist before his eyes cleared to reveal an obviously delighted marshal bowing graciously, acknowledging with a warm smile what he clearly felt to be genuine homage, a right he had perhaps earned during the bitter war years he so enjoyed reminiscing about. He was holding his hands out now, helping her up, complimenting her on her beauty, her dress, regretting the fact that he had not seen her for so long a time.

Then it was Stevan's turn. Tito's hands were on his shoulders now. 'Where have you been hiding yourself?' he was asking. 'You must come and have tea with me soon. Yes, yes. You must bring your beautiful wife to have tea with me soon, Stevan. It has been too long. Far too long.'

And then they had moved on. Someone else was standing in their place in front of the marshal whose pale eyes had rested upon them so approvingly just one moment before.

Without shame Stevan found that tears were stinging his eyes. The blood was singing warmly in his veins. He had been received back into the fold. After all this time Tito had forgiven him.

He slipped his arm around his wife's rigid waist. It was years since he had been so happy

6

'No, listen,' the doctor said. 'Don't get me wrong, now. Australia's the best bloody country in the world. It's just that I'm damned if I know what you'd do there with a degree in political science, son. We've got two main political parties, you understand, both as bad as each other, though I must admit they don't get themselves into the God-awful bloody tangles you Europeans do.'

David stared back at him a little helplessly. After having gone through all of the rigmarole with the Australian immigration authorities that had brought him as far as this very thorough medical examination, surely he was not going to be turned down by this large, kindly doctor?

'No, no,' he was saying now, as though reading David's thoughts. 'So far as I'm concerned you are in A1 shape physically. Excellent shape. But if I pass you, you understand, for the first two years in Aussie land you will have to do physical work. We need labourers, tradesmen. I'll tell you what I'll do.' He held David's papers up in the air. 'I'm going to hold these up for a few days. Give you time to think about it some more.' He winked. 'We humans,' he said, 'have got to outwit the bloody bureaucrats occasionally. This is what we'll do. Come back in a week or so. If you still want to go, fine. If you change your mind I'll tell them you've got flat feet or something.'

David walked outside into the bright Swiss morning feeling a little frustrated. As a matter of fact he was not sure whether he wanted to go to Australia. What did he know about the country? It was situated at the bottom of the world. Kangaroos! Lots of beaches. Certainly nothing bad. Plenty of sunshine, but *Ostajte ovde, Sunce tudjeg neba, nece vas grejati, kao sto ovde greje*. The words of the national poem he had learned at his father's knee crept uninvited into his mind, hitting him with the force of a sudden fever. *Stay here. The sun of the foreign sky will not warm you.* He knew with certainty that the words were true. No foreign sun would ever warm him as had his own Serbian sun. The awareness that he might never again either see his country or be warmed by its sun brought with it such an acute sense of loss and pain that he swayed, overcome by a feeling of nausea, dizziness.

For a brief moment he stood still as wary pedestrians detoured around him, then with a deep breath and an intense effort of will he pulled himself together. Australia! Concentrate on Australia! The doctor had acted in a very decent way. He had known that before the Swiss would give him a work permit they would want proof that he had exhausted all avenues of emigration. Perhaps this Australian's decency was a good omen.

A good omen! Clinging to that thought he began slowly to continue on his way. At the very least he would think very seriously about the situation during the next few days. He would think about his future very seriously indeed.

That evening he met in a downstairs bar on the rue Mont Blanc with a group of Serbian students and Yugoslav Ambassador Fotić, until recently ambassador to the United States and reputedly a good friend of Roosevelt. He was on a brief visit to Switzerland and had agreed to meet with the young Serbs and tell them what he knew of the present situation. In fact, in response to their eager questions, he spoke mostly about the past.

How could the Americans have been so easily tricked by the communist bandit, Tito? No, it was not the Americans. In fact the discrepancies between reports from American liaison officers in the field and those coming out of the

British headquarters at Cairo had caused a good deal of concern amongst US officials. He had himself talked to the president about this and had been listened to with some sympathy. Roosevelt was a man who had great admiration for the Serbs. He knew of their reputation for great gallantry while fighting with the Allies during the Great War and at one time had even, so he had told the ambassador, collected stamps from 'brave little Serbia'. Roosevelt had certainly had his doubts about the policy Churchill insisted on pursuing. He had even sent the head of the last United States' military mission to Yugoslavia, Colonel Robert McDowell, to London to try and see Churchill to explain to him the real situation as seen by American officers in the field. However, McDowell had been unable to secure an audience with the British prime minister, and had talked instead to Anthony Eden, who seemed to have a good understanding of the situation. Churchill had not, however, changed his mind and as Yugoslavia was within the British sphere of influence there was really little that Roosevelt could do. Churchill had, of course, now admitted that his decisions regarding Yugoslavia had been his greatest mistake of the war. He had, he claimed, been badly advised by his officers in the field. Men he had placed there himself such as Bill Deakin and Fitzroy MacLean in whom he had had great but obviously misplaced trust. Nor had the prime minister known that an officer at their headquarters in Cairo, a British communist called Jack Klugman, had falsified reports coming out of Yugoslavia concerning action taken by the nationalists, crediting such action to the partisans and seeing that these false reports were distributed to the foreign office and the BBC. The amazing thing was that Klugman, at least, had made no bones about his being a communist. Yet the British had let him, they had allowed him ... The very thought was too much for the ambassador who now simply shook his head.

He also talked about the sorry performance of the Yugoslav government in exile in London. Forever quarreling amongst themselves when a united front was imperative.

They had apparently forgotten that vital truth enshrined on the Serbian flag. *Samo Sloga Srbina Spasava*, the students eagerly intoned the words with him. Only unity saves Serbs! And, of course, the Croats amongst them had stoked the fires of dissension. The ambassador spoke, also, about young King Peter who, it seemed, bitterly regretted that he had allowed Churchill to bully him into making that infamous broadcast asking the people to throw their support behind Tito.

Time had flown as the young Serbs sat around him, listening with fascinated attention. All too soon, it seemed, he had regretfully excused himself, ruefully pointing at the clock, explaining that he had an extremely heavy schedule next morning.

One more question.

The war criminal, Pavelić. Did the ambassador have any news of this murderer and his followers? So many of them seemed to have apparently vanished into thin air.

The ambassador had hesitated, looked searchingly at each of the young faces eagerly surrounding him. Finally he had said, quite gently, that yes, it was known that so far as Pavelić himself was concerned the British had held him for some time in Austria. They had, well, because of his connection with the Vatican, it must be understood, they had, let us say, they had allowed him to escape. It was known that he was now under the diplomatic protection of the Vatican as were a number of the priests who had been personally involved in those terrible atrocities against the Serbs, the Jews and the Gypsies inside Croatia and Bosnia.

'The British had him?' David had forced the words out. 'But you are saying they let him go? His voice was incredulous.

Fotić shrugged, allowed one of the students to help him with his coat. 'It seems they do not want to tangle with the Vatican,' he said, adding slowly, 'besides, you must understand . . .' he hesitated.

'Yes?'

'The West, it seems, and particularly the Americans, are

now trying to enlist every Nazi they can find. For the coming war against communism,' he added in response to the blank stares facing him.

'But...' this from David's friend, Pera Lalić, 'don't they understand what he *did*? This man, all of them, they are pathological murderers. They are responsible for the deaths of hundreds of thousands of our people, not to mention the Jews! They are pathological murderers!'

The diplomat nodded. For a brief moment there was a sudden flash of anger. 'Perfidious Albion,' he muttered fiercely, but almost immediately recovered his composure. 'You must understand the Western mind,' he said. 'A British statesman once said: "Britain has no permanent friends or—"'

'Or eternal enemies,' David cut in, 'it has only its own eternal interests. Lord Palmerston!'

'Yes, yes. Palmerston. That's right.'

And these are the Western values we were fighting for? David opened his mouth to say it. Closed it. Pointless. It was all so pointless.

Before leaving the ambassador shook his hand. 'I knew your uncle,' he said. 'A great patriot. I'm so sorry we lost him.'

'Perhaps it was just as well, sir. All of this ... the things you have told us ... frankly, Mr Fotić, I think he would have preferred not to have known. He would much preferred not to have known.'

A few days later David was sitting in the outdoor section of the Canonica café drinking a cup of Swiss chocolate and idly watching a crowd that had gathered at the square on the corner of Rue Mont Blanc and Quai Wilson. They were all looking towards Mont Blanc bridge, probably expecting some international dignitary. There was always someone of note visiting Geneva.

He rose to his feet, paid his bill and crossed the street, making his way slowly towards the bridge, intent on visiting some friends who lived on the opposite side, on Avenue Grenade. He was halfway across when in the distance he saw an official-looking black convertible cruising slowly towards him. Oddly, there were hardly any other cars on the bridge. Perhaps they had cleared it for whomever . . . it was Churchill! David had now reached the middle of the bridge and stood very still, staring at the approaching car. The old man was standing in the back, quite alone. Another man, presumably his bodyguard, was sitting in the front with the driver.

Yes. I was badly advised. Yugoslavia was undoubtedly my greatest mistake. The statement the old man had made so complacently in Brussels in 1946 suddenly rang in David's ears. He could just see him chomping contentedly on his cigar as he made the admission. And that report he had read in the Swiss papers! The report that said Brigadier Maclean, no doubt in an attempt to wipe his own hands clean, had claimed he had warned Churchill that British policy might place Yugoslavia in the hands of the communists. *Do you intend to make Yugoslavia your home after the war? Neither do I! That being so the less you and I worry about the form of government they set up the better for both of us,* Churchill was supposed to have replied.

The car, still moving very slowly, had almost reached him now. The old man's pink baby face was clearly visible from the distance of fifteen or so feet. It looked tired, drawn.

Suddenly David's hand moved with the speed of lightning to his hip, to the place the Luger he had been so proud to have captured had rested for almost the entire duration of the war. His fingers encountered nothing but the thin cloth of his trousers and rested helplessly on his waist as the old warrior turned his head towards him and held up two plump fingers in the V for Victory sign. The car drove slowly past, heading towards the waiting crowd on the other side of the bridge.

For several more minutes David stood alone in the sunshine on *Le pont Mont Blanc* before he unsteadily moved on, almost blindly finding his way to a park bench overlooking the lake. He sat down heavily and found he was drenched in sweat, shivering in the warm sunshine. From across the years his Uncle Mikhail's voice boomed. *Assassins? Cowardly murderers! That's what assassins are. Striking down unarmed men! Cowards! Cowardly murderers.*

Would he have used the Luger had it been there? He did not know. What he *did* know was that his hand had moved of its own volition, before his mind had grasped the fact. His finger could as easily have pulled the trigger in the same blind way. *Would* he have done it? He did not know. He would never know.

What he did know was that he had to get out of Europe immediately. If they had turned him into a potential assassin for God's sake, then he *had* to get out of Europe.

A feeling of quiet peace flowed through him. There were no more doubts. He would not wait for a week to pass. Tomorrow he would go and see the Australian doctor.

Suddenly he wanted more than anything in the world to work outside in the clean sunshine in a country that was untouched by the machiavellian machinations of Europe.

He had not felt so much at peace with the world for years.

* * *

The weather that morning in Belgrade was heavily humid. The sky was grey and overcast. Stevan nevertheless decided he would walk to his office. He had been gaining weight lately and was not in as good condition as he might be. A walk would do him good.

He strode along the tree-lined street, erect, confident, feeling content and at peace with the world. Not that he was ever entirely free, of course, of the niggling worry at the back of his mind about Olga.

She had returned from the sanatorium a month or so ago. Undoubtedly the stay there had done her the world of good. She was an entirely different woman. Remembering the tears, the way she had pleaded with him not to send her to 'that terrible place' as she called it, he could only congratulate himself on his refusal to give way to bourgeois emotionalism. She simply could not be allowed to continue along the route she seemed to have chosen for herself. He had discussed the situation endlessly with his closest friends within the Party. They all agreed with the step he had taken. None of them could understand why a woman who so obviously had everything – beauty, position, a devoted husband – would turn to drink the way she had. It was simply inexplicable.

In any event, it was over now. She had been returned to him certainly in a much better state than when she had left. There were no more quarrels. Indeed, it was amazing how pliable she had become. She would look at him out of those beautiful dark eyes, obviously anxious to please. She was pathetically concerned that he might return her to 'that place'. As though he would! As though he needed to, now.

Yes, of course, it worried him that her eyes had lost much of their lustre, their intelligent, mischievous sparkle. But that sparkle, he felt confident, would return. And, of course, she was very quiet, given to gazing out of windows as though looking for something lost. It was only natural that for the first month or so she would be quiet. In a way it was more restful, he had to admit. If only it was not so difficult to get her to say a word.

Best to be positive. He had been extremely pleased to notice that she made no mention of the absence of Stana Radović. What a relief it had been to send that ancient, terrible old hag back to the primitive mountain village where she really belonged. The memory of the way she had flown at him when she learned he had committed Olga to the sanatorium could still send a chill down his spine. 'Godless communist!' she had hissed, the hooded eyes full of hate, the yellow nails stretched out towards his face, the sulphuric breath stinging his nostrils . . .

He paused, gulped in some fresh air, then ran lightly up the steps of the sprawling building that housed his office.

A few minutes later he was seated behind his desk, riffling through the pile of newspapers that had been placed there by his secretary. He chose one carefully from the heap, opened it to the front page, and began to scan the headlines.

In a moment he was back on his feet and had rushed into the outer office. 'Put through a call to the marshal's office,' he snapped at a startled aide. 'Tell him I'll be over there in ten minutes. I'd like to see him immediately.'

Fifteen minutes later Tito was looking up from behind his desk, peering at Stevan from over the top of his glasses. 'What's all the rush, comrade? Sit down, sit down. Has something happened? Is anything the matter?'

'Here,' Stevan was a little breathless. He handed him the paper he was still clutching. 'Read this.'

He pointed to the headline, sat down and watched as the president of the people's republic adjusted his spectacles and began to read, his eyes skimming the story to the bottom of the page, then returning to the headline which he began to read again more thoroughly.

Stevan couldn't wait. 'Two Cambridge-educated Soviet spies! A man called Burgess. And a Donald Maclean. They've both defected to Moscow. Both of them top officials with the British Foreign Office. It says it is suspected there are others, that British intelligence too has been riddled with Soviet spies since long before the war.' He paused, then began again, almost babbling with excitement. 'You know, I had almost forgotten, but years ago – it was *years* ago – Olga told me that when the communists were recruiting, you know, all those upper-class British at Oxford, at Cambridge, they were telling them to get themselves impeccable conservative credentials. She said the British establishment was riddled with Soviet spies! The civil service, politics, the intelligence service, even close to the royal family she said, and the BBC. I remembered that, I remembered that, you know when they were crediting us with action taken by Mihailović and . . .' He paused, overcome by the enormity of the implications, before asking softly. 'Those British friends of yours, you know, Deakin. Fitzroy Maclean. I always did wonder about those two.'

'What? What's that?' The marshal was not paying attention, and was once again re-reading the article through carefully, almost word by word.

'I mean, remember just after the war? They both repudiated us, claimed they had never seen us do anything other than take *defensive* action against the Germans. Claimed they had simply taken our word about our great offensives, you remember that.'

'My God,' Tito growled, 'Moscow must have known the extent ... the extent ...'

'Then, of course, when you were expelled from the Comintern and the West decided it was in their interests to admit that ours *had* been a glorious revolution, after all, they both changed their stories again. Became great experts about our fighting qualities!' Stevan shook his head ironically.

'Mmmmm? What's that you're saying?'

'Maclean! Remember when he claimed to have warned Churchill about you? It was all Churchill's fault, he implied.'

'What are you talking about? What's this about Maclean? Fitzroy Maclean?'

'Well, I just wondered. They – Maclean and Deakin – they were both with us, then?'

'With us, you say?'

'Well, my God,' with a sudden burst of impatience. 'They were either with us or ... or ... what was it they used to call those English communists? Stalin's Englishmen, that's it. Were they really Stalin's Englishmen, or were they just starry-eyed, innocent fools? Could they really have been such bloody fools?'

At the mention of Stalin's name, the marshal had looked up sharply. He dropped the paper on his desk, pushed his chair back and stared at Stevan over the top of his glasses. 'Stalin?' He suddenly began to cough, wheeze, chuckle.

'Yes, yes. I just wondered if ...'

'Stalin's Englishmen! I always liked that expression,' Tito said. He brought a chubby hand down hard on his knee, and the chuckle developed into a roar of laughter. He leaned back further in his chair.

And laughed ... and laughed ... and laughed.

Events in Sind under the British were so ambiguous and contradictory during Burton's time that one treads a shaky line in sorting out unreconcilable versions of what actually happened, who was at fault, who was the hero, why one amir was preferred over another, and why the English, who always seemed to pride themselves on their honesty, were involved in chicanery so extreme that the thieves and knaves among their enemies seemed, in contrast, like saints.

Edward Rice, *Captain Sir Richard Francis Burton*

FURTHER READING

Beloff, Norah, *Tito's Flawed Legacy: Yugoslavia and the West 1939–84*. London. 1985. Victor Gollancz, Ltd.

Deakin, F. W. D., *The Embattled Mountain*, London. Oxford University Press. 1971.

Djilas, Milovan, *Wartime*. New York. Harcourt Brace Jovanovich. 1985.

Dragnich, Alex N., *Serbs and Croats. The Struggle in Yugoslavia*. Harcourt Brace & Company. New York. 1992.

Ivanović, Vane., *Memoirs of a Yugoslav*. New York. Harcourt Brace Jovanovich. 1977.

Kostich, Dr Lazo M., *Holocaust in the Independent State of Croatia*. Chicago. Liberty Press. 1981.

Lamb, Richard, *Churchill as War Leader*. New York. Carroll & Graf Publishers, Inc. 1993.

Lees, Michael, *The Rape of Serbia: The British Role in Tito's Grab for Power 1943–1944*. New York. Harcourt Brace Jovanovich. 1990.

Martin, David, *Ally Betrayed*. New York. Prentice-Hall. 1946.

Martin, David, *The Web of Disinformation: Churchill's Yugoslav Blunder*. New York. Harcourt Brace Jovanovich. 1990.

Paris, Edmond, *Genocide in Satellite Croatia, 1941–45. A record of racial and religious persecution and massacres*. Chicago. 1962. The American Institute of Balkan Affairs.

Rootham, Jasper, *Miss Fire: The Chronicle of a British Mission to Mihailovich 1943–1944*. London. Chatto & Windus. 1946.

West, Rebecca, *Black Lamb & Grey Falcon*. London. Macmillan London Limited. 1942.

General Mihailovich – The World's Verdict A selection of articles on the first resistance leader in Europe published in the world press. Foreword by F. A. Voigt. John Bellows Limited. 1947. Gloucester.